"Dark, funny, sharp, intelligent and real-unpretentious, with a big heart and deep soul, Picardi writes from the perspective of the outsider, the out-of-town newcomer to New York, exposing the hypocrisy and mendacity of New York ambition and greed. John Picardi is Dawn Powell's soulmate."

—Kate Christensen

Writer of: In The Drink, The Epicure's Lament, The Astral, Blue Plate Special, How to Cook A Moose, The Last Cruise, 2007 *PEN/Faulkner Award for Fiction for The Great Man*

NINCOMPOOP

NINCOMPOOP

A novel
by

JOHN C. PICARDI

Adelaide Books
New York / Lisbon
2021

NINCOMPOOP

A novel

By John C. Picardi

Published by Adelaide Books, New York / Lisbon
adelaidebooks.org

Editor-in-Chief
Stevan V. Nikolic

For any information, please address Adelaide Books
at info@adelaidebooks.org

or write to:

Adelaide Books
244 Fifth Ave. Suite D27
New York, NY, 10001

ISBN: 978-1-955196-24-6

Printed in the United States of America

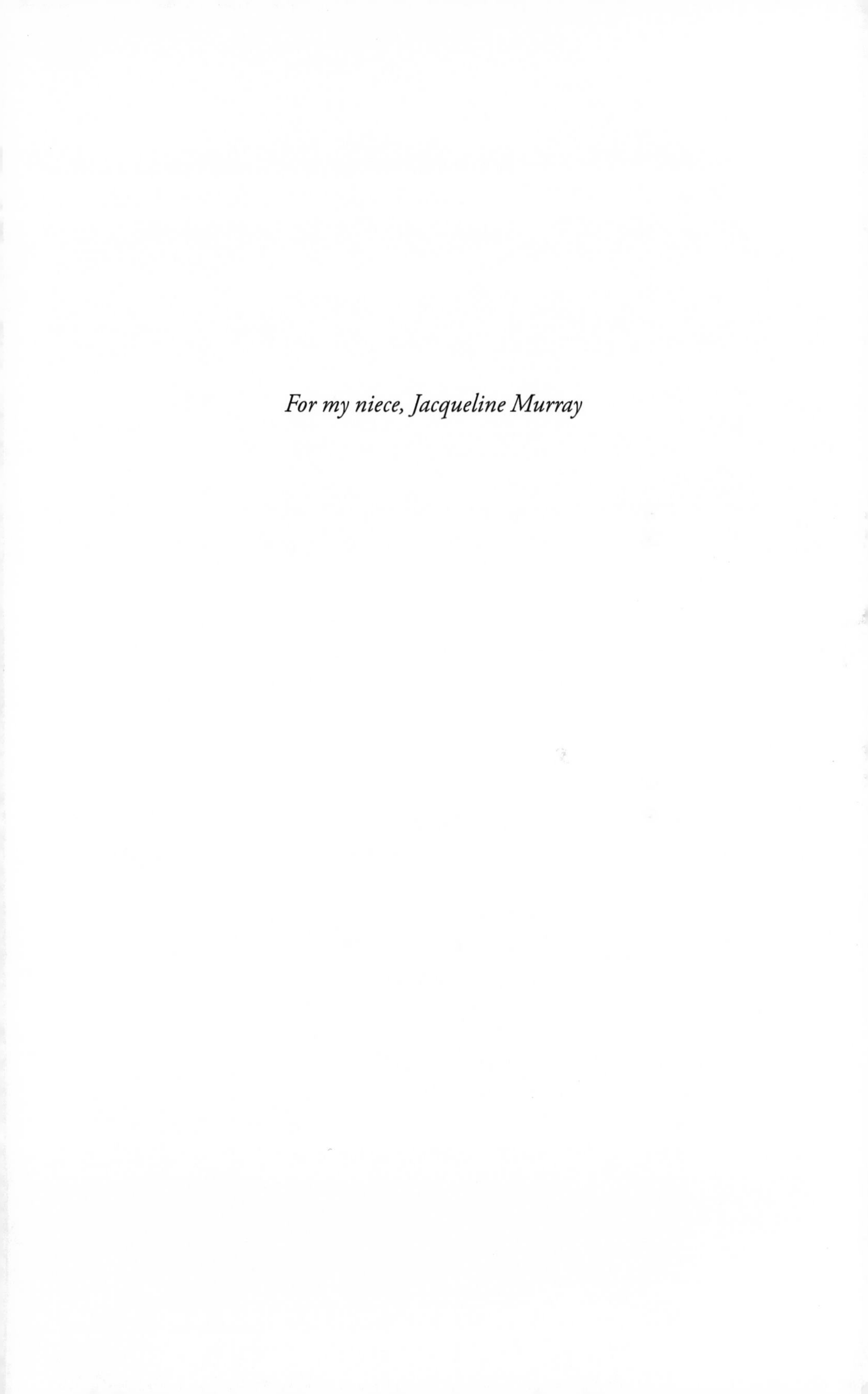

For my niece, Jacqueline Murray

Contents

The Setting

A small bar in the East Village in New York City called Bar Plato, various apartments, townhouses, bars, gay discos, and city streets. There are also small scenes that take place south of Boston, and on Cape Cod (Wellfleet), Massachusetts. One small scene takes place in Los Angeles, California in the Hollywood area.

Milieu

A suggestion would be to listen to each song that is listed before each scene. You can find these songs on *Spotify* or *YouTube* or another source of your liking (see music list page 2). Although listening to each song is not required, it will help set the milieu. Milieu is a French word meaning environment and a word that the writer failed to remember during a French exam in college; the result being the writer using the word milieu as much as possible to reassure himself that money spent for his education was well worth it.

The first half of the book takes place in New York City throughout the fall of 1994; picture falling leaves, cold air blowing off the East and Hudson Rivers, and lots of rain. It was years before iPhones, Facebook, and Instagram. It was a time when people sat across from one another and had actual conversations and eye contact. People didn't have a need to be "liked." The only thing that tweeted was a bird. There were pay phones on the streets, and you could make collect calls. Cell phones were cumbersome and funny looking and very few people had them. There were 490,600 deaths due to AIDS. As a result, the feeling of death and doom hung over the heads of most gay men. The painting, *The Scream*, by Norwegian painter

Edvard Munch was stolen in Oslo, and ironically, that painting could be used as the overall theme for this book. In other news: Monica Lewinsky said she gave President Clinton a blow job, the OJ Simpson trial commenced, the stock market did very well, the space telescope Hubble photographed Uranus with rings, the TV show *Friends* premiered on TV, the movie, *Pulp Fiction*, was the talk of the town, and every writer dreamed of hitting the screenplay jackpot like writer/director Quentin Tarantinio.

Principal Characters

Leonardo, 24, the protagonist. A gay man from Boston, naïve, self-loathing, hardcore people pleaser, insecure, and in need of constant reassurance. On first impression Leonardo, comes across as nerdy, mostly due to his conservative attire; khakis and loafers. Most everything he wears comes from the GAP or Old Navy. His hairstyle is traditionally short, parted on the side. He is nice looking. He is not "cool" or "groovy" but kindness beams from his being.

Rico, 40, Manager of the bar. Cuban, drug addicted, obnoxiously loyal to Jack Fresh, his childhood friend.

Jack Fresh, 40, married to Mara. Film actor, cocaine, alcohol and sex addict, abuses power, extremely narcissistic, self-proclaimed Buddhist.

Mara, 40, married to Jack. British, cocaine and alcohol addict, mentally unstable, abusive, dangerous in every sense of the word, deeply narcissistic, self-proclaimed Buddhist.

Charlie, 40's, Bar Plato's pianist, gay, lover of Chopin's music, gentle, wise, mentors Leonardo.

Larry, 40's, friend to Leonardo, bar customer, gay, kind, professional, HIV positive. Peter's partner.

Peter, 40's friend to Leonardo, bar customer, handsome, gay, cheery, Larry's partner.

Frankie, 50's, a regular at the bar, gay, Mara's hairdresser, flamboyant, damaged, not to be trusted.

Olena, 19, Jack's cousin, college student, confused, desperate for a boyfriend, dates Ian.

Annie, 7, Mara's daughter from her first marriage, sweet innocent, sensitive, angelic.

Cosmo, Jack and Mara's newborn son, a beautiful baby boy, adorable.

Esther, 20' s, Leonardo's first New York friend, a Columbia film student, angry, a know it all, pushy, but underneath her tough exterior she is deeply mourning the loss of her mother.

The Minor Characters

Julia, 20's, an actress, Leonardo's friend from graduate school, supportive, no-nonsense, dated Rico.

Gwen, 20's, an agent, Leonardo's friend from graduate school, intelligent, and caring.

Beth, 30's, Jack's agent, puzzled.

Dina, 60's, Jack's mother, decent and good, wants her son to be happy.

Eddie, 60's, Jack's father, obsessed with his son's career, sensitive.

Wayne Jackson, 40's, Jack's former writing partner, actor.

Emily, 30's, Leonardo's sister, concerned, loyal.

Leonardo's parents, late 50's, loving, caring, virtuous.

Susie-Q, 30's, Mara's drug dealer, flighty.

Ian, 19, Olena's boyfriend, an actor, cold and calculating.

Mickey, 30's, outrageously handsome, a gay porn actor, former gay hustler and Jack's former friend.

Jennifer Langston, 30's, Jack's co-star, beautiful, talented.

Andre Brent, 60's, former TV star, movie actor from the 1960's and 70's, accomplished, old Hollywood demeanor; distinguished, classy.

Jaffe Cash, 20's, a gorgeous, "A list" actor.

Fade In

Scene One – The Rolling Stones – *Sympathy For The Devil*

The bar phone rang. Its ring sharp and cutting, almost dangerous, it gave off an attitude of its own; a brutal harshness that stung my ears. "Shit! I bet that's her!" Rico said. He answered the phone, nodded to indicate that it was indeed her, and started repeating himself. "Yup, yup, yup," his voice carried faint tones of irritation as he glared into space and angrily twisted his mouth. He then looked at me. I felt as though he was contemplating whether or not he'd made a mistake hiring me. It was my first night working at Bar Plato and I'd been there five minutes, tops. Rico spoke curtly into the phone, his face turning red, his free hand forming a fist, "Mara please- please stop- -he's great. He's fine. What are you talking about? My judgment is fine! What are you- Okay, okay, okay! Okay!" he hung up the phone and heavily sighed. "Is everything okay?" I asked.

It was October 1994. I was 24 years old and had just landed a job at an East Village bar called, Bar Plato. It was between 9th and 10th Streets and was owned by actor Jack Fresh. At that time, there was a surge of popular actors opening bars and restaurants in the city. These were sought after jobs for show-business newbies in New York who were looking for the right connections. His British wife Mara over saw the operation of the Bar. Rico was my boss, and Jack Fresh's best friend.

"Mara wants to meet you. You gotta go upstairs in about ten minutes. You have to buy her a cup of soup from the bodega across the street and take it to her. She said she wants to make sure you're not a nincompoop. But don't worry you're hired. It's a formality. But be prepared, she will likely degrade you. She's nuts. She doesn't own the bar; she thinks she does. Just go along with her."

"A nincompoop? Take her soup? She'll degrade me?" I asked. At first it sounded ridiculous, and suspiciously troubling, but I quickly ignored it. I needed the job. It wouldn't be the first time someone would degrade me. After all, I was gay, and quite frankly, I was used to it. Rico handed me two cases of beer and told me to fill the frig under the bar in a direct, but friendly voice. Eager to make a good impression, I smiled and got right to work. He told me that Jack was in LA making a film.

"It's kind of like the same idea of Kerouac's book, *On The Road,* but only hipper, Jack's very picky about his roles. He has the soul of a real artist. You're going to love him when you meet him. He's so great," Rico's face glowed.

The thoughts of being that close to show business ignited such excitement in me that my mouth hung open, unhinged in awe. After Rico took a shot of whiskey, and coughed from the harshness of it, he started speaking to me like we had been friends for years. He talked about rude customers and his penchant for threesomes with hot babes. I wish he had spoken to me like we were lovers. The truth was Rico was the most handsome man I had laid eyes on since being in New York. He had a butt out to Milwaukee, dark hair that was shiny and black, and a pronounced sharp chin that could cut glass. Much to my chagrin, Rico was totally straight. He babbled on and on while he lined up bottles of flavored vodka. He then started to polish the bar while I continued to busily line up the beer bottles on the refrigerator's lower shelves. When I was done, he instructed me to clean ashtrays, dust the piano and cover the small twelve cocktail tables with black tablecloths. Every once in a while, he'd look at himself in a mirror over the bar and comb his impressive thick black hair back. I caught him winking at himself, and I laughed; truth was, if I looked like Rico, I would probably blow myself kisses.

"Okay it's time. Take her the soup. I'm warning you though, she keeps hounding Jack to walk out on the film because she wants him to prove his love for her. She's going to talk to you about it nonstop. Good luck."

He poured himself another shot of whiskey, tossed it down, and handed me ten dollars. He instructed me to buy soup at the bodega across the street, and then to buzz 326A. He walked me to the door.

"Look, and ahh, if she starts snorting coke and quoting Nietzsche, make an excuse and leave."

Rico's voice was blunt and bold. I started to worry for an abundance of reasons. First, if Mara was not impressed with me, she could potentially ruin the first show business contact I had since moving to New York. Not only that, I needed the job or I was going to be evicted.

I lived in the College Residence Inn on 110th Street and Broadway. I was weeks behind on payment for my rented room that looked like a padded cell in a psychiatric ward. I slept on a single bed. The mattress was old and stained and sank to the floor. Each morning I was awakened by the sounds of a trumpet; a musician lived down the hall from me, his songs so sad that sometimes I wondered if he actually existed or if the sounds were coming from the depths of my being. The phone in my room was an old 1960's model, black and bulky, sometimes it worked, sometimes it didn't. The call waiting notification a loud harsh buzz. The first time I heard it buzz, I thought I was being electrocuted. Before I started working at the bar, I'd been frantic for a job. A pile of rental non-payment green slips sat on my dresser the size of a large and tedious novel. Fearful, I desperately called my good friend, Julia. She was my Google back then. She was an actor and well connected, and knew all about jobs, restaurants, bars, theaters, and apartments. Thankfully, she called Rico, who then called me, and he said I was hired as far as he was concerned but that I had to interview with Mara who would make the final decision.

During my first months in New York, I was consumed with writing my plays. I thought money was going to magically appear like it did for my rich friends who received hefty monthly checks from their parents. I had worked minimally in New York, and had messed up every lousy job I had. I was fired from my last cater-waiter job after being caught eating a lamb chop in the pantry of a wealthy businessman downtown. The thoughts of going back to substitute teaching made me shudder to my core. I was traumatized for weeks after an eighth grader threw a desk at me.

My professional goals of becoming a screenwriter and playwright were directly linked to my personal ones. I wanted to marry a nice guy, adopt tons of kids who would run around a big house that had a screened back door that led to a massive vegetable garden. All of this cost money; I was broke and it was also against the law for gay people to get married. Most of my friends would have turned their noses up and laughed at me if they knew this is what I wanted. I could practically hear them; *poor gay, pathetic, self-loathing, unsophisticated Leonardo wanting a conventional life*; blah, blah blah. Meanwhile, at that time, my greatest accomplishment in New York was finding a dollar in change in my winter coat so I could buy a hot dog at Papaya King.

Walking to get the soup that night is etched in my memory. It had been a rainy week, but that night the rain had stopped. It was fair and cool, puddles remained on the sidewalk. Steam billowed from sewer covers and streets were crowded with people. Their conversations hit my ears in a mismatch of mid-sentences along with laughter and joy. Seeing all those happy people added to my uneasiness and excitement. I couldn't understand that eerie disconnect from humanity that seemed to pulsate around me even though I passed thousands of people on the streets of Manhattan each day.

In a matter of minutes, I was holding one of those cardboard containers full of chicken soup. Oyster crackers were in my pocket. I planned to keep those for myself when I got back to my room that night. Things were that bad.

When walking up the outside steps to Mara's apartment my hands shook, I pressed the buzzer and waited. Through the intercom came Mara's instructions, her British accent prominent. "The door is open, darling, come up. Don't knock." While climbing the next set of steps to her apartment a sense of dire dread built inside of me. What the hell was I doing?

Once at the door, I slowly pushed it open, and there she was, the infamous Mara. She was sprawled across an old ruby colored, plush sofa like she was some sort of living French painting. Mara and Jack Fresh were both forty, and to my twenty-four years, they might as well have been one hundred and ten. Her thin long legs stretched outward. Her bare feet intertwined, toenails painted red, her black hair flew every which way. In one hand she held a ball of Kleenex, in the other, a brandy snifter. She was dressed in a short black silk robe. There was an attractiveness about her, an earthy, uninhibited sexiness that was alluring, even to me. She had high cheek bones, and her eyes were hard, and salted with a well-hidden sadness,

"So you're the new waiter?" she said to me. I nodded yes.

"I'm Leonardo," I cleared my throat.

"Sit, darling." I obeyed.

"Soup, please," her long arms extended out. I handed her the soup.

"Brilliant. Cheers." She uncovered the soup. She sniffed it, steam floated to her face. She backed her head away as if she'd sniffed the most repulsive thing known to mankind and placed the soup on the coffee table.

"I cannot eat this garbage. It's going to make me bloody honk. This soup is from a can. You Americans eat everything from a can," she covered her face. "I am positively gutted over my life, devastated, really!" she declared, and sort of wept, or was trying to.

"Are you okay?"

"Darling, it's like this, Jack, is all mouth and no trousers. He's a soulless, selfish beast. Why did I marry such a damp squib? Why? Tell me? WHY? WHY?!" She then picked up a black leather zip-up boot and threw it across the room. "Bloody bollocks!" My eyes followed it as it crashed against the wall. A muffled, sleepy voice came from the next room.

"Mommy? What was that noise?"

"It's nothing, go back to sleep. Don't throw a paddy!"

"Sorry, Mommy," the little voice said.

Mara covered her face with her hands, "The point is this, to want love from my husband means to want death. He cares more about that movie he's making in LA than he does about me. Numpty bastard! God I am completely famished, darling, really I am."

"Do you want some oyster crackers?" I took them out of my pocket and gave them to her. "Oh, you're brill!" She started to eat them. "Let me tell you why life is so difficult. No one knows how to feel or how to love or how to live." Bits of crackers came flying my way via her mouth.

"I feel that way sometimes," I said. She eyed me up and down, opened a small, marbled box with a buddha on it, and pulled out a joint.

"Darling, do smoke a blunt with me," she said.

"No thank you. I'm working."

"Rico says you're the responsible type. He left out boring," she chuckled.

"Yes, I'm very responsible. Thank you."

"Stop gloating, darling, it's vile. Now do tell me, what do you want from your life?" She blew out a huge cloud of smoke that landed all around me. I coughed.

"Let's see—"

"Come on now darling, you must know what you want. This is your job interview," she had a silly grin on her face.

"Well, I want a job," I sat up straight, smiled.

"This is more than a job, don't be a cabbage. There are no chance meetings. What is your biggest desire?" More smoke came my way.

"I hope to meet someone one day. I want to have children. I love kids," I coughed.

"Some children are nothing but bloody ankle biters. What are your thoughts on that, darling?" she stubbed out the joint.

"I'm suspicious of anyone that doesn't like kids. Kids love unconditionally. They are the only hope we have for a better world and-"

"Darling spare me, I don't need a dissertation. So, what is your idea of happiness?"

"I'm a writer. I'd like to be successful at that."

"Whose your favorite writer?"

"I like Steinbeck," I said. She let out a disappointed sigh.

"It figures. Have you read any Proust?"

"I think I did in college."

"You would know if you did, his writings are life changing. Sacred, darling."

"I guess, I didn't then," I said.

"A gay man who hasn't read Proust is tragic. Yet, a gay man wanting children is unusual, but pathetic at the same time," she sipped the last of her brandy.

"Lots of gay people want children," I said.

"And lots of gay people read Proust, so there you go, darling and Bob's your uncle. Either way, you're quite charming in a sad way. It's cheeky. Do you have a boyfriend, do tell."

"No."

"Why not? Do you not want to be loved?" she asked. Her words stung my face. Did she sense that I felt unlovable? Did she sense my shame about who I was?

"Of course I do. I just don't have a boyfriend now," I said. My voice cracked.

"Well, I know why you don't. It's clear. It's because you're weak. Maybe even self-loathing. Do you know what Proust once said?"

"Ahh, don't be weak?" I said, holding back a chuckle.

"Don't be daft! This is sacred. Now, Proust said, 'Let us be grateful to people who make us happy, they are the charming gardeners who make our souls blossom' -Your soul is not ready for happiness. You do have a soul, darling, right?"

"Yes. Well—what? Why do you ask, well, yes, of course —"

"Stop babbling you're making me edgy. Just what I don't need. Another nincompoop in my life. Now listen, I have a daughter. Do you babysit?" she said this like she had a wart.

"Of course," I said.

"Good. Annie needs lots of discipline. You're officially employed, darling. Congratulations," she tightened her robe around her lanky, long body.

"Thank you," I said.

"Don't thank me, thank the universe."

"Thank you, universe," my voice a murmur.

"Did you meet Charlie? He is a real artist, the best musician you'll ever meet. Maybe the two of you can shag."

"What- -I wait -what? -Shag?"

"It means screwing. Where are you from Iowa?"

"Boston."

"I despise Boston. The whole lot of you are pseudo intellects. Now listen to me darling, go back to the bar, get us a bottle of brandy and come back up. We need to talk further. You need to be fixed."

"Fixed? But don't I have to work? I don't want to anger Rico and—"

"Anger Rico? Don't be a nincompoop! I'm the boss. Go along now, get us the brandy, please darling, hurry, my head is splitting. Make sure that tosser doesn't come up here. I want you." She then started rubbing her head, "Oh, my head hurts, it bloody hurts!"

"Would you like me to buy you some aspirin?"

"Darling, aspirin is for teenage girls with menstrual cramps. I'm a woman. Get the brandy, and please be quick! " The way she eyed me, that steely stare of hers, satisfied something unhealthy in me. I looked directly at her, looking for what I wasn't exactly sure. Approval? She pointed to the door and shooed me away like a dog being told to go outside and pee.

Once outside, there was a chill to the October air, and a small tree outside the bar was already bare, its leaves blew in small tornado-like gusts at my feet. While I walked back to the bar, I totally convinced myself that Mara wasn't that bad. She was tough, but I needed tough. I was a grown man, I could take it. Plus, she seemed to like me. Yet, the truth was, I was deeply worried. I had to find a way to somehow conceal my timidity or was it too late? Did I show Mara too much? My sister once told me I had an annoying habit of showing everyone my weaknesses and then after, wondered why people took advantage of me, "People want control over people. It's human nature," she always said. I thought she was crazy.

"How'd it go with her?" Rico asked when I reentered the bar.

"Great. She was really nice!" I said.

"You think she's nice?" Rico chuckled. "Nice my ass," he said.

"She wants me to bring her a bottle of Brandy."

"She can wait," he then changed the subject in a snap; he spoke of his love for New York City, and went on about how much he hated it at the same time. He told me he had been raised in Cuba and spoke about his childhood. He said something wicked about Castro in half English and half Spanish as he meticulously rolled up his shirt sleeves to above his elbows and then, gingerly, over his forearms. He asked me where I lived in the City. I gave him a series of yes's and no's to his 'getting to know you' questions as the bar glasses I was washing clinked and clacked. My eyes shifted right to left, hoping this new job was going to work out for me. He took another shot of whiskey and tossed me a wet rag. The wet rag landed in my hand.

"Get the step ladder in the kitchen and clean the sign out front, it's filthy. And one more thing, you can't let her get to you. I mean, she gets to me, but it's more personal, she's married to my best friend. She's crazy. Crazy! Crazy! Crazy! " Rico called after me while I grabbed the step ladder and went out front.

A dull light bulb hung over the small sign that was in gold lettering on a black flimsy board. "Bar Plato" it said in spaghetti-twirling cursive. Although only six feet off the ground I felt like a bird perched on a light post observing the world. The streets of the East Village were alive; raucous, electrifying, colorful, noisy it was all before me. The newness of the past hour suddenly invigorated me like nothing had since being in New York. Happiness washed over me like a bucket of ice water; refreshing and baptizing, the possibilities seemed endless. Enthusiastically, I washed the sign with gusto and might, my arms stretching, my hand moving in circular motions. Believing in my heart that my first meeting with Mara, for the most part, went really well. A smile from ear to ear was on my face. I was overtly proud to show the passing people below that I had a job working at a bar owned by film star Jack Fresh and his wife. Me! Could it get any better? The rag turned black from the soot, the sign glowed. I felt resourceful. Good!

The bar's interior looked like what I would imagine entering a magician's tent would be like; circa 1918 Eastern Europe. It was dark, mysterious, transporting, a bit forbidding. I pictured in my mind Houdini sitting in a back corner playing with his mirrored handcuffs. The outside door was plain, wooden, and weather beaten. The foyer was tiny, dirty, and painted black, it bordered on the verge of inexplicably creepy. It would turn the most reasonable person away, yet, the live piano music (no door fee) I guessed, was enough to entice people to step fully into the bar. After passing through the grubby foyer, walking into Bar Plato was a production itself. Customers had to part heavy, black velvet curtains that smelled like a wet goat. They were damp from the rickety old door. (There was a grate that was pulled over the entire entrance at night and locked). The curtain probably got wet countless times from gushing rain, blowing snow or the leaky ceiling above. Thick braided gold tassels hung on hooks at the entrance.

When I'd finished washing the sign, Rico went over my other duties with me,

"On busy nights you'll tie the curtains back with the tassels. It will make the flow of customers easier. Remember, Mara wants the tassels loosely tied, not knotted, she'll have a fit. Those curtains are from the 1920's, from an old theater on 40th Street. She thinks they're sacred. Oh, yeah, everything is sacred to her. Get used to it. Except how she treats human beings," Rico had said twisting his lip in repulsion and pouring himself a glass of whiskey.

Behind the bar was an expansive glass shelf; frosted curved glass, four tiers with tiny white lights that illuminated the many colorful bottles of liquor that sat upon it. It weirdly resembled a bad piece of art made by an LSD induced first year art student. All the same it was interesting in its own way; presumably when sloshed, or high on ether. Candles were placed everywhere, which was illegal, but Rico told me Mara didn't care about fire laws.

"Mara compares this place to a church, she says this bar is, guess what? Sacred! She says candles must be lit. So, make sure you light the frigging candles. You also need to know that Mara thinks she's above the law. She's probably blowing the fire marshal or paying him off, knowing how she operates. Everything to Mara is *let's make a deal* or *how can I get this for nothing."*

Maybe Rico was exaggerating. Mara didn't seem that bad, or was she? Or was Rico just a drama queen?

By all appearances the bar was a groovy place, free live music, lite snacks; crudité, pate, cheese and crackers, and top shelf booze. A strong, thick scent from incense, mostly Nag Champa gave it a druggy-den-like feel. The scent gave off a slight woody smell that was reminiscent of jasmine flowers, or a forest or even tea. Rico informed me that Mara strictly enforced the burning of incense in front of the Buddha,

"Mara, says incense must burn at all times. That's also frigging sacred. Whatever! Sacred my ass!" he rolled his eyes. "What a fucking phony!"

We stood in front of the Buddha. It was located in the far corner opposite the entrance. A blue card in a gold frame was covered in ash, it was propped up next to the burning incense. I picked it up, cleaned it off and I read it out loud. "*Three things cannot be long hidden: the sun, the moon, and the truth. Buddha.*" After I read it, Rico sardonically laughed.

"It figures that's her favorite quote considering the word *truth* isn't part of her being. If I had a dime for every time, she quoted the Buddha or writers or other philosophers, I'd be rich as Trump. You'll see soon enough. You'll see. She's enough to make anyone vomit a river, maybe an ocean. I have no idea what Jack sees in her. Personally, I think Jack is losing his mind. I really do."

Rico had handed me a feather duster, he held one too. We stood on chairs. He dusted a large bust of Aristotle and I dusted a bust of Plato. They were each on a large shelf and they faced one another and appeared to be in deep conversation and wanting no part of the bar.

"I'm just worried about Jack, you know? It's been months of craziness." Balls of dust floated round us.

"You sound like you're a good friend. Maybe she's different with Jack," I said.

"She's worse with Jack. She nags him something awful. You'll like Jack. He's a good guy. Who knows, he may help you with your writing career. He's well connected," Rico said. This was the second time he said something like this to me. My heart skipped ten beats. I did say a word, but loved the prospects of it.

We made our way over to four large Doric columns that helped block off the entry way space. Rico playful dusted one of them.

"Jack wanted to get married, he said it was time for him to grow up, but Jack changes his mind like the weather. I get it though. I want to get married one day, too. But I can't imagine being married to a woman like her. She's wicked. I'd like to marry a woman like Julia. I got it bad for her. Hey, put in a good for word for me, will you? Play me up," he said.

"Sure. Thanks for the job by the way," I dusted the other column.

Rico made his way over to the piano and sat. He pressed keys one by one, his eyes fixed on the keys. The piano was off to the side for Charlie who came in three times a week to play. I rested my head in my hand, my elbow on the piano, my eyes on Rico.

"I had dreams once. Hopes. I wanted to be an actor. I was good. I studied with HB studios. I couldn't take the constant rejection. Jack said I was good. I was in college for a while, too. I was thinking about being a high school teacher. I quit, big mistake, now look at me, forty and I got nothing. I should get a normal job. Maybe I'd be more appealing to Julia, you know? I'd like to have kids. -Hey, we have to put the rug down, help me," he said.

Next, we were on our knees rolling out a large oriental rug that adorned the wooden floor in front of the bar. Rico said it was from Iran. "This rug is Mara's pride and joy, really expensive." It was in deep reds, blues, tans and shades of yellow.

"Is the rug sacred, too," I asked, half joking.

"Probably. Every night she wants it vacuumed and rolled, and the floor mopped." I nodded swiftly to show him I understood. The truth was, when we were rolling it out, there was a small tag attached, it was made in the USA and bought at *Bed, Bath and Beyond.*

"I'll show you the garden area. Follow me," he said.

We walked down a long hallway that lead to a backdoor; Rico pushed it open. In the garden there were ten small tables. He lit a cigarette, "We launch the garden area in May and close it in September. In a week or so we'll be cleaning this up and will be storing the tables and chairs down in the basement. The garden area is where some of the customers sneak out in the winter to smoke their dope, make out, and on occasion, screw. And look, if you find a couple doing it, just let them do their thing. As long as no one is getting, you know, raped or anything nasty like that. We want no cops here."

"Okay."

Rico then flipped another switch and it illuminated another bust of Plato in the center of the garden, it was the size of a washing machine, (it was plastic, but looked like white stone). A small blue light lit Plato's face spookily with shadows, his eyes piercing and imaginably verbal. They said to me, *get the fuck out of here you dumb ass.* After that, he showed me the kitchen. It was the size of a small walk-in closet. There was an old stone sink, a beat up refrigerator and a marble counter. On top of it was a small mirror, a rolled bill, and a razor. "God damn, Mara!" Rico quickly grabbed it all and put in the microwave and slammed it shut.

"The microwave doesn't work by the way," he said.

The bar phone starting ring.

"Oh hell I bet that's her!" Rico picked up the phone and I could hear her voice; piercing and acidic, "Where's my God damn brandy! Have that kid bring it to me, now!" she said.

"We're opening in five minutes; we had things to do!" Rico said. I heard the extension go dead on the other end.

"She hung up on me, that bitch," Rico grabbed a bottle of brandy.

"I'll take the brandy up to her. You said you knew how to make drinks, right? Cash is in the small cigar box where I showed you. Do your thing. We're open for business," Rico said.

"But she told me to bring the brandy to her," my voice meek.

"Don't worry about it," he ran his hands through his thick mane of hair and left me alone with Aristotle and Plato glaring at me.

Scene Two – Ella Fitzgerald – *Wacky Dust*

Rico was upstairs in Mara's apartment for almost two hours. I figured they were polishing off the bottle of brandy. I didn't mind, in fact I was glad, it gave me a chance to plant my feet, and get used to the bar on my own. Customers came in and out. I waited on a couple who were in deep conversation over Dostoevsky's *Crime and Punishment.* They intimidated the hell out of me and I was fearful that I would mispronounce words in front of them and come across unworldly and unsophisticated. I hoped they weren't going to ask me my take on Raskolnikov's deeper motivation for committing the murder of Alyona. I was slaughtered a week prior by my new friend, Esther when I made a reference to the writer, Rainer Maria Rilke, I'd pronounced his name Rill-kee and not Rill-kuh.

I kept a close eye on the curtains that covered the entrance and thought it amusing as customers entered with regality and grandeur. Whereas other customers, the insecure ones, would pop their heads through the curtains looking like nervous vaudevillian actors peeking out at their audience. They'd inspect the Bohemian setting, their eyes would widen and a look of intimidation or fright would wash over their faces. I'd wave and give a welcome smile, but they'd quickly pop their head back and scoot off into the night. The truth was, I felt the same way when entering the bar for the first time. But my hick days were officially over; I was working at probably one of the hippest bars in the East Village!

Soon Charlie, the piano man, came in and we introduced ourselves. I was immediately attracted to him and felt myself wriggle in and out of my tortoise shell. Every self-deprecating notion of myself began to sing to me; *who would want you, you're not good looking enough, you're not sophisticated enough.* I did my best to ignore it. Charlie played mostly classical music on the grand piano, a little jazz. He only stayed for an hour because he had a gig uptown. When he was done with his set, I fixed him a plate of páte. As he ate, we chatted. I told him about my appreciation for Chopin's music although I didn't know much about it. Charlie spoke quietly,

"Although his music is in principle demanding, Chopin's style stresses fine distinction and emotional depth rather than technical genius. Chopin was Polish. Everyone thinks he was French because he lived most of his life in France."

Charlie was beautiful. He told me he was forty-five. He had the longest fingers I had ever seen. His knuckles were as round as walnuts, his eyes full of authenticity. He wore a strong cologne, something sexy and musky. I could tell he used hair gel to tame his full head of sandy brown hair; it was glossy, parted on the side, not a strand moved.

"So Leonardo, talk to me. What brings you to New York?" I told him my story.

"This is a rough place here at Plato. You seem like a nice kid. Stay out of some of the goings-on here."

"Like what?" I'm not such a kid. I'm almost twenty-six," I lied.

"Here's my phone number. Call me if you need anything." And just as Charlie went to play his second set, the bar phone rang. It was Mara.

"This lazy sod, Rico, is snoring on my sofa! I need to speak to Charlie!" I called after him and he reluctantly took the phone in his hand. He spoke calming, reassuringly to Mara, *Jack would never cheat on you- he's on location, let him do his job, ——no, Mara , you should not kill yourself, think of Annie, no, dear, sorry, I can't come up tonight, in fact, I'm leaving I have a gig uptown, I double booked, I'm so sorry… Love you, too.* Charlie hung up the phone, shrugged his shoulders, smiled and pointed to me.

"You have my number, use it! I'm leaving. I'm in no mood for her. If she comes down asking for me, remind her I had another gig uptown and had to leave." He put on his coat and off he went leaving a trail of his delightful spicy cologne behind.

Two customers came in. They were business types, conservative, each wore a suit and tie. They looked out of place, and almost apologetically told me they wanted a quick shot of booze before meeting their girlfriends. I poured. They congratulated each other over some contract that was signed, clanged their glasses, chugged, laughed, and left me a twenty dollar bill. I was alone again, and immediately called my sister Emily in Boston on the bar phone. "I got a job working for Jack Fresh and his wife!" She had no idea who Jack Fresh was, and so I explained.

"Oh that's good. Good for you." Emily sounded preoccupied. I heard my niece and nephew screeching in the background. "How are the kids?" I asked.

"They miss you. They ask for you all the time."

"Tell them I love them so much." Homesickness came crashing in. But I immediately stopped those feelings, kicked thoughts of home and my family out of my head because I refused to be that pitiful homespun person, even though every inch of me wanted to be home. I wanted grass and trees. I wanted to see familiar faces in stores. I wanted to buy Mrs. Coletti's chocolate chip cookies at the church bazaar. Yet, all the same I felt the people at home were common and ordinary, and pathetically boring. I had to be different than those people. I had to show them I was better than they were, and more sophisticated. I was protecting myself. They had injured me so much that I was forever trying to prove something to the world as if the world cared or was even watching. My ego wouldn't allow me to give up. I would suffer through homesickness and prove some lame point to people who hadn't been nice, and probably weren't even thinking about me anymore. I didn't want to hear Emily's voice any longer, it filled me with sadness and a deep longing for familiarity and safety. Love.

"Emily I have to go. Tell mom and dad I'll call them." As soon as I hung up the phone, it rang again.

"Hello, Bar Plato."

"Rico, that you?" The voice was thick, deep, sad, haunted, and sounded heavily drugged.

"No. May I take a message?" I asked.

"This is Jack Fresh. Whose this?" he said.

"It's Leonardo. I'm new."

"Oh, hey, Julia's friend? Rico says you're a fantastic writer. When I get back from LA I'd like to read some of your stuff. I'll be back in a few weeks. Listen, don't tell Mara I called. I gotta go." Click.

I was floating on air. Jack Fresh wanted to read my stuff. At that moment the potential possibilities for my writing career ran through my mind; screenplay, plays, TV shows. I told myself I was on my way. I turned on the stereo and Queen blasted, *Don't Stop Me Now*. I washed glasses and danced around using a beer bottle for a microphone. I imagined I was Freddy Mercury as I sang and danced around the tables to my imaginary audience. The busts of Aristotle and Plato seemed to be laughing at me so I shot them the bird with both hands. When Rico came angrily storming into the bar, I immediately stopped and pretended to be cleaning off a table.

"You! She wants you up there! She's crazy!" he shouted. He pointed his thick finger at me like I had killed a small child, "Go! Go before she calls looking for you! I can't speak to her again tonight!"

Once outside, I excitedly dashed up the stairs to the apartment. I stopped and walked back down. Something pulled me back. Something strong like a huge arm that had wrapped itself around my waist. It prevented me from stepping forward. A voice inside of me told me to go home and to ditch the new job. Scram! Bolt! Skedaddle! I sat down on the bottom step to catch my breath. I looked up the avenue. What did Charlie mean the bar was a rough place? Cars sped by, lights flickered. Why did I feel so honored that Mara wanted to spend time with me when undoubtedly she was off her rocker? And, not only that, but from what I was gathering she was abusive. I'd be a fool to leave, I told myself. This was my chance, my opportunity to network, to get what I wanted. The apartment building loomed as if it were going to crash down on me. I stood, regardless of my apprehension, and walked up the stairs while every bone in my body told me to run and to never look back.

The unsettled feeling I had that night was with me throughout the years I knew Jack and Mara. It was like a TV left on by a neighbor; its volume unpredictable, it went from low to medium to high at any given hour, but could always be heard and always kept me up at night.

"I specifically told you not to send that berk up here," she yelled. It was like a hard cold slap to my face.

"He insisted. I'm sorry," I said.

"Bloody hell! Do as I say! Rico doesn't understand women. Only gay men understand women. Gay men are half man, half woman," she snapped. I immediately pondered working for a circus if this writing thing didn't work out for me.

"I'll need your phone number. I might have you run an errand here and there for me. I'll pay of course. Would you fancy that?"

"Really? Well, yes, sure. I'd like that." She slid a pad of paper my way and I wrote down my phone number.

"Sometimes my phone works and sometimes it doesn't. It's old and calls first come through the front desk. Like the old days. It's pretty cool. It's kind of like a 1950's movie. It's charming in a way. I guess. I think. Maybe?" I said. She turned her lip up, annoyingly sighed and crossed her arms over her chest. She looked at me as if the sperm cell that swam into my mother's fallopian tube and created me had made the biggest mistake known to mankind.

"You're not the type of person whose going to talk and talk and talk, are you? I can't take a lot of nattering. I have enough with Annie- God she's so demanding!"

"No. No. No. Absolutely not."

"Good because I can't take much more from people. Not to mention that Jack is being a real knob, too! I'm surrounded by nincompoops! I advise you to never get married!" When she started to slip out of her robe, I looked away, and sensed she was naked. My heart beat so fiercely I was positive people in Brooklyn could hear it. Was she trying to seduce me? Thinking she could 'fix' me? She took a swig from the bottle, and fumbled through a pile of clothes until she found what she was looking for. A pair of clean panties. From the corner of my eye I saw her pull off the pair she had on and put on the clean pair. She flung the dirty pair across the room and they landed next to me. She then put on a pair of leather pants and a red top that was cut in a sharp V. She bent over a small mirror with coke on it and her nose sucked up a line of cocaine, her nose more powerful than my mother's Dyson DC17 Animal Bagless Upright Cyclonic Vacuum. She was now hammered.

"Aristotle," she said.

"No, I'm Leonardo," she roared with laughter.

"You really are a nincompoop, aren't you, darling?" she said. I was stunned.

"What? I'm confused," I said. She made a sound like she was swallowing a baseball and rubbed her nose. "I said, Aristotle. Do you read him? Have you ever read him?" Her eyeballs looked as if they were freely floating in their sockets.

"In college. Once," I said.

"Oh, God! GOD! I hate America! Once? You must read him every day! His writings are sacred! Plato too!"

"I will, I will tomorrow. I will read Aristotle and Plato tomorrow. First thing."

"And Proust and Kafka! Dostoyevsky! Tolstoy! Gogal and Dante! Make sure you do if you want to call yourself a writer!" She leaned back over the mirror.

My hands properly folded in my lap, waiting to see what she was going to say or ask me to do, next. I was eager to please, scared, but at the same time, quite intrigued. She jammed a Kleenex wrapped finger up her nose, twirled it and squeaked in great pain, small specks of blood appeared on the Kleenex. "Stop staring at me like some kind of sappy puppy!" I took my eyes off her. "Sorry," I said. I scanned the room. She had taken a small unattractive apartment and made it livable with silky purple curtains, candles, ornate lamps, dramatic old paintings, and a mixture of antique furniture. "I like your apartment," I said. "Thanks, darling, we're looking to buy a building in a few years. We're saving like mad! We're cramped like sardines, but for now this will do."

There was a portrait that hung over a small mahogany dresser that resembled Jack Fresh, it was very old, set in a gold baroque frame.

LET'S MAKE THE WORLD A HAPPIER PLACE, ONE DOG'S SMILE AT A TIME.

JULY

FRIDAY

30

S	M	T	W	T	F	S
27	28	29	30	1	2	3
4	5	6	7	8	9	10
11	12	13	14	15	16	17
18	19	20	21	22	23	24
25	26	27	28	29	30	31

"Is that a painting of Jack?" I asked.

"No, that was done in the early twentieth century. About 1901.I bought it at the Chelsea Flea Market years ago. Isn't it brill?"

"What a strange coincidence. It looks so much like Jack," I said.

"Darling, there are no coincidences. It was a cosmic happening. Sacred. The Gods were talking to me when I bought it. Our love was destiny, but my dear Jack is messing up. Right now I want to slice that painting with a razor because I know he's in LA sucking on someone's willy! Our marriage is all to the pot, I'm telling you. Really it is."

I watched as her hand went for the razor on the mirror that held the coke. She eyed the painting. My eyes widened. She brought the razor down and started cutting more cocaine. She did another line. I wondered if it was humanly possible for someone to snort that much cocaine.

"Maybe, you should take it easy with that stuff," I said in a mere whisper.

"What? What did you say? You're mumbling! Out with it!" she barked.

"Oh," I said. "It's easy to relax here with all this nice stuff around," I smiled wide.

"This jolly manner of yours, it's alluring and cute, but stop it, darling, really."

"Sorry. Esther says the same thing to me."

"Who the hell is... Esther?" The word Esther rolled off her tongue as if she'd licked the bottom of a dirty shoe.

"Esther is one of my friends."

"Stop! Please don't say, Esther, I hate that name!" She motioned to the mirror with lines of coke on it as if to offer me some.

"No thanks." She then indulged another line of coke. I was certain she was going to go into cardiac arrest at any moment. Beads of perspiration where forming on my forehead. I glanced at my watch.

"You know, man, it is like we are all here on earth under the same sun, and it is like Nietzsche said, all credibility, all good conscience, all evidence of truth come only from the senses to one heart, do you know what he means, darling? It's like we suffer all into one's loving arms and we render the joy of life but only on a peninsula that we can understand. It's all sacred."

"Yes, I agree completely." I had no idea what the hell she was talking about.

"You need to know, darling, for some reason Jack is not taking our love seriously. He will be punished when he returns." She paused. I nodded sympathetically. She snorted more cocaine and clutched her nose and winced.

"I met Jack in a Drag *Bar* on Christopher Street. He was on the pull. He likes chicks with dicks, you need to know the truth of him. He likes it all and good for him, women, drag queens, the works and quite honestly so do I. But sex aside, there must be love and devotion. I wonder if I made a big mistake marrying him. It's clear he cares more about acting in that movie in LA than he does about me. Our love is sacred, he doesn't understand."

"Well, I'm sure he loves you," I said.

"You sound very petite bourgeoisie. Darling, really, how do you know what my husband feels? You Americans are all the same." I could feel her approval rating of me dropping. I decided to be quiet and smile and nod in agreement.

"When we first met, we shagged like two wild dogs, it was purely animalistic. When we were done, he begged me to beat him up, so I beat him until he was covered in black and blues.

I done him up like kipper. Then after I'd beaten him, we got properly smashed. We drank brandy for hours. We drank so much he honked on the sidewalk. I knew that I loved him at that moment. It was so human. It's impossible for the average person to understand." Her face serious, and intense. My head could no longer move. I did everything to remain still, and not laugh. I curled my toes, and pinched my thighs.

"It was very intense, man. You wouldn't understand."

"No, I understand. That is really intense. Sacred," I said. She then started putting on her long black boots. She zipped them up and stood.

"Darling, I positively need to get out of here, do you mind sitting for a while? Annie is sleeping. She will never wake up, and if she does, tell her to get back to bed." This made me feel uncomfortable and I didn't like it, but before I could say anything she was out the door.

After she left I sat on the sofa pretty upset, but on the other side; everything was falling into place. She liked me, left me with her child, she trusted me. I peeked in the room and there was Annie, small and cute, soundly sleeping. I shut the door and fell asleep on the sofa. Two hours later the phone rang. I was exhausted, and shivered from the drafty apartment.

"Hi, it's Jack. Did I call the bar again?"

"No. I'm babysitting. Mara went out."

The phone went dead. My teeth started to rattle from the chill. I started looking for a blanket. Off to the side was a small wooden chest. Inside it was filled with papers and peeking out was an envelope with photos inside. I flipped through them. First photo was Mara in S&M gear; black leather tights, and a corset, the works. She held a whip. Another photo was of Jack. He was tied up like a pig ready for barbecuing. He was in his underwear. His chest full of thick blonde hair. The last photo was a close up of Jack's face. A pink sex toy in his mouth. He looked like he was gagging, his eyes bulged, Mara's foot was on his forehead. The last photo was of Jack, Mara and another guy with bleached orange hair, all of them fully dressed, all in leather coats, smiling. It was a perfect sunny day, they were standing by a canal somewhere in Amsterdam. I closed the wooden chest, and a small black leather bag caught my eye. Perhaps there was a blanket in the bag, I thought. No, there were handcuffs, a giant whip, two pink enormous dildos, a large black cone that at first I thought was a drain plunger. (I later learned it was a butt-plug.) There was something inside a bundle that was unopened. It said electric anal bullet. Hastily, I put everything back. I felt guilty for snooping, but at the same time it was delightfully naughty, and interesting. I liked that they were sexually liberated.

At 5:00am I was awakened by an unsteady on her feet, Mara. A strange and odd grin glued on her face. "You're brilliant, really you are, darling," she slurred, and handed me a one hundred dollar bill. She stumbled to the sofa. Her eyes rolled to the back of her head, and she was out.

Scene Three – Stevie Wonder – *For Once In My Life*

That first week at the bar I noticed that Rico's moods were unpredictable. I contributed this to his many quick dashes to the kitchen to snort cocaine. His nostrils red, there was always a small spot of white powder that lived under his nose; on occasion crusty specs of blood. His moods shifted without much notice and it worried me. Soon I figured out what to expect by the music he played. If Charlie wasn't playing the piano, Rico controlled the stereo. When he was flying high, he played mostly Queen, Bowie and Aerosmith, and we'd sing along, do whiskey shots, laugh, and he'd do imitations of Mara. He'd put his two hands over his heart, tilt his head dramatically and do his best British accent,

"Oh, darling, the flowers looked so lovely at the market today, so colorful. I wanted to buy them all. It was a sacred moment. I felt like I was in a Woolf novel and I was Mrs. Dalloway."

I would applaud and Rico would bow and growl. When he was in a bad mood, he played Tom Waits, Leonard Cohen, Elvis Costello, and Mazzy Star. At those moments I remained quiet, and stayed clear of him. I'd watch as he frustratingly slammed things around and sucked air through his nose and clenched his jaw bone in a way that made it noticeably pulsate. His sour moods were also instigated by phone calls from Mara who yelled at him for an assortment of silly things like not tying a trash bag tight enough or not ordering the correct wine. Then there were the calls from Wayne Jackson who was an actor/writer friend of Jack's. Rico spent a lot of time on the bar phone with him. There were always proclamations that sounded like mutual agreement. Rico would always repeat, "He should never have left Cora." He was talking about Cora Tanner, a famous and well-respected actress who had lived with Jack for years. At the end one of those conversations with Wayne, I sat at the bar and sipped my complimentary cocktail. Rico rambled as if thinking out loud, "This thing with Wayne Jackson is outrageous. Mara's trying to control that too. Jack and Wayne wrote a screenplay together. Mara is destroying it. She is purposely going out of her way to ruin all of Jack's friendships. Jack should never have let Cora Tanner get away. Cora loved Jack. He royally messed up when he left her."

Rico swallowed down his third drink, and made himself another,

"Cora was great to Jack. He treated her like crap. Cheated on her all the time and she's the one that got him into films, well, that and other things. Like hustling his ass everywhere. Crazy bastard; everyone know he was a hustler. Common fucking knowledge. He let anyone fuck him up the ass for cash or a part in a film. Miracle he's alive. Poor Cora." Rico slurred the last part. He was ripped drunk.

"What?" I asked, even though I heard him.

"Nothing. Forget it. Jack just gets away with shit, he just does."

"Cora Tanner is an awesome actress. She was great in, "Last Train to Memphis," I said.

"Christ on the cross! Leonardo, listen to me, don't ever mention Cora Tanner's name around Mara. She fired a waiter last week because he told her he saw Cora in Soho. And that waiter was Jack's cousin, Bobby, great guy," Rico slurred his words.

"He fired his own cousin?" I asked.

"Flesh and blood. Mara wanted him out. Bobby and Jack were real close. He took off to Florida. He told Jack not to ever contact him again. There was a big blow out. I blame Jack. He allowed it. You'll learn soon enough that Jack doesn't have much of a backbone. I love him though, I really do. He's like my brother." Rico said. The bar phone rang, he answered and held out the phone to me.

"It's her. She wants to speak to you," Rico said. I took the phone in my hand.

"Darling, I would be eternally grateful if you would watch Annie. She's sleeping and will not wake. Just a few hours?"

"Sure, of course," I said.

Mara came home so high the next morning, I wondered if she'd floated in on a magic carpet. She could barely stand. Her hair was askew like a ravaged plastic doll found at the bottom of a toy chest. Her eyes were watery, red and coated with running mascara and her nose streamed with snot. She looked like something you'd hang on a stick in your garden to scare crows away. I was worried and scared for her, had never seen anyone that obliterated before, "Cheers, darling, off you go," she burped, and handed a one hundred dollar bill. "Darling, I love you! Truly I do!" And, boom! She was out cold on the sofa as if someone had clobbered her skull with a baseball bat. I covered her with a blanket, tucked her in. She woke for a bit, slurred in faint splintered sentences while I stood over her. Her pupils like two sleek black olives.

"You're a kind bloke aren't you? So dear and kind. My mother never tucked me in when I was a girl. Sorry excuse for a mother, off her trolley, she was. And my father...barmy bastard. They never knew how to love. Neither one did. Barmy bastards..." She took exasperated breaths and tousled around.

I left her with such great sorrow in my heart that I actually wanted to sit on her outside stoop and bawl; her loneliness and desperation so obvious to me, it seemed to leap off her body as if it were some sort of separate entity that grabbed me by my shoulders and shook me. Walking to the curb to catch a taxi, I felt rattled, emotionally wounded, exhausted. Once at 110th Street, I walked into my building and up the stairs to my room; my legs like two lead poles, my body tired and my mind weary. I threw myself on my lousy bed. I dreamt that the marionettes from the movie *The Sound of Music* were chasing me with small axes. I was dressed like a nun. I woke startled, wondered what I was getting myself in to; my respiration deep and laborious, my heart pounded rapidly. Soon sleep arrived again and I woke to the sound of my phone ringing.

"Yup," I answered groggily.

"Hello? Darling is that you? Hello! Hello!" her voice was full of panic.

"It's me. I'm here!" I said.

"I've been calling and calling!" she said.

"It's my phone, it doesn't work all the time, remember? I told you when I first-"

"Please stop with the nattering! I beg you ! Now listen to me. I need you to come to the bar immediately. I need company, some support. I have this inexplicable need for company. Truth is, I'm in a snooker. I'm fearful. I can't explain it! Get here!"

"What's wrong?" I sat up in bed.

"Are you not listening! I need you," she said. I loved that she called me. I loved it so much that I wanted her *need* for me to be tangible, like a thick lotion that I could rub all over my body until it seeped through my skin and into my bones and became part of me. But in the midst of such glee, way in the back of the darkest corner of my mind, I felt myself speedily fly into an intricate web of tangled and gluey threads that coated and trapped me.

"Jack's family is out to get me. I feel it plain as day. I think they may have a plot against me. They want Jack to leave me. I feel it. I know I sound like a nutter, but it's true. Please come, darling. Everyone hates me."

"Who could hate you?"

"People who are jealous and small. I'm an intellect, darling, it scares the working classes. This is why Jack's family despises me! Are you coming?"

"Yes, I'm leaving now!"

"You're my life saver, I love you, darling. Our friendship is sacred." Click. My God! She really loved me! I hurriedly threw on my clothes. My phone rang again. It was Gwen, one of my friends from graduate school. She was the warm and cozy type; motherly, the person everyone went to with secrets and needs of comfort. She now lived in LA. After graduate school, she'd landed a job as an agent. She loved my thesis play, *Come and Get It.* At graduation, she told me to stay in close touch with her and keep her updated on my writing career.

"I've been calling for a few days, but each time I call, I get disconnected. You have to get your phone fixed," Gwen said.

"Sorry, but guess what? I'm working at a bar owned by Jack Fresh and his wife. I really like her. She's this eccentric British woman. I have a great feeling about all of this. I haven't met Jack yet, he's still in LA making a movie. He's coming home soon. I'm pretty excited to meet him! His wife, loves me. Have you met anyone famous yet?"

"I had lunch with Julia Roberts yesterday. I was at a party and Madonna was there."

"No. Stop. What? Julia Roberts? You ate with her? She ate food? Party and Madonna? Give me details!" my voice was full of enthusiasm. My eyes fixated out my small window, 110th Street and Broadway below me, the sounds of car horns and sirens fed my adrenaline. My head was spinning.

"There are no details. It was like having lunch with a human being. And, I saw Madonna for a second. You can't get near her. It was no big deal. My call waiting buzzed.

"Gwen, I gotta go. It might be Mara!" Click.

"Are you coming?" Mara sounded more despondent.

"Yes! Yes! I'm leaving this instant! Are you okay?"

"Darling, go to the Carnegie Deli and get me a sandwich."

"What kind of sandwich?"

"Anything! Anything! I don't know, tuna? Get here!" Click. At that moment I remembered I had made plans with Esther. We were going to hang in the East Village. I called her, and spoke quickly.

"I have to break plans. His wife, Mara, Jack Fresh's wife, needs me and I'm in a hurry. I'll call you later."

"Wait, numb nuts, how's it going? It's been a week! I haven't heard from you!" Esther said.

"I didn't meet Jack yet, but his wife digs me. I'm buying her a sandwich. Plus, she needs me today. She didn't tell me what for, but she wants me there. She's having some sort of family emergency. I can hang tomorrow. Is that good?"

"Whatever."

"It's pretty great Jack's wife likes me so far, right? She told me she loved me.

"Well, let's see if this pans out. We need to make a plan for you."

"What do you mean? Make a plan for me?"

"Look, at this point do what this Mara person says. Don't speak. Don't start going on about Meryl Streep and Julia Roberts. Jack Fresh is fierce. You need to start thinking about more edgy type of actors like Frances McDormand, Catherine Keener, Steve Buscemi. Take my advice. I'll coach you. But for now, shut your mouth." My call waiting buzzed.

"I have to go, I'll call you later." Click.

"Bloody hell you haven't left yet!" Mara yelled.

"I'm out the door! I'm practically there!" I said. She hung up on me. I ran out and jumped into a taxi.

Once at the Carnegie deli I impatiently stood in a huge line pacing in my space; looking at my watch, my stomach bubbling with fear that I might not get to the bar quick enough. When it was my turn, I ordered a tuna fish on rye. As the word "rye" spilled out of my mouth I heard my name being paged by the woman at the cash register.

"Is there a Leonardo in here? Leonardo? Emergency call from a Mara. Leonardo! Emergency call!" I turned and the cashier, a woman, blonde, big and heavily made-up in blue eye shadow held up the phone's receiver. I took the phone in my hand. The woman looked at me, shook her head in disgust. "Make it quick. This isn't an answering service." she grumbled.

"Mara is that you? Are you okay?"

"Pick me up some good wine, something expensive. That idiot Rico ordered plonk! Please, hurry. And get me a corn beef on pumpernickel. Dark bread. Make sure they put mustard on the sandwich. I like when the heat of the meat absorbs the mustard."

"Okay. But I ordered you a tuna, you said-" I said

"For Goodness sake, hook it! My blood sugar is low. I'm going to pass out. Make sure they give you pickles. They always forget the bloody pickles, and get a cheesecake, too. No fruit. I swear they use canned fruit. It's a travesty really. Please hurry." I handed the phone back to the fuming cashier and ordered another sandwich. I then urgently ran to to a wine store. The clerk suggested an expensive bottle of wine, Chateauneuf-du-Pape. I used the one hundred dollar bill she gave me the night before.

When I arrived, Mara was madly pacing in front of the bar. She acted as if she were on fire. She rubbed her arms and scratched them. She moved her tongue over her lips and lapped them like a hungry dog.

"What took you so long, darling?"

"There was a lot of traffic. At first I got you tuna and then you called and ..."

"Darling, please I can't take your babbling. Not today. It's going to drive me as mad as a bag of ferrets." Her leather boots clacked on the sidewalk as she went back and forth in small circles, huffing, puffing, pacing. She then kept obsessively running her fingers through her hair and making spikes on the back of her head. It made her look like she was caught in the wind. She then snapped out of whatever kind of trance she was in and looked at me as if she didn't know who I was. "Come inside with me." I handed her the wine, she read the label, "Chateauneuf-du-Pape, and Bob's your uncle! Good job, cheers, darling!" She took a corkscrew to the wine. The cork came out with a loud squeak. She poured us both a glass, and clicked my glass with hers, "Cheers," she gulped the wine as if it was water. "This is perfect!" She then poured another glass, unwrapped the sandwich, bit into it and swallowed.

"This is beastly! Why did I tell you to get me meat, ugh!" She then unwrapped the cheese cake and broke a piece off with her finger. She swallowed that down with more wine.

"What else is in that bag?" She stuck her hand inside the bag rustling and crinkling about and pulled out the tuna sandwich. She opened it and took a bite, chewed, mayo gathering on her upper lip. "I have to force myself to eat. This is all Jack's fault. All of it. I can't concentrate. I'm nothing when he's not around."

Rico was coming in and out of the bar carrying chairs from the garden out back; they were closing the garden up for winter.

"Hi, Leonardo," he grumbled. He looked exhausted, disheveled, and discontent. He put a chair down and returned to the garden area. Mara took another bite of the sandwich.

"This tuna is from a can, bloody hell. Everything from a damn can." She pushed the rest of the sandwich toward me. I ate it slowly. She stood, started pacing around the bar. She spoke to me very swiftly. It was hard for me to keep track as she went from subject to subject, "Now listen, Jack's cousin, Olena, is picking Annie up from school. She'll be here any second. Olena is lovely but she has a face like a chewed piece of toffee, warts and all. She tends to have crushes on weak men. Make it clear to her you're a poof. I need you to spend time with Annie. I need to help Rico in the garden. Annie needs to be around someone who is well-read. You are well-read aren't you? You had to have read books in those fancy universities you went to, correct? Correct? Huh? Huh? Are you listening? Huh?"

My head was spinning. Not long ago, Mara told me that she didn't like my choice of authors. She told me I *wasn't* well read. She called me weak. "Yes, sure, I'll help with Annie, but what was the emergency? You told me there was an emergency and I rushed down here. Are you sure you're okay?" I said.

"I never said there was an emergency, darling. I said I needed people around me. Is it so wrong to want mates around? To feel loved? To be needed? What don't you Americans understand about friendship and love? Huh? Tell me? You must embrace people when they come into your life. Why don't you know this? I'm starting to think Americans are worse than us Brits. I won't call if you don't like it," she let out a sigh like I'd hurt her feelings.

"No. I didn't mean it like that, call me anytime you like." She waved her hand at me like she was done with me and walked away. I sat alone. Looking up at me was a messy tuna sandwich, an oversized corn beef on rye, a humongous piece of cheese cake and a half empty bottle of expensive French wine. Within minutes Olena arrived holding Annie's hand

Olena wore jeans and a navy-blue wool cape. She was eighteen and a student at NYU where she studied business management. She had long curly brilliant red hair. Her body was Amazonian, but it coordinated nicely with her thin face. Her eyes were wide and deep green, full of enthusiasm, and innocence. She seemed untouched by life. We shook hands, and chatted a bit. Annie hid behind Olena's hips, and intermittently looked up at me as if playing peek-a-boo. I indulged her by making funny faces. Her eyes were a glowing light green; they were almond shaped, and curious. Her chin was square, and her nose was curled. Each time Annie looked up at me she playfully crinkled it. She was a strikingly attractive little girl with short blonde hair that was almost white, it gave her an angelic quality.

The sickly skunky smell of pot floated into the bar from the garden. I could hear Mara and Rico discussing business and arguing about the pros and cons of buying a new ice machine for the bar.

Annie finally came out from behind Olena. "Hello, there, I'm Leonardo. I babysat you a few times and you didn't even know it, how about that? You were sleeping. I heard you are very smart."

"Mommy says I'm a nincompoop."

"I know a smart girl when I see one." A slight smile was forming on her face.

"I have to go to the bathroom." Annie ran to the bathroom.

"As you'll soon find out, Mara is pretty tough on Annie. I do all I can to make things better for her. We all do," Olena said softly as to make sure Mara wouldn't hear her.

"I understand."

"Mara doesn't want to raise a weak girl. There's a side to Mara that's really good. After all, she brought Jack and I together. My father and Jack's mother are brother and sister. They're not close. Jack's mother is the only girl of seven brothers." She spoke quietly as if it were all a big bad secret. "Between you and I, Jack's parents don't like, Mara." Annie came skipping back from the bathroom.

"Olena, I want to play with Hunter. I really do. He's my best friend."

"Annie, you know the rules about Hunter."

"Mommy hates everyone," she whimpered. Olena told me about Hunter in hushed whispers while she cautiously kept an eye on the entrance that led to the garden.

"Hunter is Wayne Jackson's son. There's a big fight about a screenplay."

Mara walked in from the garden, looked at us, put her hands on her hips. A stream of light from behind her made her look surreal, devilish.

"Annie! Why are you crying!" she asked.

"I'm not," she pouted.

"No crybaby stuff today! I mean it!" Mara screeched.

"Olena, come outside with me. Annie stay inside with Leonardo." Mara put her hands to her mouth indicating to Olena she had a joint to smoke with her in the garden area. Olena gathered her bag and joined her.

"Annie start your homework. I'll be back in a bit. Stay inside," Olena said.

"But Olena, why do you have to go out there, why can't you stay with me," Annie wept. Mara briskly walked toward Annie.

"What did I tell you about whining? It's for weak girls. Do you want to be weak and have everyone walk all over you because you're a girl! Now listen to me. I need to speak to Olena in private. Stop being selfish," Mara said as she stood over Annie.

"Stop it, Mommy," Annie was sobbing.

"Oh poor little Annie. Her mother is so cruel to her. I'm so bad, tell Leonardo and Olena how bad I am," Mara paced. She became spookily contemplative again, then immediately hyper. She poured herself the rest of the wine. "Why isn't Jack answering his phone. It's all bollocks, really it is."

"Mara, you're tired. Let's go outside for a second," Olena said.

"Mara, can I take Annie out for a walk. Maybe buy her a chocolate bar?" I asked.

"Darling, you don't have to buy candy to endear her to you. She's impossible. See what you did, Annie? Why do you do this to me?" she gulped the wine.

"What did I do, Mommy?" Annie asked with more tears.

"Stop it, Annie! Damn it!" Mara screamed as the wine spilled out of her glass.

"Let her go with, Leonardo, Mara," Olena said. Mara's head turned from Olena, to me to Annie. She took deep, dramatic, contemplative breaths.

"Yes, you may go." Annie ran to her and hugged her. Mara lovingly stroked her face. "Now that you got your way, all is good. Have fun, darling."

As we exited the bar, a young man passed us. He was strikingly handsome. I assumed it was Olena's friend, Ian. Olena told me earlier that he was eighteen, a freshman like her, at NYU. He was well-built and had a lantern jaw. "Ian!" Olena screamed. "You came, hi!" She ran to him. Mara wrinkled her eyes as if Ian was nauseating. Olena was quivering, "Mara, uh, uh, Leonardo and uh uh, Annie, this is Ian."

"Hi, everyone," he said. His voice was perfect, deep and studied. He firmly shook hands with all of us. His hand bony, but soft. He smelled like *Downey* fabric softener.

"Nice to meet all of you," he said.

"The pleasure is ours," Mara said bitingly.

I bought Annie an ice cream and when she was done with that I bought her a pack of colored pencils. She finally smiled. I had only known Annie for about an hour and as far as I could tell she was bashful, scared, and insecure. It didn't take a genius to know why. I held Annie's hand firmly as we walked down 2nd Avenue. In her other hand she held colorful pencils.

"Are you going to babysit me like Olena?"

"I think so."

"Do you like to play checkers?"

"Oh, very, very much."

"Do you know my real Daddy?"

"No I haven't met him."

"He wants me to live with him, but I'm afraid to tell Mommy."

We passed a small playground on 19th and 2nd, and even though there was a chill in the air, we sat down under a tree. We watched other children joyfully play; some chased balls, others swung on swings, some slid down slides. Annie sat next to me. She moved closer to me as some of the kids asked her to play, "Go on, have some fun," I said. She nodded no, seemed frightened and unsure of herself. I didn't push her to play with the other kids because I was certain of one thing. I was sitting next to the little kid version of myself, and I wanted to rescue her and wasn't quite sure how.

Scene Four – Diana Ross – *I'm Coming Out*

I'd met Esther the first week I was in New York. We were both in a coffee shop on the corner of 114th Street and Broadway. I was working on a play. She sat across from me and acted tormented as she read *The Unbearable Likeness of Being.* She cried, and sniffed. I offered her a cup of coffee to help console her. She said it was evident that I wanted to have sex with her. I told her that wasn't true because I was gay and reassured her that I would be a lousy lay. She asked if I wanted to get high. I enthusiastically obliged. "That I could do," I said. We headed over to Riverside Park where we sucked on a huge blunt until we could hardly move. She told me she was a film student at Columbia studying for her MFA. She spoke of Bergman films, and all the other cliché's that film students speak of; storyline, cinematography, black and white films versus color, and the best screenplays ever written. She went on about her love for the films *Battleship Potemkin, Duck Soup, Citizen Kane, The Conversation*, and the *Bicycle Thief*, and of course she went on about *The Godfather.* After another blunt, we picked maple leaves, and slowly tore them apart. We talked about how amazing nature was, and we each ate an acorn. We gagged and howled with laughter. At one point, Esther pulled down her pants and peed in front of me, right there, as cars zoomed by on the West End Highway, "Peeing is such a natural thing. It's one of the only things that we really know is natural to us, that and screwing, shitting, and making babies," she said. We then walked to Grant's Tomb where we knelt and prayed to him for no apparent reason. Then we smoked a bit more. Soon, I couldn't feel any of my limbs. We rolled on the grass and laughed until we couldn't laugh anymore. We sat and stared at the sky. It was clear and blue. We didn't talk much, but had somehow determined we were soulmates, and that it had nothing to do with the fact that we had smoked three joints the size of polish sausages. Esther told me that our friendship was fate. Mara said the same thing about us meeting and I'd believed her, too. She said the Universe brought us together. I heard a lot about the Universe my first year in New York, and how it would give me exactly what I needed. I seriously hoped it was going to do more for me than bring me into contact with an imbecilic, British, cocaine addict and a lonely film student who had excellent marijuana.

I soon found out that Esther lived on cases of *Coors Lite* beer, cigarettes that she rolled herself with *Sir Walter Raleigh* tobacco, and slices of pizza from Kornet Pizza on 111th Street and Broadway. Esther liked to pontificate about show biz, non-stop. One night after watching a screening of *Annie Hall* at Columbia (they were doing a retrospective), Esther went on and on as we walked back to my place. "See, Woody Allen had nothing to do with that Hollywood bullshit. He made that movie in '77. He could have sold out. Everyone did in the 70's. But he never did. He makes movies on his own terms. It's not about fame for Woody. It's about art. You've got to have integrity!" Esther lived in a glamorous, doorman apartment that had a spanning view of the Hudson. It was between Broadway and Riverside Drive. Her father, a hotshot New York lawyer who was on the cover of *Time* in the 1980's, and who she hated, paid her rent and sent her expense money weekly. I wanted to have integrity like Esther. She told me her mother died of cancer when she was ten. In her next breath, she boasted that her mother's death didn't affect her because she was a super strong person and could handle anything life threw at her. I didn't react. Sadness hung over Esther like the sun over the earth. Her living room and bedroom were obsessively covered with photos of her mother. So many, that it was heart wrenchingly difficult for me to go into her apartment.

After I told Esther that Jack was home from LA and that I was going to meet him for the first time she told me she had to 'coach' me. "Dude, you can't screw this up!" she said. She instructed me to meet her at a bar on the corner of Columbus and 106th Street. She said she had her father's credit card. "We're going to drink beer, eat and talk, and it's all on me. Well, on my Dad, but who cares."

The bar was full of deadbeats. One man at the bar had his head slumped in his hands. A woman next to him was putting lipstick on her nose and laughing like a lunatic. Bruce Springsteen was blaring *Born to Run* from the jukebox. The lights were dim. A strand of colorful lights were strung across the back of the bar. They were strikingly vivid as they blinked and reflected off Esther's chalk white face that she heavily powdered. "I've been watching Romero's, *The Night of the Living Dead*, I swear it's effecting me!" she said.

"Your Dad is so nice, buying all this food for us," I said. Before us were mugs of beer, burgers, and jalapeno poppers.

"He's loaded he doesn't care. He drives me nuts. He says that he loves me. How can he love me? He doesn't even know me. Such bullshit!"

"He knew you before you even knew yourself. Esther, for crying out loud, he takes care of you because he loves you."

"Enough about my father. So you need to get ready for Jack Fresh tonight."

"What do you mean, get ready?"

"He chooses really cool people to work with. Look at you."

"What does that mean?" I chugged my beer.

"You're not cool."

"I'm cool," I said. She laughed so fervently she nearly fell off her bar stool.

"Leonardo, you're not cool."

"I am too."

"Dude. You make Tom Hanks look like De Niro in *Taxi Driver.*"

"Are you serious? What the hell. Seriously?"

"Look queen, these are the facts, the minute Jack sees you in your khakis and that shirt, he's going to think you're a nerd. Plus look at your hair, it's like a little boy's haircut. Dude it's like you walked off the set of *Family Ties*.

"Mara *does* call me a nincompoop."

"Of course she does, and who could blame her? But Jack hasn't met you yet. Screw what those other crazies think. Jack's the one you need to impress. Look, placate his nutty wife. If she says jump, you say how high. Get it? But in the mean time you need to De Niro it up a bit. "

I swigged from my mug of beer and contemplated pouring the rest over her head. I sighed. "Okay, so how can I make myself look better?" I wondered what Esther was *really* trying to tell me. That I was unattractive? Was I a dog in denial? Was I hideous looking? My eyes were blue. My hair was curly and parted to the side. My eyebrows were a bit bushy, but not bad. My chin was pronounced. I admit my nose was maybe a little too big, but I wasn't ugly. I wasn't exceptional either. I was okay, so I thought. I hoped.

"Let's get out of here, queer. Your geek days are over," Esther said. She got up and walked out of the bar and I followed. We started walking up Amsterdam.

"When you call me a queer, it brings me right back to high school."

"Dude, being called a queer is an honor nowadays."

"It still hurts."

"You're queer, you're here, get used to it," she said and poked my shoulder.

"I don't want to come off as woe as me, but I don't think you understand how bad it was for me back in high school. You may think I come from this white picket fence place, but inside that white picket fence, gay people weren't allowed. Boston is Catholic land."

"Get over it bitch, this is New York City. Gay people have power in the world. Forget those people in that dumb place you're from. Gay power!"

"It's not easy feeling like a freak and having the world confirm it all the time."

"Boohoo! Poor Leonardo! Buckle up, you belong here, queen! Why do you think half the people in show biz go into show biz in the first place? Everyone is trying to show the world that they're good and decent and all that crap. Show biz is like the land of misfits. It's about social acceptance, '*look at me world, I'm not so bad after all.*' It's about repairing feelings of inadequacy and showing every dickhead in high school that you're now a superstar. You see, seeking fame is a big 'screw you' to all those losers who have kicked anyone to the curb."

"I'm an artist. I'm not here to prove points."

"Yes you are. There are very few artists, but lots of narcissists. There's a difference. You're an artist because you feel pain more than the average person. That's it."

"I'm true to my art. I don't need to be loved or accepted. I'm like Meryl Streep." I said, knowing I was completely full of shit.

"If you say so, Meryl. But you told me you wanted to be famous."

"You told me to have integrity."

"After you make it you should have integrity, not now when you're fighting your way to the top, numb nuts!"

"The last thing I need is to feel even worse about myself. Give me a break!"

"Leonardo, I'm trying to help you. You need to get tough. Besides I bet half your high school classmates are working at Dairy Queen or cleaning toilets."

"No, you're wrong. Some of them are quite successful. "

"So why continue to be a loser?"

"Now you think I'm a loser?"

"I'm saying being true-blue isn't always the best thing. At least, not while you're in the midst of your nonexistent writing career. Doing what's necessary to survive and to make it in New York is where it's at. It's reality. Look, I'm sorry you were bullied. People are mean and cruel and they suck. But that was then and this is now. You're no longer the lone, gay boy in high school. You're surrounded by gays here. New York is the queer magnet of the world. Get tough. Be proud. And, PS: you have a great ass. The queens are going to love you, but you're not going to get any action with those baggy jeans."

"Maybe you're right."

"I love that you're sweet and charming. I feel safe with you, but that's not going to fly with New Yorkers. We need to transform you into someone hip and confident. This has to be drastic. You need to shave your head; shaved heads are very *in* now."

"No way. No. absolutely not."

"Do you want people to take advantage of you your whole life or do you want to be a winner? Do you think Meryl Streep was always nice when she was struggling? I bet she was ruthless and behind that sweet persona of hers there was a tigress who would do whatever it took to be America's leading actor. Then after she made it, she became this nice girl from New Jersey who loves her children blah blah blah… And look at Rock Hudson, bless his heart, do you think he didn't do what needed to be done? I'm sure he spent a lot of time on his knees before making it big. And look at Tennessee Williams and William Inge. Hello? They were gay. Tennessee helped Inge make it big. I'm sure it wasn't from the goodness of his heart. I bet those two queens were banging each other left and right. It's called show biz, baby. The fact is this, tonight you're meeting Jack Fresh. You need to be fake, callous, and maybe drop to your knees. Think of yourself. Then after you make it, go back to being that nerdy gay guy from Boston and go to church or do whatever creepy conventional thing you said you wanted to do. Dude, we have work to do. Stop fighting me."

"I want children, and a partner. It's not creepy." I stammered.

"Whatever, follow me."

An hour later Esther covered my head with shaving cream and shaved my head. I had not shaven my face in a few days and so she out-lined the shape of a beard with a razor. Then we went to a thrift store on Columbus. She bought me an old puffy looking jacket that I think belonged to a paratrooper at one time. She picked out some very old jeans that were two sizes too small. I looked like I was sporting a huge package. She also bought me some t-shirts that had holes in them, with a variety of nasty, aggressive and hostile sayings across the chest, *I screwed your mother so what?*, *What are you looking at?*, *Top Man*, and *PIG.* She also picked out a small black knit hat. When she was done with me, Esther said that I was the emblematic East Village gay boy. I thought I resembled a rapist.

"Esther, I look like a sexual predator. Is this one of your jokes?"

"I wouldn't joke around about this. Your ass looks amazing, even I want to tap it. You're now a sexy mofo. Dude, you could do gay porn." She pinched my buttocks, hard.

"Great, now I look like a porn star. Perfect," I became irritated.

"You need to chill out. You look great."

Esther walked me to the Number 1 train. I stopped at the subway entrance

"Are you sure I look okay?"

"So hot! Jack is going to think you're super chic! Don't speak much. Your big nose and droopy eyes work. They give you a sinister, mysterious, freaky look. Oh, and whatever you do, don't talk about your family and how much you love them. Don't go on about how you want kids and a partner and a big house with a yard. That is so not right. Act like a rebel. Every hip person hates their family. Saying you love your family will make you look, well, provincial. There are certain buzz words you can casually bring into conversations to look fabulous. Say something political about South Africa and apartheid. Say you love the poems of Pablo Neruda, everyone is into him nowadays. Maybe say you're vegan. Mention that you're thinking about converting to Buddhism. Always say Cohen is better than Dylan. You love sushi. Oh, say you were part of ACT UP. Remember Jack Fresh is cool, you've gotta think cool, you've gotta think glamorous, in a grungy way."

"Okay, thanks. I think," I rubbed my freshly bald head.

"Remember try to have an intense look on your face. Get rid of that wide-eyed *Tweety Bird* innocent look. Call me. If I don't answer, it means I'm trying to finish my dumbass thesis."

Esther was perpetually on page one of her thesis. The page was blank except for one lone word on the top that was indented two spaces. The word was "The."

"Thanks Esther." I gave her a quick wave and walked down the stairs to the train. She called after me when my foot touched the bottom step,

"Go get'em! And honey, you are not a loser!" She smiled widely and blew me a kiss.

Esther could be hard, cynical and rough, but I couldn't really get angry at her. I kept thinking of her apartment and all those photos of her mom. That night on the train ride down to the bar I seriously asked myself why I was always attracted to tragic, lonely and desperate people. What was the draw? I couldn't come up with an answer.

Scene Five – Talking Heads – *Pyscho Killer*

Rico was behind the bar when I showed up for work. He was washing glasses. His hands plopped in and out of the the sink; splattering water hit his face. He looked directly at me and stopped what he was doing. His eyes protruded lividly at me. He went back to washing the glasses. Immediately paranoia started to tango in my head in full boogie with gymnastic lifts, kicks and drops and there was no mercy. Did I look too radical to work in the bar? Was Rico pissed off with my new look? He looked at me again, squinted his eyes, and gave me a second once over. "You look good. Nice haircut." I let out a puff of relief that took four inches off my belly. "You seem angry, are you okay?" I asked. He rubbed his wet hand over his face. "Jack's not home yet, well, he was and he went back to LA. Everything is a mess." He grabbed another glass: Swish and splash. "Are you okay?" I asked. He took the glass he was washing and whipped it at the wall; crash, boom! "Stop asking me if I'm okay!" There was a pile of shattered glass below the wall, evidently, he'd been breaking glasses before I showed up. He then threw four more glasses. Frightened, shocked, my eyes wide open, I kept jumping back with each exploding smash. "I fucking hate her! Things are crazy! Insane!" he bitterly grabbed a dust pan and broom and went to clean up the shattered glass. I took the broom from him, "I'll do it." I said. My voice a mere traumatized whisper. I swept the glass pieces into a dust pan while Rico, who had lit a cigarette, held the trash can as I emptied pieces of glass into it. The sound of the rattling glass gave me a weird prickly feeling down my spine and into my ass bone. "She took some sleeping pills. I hope she never wakes up. I mean it. I hate her. Let's grab some dinner. We can open the bar a little later tonight. Screw this joint."

We walked to a Russian restaurant on 10th Avenue. Panic came to me; sleeping pills? What? "Is she okay?" I asked, while trying to keep up with Rico's quick, aggressive strut. "She's fine! She'll always be fine! Okay? Okay! Okay! You're always asking if this and that one is okay, what if they're not? What the hell are you going to do about it?" he said. I shrugged and said, "I dunno." My pants were so tight that when I walked it felt like my skin was being rubbed off my bones by an electric sander. "I'm sorry." I said. Rico held out his hand to me as we walked; resting in his palm was a cell phone, "Look at this. Mara bought it for me. I shouldn't have accepted it!" It was black and about the size of his hand. He was carefully showing it to me; flipping it over, pulling out it's small antenna, running his fingers across all the buttons and small screen. "It runs on a battery and you recharge it. Mara said it was a gift. Ha! Bullshit! I know it's for me to be at her beck and call. She's been frigging calling me non-stop!" he said. We slipped into a booth, "Look Leonardo, I need to talk to someone. I'm pretty upset. This is madness." He sounded exhausted and had brown circles under his eyes. He kept running his hands through his hair. Then he hungrily spooned Borsht into his mouth, he sighed deeply, "I've been up all night and all morning." His lips turned a deep reddish, purple from the soup.

"Jack flew home from LA and spent 4 hours with Mara. Then the shit hit the fan. Jack was called back to LA to do a reshoot of a few scenes. Something happened to the camera. Some scenes were lost. Mara went nuts. She warned him not to go back to LA. She said if he did, she was leaving him. But since it was a low budget film, he had to go. Things got worse. She literally wouldn't let him out of the apartment. She blocked the door. She said she was going to kill herself. She held a knife to her throat. He finally calmed her down."

"That's intense," I stopped eating my rolled cabbage.

"When Jack started to leave again. She went completely bonkers. It was really bad. She started throwing stuff at him in front of Annie. He ran out and kept running. Mara then called the airport and paged him at Kennedy because his cell phone wasn't working. He finally called her. He was furious. She accused him of having an affair with one of the male producers. Jack called me from Kennedy, crying. He told me he couldn't take it anymore. Then, my new cell phone beeps. Get this, it was Annie in hysterics. She told me she was scared of her mother. So, there I was trying to calm Annie down until Mara got on the phone. She was going bananas. I spent two solid hours going back and forth between all three of them. It went on until Jack's flight left."

"Why do you think Jack stays with Mara?" I asked.

"I don't know. I heard that as well as having a vagina, Mara has a dick." We both cracked up. Then we stopped. "It's true. It could be a rumor, but who knows." Rico looked serious.

"Wait, hold on, Mara is a hermaphrodite?" I said.

"This is what I heard," Rico said.

"Are you serious? No way, she wouldn't be able to have kids."

"In rare cases, they can. If she has a uterus and ovaries, it's possible."

"Maybe life's been tough for her. We shouldn't laugh," I said.

"She's fine. Don't worry about her."

"On the other hand, maybe she likes it. Good for Mara. And, I guess Jack too," I said.

"If it's true. It's typical Jack. He gets the best of both worlds. He always gets what he wants, nuts and all," Rico said. We roared.

He then looked up from his cup of coffee. He became somber, and flustered, "So anyway this afternoon Jack asked me to go check on Annie and Mara. I go into the apartment and Mara is telling me she's going to kill Annie and herself. She says it's all Jack's fault. At this point I'm real scared. I look for Annie and I can't find her. I'm shaking Mara and I'm screaming at her like a lunatic. I kept screaming, "Where's Annie!" I had visons of her stuffing Annie in a closet or a bag, but soon enough I found out that Annie was with her father, thank God. Next, Mara is writing something on her stomach in black marker. She's walking around the apartment in a crazed state. She's doing coke. She's only in her bra and underwear with this crazy thing written on her belly."

"What did she write on her belly?" I asked. Rico became distant, he gazed out the restaurant window. Then he turned to me. His voice cracked when he spoke. He sounded like he agreed with what Mara had written on her belly, "Loving Jack means death," he said. Our eyes met. I looked away, flagged down the waitress and ordered myself a bowl of Borsht. When it arrived, for some reason it was a deeper red than Rico's. I pushed it away.

Scene Six – Queen – *Don't Stop Me Now*

It was a Sunday in November when Rico got the phone call from his Aunt Cailida who lived in Miami. It was damp and gray, fog floated over the streets. Jack was scheduled to be home from LA by Wednesday. The bar was dead. I was killing time by going through piles of old tablecloths looking for rips and cigarette burns. In the morning Mara was going to order new ones. When Rico hung up the phone, he shouted to me across the empty bar, "My old man died. Shit. Fuck." He put both hands on the bar. A lit cigarette hung out of his mouth. He shook his head as if trying to comprehend the news, and figure out how to react. "He died in Argentina from a heart attack. Shit," he said.

"Rico. I'm really sorry." I made my way over to him.

"It's not like I was close to him. I haven't seen him in years, since I was maybe a teenager. When I was eighteen? I dunno."

"That's still not easy. Are you going to Miami?"

"No, no. My aunt said he'll be cremated in South America. Poor bastard. Everything was taken from him in Cuba. His job, his kid, his life."

"That sucks. I'm really sorry." I was searching for words of wisdom. I had no experience with death. Anything I said would have sounded as lame as my constant murmured, "I'm sorry." I figured it was best for me to keep my mouth shut and listen. The thought of losing my parents to death was unfathomable to me. They were my touch stones and one of my many reasons to succeed. I wanted to make them proud and to somehow ease my imagined disappointment they had for having a gay son.

"Dude, let's close this joint. Let's go to Victor's Cafe and eat Cuban food in honor of my old man. Fuck this place," he said. I nodded quietly while thinking what my world would be like without my parents. Lonely. Desolate. Fearful. They were truly all I had. My sister had her life, her husband, her children. I'd be all alone. No one would care if I were alive or dead. I needed to get my own life. I needed to be needed, or loved.

We locked the bar, and jumped in a taxi. I kept my eyes on Rico, and looked for tears, but there was only a hard uneasy stare that told me he was emotionally paralyzed. His breaths slow and steady, his unexpressed pain scared me. It made me feel even more lonesome and desperate. My mind going directly to sixty years from then; I saw myself old and drooling in some state nursing home eating *Cream of Wheat* while sitting in dirty diapers all day. After only seconds in the taxi I found myself holding back tears, not only for Rico, but for myself and for all the lonely people in the world. It made no sense to me; what was that constant unexplainable feeling of lonesomeness that seemed to devour me daily? Was I the only one who felt this way? When Rico finally spoke his voice became harsh, "When I was a kid I always hoped I'd see my father again. Now I never will. Oh, well. Fucking life." I wanted to tell him it was okay to cry, but Rico was the definition of macho and I thought if he heard me say the word "cry" he would make fun of me or vomit in my face.

We chowed on slow roasted pork, shrimp in a creole sauce, ham croquettes, fried plantains, and yuca with olive oil, garlic and parsley. We drank mojitos, and each time a new one came, we toasted his father, "To Manuel!" I said drunkenly. "To my old man!" Rico said. We got quickly plastered, but ate slowly and kept ordering more food. By the time the flan came, we were drinking strong dark coffee and our heads were screwing back on. Rico told me stories of his childhood in Cuba, "I remember the fruit on the trees; the mangos and avocados and papayas." He started talking about his father, they were more like snippets, like the shuffling of old photos. "He caught me an Iguana. I kept it in a little box." He'd stop and think. "My Dad loved mangos," he said. And then, Rico told me about the ocean and how blue and clear it was, the time his father taught him how to swim. "I have this image in my head. My father's face is really close to mine. Both of us are in the ocean. His big hands under me, holding me afloat. He's telling me to kick my legs. We were both laughing. He had a real solid laugh, like it came from his chest, from his heart, right where he lived, you know? Sometimes I still hear the water splashing around us. Sometimes I see his face." His tone of voice was deep and it mixed with sorrow and the Cuban music that played in the nearly empty restaurant,

In 1962 when Rico was eight years old, he left Cuba for America through a Catholic Charities program in Miami called the Pedro Program. It was used mainly for parents who were fighting underground against the regime. Soon the program was expanded to all families who feared Castro and who wanted to get their children out, even if that meant not seeing them for a few years. When Rico came to the U.S., he was placed in a foster home in Miami. A year later distant relatives from upstate New York sent for him.

"They were nice people, they were like fourth cousins, something like that, devout Catholics. They were the sickly sweet types. White as bread. They were Americanized Cubans. Meanwhile, I wanted to be a badass. I felt like a specimen though. Like a prize. I was paraded around to their friends. I was their, 'good deed.' I hated it. Don't get me wrong, I was grateful. But I wanted to be with my parents. I wanted to be back in Cuba. I didn't know what the hell was going on. Anyway, I didn't see my parents for four years. They couldn't get clearance to leave Cuba. By the time I finally saw my parents it was like we didn't know each other. I wasn't a little boy anymore. They weren't the parents I remembered. Four years is a long time in a little kid's world. You know what was really bad? A part of me hated them. I thought they'd abandoned me. I know now it wasn't their fault. As a little kid, I didn't know they were doing what was best for me. Years later, we were all together in the states. We moved to New Haven, Connecticut. We lived next door to Jack and his parents. Things were never the same in my family. It was a mess. We were broken. I always feared my parents were going to leave me again. I'd wake up in the middle of the night and peek in their bedroom to make sure they were still there. It's a rotten way to live, thinking your parents could up and leave you alone in the world. One day my father did. He left us. He hated America. He hated the bigotry here. He was educated, but was treated poorly. He hated the winters and the snow. He took off for South America. And my mother, well, she had no use for me anymore. The entire Castro thing ruined her. She wasn't strong. She lost it. Her own family was separated. Some were here, some were in Cuba, some in South America. My mother had all these nervous breakdowns. When I was eighteen, she split to be with her family in Miami. She wanted me to go with her but I didn't want to go. Whatever. I see her a few times a year. My saving grace through all that bullshit was Jack's parent's house. I was on my own at eighteen and they were there for me. They provided me with a safe haven, security, a feeling of home. Jack was a few years younger than me, I thought of him as a little brother. Jack's parents treated me like I was their son. I'll never forget their kindness. Jack and his family are everything to me."

Jack came home four days later. Mara had planned a coming home party for him in the bar. That day Rico was crazy excited. "Finally my brother is coming home!" he said. Early that evening he washed glasses, proudly polished the brass around the bar, his strong arms going back and forth, his face intense, yet happy. He bought a bottle of brandy for Jack that was not normally sold in the bar, something expensive and French. When I got to work, Rico sent me back out to buy Jack's favorite snacks; cashews, a hunk of Stilton cheese, pretzels and a bunch of chocolate bars: *Ritter Sport* chocolate rum raisin.

The first to arrive at the bar were Larry and Peter. They were a gay couple in their forties who had been together since 1975. Rico had told me about them. I felt that I needed gay friends and the idea that Larry and Peter were older appealed to me. Being young and looking for some direction and purpose in my life, I viewed older gay men as having some secret key to happiness. Older gay men, in my, eyes were kinder than my peers. I assumed it was because of age and experience. I had a hard time making gay friends my own age. Maybe because my defenses were up. I didn't want to get hurt. I didn't want to be rejected and didn't want my desire for friendship to be misinterpreted as a come on.

Larry and Peter had patronized the bar from its inception. They had become friendly with Jack and Mara. Both of them were outrageously handsome. They greeted me with warmth and friendliness, and when they found out I was from Boston, we immediately started talking about Provincetown and their favorite bars and restaurants there. I had been to Provincetown only twice prior to moving to New York City. It's a gay mecca on the tip of Cape Cod and going there for vacation is a rite of passage for most gay people. I was glad we had something in common and quickly felt connected to them. Larry had a big toothy smile that was permanently on his face. It would be virtually impossible to dislike him. "We'll have to go dancing some night!" Larry said. His eyes were as green as the leaves of summer. He was a chiropractor, and was forever cracking Mara's back, cost free. Rico told me weeks after I met Larry, that Larry was HIV positive and had been for a long time. He'd almost died years ago. The new cocktail of medications seemed to be working. Peter was five years younger than Larry. He was a financial consultant. A Penn State grad, from Delaware. He was affectionate and charming, and smelled like ivory soap; pure and clean. Peter was always well put together. He reminded me of Patrick Swayze in the movie *Dirty Dancing*, in both looks and stature. When I told him that, he'd forever tease me, "No one puts Leonardo in the Corner!" The first night we met, we swapped numbers and planned to have dinner the following week with Charlie. After phone numbers were swapped, Frankie made his grand entrance. He made cat calls, and whistled and snapped his fingers, all eyes were on him. Frankie was Mara's hairdresser. He was semi-famous. He had a few B movie stars as clients. He was fifty. He covered his face heavily with make-up to hide a bad case of adult acne. Frankie's wardrobe consisted of a variety of red pants, and red patent leather shoes. His hair was gray and at first glance you would think he was Andy Warhol, but on close inspection he looked more like Debbie Reynolds.

Frankie pranced through the bar, kissing everyone. He stopped when he came to me, "And who might you be?" I introduced myself as the new waiter. He told me to get him a dirty martini, and fast, "I had a bitch of a day! If I had to do one more blowout for a rich 5th Ave debutant, I swore I would shoot myself!" I obeyed and brought him his cocktail. He sipped it and told me that his dream was to be Madonna's hairdresser. I nodded and did my best to listen to him. He moved closer, trapping me, his breath on my face. Panic was emerging from the tips of my fingers, "You're a sweet little thing. Let's go to the basement. I want to suck your cock." He then growled like Eartha Kitt as Catwoman and at the same time ran his hand from my belly button to under my chin. I backed off, wanted to push him away, but remembered how Rico warned me about Frankie. I then felt an arm around my shoulder. It was Larry, "What do we need to do to get drinks around here?" Larry guided me back to the bar and playfully hummed in my ear, "Remember me in your memoirs, kid." Rico's words from earlier rang in my head,

"Frankie's an angry dude, don't mess with him or trust him. He has Mara's ear. But Larry is a prince, he's everything around here. He takes care of all of us. Frankie can be bitchy about that too. He's jealous."

In the early 1960's when Frankie was a young teen in Minnesota, his religious parents caught Frankie having sex with a neighbor, an older man who had a wife and three kids. The man killed himself. Frankie was carted off to a psychiatric hospital outside Minneapolis where he was mistreated; beaten and raped. When he was discharged almost a year later, he ran away to New York City. He was fifteen and prostituted himself. By the mid-1970's, he became quite a popular gay porn star, his most famous film, a gay cult favorite, "*Filling up Frankie.*" He played a gas attendant in a garage full of greasy, perspiring, hunky mechanics. I was fascinated. Of course, I rented the movie the very first chance I had and watched it on the crappy

T.V. and hardly working VCR that came with my rented room. And there was Frankie, young buff, blonde, beautiful, being gang-banged by six auto mechanics on the hood of a red mustang convertible. Rico told me not to ever mention the porn to Frankie. Once some guy said something to him at a bar downtown, and Frankie nearly tore the guy's eyes out of his head.

"Where the hell is the man of the hour!" Frankie screeched. Everyone in the bar followed his lead, and asked about Jack's whereabouts.

"With Mara upstairs in the apartment. They're coming down soon!" Rico shouted back.

I busily served drinks and watched people in pairs of threes or fours going into the small bathroom to snort coke. Soon the bar was packed and I weaved my way through the yapping crowd while the music of Chopin played. I glanced at Charlie, both of us exchanged smiles, winks, and when I passed him, pleasantries. A solid camaraderie was quickly building between us and I was excited and confident we would be friends for years to come. While waiting for Rico to make my drink orders, Frankie held his two hands around his mouth and muffled words to Rico. "So what's going on with Wayne and the screenplay? Did Mara tell him she was going to gut him like a fish yet?"

"Wayne's fucking furious that Mara is interfering with the screenplay. Who can blame him? Wayne's insisting that Jack didn't do that much, and Mara is saying Jack wrote the entire thing. It's such bullshit. I was there, it's not true. Wayne wrote the first three drafts. It's fucking absurd." Rico said. He was filling two glasses with Margarita's for Larry and Peter. The light greenish liquid glowed off the dim lights of the bar and the limey scent hit my nose. I took them to Larry and Peter who were leaning over the piano as Charlie played. "So is New York being good to you?" Larry asked. "How are the guys? Anything good lately?" Peter said to me, "Wouldn't you two queens like to know," I snapped my fingers and Larry laughed, "Oh, oh, oh, we have a live one here! I think I'm going to like you!" I stuck my tongue out at them and walked away.

When the big moment came. Mara walked in first. She wore her black leather pants and a tight short black leather jacket, she was braless and shirtless. Her cleavage demanded attention, her body squeaked when she walked. Jack followed. He wore dress pants and a deep navy blue button down shirt. His large nose led the way, his lips were thick. They seemed to quiver. His blonde curls framed his round moon shaped face. He was super tall and lanky. His voice was soft, melodious, pronounced. He had strong looking legs, big thighs, and full buttocks.

When Rico spotted Jack, he came from behind the bar and hugged him, "Welcome home brother." Jack patted his back and then, one by one, everyone flocked to him like hungry seagulls fighting over the lone french fry on a beach. Mara motioned me to go behind the bar, "Leonardo, open a bottle of Dom Perignon," she said. I immediately did what I was told. I lined champagne flutes across the bar. I then twisted the cork off and a loud pop and squeak come from the bottle's neck, "You never open an expensive bottle of champagne like that! That sound is vulgar!" Mara barked. I gritted my teeth. I was embarrassed. "Hey Leonardo, I'm Jack Fresh, how are you doing?" When I reached my hand out to shake Jack's hand, the bottle of champagne almost fell from my hand and the bottom of the bottle hit the top of the stainless steel sink. Champagne starting spilling over. I briskly pulled my hand away from Jack's and tended to the bottle. Mara saw everything. I soon learned, she kept a close eye on anyone Jack was talking to. So did Rico. "Darling! What are you doing? You first make that vulgar popping noise and now you waste all that expensive champagne!" Rico heard her and came behind the bar almost bulldozing me down. "Get back on the floor. We have a few new customers," his voice had changed. He used an angry tone that he'd never used on me before. My face heated up, Jack was looking at me. I felt like a loser. I came from behind the bar as Jack was on his way to the bathroom. He patted my shoulder, "Don't worry about them, man. They're highly strung." He then disappeared into the bathroom.

Rico was by my side within seconds.

"What did you say to him?"

"What? What do you mean?" I said.

"Don't bother him with stuff."

"I didn't say anything. What do you mean?"

"I'm just saying. He's tired. Don't bother him," Rico said. He left for the kitchen and I knew what that meant. I took drink orders, and by the time I was finished Rico was back behind the bar. I gave him my order. He was now smiling. His mood toward me drastically changed for the better in a matter of five minutes. "Right on it, Leonardo!" he went cheerfully about making the drinks. I noticed a speck of white powder under his nose. The shifting of moods due to the use of coke was mind blowing. Being around cocaine addicts was like playing Russian Roulette and Pop Goes the Weasel all rolled into one staggering game of not knowing if you needed to take cover from the vicious verbal bullets or extend your arms to embrace the tremendous love that came your way.

Soon Jack, Mara , Rico, Larry, Peter and Frankie went to the basement of the bar where Mara's desk sat dead center. A single light bulb was covered in a red paper Chinese shade. It hung over the desk and cast reddish shadows on people's faces. Scattered about the basement were endless boxes of receipts, lamps, tables and other objects Mara had bought at different flea markets. It was an old and cold space constructed with small thin bricks that were lopsided and stuck together with cement that had oozed over a hundred years ago, now frozen in time. The night ended with me being alone in the bar washing glasses, and sweeping. Rico called the bar phone from the basement, "You can go. Lock the door." His voice was curt and rude, he hung up abruptly. I barked at the dead phone, "Fuck you!" and I said it again. The sound of robust laughter made me jump and turn. Jack had exited the bathroom door, "Good for you. Good for you," he said and exited down the steps that led to the basement. His laughter carried up to me and I felt a small gust of joy. I think he liked me.

Scene Seven – Tom Waits – *Innocent When You Dream*

After working at the bar those first weeks, I realized that bar was a place for artists to congregate, listen to music, chat about how deeply devoted they were to their artwork and every so often sneak off to the bathroom to snort lines of cocaine. They knew the right things to say, buzzwords, names to drop, and they wore black. Most nights the bar was humming with analytical interpretations of the works of Joyce and Whitman, as well as the works of Rodin and Gauguin who they referred to as, "geniuses"… a word I heard so much while being in New York that each time I heard it I wanted to take a hot poker to my eardrum. Genius! Most of these conversations ended with everyone proclaiming their love for Patti Smith and Mapplethorpe. More than once, I heard the same customer speak of his deep understanding of Faulkner's *The Sound and the Fury* when he read it in college and how he couldn't understand how his classmates didn't "get it" alluding to how brilliant he was because he did. The bar also attracted a lot of pseudo socialists who lived in Alphabet City. Alphabet City was a part of the East Village where the Avenues were named with single letter names, A, B, C, and D. This was a super cheap neighborhood to live in and easy for most trust fund kids to live there and pretend to be living a poverty stricken, artistic life. Some of those people were the worst. Their conversations consisted of the evils of capitalism and government conspiracies. In the meantime, their rent was being paid by their "capitalistic pig" parents. Everyone spoke endlessly about their diets; veganism, vegetarianism, fruitarian diets, semi-vegetarianism, lacto-vegetarianism, ovo-vegetarianism, and ovo-lacto vegetarianism. When I had to run to the bodega to buy supplies, I'd sometimes pass the diner two doors up and see those same people chowing down on giant juicy cheeseburgers that dripped with orange American cheese.

A week after Jack came home, he stood in a corner of the bar and looked as if he was waiting for a bus, "Is Charlie coming in tonight?" his voice was gloomy and slow. "Charlie will be here soon, do you need anything?" Rico put his hand on his forearm. Jack muttered, "No thanks." A lit cigarette hung from his mouth. Smoke swirled over his head in slow gray slivers. The bar was practically empty and I was bored. I went over to Jack, "Need a drink, Jack?" I asked. Jack nodded, "Sure grab me an Italian beer, if you don't mind." His body started to slowly move from right to left unsteadily as if his movements were controlled by a computer chip installed in his head and it had gone awry. I went behind the bar, grabbed a beer and cracked it open. I handed it to Jack. I went back to the bar to count my tips. Rico stood next to me. When he spoke his voice was fiery, "I asked Jack if he needed a drink. Why did you ask him again?"

"Because he looked thirsty." I put my tips back in my pocket and walked away. Rico came after me, and tapped me on my shoulder in the middle of the bar,

"Listen, don't wise off to me. I get Jack his drinks. No one else does unless I say," he said. I held my hands up like someone had a gun pointing at me, "You're the boss applesauce." I walked away knowing that Rico might have been the biggest moron I had ever encountered in my twenty-four years of living.

Olena came in very late, kissed all of us, and sat at the bar. She had a fixed smile on her face. We chatted about her college courses and, as expected, she talked about her undying love for her boyfriend Ian. "I am so in love with him!" she covered her face with her hands and giggled and knocked feet together. It was obvious that Ian, who was an actor, was using Olena to get to Jack. Most of the time when he came to the bar the first thing he would ask was, "Is Jack here tonight?" and if he wasn't, he'd make excuses and leave. Other times, if Jack was around, he'd stay and they would swap small talk.

When Charlie arrived I was elated. His presence gave me a sense of protection. He watched out for me. "Always have safe sex," he'd say when we spoke about dates and our sexual conquests. I had a little crush on him, and that made me feel happy and alive. I'd often fantasize about us being together. That night, he chatted with Jack for a long time by the piano until he did his set. They were friends from years ago, and memory lane was being traveled by both of them. Mara came up from the basement, taking her usual break from snorting. She tried to get Jack to come to the basement, but he refused motioning that he wanted to continue to hear Charlie play. Mara stood and carefully glared at them both, her mind busy contemplating, without a doubt, something wicked. She stood holding a brandy glass. Her eyes went from Jack to Charlie. Later that night I was carrying a case of Amstel Lites up from the basement when I passed Jack and Mara going down the steps. Mara said to Jack, her voice venomous and mean, "You want to suck Charlie's cock? I see the way you look at him and the way he looks at you! Those days are gone!" She then slapped him upside the head. Jack's voice carried up to me, "Will you please stop, Mara." His voice submissive and beaten down. I heard a loud, horrid slap, and Jack letting out a little cry, followed by Mara, yelling, "You're bad and you will be punished."

A half hour later, the bar phone rang. Rico answered. It was Mara from the basement. She wanted to speak to Olena who took the phone from Rico. He lit a cigarette and eyed Olena closely. Olena spoke in a string of "yups" as she listened attentively. When she was done, she hung up the phone. She called over to Charlie who was getting ready to leave.

"Charlie, Mara wants to see you in the basement."

"No way, not tonight, tell her no thanks. I'm meeting friends uptown." Charlie started to put his coat on. Frankie played with a brass candelabra that sat in the center of the bar, it had six melting candles inside of it, he carefully eyeballed Charlie.

"Mara adores you, Charlie," Frankie said, "I think she gets hurt when you don't speak to her. You need to be more thankful." He took an olive out of his martini and plopped it in his mouth.

"Then why don't you go down and talk to her, she likes you, too," Charlie said. He winked at me. Frankie twisted himself off his bar stool, "Don't give me your attitude, queen, I'll do what I want, when I want!" Frankie headed for the basement. I handed Charlie his wool hat and walked him to the door.

"I want you to listen to me. And this is not a come-on. You're young, gay and stunning. You don't know it, but you are. So, listen to me. Find a nice guy, get another job, and get the hell out of here."

"But why do you stay here?" I said timidly.

"That's too complex to explain right now. I have to go. One day I'll tell you. Just get another job," he said.

About three in the morning the place was starting to empty. Rico and everyone else was in the basement. I sat alone, tossed down a few drinks and waited for the last customer to pay his bill. Jack called from the basement phone and told me to make a pitcher of Cosmopolitans for everyone and to bring them down to the basement. I went to the basement with the drinks, set the glasses on the desk and poured. All eyes were on me. I started to shake. Some spilled on Frankie's leg. He jumped.

"I'm sorry!" I said. "What the hell, queen, do you know how much these pants cost? But then again, I suppose you wouldn't. Where are you from anyway? The Bronx?" I started to clean off his leg. "I'm from Boston," I said. The napkin I was using started to crumble on his pants, "Bitch, stop, I'll do it!" Frankie flicked my hand away.

"Frankie, for crying out loud leave the kid alone!" Larry said.

"Do you want to buy me a new pair of pants?" Frankie barked.

"You're being ridiculous. Leave him alone," Peter said.

"Where did you find this nincompoop?" Mara said. Jack clandestinely put a twenty dollar bill in my hand. I speedily climbed the stairs, telling myself I was the biggest dork known to mankind. Except of course, for Frankie and Rico, who had proven over the past few weeks that they were in a close tie for the number one spot with Mara following only centimeters behind. All three of them had shown me who they were, desperate and controlling, all vying for Jack's approval and love.

I went into the bathroom and splashed cold water on my face. Water ran down my shirt and it chilled me. I was going to be fired without a doubt. My hands shook. When I came out of the bathroom, Larry was standing in front of me. "Look kid, I wanted to come up and say you're terrific. Pay no mind to them, you're doing a fine job!" He handed me five twenties. "No. No it's okay," I said. "Take it, go on, take it." He pushed the rolled up bills in my hand and high fived me. "I got your back, kid!" He ran back to the basement.

I locked the front door and went to the stereo and found something dark to play to fit the sad state of my affairs. I found a Tom Waits CD, and played *Innocent When you Dream.* As Waits sang, I stacked the tables and chairs, rolled up the giant oriental rug and started sweeping the floor. Then I heard single notes from the piano being pressed. Each key echoed and knocked off the tune of the Waits song. It was Jack.

"I wish I knew how to play." His long back hunched over the piano. "Sorry about Frankie, he's a pain in the ass."

"It's okay," I said.

"Let me sweep. Sit down," Jack said.

"It's okay," I said.

"I want to. Really."

I gave him the broom, sat at the piano, did the same thing he had done, pushed one key at a time. I watched as Jack swept. It seemed wrong to see him clean. I thought of him as royalty, too good to clean messes.

Those first weeks of meeting Jack were difficult, it was hard to capture who he really was. He was either drugged or drunk or in a blank state. The only thing consistent about him was the gloominess that emanated from his being.

"What are you writing?" he swept slowly, his eyes on the floor.

"I'm working on a play about a mother and daughter. It's about control and coming of age. I'm setting it in a tiny claustrophobic apartment. I like the idea of people thrown together and then watching the dynamic play out."

"Sounds good. I like to write too. It's very hard, but I like it," he said.

Then from behind me I heard a shout.

"What the hell! What are you doing, Leonardo?" Rico stood over me.

"Easy Rico, I wanted to sweep," Jack said. I immediately stood and went for the mop and bucket. Mara was now standing beside us, "Jack, why are you sweeping?" She whisked past me as if I didn't exist. She had a hard, silly grin on her face. She turned to me, "Look mate, I'm not interested in getting into an argy-bargy over this, but Jack doesn't clean." She then took the broom out of Jack's hand and threw it to the side. She snatched Jack by his face and gave him a deep kiss. "I wanted to sweep," he said. Mara took him by his hand and dragged him off, "Come baby let's go, you don't sweep floors. Have you gone bonkers?" and they both went to the bar's door. "I wanted to sweep," he said over and over as they walked out. "I wanted to sweep, I wanted to sweep." His voice carrying off into the night as the bar door closed. "You sound like a Ninny! Be quiet!" Mara said. The bar door slammed shut.

Rico poured himself a Vodka rocks and sat at the bar while I swished the mop across the floor. He asked me if Julia had called me. I garbled, "No."

"I think she's going to break up with me. Do you know anything?" he said.

"All I know is that she's in Ohio doing a play," I said. He gulped down his drink, "You better be careful. You're messing up. Mara is thinking about firing you," he then left for the basement.

Alone again, I looked inside the bucket. The water was grayish, dirty and it smelled like ammonia. I was tempted to drink it slowly with a straw.

Scene Eight – The Staple Singers – *I'll Take You There*

Still convinced I was going to be canned, I woke the next day in a horrible mood. I had one day off and I'd planned to spend it with Esther. Yet, I was fearful she would say something rude to me, leaving me with no other choice but to gnaw her into two pieces.

Esther's father spent ninety-five dollars each on tickets for us to see the "hot" new play by a "hot" new playwright. After the play, Esther said to me, "Wow, that playwright must be terrific in the sack. That play was the worst piece of crap I have ever seen in my life." I wholly agreed. The play was getting mega attention. Critics loved it. Newspapers and magazines were glowing with words like, "A must see!" and my favorite, "A transcendental experience!" Awards were predicted for that coming spring. Oddly audience members, the ones who didn't walk out, the ones that didn't fall asleep, the ones buying the tickets, buzzed outside the theater about how bad the play was.

Esther and I stood in front of the Lincoln Center Fountains. I was mad, jealous, bitter, and angry. Why not me? I wanted to drown myself in the fountain or roll my playbill up and choke myself with it.

"I don't get it. That play reminded me of something a freshman in college would write. It was like a first draft. This is a dying city. This isn't the New York I dreamed about," I said. Esther tugged on my coat and tried to pull me away from the fountain. I wouldn't budge.

"I think you should start schmoozing more with Jack. Ask him to read one of your plays. Granted, he might laugh at it, but it's worth a try."

"That's it! I'm in no mood for that kind of shit tonight. You're being mean."

"Jesus, Leonardo, it's some dumb play. The playwright got lucky. Dude, you'll get your day."

"I shouldn't be around people. Everyone makes fun of me. I'm awkward and pathetic and lonely. I'm a horrible writer. Seeing this rotten play has been the decaying cherry on top of the lousy frosting called my life. I need to be alone."

"I think you feel that you don't deserve success. It won't happen if that's what you think," she said.

"Oh, to hell with you, don't psychoanalyze me. What about you? Would you like me to point out your weaknesses and all your bullshit? Miss know it all! Miss frigging New York! You need to call your dad and thank him for all he does for you. The guy loves you, and you don't even see it. Maybe because you don't think you deserve his love. Huh? Did you think about that? Doesn't feel very nice, does it!" People started to notice my craziness. I stopped myself. Esther was on the verge of tears, my heart sank, "I'm sorry. That was wrong of me," I said. She then burst out crying and ran off. I chased after her, but it was too late. She was in a taxi and gone.

That evening I was so despondent and frustrated, so lost and empty, I didn't know quite what to do with myself. Left, right, center, I didn't even know what direction to walk. I wanted to feel good. I decided at that moment that sex was in order. Hot, steamy, sex, pure and joyous and magnificent and wonderful and fantastic. Sex! I jumped into a taxi and headed to a bathhouse in Chelsea, a place Larry had told me about, "Every gay man must experience a bathhouse at least once or fifty times." He'd said with a hearty laugh, adding, "But always play safe! You don't want to be on all these meds like me."

I dared myself to go, and off I went. The thoughts of contracting HIV scared me, always sent me into a panic after I had sex. I was strident in my practice of safe sex. I didn't want to die. I didn't want to be diseased and ostracized. I didn't want to hurt my parents. What would people in the town I lived in say? "I knew it! AIDS!" Although I was gay, I too had fears and prejudices against people with HIV even though it made absolutely no sense because more than likely I was having sex with HIV positive men and certainly susceptible to contracting it. I hated myself for feeling this way.

On the ride downtown I was scared. I didn't know what to expect. I'd heard the stories of bathhouses, but the reality of things was always different from what people talked about. My fear soon vanished with thoughts of another warm body close to mine. I was on a mission, a much needed one, one that had been ignored for weeks because I'd been working so many hours at the bar. Once inside the bathhouse I went directly into the sauna, took a long steam bath, and after, I cruised the corridors. Men, hunky men, passed me with towels wrapped around their waists; fat and skinny, short and tall, white, brown and black, young and old, hairy and smooth. They were all looking for sex, love, touch, and despite being told almost all my young life by my church and high school classmates and the world at large, that I was a freak, an abomination, and a disgusting human being, it was all good and unapologetic. The experience was new, fun, and exciting, an experiment, and a part of the gay culture I needed to explore. I loved all the men I saw that night, all their stunning faces, their bodies, their smiles, and I was them and they were me. I took a warm shower, wrapped a towel around my waist, cruised past rooms where doors were shut, and past open doors where, inside, men were having sex with one another. My heart beat with excitement. Disco music played, and at that moment, I was a million miles away from the bar. All my troubles and worries were gone. It felt free and good. Silly. Pleasurable and a whole lot wonderfully mischievous.

I met a man from San Diego. We chatted, and ended up playing most of the night. My first words to him were, "I play safe only," and he said, "Me too." His voice sincere serious. I trusted him. He was big and brawly, handsome, and we kissed and talked, made fun of ourselves, and the awkwardness of cruising and the fact that we didn't know one another's name. It was his first time in a bathhouse, too. "I'm Matt by the way. This is wild!" and I smiled, "I'm Leonardo."

It was something I needed, something that relaxed me. I loved being gay that night. I loved the freedom, the love, the sex, the intimacy, and the mutual acceptance. My frustrations were gone. I could breathe again, was human, a proud gay man and my guilt wasn't as bad as it usually was. Progress.

Scene Nine – Janis Joplin – *Piece of My Heart*

Julia called me. She was going to call things off with Rico. I figured the only reason Rico kept me around the bar, was to keep tabs on Julia. I was a goner. When I returned to work the next night, I prepared myself for the worst. I told myself it would be okay if I were fired. After all, I wasn't the first writer to totally mess up his life. Look at F. Scott Fitzgerald, Oscar Wilde, and Carson McCullers, the list was endless and impressive. I was going to be okay. This was all part of my legacy.

Before going into the bar, I took a deep breath and walked in. Rico was polishing glasses. He smiled, "Hey Leonardo, how goes it?" I smiled back suspiciously. Rico's hair was wet, and freshly slicked back. The smell of cheap cologne dominated the bar. I knew what it all meant. He'd spent the night on the sofa in the basement after a night of heavy snorting. While in that condition, he didn't like to take a taxi home because the coke triggered his paranoia. More than once he had gotten violent with taxi drivers. "It's best I lock myself in the basement, the Mr. Hyde comes out in me." The next afternoon when he woke in the basement, he would give himself a quick wash in the men's room, then drench himself with a cheap bottle of cologne that he bought from the CVS around the corner.

I started to set up the bar. Mara came up from the basement. My mind went into overdrive and I tried to clear the phantoms from my head. Maybe, I thought, they were going to fire me together. Maybe, put me in front of a firing squad. Instead, she called over to me while she covered her lips with blood red lipstick and sniffled, "Darling, we need you to babysit next week when Annie gets back from London. She's been with her daft father for the holiday. Olena has finals and she can't." I nodded yes to her. "Perfect, darling," she snapped her fingers at Rico, "brandy." He poured her one and slid it over to her. "Rico, pour one for Leonardo, too. What is wrong with you?" Mara said to Rico. He gritted his teeth and poured me a brandy. I took a small sip and enjoyed the burn and the much needed relief. She had her forefinger up her nose picking away at her cocaine crust. I was trying not to pay attention as she rolled small balls of crust off her fingers. I pushed my brandy dispassionately away. The phone rang and Rico answered it, "Oh, hi, Wayne." Mara waved her hand as if to tell Rico she did not want to speak to him. "No one is here, sorry Wayne. Ok. Later," Rico hung up and began to dust off the bottles behind the bar with a feather duster.

"Next time he calls, hang up on him," Mara said.

"He said he's coming by this week to talk to Jack about the screenplay."

She gulped down her brandy, took mine, and chugged it. I started to polish the piano. Thoughts of Charlie made me smile.

"Why don't you let Jack handle the situation with Wayne. He wrote the screenplay with him. Not you. It's too much for you. That's all I'm saying," Rico said.

"Jack and I are a team. You don't understand love. You're still a child. You'll never understand Jack's journey with me, it's metaphysical. The screenplay he wrote with Wayne is now *our* screenplay because it came from Jack. Therefore, it came from me, Jack and I are one. There is no Jack without Mara and no Mara without Jack. Darling get it through your thick skull!"

"But they wrote the screenplay way before you were in the picture."

"It doesn't matter," she motioned to be poured more brandy.

"As Jack's best friend, Mara, trust me, stay out of it," he filled her glass.

"As Jack's wife, I am telling *you* to stay out of it. Besides, mate, you have other things to be concerned with, like ordering more brandy. And besides your clothes look dirty. You're going downhill. It's sickening. You don't know how to handle your drugs. You're starting to look like a junkie." She looked at herself in a small compact mirror she had taken from her bag. She fixed her hair, moved her head left to right.

Rico left morosely for the kitchen shaking his head in frustration.

"Nincompoop," she exhaled groans of disappoint and disgust. I was on my knees wiping down the legs of the piano.

"Wash the window, too, darling, you do such a good job." I smiled up at her. When Rico came back to the bar she gave a swift, neat kiss to Rico on his lips, "I hate when you make me yell at you. I love you, I only want you to be your best. I have to run."

"I love you too," he said with as much sincerity as a murder victim thanking his murderer. Mara gave me a kiss on each of my cheeks, "Be good, darling, I'll give you a bell later. Cheers." As soon as she left, Rico plucked a wine glass off the drying rack and whipped it against the wall. Glass exploded everywhere as he did it three more times,

"Screw her! I hate her!" he said. I went for the broom and started to clean up the broken glass.

"Have you talked to Julia? She told me she wanted to take a break for a while. I don't know why. I can't figure her out. What the hell did I do wrong? She just wants to leave me like that?"

"She's really busy, Rico. That's all." I started to wash the inside of the window.

That night, Jack supported himself against the piano. He was mesmerized by Charlie who played mostly Mozart. Charlie performed sharply and with passion, his fingers skillfully prancing along the keys. It fascinated me. When he stopped, he said, "This one's for Michael" He played Mozart's Requiem. While he played tears formed in Charlie's eyes. Jack was motionless. I wondered who Michael was. Former lover? Mara walked into the bar and stopped when she noticed Jack standing over the piano. She stormed past him, and into the kitchen. Seconds later she stormed out. My eyes closely on her. She went directly to Rico. She clandestinely scolded him and he followed her to the kitchen.

Rico told me he forgot to put her coke supply in the hiding place in the kitchen. In addition to his other duties, Rico was assigned the task of calling Mara's drug dealer, Susie-Q, whose high teased hair and retro 1960's clothes made her look like a cast member from Valley of the Dolls. Rico was also responsible for cutting it, and making sure lines were ready to go on a small mirror before Mara went into the kitchen. They kept a small mirror inside a broken microwave in a corner of the kitchen. Rico also had a stash in a cigar box in the basement that he kept on a ceiling beam above the desk. He kept both cocaine hideaways stocked well. He didn't seem to mind. He called it one of his perks, "free drugs." When Susie-Q was around, I usually hoped for an open sewer to jump into. She referred to me as "sweetie," and constantly patted my back as if I were a kitten, "Hey sweetie, would you mind fixing me a ginger-ale with lime." "Hey sweetie, where's Mara?" Mara made it clear that she didn't want to be around Susie-Q because she disliked her. But the truth was, Mara, and Susie Q had been lovers years ago. Susie Q had a hard time letting Mara go, but her coke was good so Mara kept her around. "Her stuff is so pure, darling." Not only that, Mara had said to me many times, "I can't risk getting caught. I'm a mother." Clearly she figured getting busted for the possession of drugs was Rico's problem. And he was more than willing to take the chance. "I'll do anything for Jack and Mara. I love them. When you love people, you take the bullet for them," Rico often said.

Mara stood in a corner and observed everyone in the bar. Jack was still at the piano. His eyes fixated on Charlie. The bar was in full swing. Mara made her way in and out of the kitchen and at different intervals went down to the basement. Then, she'd be back up, kiss Jack, and prowl around the bar again. She'd grin baring the slightest amount of her teeth, talk to customers, or act like a zombie and stand very still. Her eyes always landing on Jack and Charlie.

When Charlie finished the set, Jack clapped fervently. He was awake and alive. He smiled and placed his arm on Charlie's back as they quietly chatted. Across the bar, Mara stood, her hands folded over her chest, biting the inside of her mouth. She made her way to me and spoke directly into my ear, her voice so penetrating I was surprised wax didn't come shooting out my other ear. "Charlie is playing horrible tonight, each night he gets worse and worse. Don't you agree, darling?" She didn't wait for my answer and started her slow skulk around the bar again.

When the bar closed, I was ordered to fill glasses with brandy and bring them around to everyone; Larry, Peter, Frankie, Jack, Mara and Rico as they stood around the piano. Charlie played *Chopin's* waltz in A-flat minor while I played servant. Mara had a nasty smile across her face. When Charlie finished playing, Mara held court. She decided to tell us the life story of *Chopin*. By that time, she had probably snorted about six kilos of coke. She looked like a corpse. When she had an audience and started to pontificate, there was no telling how long you'd have to stand and hear her cocaine induced babble. If you dared to walk away while she spoke, she took it as if you were literally peeing on her. That night, when she began her nonsensical hubbub, everyone had the look of horror on their faces. Larry and Peter had one foot out the door. Even Frankie whose lips were permanently attached to Mara's ass, looked like he wanted to run for Murry Hill. Charlie got up from the piano, and grabbed his coat, and corrected her.

"Mara, Chopin was born in Poland, not France."

There was dead silence. Larry and Peter coughed timorously, and Frankie puckered his lips and gave Mara an approving nod. Jack sat at the bar, far off in his alternative cocaine universe, tapping his fingers on the bar.

"Well, Charlie, dear, mate, wherever Chopin was born, you have no right playing his music. Tonight your work was very pedestrian, you played like a daft cow. You lack passion and your coldness is obvious. It's quite telling, plainly put, you're not as talented as I once thought. It's like you have no heart. If you don't improve by next week, you should find another place to work."

Charlie smiled nonchalantly, "Mara, you're out of control as usual, and you need to go home and go to bed." He put on his coat, wished us all a good night, and left. Mara marched off to the kitchen pulling Jack with her. Death and destruction had arrived. Mara came back from the kitchen, along with Jack, rubbing her nose frantically. She forcefully nabbed Jack by the wrist and pulled him along as they made their way to the door. She spoke noticeably to Jack so we could all hear,

"Charlie is part of your old life. He must be gone now. Enough of this." Jack followed her out as if he were on a leash or would soon be on one. I learned the next night that Charlie had been fired. I was completely heartbroken, torn apart, devastated. That night there was such sadness in the bar that Rico didn't even play music on the stereo. After hours, Rico told me that when Jack first moved to New York, he waited tables at a restaurant in Brooklyn where Charlie played piano. Jack was young, and struggling. Charlie helped him out by letting him sleep on his sofa and by giving him money. Charlie was one of Jack's oldest and dearest friends, their connection was meaningful and binding. I also learned the next day that there was much more that Rico didn't know about Charlie and Jack.

First thing the next morning, I called Charlie. I met him in Brooklyn for coffee at *Sugar Darling*, a hip new bakery in Brooklyn known for their humongous lumpy sugar doughnuts. They were made by bearded flannel shirt wearing quadruplets. Their doughnuts were the size of basketballs. Everyone loved them, and so I pretended I loved them too, even though after eating one it lay so heavy in my stomach I feared my body was going to sink into the earth's core. Coffee was served in used tin cans. Their coffee was from another famous place in Brooklyn where coffee beans from Jamaica were roasted and processed by another set of hipster type bearded brothers.

"She sucks. She's terrible. I can't believe you're not going to be there anymore," I said. A huge doughnut between us. Two tin cans filled with coffee sat at our place settings. He started ripping the giant doughnut apart with his large hands.

"It's not a big deal, it was more of a hassle than anything. I didn't need the job. Jack wanted me there. I have gigs all over town. This summer I have fifteen weddings. I do my film scoring. I'm fine." He sipped his coffee. His eyes were the bluest I'd ever seen.

"Well, I'm going to miss you," I took a sip of my coffee, and almost cut my tongue on the edge of the tin can, "My coffee tastes like cream of celery soup," I said. He roared. I padded my lip with a napkin.

"How are other things going, your writing, your love life. Remember what I said. No matter how in love you are, or how hot the guy, always play safe."

"I do. I swear," I said.

"Think of me as your gay mentor," he winked at me.

I ripped a hunk off the giant doughnut and shoved it in my mouth and immediately wanted to spit it out, instead I chewed slowly.

"I don't mean to come off as condescending. I'm older. I've seen all this before. Young gay man comes to New York. He's sincere and gentle like a baby cub and then he gets eaten alive by the tigers. I wish I'd had a gay mentor."

"Am I that obvious?"

"You practically have grass growing out of your ears."

"Can we get out of here. This doughnut tastes like shit. I don't trust these cups. I hope I don't get tin poisoning if there is such a thing."

We walked through Williamsburg, and made our way to the waterfront. The wind was fierce, and the sun strong. The twin towers were illuminated in a bluish haze. I loved having Charlie by my side. It was nice to see him in daylight out of the realm of the bar at night. Before us, tug boats were coursing through the East River, their horns blowing, making foamy waves of white. There was something majestic and awe inspiring about Manhattan from this point of view. It was distant but close. I imagined that if I stuck my hands out I could run them along the top of the buildings, gather the city in both my hands and squeeze out all I wanted. I felt like I had power at that moment. Even though I knew that once I was back in the City, everything around me would swallow me whole, take away my identity and confuse me again. I was learning, with each passing day, that New York was a difficult place; lonely and exciting, sad and thrilling, bright and gray, wonderful and awful. On that day, with Charlie next to me, New York was simple and good, all was possible, and I could have what I wanted.

"I wish I was young and starting out. If I'd only known then what I know now..."

"Known what? Tell me."

"That I was worth so much more than I thought. I could've had more. Lasting relationships, a bigger career. When I was a kid I was bullied terribly. It tore me down and it broke me. All I wanted to do was to get the hell out of Virginia. I came to the City in the mid 1970's, I was only twenty. I went wild with my new found freedom. For the first time I was around tons of other gay people. It was unreal! Yet, I had really low self-esteem. I attracted some shady characters. It took me years to understand the laws of attraction," he said.

"And what are those laws?" I asked.

"You attract what you think you're worth," he said. We started walking toward the Brooklyn Bridge.

"Charlie, are you sure you're okay?" I looked at him as he looked straight ahead,

"It's been a messy week. My dearest friend died a few days ago. I'm pretty upset. His name was Michael. He designed clothes. He was a good person. Very talented. He thought he would never achieve what he set out to do, and he did. It still wasn't good enough for him. Poor Michael. It's heartbreaking. I had to call his parents and tell them he was gone. They were devastated. His mother wept on the phone. She kept saying over and over that she didn't understand, that her son was only forty-four. Poor Michael had hung in there. He had AIDS for almost ten years. I can't believe another friend is gone. Jack and Mara knew him well too. Maybe Mara was upset, who knows."

"And they fired you knowing this?" He put his hand on my back as if to calm me down.

"Jack's always been passive. He allows people to do his dirty work, and then he comes out smelling like roses. It's Jack's way. I knew it was only a matter of time before Mara would come after me, and I don't blame her. Leonardo, this is complicated and I'm telling you this so you can get a larger picture, so you can fully understand what you're dealing with. Trust me when I tell you that you need to find another job and move on. They're going to eat you alive," he let out a long sigh,

"I shouldn't say anymore because if I do, then I have to go into my dysfunction and you don't want to hear that," he chuckled sadly.

"Sure I do," I said. There was dead silence as we walked another block.

"You can tell me anything," I said.

"Jack and I met about six months after a roommate of his died from AIDS. It was the early eighties and the beginning of all that horror. That whole experience screwed him up. He felt guilty about that guy's death for many reasons and he was doing a ton of drugs and drinking. He was young and exploring his sexuality and filled with self-hatred and guilt. Anyway, I met him at this funky party I'd stumbled upon. I saw this guy in his 50's dressed in leather garb, and next to him, was Jack, who was dressed like a little kid. He had a pacifier in his mouth. It was absurd. I was naïve. I didn't understand what was going on. The guy kept calling Jack names and belittling him. He called him a filthy faggot. Stuff like that. He started smacking Jack around. I tried to stop it, not knowing it was some kind of kinky role playing thing for everyone there to get off on. I made an ass of myself. I was kicked out. Anyway, I was walking home and Jack ran after me. He said he thought my kindness was amazing. I often wonder if it was actually my kindness he liked or the fact that he knew he'd found a sap. That night Jack and I hooked up. We fell in love. He soon moved in. It lasted a summer. It was a great time. It was a hot summer, record breaking, our air conditioner blasted. We hung out in the park, Fire Island, we danced at night, we went to the movies. It was one of those times that you never want to end. It was a scary time too though, so many guys died that summer. So to be in love and to feel that good in the middle of such darkness, well, it was a miracle. When our affair was over, it was hard to let go. I mean all I was doing back then was saying goodbye to people. Every week a friend died. Jack was really the only happiness I had for a long time, so I have this deep bond with him. Anyway, he was young, he didn't want to be tied down. I wanted a commitment. He was unable to give that to me. I was madly in love. Look, it's no secret that Jack started to hustle back then. I wanted him to stop. He didn't want to. He confessed to me one night that he liked the attention and the money. It was always about the money with Jack. He moved out and found himself a room to rent. He auditioned by day, took acting classes downtown, and worked at night. He messed around with important film executives, and at a party one night he met Cora Tanner. She was very hot at that time. Jack used his charm on her. They started dating and he moved in with her. Cora advocated for him, and within a matter of a year Jack was a film actor. He still came to me when he needed me, or as I told myself, when he needed to be loved. Not that Cora didn't love him, but we had this bond. Cora was good to me, she never knew about my affair with Jack, but when they broke up Cora came to me. She told me a lot of stuff. Jack is complicated.

I don't know how well he is mentally, to be honest. Poor Jack, he's not emotionally able to commit to anyone or to himself. It's like he's half here. When he came to see me he was usually drunk or high. I'm no fool. I knew he was emotionally limited. Maybe I'm the same way. Maybe that was the attraction I had to him. Mara knows in her heart who Jack is and she's not willing to love him on his terms. So she keeps him drugged and drunk. Look, you can't blame her for not wanting me around. She wants her marriage to work. She's desperate. I know what Mara goes through with him. I know what Cora went through. It's hard for you to understand, but Mara has a crazy past, too. She was absolutely beautiful when she was young. When they first met, Jack told me all about her. She came from Liverpool. She was a very poor, working class girl. Her father was a terrible drunk. He was jailed all the time for violent behavior. She was sexually abused by him most of her young life. When her mother found out, she took Mara to Oxford. They both lived with an aunt who worked for a professor as a housekeeper. Mara said her mother blamed her for her failed marriage and they fought all the time. Mara started taking drugs, got into the Punk scene, ran away to London, then went back to Oxford. Eventually her mother began cleaning the home of a very well educated, wealthy man who was an art history professor at Oxford. He ended up leaving his wife for Mara's mother and they married. He changed their lives. After a year, he started to have a special interest in Mara. He taught her everything about art and music.

"It was a real life Pygmalion story. He fell in love with her. She was a teenager. Mara didn't think that what her stepfather did was wrong. She claimed he no longer loved her mother. Mara hasn't spoken to her mother in years. And of course, in time, Mara was ousted by someone younger and prettier and as the story goes, Mara stabbed the girl. She didn't kill her, but it wasn't good. Long story short, after a period of time, she met Annie's father. He was a Chef, and soon they moved to New York, and Annie was born. Mara met Jack and within weeks dumped Annie's father. To be honest, Jack has the same kind of sad stuff in his life too. He has a history of sexual abuse. I'm unsure by who. He was never clear. I thought it was a priest or a family member, but he'd never tell me. He was very protective of that person. He'd whimper about it when he was drunk and in my arms but I couldn't understand him through his sobs. Jack and Mara have common ground. A sadness that binds them. They're one in the same. It's the law of attraction."

"Has Jack been coming to you all these years?"

"Let's put it this way. Jack is my bad habit. He's remnants of the old me. I'm not in love with him and don't want him back by any means, but I love him. And so, to answer your question, yes, he still comes to me. He came to me last week. We're not intimate, that was over for us years ago. Usually, I hold him, and sometimes he cries, sometimes he sobs like a little kid who has been hurt. We spoke this morning. I told him we both needed to move on and he agreed. He's a married man now. It's over, it's not healthy for either one of us."

We walked in silence for another block. I wanted to know more about him. I felt close to him. I hadn't had that feeling since my first college boyfriend.

"You mentioned you were picked on in school. I was, too," I said it like it was a badge of honor; the two of us wounded soldiers sharing stories of our battles.

"Most of us gay boys were. I've heard the most horrific stories in my life," he put his hand on my shoulder.

"I actually confronted one of my bully's after school one day. He was a neighbor, Howard Camp. Little asshole. We were actually friends when we were kids. I pleaded with him to stop bullying me, and he spit in my face. I remember standing there with his nasty spit dripping off my face. I couldn't move. I don't know how I survived those years. I knew that if I ever complained, it would be turned around, and I would be the bad one. It seemed perfectly acceptable to treat a gay kid in that way. Even my teachers did it. My gym teacher, Mr. Millis, was the worst. He used to call me fag boy. The other boys would laugh. I was powerless. I hated myself. I couldn't understand why I was gay -why I was created this way," I said.

"During a high school rally a bunch of kids tore my clothes off in the locker room and wrote 'queer' and 'fag' all over my body in black marker," Charlie said. "They carried me out into the gym in front of my entire class. I stood there shivering in the middle of the gym, stark naked. No one, not one single person came to help me. One teacher came up to me and he told me to get out. Everyone cheered. The principal said it was my fault, after all, I played piano. What could I expect?"

"Shit, Charlie, I could go on and on. Boys would walk by me, and whack my head; they'd write stuff on my locker like *faggot, queer*, and *girl.* I'd go home and fake that all was good. I was too embarrassed to tell my parents. How do you tell your parents that kids are calling you fag? I hid and cried a lot. After a while, I was convinced I was a freak. When I went off to college, the bullying was over, but that pain still lived inside of me. It still does. It's nuts. I'm twenty-four years old and I still worry about people not liking me because I'm gay. Every time I meet someone for the first time I wonder if they're going to hate me, reject me, or kill me. It's a horrible way to live and I try not be aware of it, but I'm pissed I even have to put effort into not being afraid of people. Do you know, that even now, when I walk past a group of fifteen-year-old boys, I still think I'm going to be attacked? It's so messed-up. But hey, guess what?

I actually had a boyfriend throughout college. His name was Josh Watson. He is in Oregon now. He's a teacher. Good guy. I should call him. …Anyway, my parents adored Josh. It was a happy time for me. When we graduated, he wanted to move back to Oregon and I wanted to stay on the east coast," I said.

"Gay people are stronger and more powerful now then ever. We're fighting back. This is a different time. Things are changing. AIDS is bad, it's a nightmare, but because of it we're being noticed, we exist, we're not invisible anymore. My friends who've died are martyrs as far as I'm concerned. I feel great change coming. I do," Charlie said.

"I want to kiss you," I said. My voice meek. He pulled me close to his chest, hugged me so hard his rib cage pressed into me. He smelled like spicy musk. He rubbed the top of my head, and let me go.

"Why did you let me go?" We were in the middle of the Brooklyn Bridge, gusts of wind blew our jackets haphazardly. He smiled. Took me by my chin, and we kissed. He was warm and tender. I brought one hand to his and held it in mine. His big hands, soft, and tender, I wondered if I'd ever see them prancing along a piano's keys again.

"I want you to take real good care of yourself, do you understand?" he said.

"When can I see you again?" I said. He became nervous, and stuttered.

"Not for a bit, I've decided to go to Florida for a while to spend time with my folks, and do some relaxing. I need to get out of the City. I'll be back in a few months. Listen I'm an old guy."

"I'm really sad," I said.

"Leonardo, listen to me. I'm an old man, and you're young. You don't want me. Everything is going to be fine. I promise," he said, and winked.

"How do you know?"

"I have faith in you. Just know your self-worth, and then go fly like a bird."

"Are you HIV positive, is that what this is about? That wouldn't bother me."

"No. I'm negative. It's about you being young and me being old. You'll understand one day," he wiggled his fingers in front of me. "Behave yourself and goodbye." He smiled, turned, and walked back into Brooklyn. I walked toward Manhattan. My final steps off the bridge, I heaved with rejection and cried.

Back at the bar, I started to clean up for the night and close things down. Rico sat at the bar, his face in both hands, his Scotch under his chin; he had put on Leonard Cohen's, *Paper Thin Hotel.*

"I have done so much cocaine and have drunk so much since Jack met Mara, I feel it's getting worse," Rico sipped his Scotch.

"Try and stop." I was closing the velvety curtains and starting to stack chairs.

"It's like I want to, but then Mara has me call Susie-Q and I find myself back at it."

"You can't blame Mara. She's not forcing you." I started rolling up the Oriental rug.

"I feel worried about Jack. Did you know that Jack had five years of sobriety when he was with Cora? He went back to drinking when he met Mara. She could drive anyone to drink because it's the only way she's tolerable."

We both laughed boisterously.

"Everyone is free to do what they want." Who was I to advise? I was in a horrible situation by my own free will. I chose to be around some massively dislikable people. I allowed my own imprisonment while waiting for a chance, a lucky break.

"Want a drink?" Rico asked.

"Sure," I said. Might as well, I thought. I asked Rico for a shot of *Maker's Mark* and Italian beer. I finished mopping and sat next to Rico. It was early in the morning and I could see the sun coming in through the cracks in the curtains. Small thin gleams of light lit the bar harshly. I started playing with the candelabra, the six candles still burned from the night before, the lights were dim and the place smelled like ammonia from the mop water.

"It's almost like he doesn't know who he is. He was like that as a kid. If Jack dated a vegetarian, he would be a vegetarian. When he dated someone sober, he joined AA. Now he has a major coke enthusiast as a wife, and that's who he is. When we were in our twenties, all Jack wanted to be was an actor. I remember when the movie *Fame* came out. We'd all dance in the street to the soundtrack. I can still see Jack dancing on the cars parked along our street. I knew he would be famous. I knew it. Soon after, he left for the City. Years later, he met Cora Tanner. All his dreams started coming true. It was awesome to see Jack progress as an actor. Cora made sure that when she was in a film there was a part for Jack. Man, she loved him. Then, Jack started cheating on her. Cora found out, and that was the end of that. Cora won't talk to him anymore. That's what Jack does. He has a remarkable ability to draw you in, and then toss you away and forget you."

"Why do you love Jack so much?" I asked.

"Because inside, Jack is a good person." At that moment I understood why Rico was infatuated with Jack. It wasn't about love, it was about need. I understood why Mara put up with Jack. I understood why his family did, why Charlie did, and why everyone else did. Jack was so withdrawn from everyone, so out of touch with people, that he was a challenge for everyone, a puzzle to be solved. He stirred in all of us that basic human necessity of needing to be needed, approved of, and to be loved.

Scene Ten – Bette Milder – *Baby Mine*

"Where the hell have you been? It's been weeks!" It was Esther on the other end of the my phone, her call woke me up.

"Ugh…I am so hung over. Sometimes my phone doesn't work," my voice was groggy.

"You sound rough."

"You have no idea; I think I drank a case of whiskey and a million beers this week."

"I'm impressed. Hey, look, I have tickets to some lame show on Broadway tomorrow night. Wanna go with me? My dopey father got them from some gross capitalistic cow he does business with."

"I probably have to work and if Mara needs me, I can't say no to her."

"Wow, you've really been pulled into their life, big time."

"Whatever. Can I call you back?"

"Why are you sleeping so late?"

"What time is it?"

"Hello, its 6:30."

"In the morning? It can't be."

"It's 6:30 at night! What is wrong with you?"

"I was supposed to be at work a half hour ago! I gotta go!"

As soon as I hung up, Mara called.

"Where the hell are you? I've been waiting for you! And calling and calling, no bloody answer! I have a surprise for you. Come straight away! Of all days you decide to be late!"

"On my way! Sorry!"

"Do you not take this job seriously? I'm running a business here. You're messing up again and again." Click. I hailed a taxi and in my bleary state of mind instructed the taxi driver to cut through every opening between cars, encouraged him to run lights, directed him down a few cross streets, and shouted at him to beep his horn. Finally, I got out of the taxi because traffic was so heavy. I ran toward the bar dodging people, cars, dogs and small children, telling myself over and over, "I could not let myself get fired." When I arrived, Mara was sitting at the bar, a sad grimace was on her face. Rico was setting up the bar. I was huffing and puffing completely out of breath. A small box sat in front of her.

"I am so sorry!" I said.

"Sorry is not an excuse. I called and called and there was no answer."

"I must have been out cold. My phone never works, I swear and..." I said.

"Blah blah blah. Spare me, darling! This must never happen again. I was so excited to give you this and you spoiled it." She slid the box over to me. It was a cell phone.

"What's this?"

"Darling really, what does it look like? It's a cell phone. It's your surprise. You ruined it. I was waiting and waiting for you! Surprise ruined!"

"I'm surprised! I overslept and I-"

"Blah blah blah! So anyway, since you're officially employed, we've decided it would be best for you to have a cell phone since you can't manage to get your own phone to work correctly. Clearly this gift has come at the right time! Anyway, Jack and I will cover the bill. But it's a work phone, only. Of course we expect you to call that bourgeois town you're from so you can speak to those parents you love so much, but limit the calls," she said. I took the phone out of it's box. It was fairly big, and covered with buttons. It was confusing as all hell. I was completely engrossed; turning the phone, pressing buttons.

"Can you babysit for Jack and I tonight? We have a party. Hello? Hello? Are you listening to me, damn it!" She harshly snatched the phone from my hands. "Bloody hell! Did you hear me! I need you to babysit for me tonight!" she barked.

"Yes. Yes. Of course," she handed the phone back to me.

"Wow, my own phone. I'm stunned."

"Don't call China or anything silly like that," she rolled her eyes.

"I don't know what to say."

"Most people would say, 'thank you'. Rico, show him how it works." She then pointed at me. Her finger almost touched the tip of my nose. "When I call, answer. Don't disappoint me. I'll call you later tonight when I want you to come babysit," she shot down the rest of her brandy and left. For the remainder of the night Rico explained how to use the phone, loaded his phone number inside of it, then Mara's and Jack's number. We made tests calls and made jokes. I'd go into the garden area and he'd call me, "Fuck you," he'd say and hang up. When I was in the basement getting beer, I'd call him, "Eat shit and die" I'd say and hang up. We thought we were a laugh riot. Finally, I told him I wanted to walk blocks away and call him. I ran up 2nd Avenue three blocks away and called, "Hello asshole central," Rico said when he answered the phone. "I'm looking for the head asshole?" "Oh, she can't come to the phone right now she's busy snorting a kilo of cocaine. How can I help you?" Rico said. Our laughter going through the cell phone waves of the universe, people on the street looking at me, I had entered into the modern world. What was next for me? Email? The feeling of self-satisfaction I had at that moment was incredible, but at the same time nauseating. Sure, I had seen plenty of people walking the streets of New York talking into cells phones. I always assumed they were business types, sophisticated, better than me, wealthy and naturally I made fun of those people. I referred to them as self-important douche bags. But look at me now, I had a cell phone! Christ, I was thrilled. I felt indebted to Mara and Jack. Forever. Obviously they loved me. They really loved me! Walking back to the bar, I called my parents.

"I have a cell phone. My own phone! Jack and Mara bought it for me. Can you believe it?" I said. They were both impressed and congratulated me. After giving them my new number I warned them about limiting their calls to me because the cell phone was mostly for work. My voice condescendingly boastful, I wanted to prove to them I was on my way to superstardom. That I was important.

At midnight, Mara called me on my new phone, "We're waiting, get up here!" Click. I told Rico I was leaving to babysit, and while getting ready to dash, Rico stopped me, "Don't feel too special. I know Mara, she looks for as many tax write off's as she can. Our phones are write offs. We're doing them the favor. Trust me." I shrugged it off and thought Rico an ungrateful swine and left.

When I arrived at Mara and Jack's apartment to babysit, Annie was sleeping. Mara told me they were both going to a very "private" party. They wore tight black latex outfits that made them look like they were starring in a science fiction porn movie. Mara left holding the black bag filled with sex toys.

In the morning, when Annie noticed her parents weren't home, she found me.

"Leonardo. Are you staying with me forever? Can we get pancakes at the diner? Can we? Can we?" her voice jubilant. She played with my new phone.

In the diner, I faced the window outside and Annie faced inside the diner. I happily watched her eat her stack of pancakes. While finishing breakfast, Jack and Mara walked by. Both were visibly strung out. Mara was drumming Jack on the shoulder repeatedly, screaming at him. I couldn't hear what they were saying, their voices were muffled. I kept giving Annie a big safe smile, grateful her back was to the window. I didn't tell her that her mother and Jack were right behind her. Jack went up to Mara, put his hand on her chin and shook it. She kicked him. He pushed her and she fell to the curb. People walked by, some nonchalantly, some stunned. Jack helped Mara to her feet. She swung the black bag at him and all the sex toys went flying out of the bag; two dildos, a butt plug, handcuffs, lube and the electric anal bullet. Jack went to pick them all up and Mara picked up the biggest dildo and started whacking him over the head with it. He started laughing at her, and that is when they both noticed me sitting with Annie. I gave them a slow and long nervous wave. They composed themselves and came into the diner. Mara came in first, looking ferocious as her eyes kept shifting. Jack followed her, stopping to pick up a *Village Voice* in the diner's entrance.

"Oh, look there's your Mommy," I said. Mara slid into the booth.

"Order me coffee. I don't want to speak to the waitress." I raised my hand to the waitress, "Coffee, please." Jack slid in next to me, "Make it two." Jack said to the waitress. He began to read the paper.

"Hi Mommy. Mommy can I stay with Leonardo forever?" Annie said.

"Why would you ask me such a stupid question? Of course not!" Annie's body looked like a deflating balloon. Mara ripped the paper out of Jack's hands, "You are such a wanker! I want to know, where you were you for one hour!" Mara said. Her voice piercing, low, cutting. She glared at Jack as if she was going to strangle him with one hand.

"Not now, Mara ."

"Big show off, big actor, dodgy bastard you are! You make me want to honk!"

"Not now, Mara," his voice low. Annie's shoulder's started to bend inward, people were looking. Huge tears came to Annie's eyes. Jack's body rocked slightly, "You do too much of that stuff and it makes you crazy." His voice was monotone, deep.

"You're a daft cow!" Mara picked up my glass of water and tossed it in Jack's face. She abruptly slid out of the booth, almost knocking the two coffees out of the approaching waitress's hands and stormed off. Jack wiped his face off and spoke to the waitress, "Can you please get him another water? And, could I have some eggs, over easy," he said.

When Jack was done with his coffee and eggs, he took Annie home. I stood on the sidewalk and watched as Jack took her by the hand and walked off. Annie turned her head, looked at me, and waved until they disappeared in the crowd on the sidewalk. My cell phone rang. It was Mara. "I'm glad you witnessed my husband's shitty behavior! He's a disgusting animal! A real pig. I ask myself every bloody day why I married him? Why? Have you ever felt like you made a colossal life mistake? I do every day. My life is a mess, truly it is! Men! They have always used me. I know it sounds cliché, but it's bloody true. I'm telling you Leonardo, don't trust a soul in this crappy world! Men! Huh, they all cheat. They all lie. Let me ask you this, is it too bloody much to ask to be loved? Is it? I see that in you, Leonardo, I do, I see that you want to be loved, but are terrified. We're a lot alike you and I. You poor dear."

"Well. I will, I mean, I don't know," I stuttered. If I was like her, I thought, I might as well run into traffic and call it a day. She went on and on as I walked up 2nd Avenue. My new phone pressed against my ear. For one hour I listened as her emotions run from absolute murderous anger, to sorrowful sobs. She jumped from subject to subject in her usual nonsensical fashion. A part of me wanted to run back to her apartment and rescue and console her. The other part of me wanted to tie a cinder block to her waist and throw her in the East River. She would not stop talking and I didn't know how to stop her.

"To hell with bloody love, maybe I should be like you, maybe I should protect myself and avoid love. My parents never loved me, they didn't. I really believe they were jealous of me. I really do. You see, darling, I know things. I have a great intuitive sense. It scares people. To hell with people and life! Maybe you're the smart one! I should avoid love like you!" And on and on she went. When I arrived home, depression stomped it's ugly way into my brain and all I could think was what a damn lousy place the world was and how the hell did Mara always seem to know exactly how I felt inside? My phone battery died and her voice was gone. My excitement over my new phone was replaced with dread and an annoying buzz in my ear.

Scene Eleven – Perry Como – *There Is No Christmas Like a Home Christmas*

I was going home for four days over Christmas. Esther came to my place and watched me pack my small duffle bag. She sat on a gift that was wrapped in striped red and white paper. It looked like a book. She'd bleached her hair a snowy white, wore a black mini skirt, a white angora sweater, and high, red, patent leather boots. By her side was on open beer can and a smoldering cigarette in an ashtray. She examined my cell phone in her hands. There was a hard, indignant expression on her face that told me there was something on Esther's mind. Either I did something unsophisticated, or she had a fight with her father or she was jealous I had a cell phone, or it was all three reasons.

"My father is buying me a cell phone. Like yours. We can talk more. I miss you."

"Awesome," I said.

"So, I got laid last night," she said. She puckered her lips and sucked in some smoke.

"You don't look happy for someone who recently got laid," I said.

"It was fun. Why do you say that?" She sipped her beer, crossed her legs the other way.

"Who was it?"

"I don't know. Some guy I sat next to at this bar last night."

"Were you safe? Did he come to your place or did you go to his?"

"Are you a complete moron? Like I would take some psycho back to my place and let him screw me without a condom? Hello! We went out the back door and down this small alley, he put me on a trash can, covered his junk, and we did our thing. All these boxes of empty beer bottles next to us were rattling. It was kind of amusing until he started grunting like a dog."

"You need to be careful," I said.

"It's not like I do that all the time. He was cute, so I went for it."

"Well, good for you then."

"So Merry Christmas, even though I'm an atheist," she handed me the gift she had been sitting on.

"I feel bad I didn't get you a gift." I unwrapped it. It was a book entitled, *So You Want To Be A Writer.* "Thanks, I think…" I said.

"What? You don't like? Study it while you're home. Come on, I'll walk you to the subway."

Christmas trees lined the sidewalk. Pine needles were at our feet. Snow started to wistfully blow through the air and as we spoke, our breath wafted above us in haphazard clouds. Esther hadn't worn coat so she kept her hands in the pockets of her skirt. She shivered as we walked, "I feel like you're dumping my ass for Jack and his wife. I have to be honest."

"I'm doing what you told me to do. I'm networking and kissing ass."

"Dude, I said kiss their ass not stick your head up their butts and look for polyps," her teeth started to chatter.

"I'm sorry. I swear we'll hang out more when I get back. They're demanding. I'm always babysitting. I worry about Annie. I'm not crazy about leaving her with them. I feel badly about it. I can't explain it, but it's like I want to save her from them."

"She'll be fine, kids are resilient."

"I know, I know, I know, but they're both crazy. I feel like I need to do the right thing, like call social services. I'm serious. What kind of person lets a kid be exposed to this kind of crap?" I said.

"So go ahead and report them. Then, you better go into hiding for the rest of your life and say goodbye to any chance of having a career in show business."

"Kids come first. Always."

"Then call social services since you have so much integrity."

"You're not making this easy for me."

"The reality is this, it's worse when a kid is taken away from a parent. They end up going to foster parents who are complete strangers. I bet some are total creeps. I'd stay out of it. Messing with a parent and child relationship is tricky territory. If you call Annie's father, he'd call Mara. If you call social services, they'd investigate her dad too. In the long run it would be worse for Annie. It's not worth it. That stuff is very hard to prove. In the end, you'll be the bad guy."

"I feel sick about it, I really do," I said.

"It's not your fault. It's the system. It's America. We're all responsible for this bullshit. Look, Leonardo, it's like I've told you over and over. Americans love their celebrities. You call the authorities on a hip and beloved New York film star without any real proof, it will be looked at as hearsay. You'll be screwed. You'll be lynched in Central Park. You'll be the victimizer. I can promise you this, Jack and Mara will come off as the saints. The victims. Plus, from what you're telling me about them, they'll make stuff up about you, and the public will believe them. Anyone who ever worked with Jack, and he's worked with some 'A' list actors, will come forward. They will contest how wonderful and kind Jack is. You'll be the bad guy. The wanna be writer. The guy who is jealous. The guy with some weird agenda.

Keep your mouth shut, love Annie, be there for her, do what you can, encourage her to live with her Dad."

"That's a good idea."

"At the end of the day, Annie might be okay. We all face stuff, we all have to survive in an unjust world. You can't take it all on. This is much bigger than you." We stood at the entrance of the Number 1 train at 110th Street. She bounced up and down as we said goodbye. "So, have a nice time," she said. I put my duffel bag down and hugged her.

"I feel like shit. I shouldn't have had sex with that guy," she said.

"It's okay. Forget about it."

"So what are you going to do over Christmas?"

"I dunno. My Dad is begging me to have dinner with him. Ugh, I hate him. He's always telling me he loves me. He's always asking me why we're not close. It's so annoying."

"You need to be nice to him. He pays your rent. He sounds like a nice guy."

"Be quiet. Go. I love you."

I started down the subway stairs. She tugged on my duffel bag, "Wait!" I went back to her. A snowflake was caught on her eyelash and I pushed it away,

"Do you think I'm a slut for what I did?"

"No. I don't. I think you're great."

"Truly?"

"Yes. Truly."

"Can you give me another hug?" I pulled her very close to me. She melted in my arms,

"I'm an idiot," she said, and I let her go.

"You're not. You're wonderful and wise. You're a pain in the ass, but I love you. I'll call you from Boston. Goodbye." I kissed her, and walked down the steps that led to the train. She called after me.

"See you soon! Merry Christmas! Love you!"

"Same to you, Miss Atheist, love you too!"

And that was the last time I saw Esther for quite some time.

Walking through Penn Station that night I was beyond elated and could not wait to get home. The thought of getting into my old bed thrilled me. I was going to decorate our Christmas tree, eat good food, be with my family, go to the movies and sleep and sleep some more. I found a seat and waited for my gate to be called. I started to read the first fifteen pages of a play I started weeks ago. It wasn't good, and was giving me a lot of trouble. My cell phone rang. It was Mara. I contemplated answering it, and didn't. No way. Not now. I'm going home. I was determined to be free of her for four entire days. My cell phone rang again. It was her. I didn't answer. I was proud of my restraint. It rang again, and quickly it went dead. Seconds later, it rang again and again, and then it stopped. Glory be to God! Shit! Mara had advised me to always answer the phone when she called, what if I didn't answer? What would Mara do? Finally my gate was called and I was on my way home. I convinced myself she would get over it. I forced a smile that was wide and gleaming, it ran across my face although I knew I was somehow doomed. I descended the steps to the tracks. My phone rang again. I told myself I was a gigantic idiot the second I answered it, but Mara's warning to always answer the cell phone kept needling me and I was weak.

"Hello?"

"All right darling?"

"Hi Mara. I'm about to get on the train for Boston."

"Take a later one, darling."

"Well, the next one is at 9pm."

"Brilliant! Jack and I want to have a holiday drink with you. We have important things to discuss. Don't fanny around. Get down here."

"But I was—I don't—"

"What's the problem? There's a 9:00 pm train. Tis the season. You come visit with us for a while, we have drinks, we wish each other a Happy Christmas and Bob's your uncle. Please, darling, do come."

"My father is meeting me at the station and—"

"It would mean a lot to us. Ring him on the new cell."

"Okay, okay I'll be there in about 30 minutes."

"Luvvly-jubbly! See you soon, brilliant! Click.

I called my Dad, told him about my change of plans, and walked up 8th Avenue. My phone rang again.

"Darling, it's monkey's outside, would you mind picking up a bottle of brandy? Jack is getting a cold and right knackered. I don't want to send him out. We don't want to ask that bumsucker, Rico. He's undependable. The bar is busy, and every person has up and left town.

"No problem," I managed to say.

"Smashing! See you soon, love." I wanted to reach through my cell phone and strangle her, slowly and unmercifully until her eyes popped out of her head. But the truth was, I should have strangled myself, right then and there.

Annie was in England with her father. The house was very still. Mara had Chinese delivered. Jack took the brandy from me without saying hello. Poured three glasses for us while Mara was fixing plates of food.

"Mara and I were talking," Jack said.

"We wanted to share some brilliant news with you," she said.

"So much is happening," Jack said.

"The Universe is one with Jack and I. It's sacred."

"I signed with a great agency today. The biggest one in New York and LA," Jack smiled.

"They think he is the actor of his generation. We're gob-smacked!" Mara kissed Jack.

"We will need help this coming year, with Annie and such," Mara said. She handed me a plate of food and I dug in.

"I got another film too."

"It's filming in New York. It's the lead and there are some possible writing opportunities," Mara said.

"I always wanted to try my hand at writing," Jack said.

"Tell him about Budweiser," Mara said.

"I got this commercial for Budweiser for the Chinese market."

"I hope to close the bar in two years. We hope to purchase a townhouse soon," Mara said.

"Plus there is some talk of a TV series for one of the cable networks," Jack said.

"We like you Leonardo. We're happy you're in our lives. We love you. This is our Christmas gift to you: our dedication and love. To our dear Leonardo," Mara said. We all toasted to me, I guess I should have known better, but such proclamations were not common, so I went for it.

"Here's to me," I said. They laughed.

Jack poured us more brandy and we toasted. Mara curled in a ball on the floor and went in and out of sleep, tossing and turning, scratching her arms. She reminded me of a cat. A lazy one. Jack asked me questions about my life, family, dreams, artistic goals, the same old stuff he always asked me but always seemed to forget my answers to because he was consistently high or drunk. In a way it was amusing, it was like talking to my great Uncle Bruce who was 94 and couldn't remember anything. I glanced at the time on my phone.

"Well, thank you so much for everything. It's 8:30 and my train leaves at 9. I'm going to get going." Mara's face became forlorn. She sat up,

"Oh phooey! Can't you take another train, darling? This is a special night."

"But the next train is not until 4am."

"Perfect! We have something else to tell you something we're contemplating."

"Mara, not now," Jack poured more brandy. He was slowly disappearing, tuning out. I was used to that look. Something was up.

"We're going to try and have a baby!" Mara said. She rubbed her nose and smiled happily. I didn't know whether she was making a joke or not. Was she going to ask me to watch her and Jack make a baby and photograph the event? I wouldn't have put it past them. I cracked my knuckles.

"Wow — Hey — Well, that's great news," I said.

"It's only a thought, we're not sure yet," Jack said. His voice low, almost troubled.

"What do you mean, we're not sure, you said you wanted a baby earlier," Mara said.

"I said we should talk about it," Jack said.

"Don't listen to him, he's bonkers, Leonardo, we knew you'd be happy for us," Mara said.

"I'm thrilled. Congratulations," I said.

"I'm beat. I think I need to go to bed," Jack said.

"Yes, I agree, let's go to bed. It's been a long and exciting day. So Leonardo, do stay on the sofa, and see yourself out, give us a bell the second you get back to New York," Mara said. She kissed both sides of my face. "Do have a nice holiday, cheers darling." Jack gave me a hug, "Merry Christmas, man," he said. She then guided him to the bedroom, and shut the door.

It was 8:45 pm. I would never make my train. I was dumbfounded. Why couldn't their decree of love for me and career news wait four days? Why beg me to stay only to go to bed? I rationalized the ridiculousness of it by convincing myself that it was an honor to be so valued by both of them. Either that, or they couldn't find a liquor store that delivered. I lay on the sofa, set the alarm on my phone, and fell asleep. I was stirred later by whimpering and squealing coming from their bedroom. My mind went to that place. Was Mara smacking Jack's ass with a paddle or a baseball bat? The sounds were loud and frightening. I couldn't decipher whether the moans were of passion or pain, whichever, it didn't sound like fun to me. I hope a baby wasn't going to be the end product of some weird and kinky sex session. It seemed disturbing, yet twistedly amusing, and I couldn't help but giggle. I soon left, and made my way to Penn Station, drunk, a little pissed off, a little wigged out, and a lot perplexed.

On the train home, my mind did flips. The idea of Mara having a baby frightened me, but maybe it would provide the change she and Jack needed. Maybe a baby would get them both off the booze and cocaine. A baby could provide them with a new beginning, and that could ultimately benefit Annie. Poor Annie. I hoped she was having fun in England, hoped all her Christmas dreams would come true. I soon fell asleep and a nightmare came; I was being chased by a ferocious barking dog with fanged teeth and red eyes, and no matter where I hid, the beast found me, and off I'd go running from it again and again and again. There was no escape.

I arrived in Boston exhausted, and disgruntled.

In my father's car, driving on the highway, I looked in the mirror above the dash, the circles under my eyes were deeply brown, my face was bloated and my skin chalk white.

"You smell of booze." My father's attention was steady on the road.

"Nice to see you too." My head hurt, and my hands shook. My father remained silent which meant he had a lot to say. To ensure silence, the idea of faking sleep came to me, snoring sounds were included to maximize effectiveness. When we pulled into the driveway my eyes focused on my childhood home longingly; a small, neat cape, white and merry, a place that provided a sanctuary from my horrid school days, but mostly that house contained happy recollections of family, and holidays, my nieces and nephews and good food and cheer. My home.

My mother had hung Christmas garlands on our front door and on the large hedges by the brick front steps. Tears of grief came to my eyes, I felt shame. Nostalgia hit me in the softest part of my belly and it stung badly. My behavior in New York did not represent how my parents raised me. My father, a high school principal, my mother a floral designer at a local flower shop; both were liberals.

In their house there were morals and good will toward all. There was church on Sunday. Even though they disagreed with any dogma that oppressed people, they expected me to go to church right up until my teens. In my parent's home, there was innocence too, a provincialism that was both good and bad. It aided in my unpreparedness for the bigger world. The longer I was away from it, the more evident it became, and the more falsely superior to my family I thought I was.

When I was twenty and a junior in college, I told my parents that my best friend Josh was more than a friend. They said they had known I was gay and they reassured me that they loved me. I told them about my high school troubles. The torment I'd endured by my classmates, my fears, and of the profound embarrassment about being gay. My parents were more angry at me for not letting them know about my school difficulties than for being gay. I explained my faked happiness back in my teen days, reminded them of my professed shyness and how it was used as an excuse for my lack of friends, for not attending high school activities; dances and proms, "I didn't want you to think you had a loser for a son. I wanted you to think of me as happy." When I finished speaking, they told me that they felt as though they had failed me, "Why didn't you tell us who you were, you knew we would have accepted you." My mother had said. They didn't understand that it wasn't only about their acceptance of me. It was about my own acceptance of myself and my profound shame about who I was that was reinforced by the world and the church we attended every Sunday. It was about my sadness over the fact that I would not be married and have children. It was about the times we lived in; young gay men were dying of AIDS at a rapid rate. I didn't want them to think my death was imminent. I loved them both so much. I wanted them to think I was content, and that I was a winner, not some pathetic gay man destined for a life of ridicule and loneliness and disease.

My mother was in the living room watching TV when I walked into the house, "Hi mom! I have to go to the bathroom, I'll be right back!" I gave her a quick kiss, and ran up the stairs, put my head in the toilet bowl and puked. The smell of brandy floated back to my face. It felt weird and wrong to have carried something in my belly from New York back to my parent's home. I stood at the bathroom window, trying to steady myself, the side of the house faced east, and the sun streamed into the house cheerfully and there I was coming from a figuratively bleak, sinister, and dreary place in Manhattan; it all seemed incompatible. Did I fit in here anymore? Did I fit in in New York? Where did I belong? I wanted to be artsy and on the cutting edge, but at the same time I wanted grass, warmth, silence. I ran a steaming hot shower and stood under it, hoping to extract the brandy smell from my pores and to activate blood flow to my face so I could at least look alive.

"Hi mom," I said. Her blue eyes wide. She smiled and gave me a kiss.

"You smell like alcohol," she said.

"I was working at the bar. I spill drinks on myself."

"Well, even with a shower you stink of it! I guess that's some strong booze," she said.

At the kitchen table my mom handed me a plate of scrambled eggs and bacon. My Dad sat across from me reading the morning paper, and every so often he looked up from it and glanced at me as if trying to figure something out. He was graying, and a small strand of hair fell over his forehead. They were worried, it was clear, and it seemed overwhelmingly unfair that all their love, acceptance and investment in me was turning to shit right before them. I had faked happiness in front of them all through my school days, and now they knew the signs of my tricks.

"So let me tell you about Jack!" A loud and excited pitch came out of me while chomping on bacon. I showed them my cell phone. My father put his newspaper down, my mother stopped stirring her coffee. They both looked it over inquisitively. My voice went on about how well respected Jack was as an actor, about me working in their bar, and all the funky characters that came in, and the famous people. My parents seemed impressed. I went on and on about Mara, how wonderful she was, followed by imitations of her, using a British accent, "Really now darling do have a lovely holiday" and "That Jack is a daft cow!" and "Sweet Fanny Adams!' and they roared.

"Oh, and everything is sacred to her. They're Buddhist," I said.

"Interesting. So the buddha is like their Jesus?" my mother said.

"Yes, like that statue at the China Star restaurant. That's Buddha," my Dad said to her.

"So interesting. But you're Catholic. Still. Right?" my mother said.

"The church doesn't want me, Mom. I'm gay."

"Jesus loves you. To hell with the men who run the church. You're Catholic."

"Can I finish telling you about my new friends please?" They both nodded, yes. My father put his hand on his chin. I then told them about Jack, how he really took care of me and how they wanted me in their life. I told them how they said they loved me. We spoke about the film Jack was going to make and about Jack's new agent and all the exciting changes that were coming his way.

"What's going on with your own career?" Dad asked. My mother nodded, she had a confused look on her face.

"Shouldn't you have more than one contact?" Mom said.

"It's great you have this connection. Don't put all your eggs in one basket," my Dad said.

"Oh, Jack is going to help me. It's hard breaking into show business. You need someone to help you. I have other connections, too. There's Gwen in LA, she's a big agent now."

I changed the subject and told them more about the eccentric people I knew and how much fun it was. I told them how Frankie only wore red, how he was bitchy and mean, and did an imitation of him, "Look, queen, I paid a small fortune for those pants!" They both howled, "It sounds so exiting. It's so dull here compared to all that," my mom said. My father kept eyeing me. I told them about Charlie, and how talented he was, went on about Peter and Larry and how they were older gay men who protected me, and how much I admired them, "They're the kindest three men I've ever known. They advise me and really care for me." I told them about Esther and her dad, and all her quirkiness, and how she lived off his money and resented him for it. My Dad made an "ah ha" sound.

"Okay, Dad, what's up, really, you keep looking at me. Say what you have to say."

"I didn't want to say anything, but why did you shave your head?" he asked.

"I knew you guys weren't going to like it. It's very in."

"I don't understand why you had to shave your head. You have such nice hair. But suit yourself. Do you plan on keeping the beard?" Mom asked.

"Yes I do plan on keeping it. My friend Esther shaved it. She says I look amazing. It's something I wanted to do. Sorry you don't like it, but I do. It's New York. I don't belong here anymore."

"So Esther…she's the one with the rich father that she hates?" Mom said.

"He pays her rent, right?" Dad asked.

"Yes, that's her," I started to sigh.

"She's the one who dyes her hair different colors, orange and pink, or was that someone else? Was that Frankie or Larry?"

"No that's Esther. She's great though, she's been a good friend."

"How great can she be if she shaved your head and hates her father who pays her rent? But then says everything is sacred," Dad said.

"I agree with you!" Mom said.

"Oh, my God! Will you guys please stop, seriously. Mara thinks everything is sacred, not Esther," I said.

"Sorry. It sounds like you've got quite an interesting crew in New York," Dad said.

"Yes, as long as you're happy. Are you happy, Leonardo?" Mom had one of those forced smiles on her face.

"How can I not be happy? I'm doing what I love. Okay, I admit that some of my new friends are a little strange, but not all of them are. Take Charlie for example. He's totally normal, you guys would love him, but he was fired from the bar. He was flirting with Jack, and Mara was jealous. Poor Charlie. He lost his friend to AIDS."

"Mara fired him because he was friends with a man with AIDS. Terrible!" Dad said.

"No, Dad!" I said,

"Weren't you listening, George? He said because Mara was flirting with Jack. So Jack fired Charlie," Mom said.

"No, Mom! Jack was flirting with Charlie, so Mara fired Charlie. Are you not listening to me?"

"Don't raise your voice! What the hell is wrong with you!" Mom said.

"Oh here we go! Now you're going to start yelling at me!"

"You're the one who is yelling!" my father said.

"Everything I say is wrong!" my mother said.

"I never said that, Ma! But you don't listen to me. I said they weren't really flirting, it was because Charlie and Jack were together at one time. Mara is possessive of Jack."

"Wait, I thought Jack was married to Mara?" Dad asked.

"He is. For crying out load!" I said,

"But he had an affair with Charlie?" Dad asked.

"He's bisexual! Oh, my God!" I said.

"So Jack likes both?" Dad asked.

"Yes." I said.

"Larry and Peter and Frankie are what?"

"They're gay."

"I'm glad you have gay friends," Dad said.

"But you could always get a teaching job and write on the side. There are plenty of nice gay guys here. I'm hearing that Cambridge is very gay now," Mom said.

"Mom, it's always been gay."

"That's true," Dad said.

"Oh, I meant to tell you. Jefferey Calabrio came out of the closet," Mom clapped.

"Everyone's been talking about it. Good for him. And guess what? A lesbian couple moved in two houses up the road," Mom said.

"Jefferey does come from a good family. Maybe you should call him," Dad said.

"For what?" I said.

"He makes a lot of money and he's handsome," my Mom's voice sing songy.

"He's 56 years old, not that I have anything against older gay men, but he lives with his mother, and it was no secret he was gay. Ten years ago he was arrested for cruising a rest stop on Route 3! Plus, I'm twenty-four. Hello?"

"I forgot he was arrested! Poor Jefferey. If people were nicer to gay people and didn't make them feel so ashamed, they wouldn't have to sneak around at rest stops to have oral sex," Mom said.

"Mom, seriously, oh my god, oh my god, you didn't just say that to me!"

"It's the truth, isn't it. We're all adults."

"People love the gays now. Not like back in my day," Dad said.

"I meant to tell you! Guess what?" Mother said.

"Oh, Jesus, listen to this, Leonardo," Dad said.

"I had a fight with the new girl at the flower shop. She made some nasty comment about gays wanting to get married, and I told her my son was gay and we couldn't be prouder and that gays should be able to marry. Anyway, she hates me now and I don't care. Ignoramus!"

"Mom, don't fight with people at work. Honestly," I said.

"She's so rude," she said. My father started tapping his fingers on the table.

"Listen I'm really tired. I think I need a nap."

"We love you. We want you to be happy," Mom said.

"Sorry I yelled," I said.

"It's okay, you've always been touchy. It's okay to be sensitive." Mom said.

"Look, I know you're worried. I'm happy. I'm going to make it. I'm fine. The end."

"Well, like the song goes if you make it there…" Dad said. He flicked his newspaper as to get a better grip on it. He knew I was full of big mounds of globby straw filled horse manure. "I have to make some calls," I said, and left them. I went to my old bedroom, jumped on my bed and covered my face with a pillow and contemplated how long would it take to suffocate myself.

The scent of pine from the Christmas tree perfumed the house. Soon the soothing sound of Bing Crosby singing *White Christmas* traveled to my room. I sat up in bed and decided to call Gwen in LA as reassurance that Jack wasn't my only connection to show business and that I did have more eggs in my basket.

"Merry Christmas! I'm checking in. Things are great! Jack and I are becoming really good friends. I'm home now, but can't wait to get back to New York to start working on my career."

"I met this other agent. We were chatting and one thing led to another. I mentioned I had a friend who was friends with Jack Fresh. This agent didn't say much. People are so careful out here, but there was something funny in his tone. He said he heard Jack Fresh worked on a screenplay with a character actor named Wayne Jackson. He said things got funky between the two of them. The writers guild was involved. He didn't say more than that. It didn't sound good though."

"Wayne is a complete psycho. Forget about it," I said.

"That's interesting. My agent friend said Wayne was a great guy."

"I'm staying out of that," I said We chatted a bit more. Gwen was getting married the following year, was up for a job promotion and was representing some major talent. Our conversation ended with us hoping to see one another soon. I then called Julia to wish her a happy holiday. She said she was home briefly but was going to Oregon to do Macbeth. She said nothing had changed between her and Rico. They were going to meet for drinks that night, but she was off to the Northwest the day after Christmas to start rehearsals, "The last thing on my mind is a relationship. It's so weird I never saw him that much. I think we had five dates, but in his mind he thinks we're still dating. It's a little scary. I care for him, he's always good to me but I don't see us together. Does he do drugs?" She said.

"I'm unsure," I said.

My sister Emily was busy preparing for Christmas when I arrived at her house. Her brown hair was tied back, she looked exhausted. We stood in her large foyer, her Christmas tree, bigger than life, was in the far corner of her living room. She worked out regularly, her arms strong and smooth, her shoulders were broad.

"How's it going?" She hugged and kissed me. Her body hard and fit. She eyed me up and down, and crossed her arms. She was trying to see if I was going tell her fibs too. "Mom and Dad said you're unhappy." I ignored her and said. "The house smells so nice. Like pine."

"Leonardo, seriously, what's up?"

"I'm doing really well," I said, forcing a smile.

"You don't look it," she said.

"Must you be so confrontational?"

"Okay, I'll lie to you. You look really, really happy."

"Good. Thank you," I said.

"Did Mom and Dad say that to you really?"

"Yes they did. They think you're full of shit," she said. I cracked my knuckles, and called out the names of my niece and nephew, and they came running toward me, and jumped all over the place. The kids begged me to take them to the mall. Not being able to get away from my sister and her haughty, worried glare quick enough, I piled the kids in the back seat of the car.

I took them to the movies, then to *McDonald's,* where we ate cheeseburgers, downed fries and drank too much soda. We chased each other through the Mall, and they sat on Santa's lap. They jumped on me some more and pulled on my arms, and wiped their boogers on their sleeves and on me. While driving home that late afternoon the sky turned into hues of orange, I glanced at the kids in the back seat of the car. They slept in a big lump. I soundlessly hummed Jingle Bells to myself as we passed streets lined with perfect houses that were illuminated with colorful Christmas lights. My heart warmed, I knew I was lucky, and immediately wondered about Annie in England. I wished that she was with us having fun. With those thoughts, I dreaded the idea of going back to New York. I wanted to stay home. Why was it wrong to stay around my family, my roots, and their sometimes imperfections that drove me crazy. My father and his controlling ways, his old Yankee thriftiness, his bad joke telling, and his stinky cigar. My mother who nagged at my Dad relentlessly, and her constant worry, "I don't want people to hurt you because of who you are." Her telling me non-stop how she wanted me to meet a nice fella. And there was my sister who was exceedingly kind, but at times, thought she was an aristocrat, and could be obnoxiously bossy and dreadfully stubborn. She disappointedly married a Republican. Yet, all of our family troubles were manageable, light and easy, there was nothing overtly dismal like the sad and troubled troop of people I chose to expose myself to in New York.

Life was simple here. The place that I once thought provincial and stifling, didn't seem so bad. After all, there was love, family, trees, grass... a sense of community. But with all of that goodness around me, I was still aware of my inner turmoil and so beyond my hometown, and the family unit that I belonged to, I was spooked by bad memories and still wanted to run from them. I feared that if I was in a market, the gym, or other public place, and was seen by a former high school bully, that I would be called a queer or a faggot, and be publicly shamed. Or, maybe even be in danger of losing my life. In reality, high school was long gone, gays lived all over town. Times had changed, but my fear still lingered in gigantic, unhealthy proportions. I still felt like the town queer, and no matter how strong my desire to be back home, I refused to even consider it until I was a somebody. That principle fiercely fed my mission to do whatever it took to succeed in New York.

The afternoon after Christmas it snowed like mad. Earlier that day, I'd rented all of Jack Fresh's movies. We made giant left-over ham and cheddar cheese sandwiches on French baguettes, mugs of hot chocolate, and bowls of popcorn. My parents and I sat on the sofas and covered ourselves in blankets. We had a Jack Fresh film festival. My parents were immediately excited. Surprisingly, they knew who Jack Fresh was by his face and not name, "Oh my! I've seen him on that TV show, *Busted in New York*!" Wham! They were impressed with the idea of my new famous friend. The rest of the night a smile was on my face from ear to ear. When I started one movie, my father became excited, "Hey, wait a minute, what was I thinking, I've seen this movie! I love this movie! He's great! How about that!" and when another movie was over, and I played another, my mother said, "I can't believe you know him! I can't wait to tell my friends at the flower shop, this is great!" Before they went to bed, my father said, "Well, if you say this guy can help you out, then good luck. I'm really impressed. We're proud of you son." I was left alone in the den, flicking channels. I found a movie, and decided to watch it. It was *Rosemary's Baby*.

Scene Twelve – The Cars – *Good Times Roll*

Back in New York things were routine. I waited tables at the bar, ate in diners at ungodly hours, and watched the bar crew snort cocaine until they were comatose. Each day I forced myself to write for a few hours, but usually my mind was cloudy; everything I wrote was shit. Sunday nights after work I went to various gay bars in the West Village. Sometimes I'd meet Larry and Peter and we'd dance all night. Other times I went alone, going in and out of gay bars, cruising, flirting, and picking up the occasional guy. I had affairs that lasted a week or a few months, but nothing longer than that. I made every excuse not to give my heart away. Fearing that guys would eventually find out that I was a bad person or whatever, crazy, self-deprecating thing I was cooking up in my mind about myself. Regardless, my uncertainties were rooted in abandonment and rejection. I drew archery targets all over my body and handed people arrows. I made dating complex and confusing and thrived on the chaos. It felt fitting to emotionally torment myself for days and weeks and so I sought out guys who would bend and bruise my ego. I believed that's what I deserved. Most of the guys I dated were swingers, bar flies, and party boys, all extremely good-looking, hard to get, challenging, unable to commit, perfect narcissists leading me to dead ends and obsessions of how undesirable I was to the entire gay population. Soon I knew the truth, those guys wanted open relationships. At first this bothered me and I took it as an insult. How come not one guy wanted to commit to me? Yet, if a guy was sincere and liked me, and wanted to commit to me I'd freak out and use every excuse to end the relationship. The reasons were endless; bad breath, hairy back, a pimple, bad manners, they farted, they had a strand of hair hanging from their nose, they liked sushi, or they didn't hold their fork the correct way. And still I cried to myself that no one wanted to love me. Soon sex and making myself sexually desirable to other gay men replaced my need for love and I thought it exciting and fantastic because New York was teeming with sexual enticements. It was a hunting game and an easy one. There was a gorgeous guy on every street corner to cruise and say hello to and swap numbers or to follow home to their apartment or to my room, or hook up inside a booth inside a triple x video store. There was someone for everyone. There was no need for the buying of drinks and dinners, no wasting time on dates, and no need for the breaking of hearts. If a gay man wanted sex they would cut to the chase and get it in a variety of ways and in a short matter of time. I pretended that I loved my tricks and that they loved me. It helped satisfy that raw human need I had to be wanted and loved. I hated my sex life and felt ashamed of it, as much as I adored it; skin on skin, gay men, sex, dating, at times my quandary. In the end, I chose to believe that I had no time for a serious relationship until I was a somebody. No one seemed to mind. Nevertheless, no matter how much I analyzed or philosophized and made excuses about my sexual conquests and my failed love affairs, my sole foundation was steeped in the belief that I felt unlovable and underserving of good things in life because the world said gay people were worthless sinners, freaks of nature, immoral and disgusting and I was sensitive and unsophisticated enough to believe what I was told. How could anyone see anything redeeming in me when I couldn't see anything positive inside myself? As far as I was concerned, I was only some insane lady's bitch boy, and it was just fine. Her husband was famous, and in a twisted way, I thought it validated me. My servitude to Mara and Jack became as natural to me as eating and defecating. I thrived on them using and abusing me because it reinforced my inner belief about myself. It got to the point that when I didn't hear from Mara, I became fearful. Was she okay? Did she still love me. Was I still good enough? Did she find me out?

By mid-winter I had massaged Mara's feet endless times and pulled globs of hair out of her bathroom sink and had cleaned her frig of all 32 to-go food containers that had rotten food in them. She insisted they be washed and used for bar customers who wanted to take the crappy food she served home. I scrubbed, shopped, served and together we conditioned her hair with mayonnaise once a week to soften it. It was something she did since she was a small girl in Liverpool. It never worked because gasoline ran through her veins and everything that grew off her body was burnt or dead.

By the time February rolled around, the precarious situation with Wayne Jackson and the screenplay evolved into a tornado of trouble. This is what I learned. A year or so before Jack met Mara, Wayne Jackson had gone to Jack with a completed screenplay. It was a story of a family living in Providence coming to terms with a missing son and his dog that helps find him. It was a riveting, dramatic story, titled "Follow The Bone" Wayne asked Jack for help because Jack had worked with some well-known, edgy, directors. Jack and Wayne sharpened the script and sold it after the film director, Robert Cain, a popular French Director, who attached himself to the project. Jack insisted on top billing for writing the film and wanted more money than Wayne because Jack said he was a bigger name. Jack's main argument was that he got Robert Cain attached to the project. Wayne argued that he came to Jack with a fully written script. Both of their agents were in a horrid battle. Wayne's agent called the Writers Guild. Then Jack's agent was questioned by the Guild about who the original writer of the screenplay was. After that, Jack started to slowly tarnish Wayne's reputation. Many nights Jack would stand at the bar and talk softly to his famous friends about Wayne. His voice docile, full of sadness to evoke pity, his carefully measured words logically and steadily convincing his famous friends that he was the victim,

"The script was a mess. I was only trying to help him. I felt badly for him. It wasn't very good, and he was so proud of it. I rewrote the entire thing. I should have known better. Every time I help someone I get in trouble, but I guess that shouldn't stop me." The night unfolded with Jack being coddled by his famous friends. He was told how wonderful and kind he was, Gandhi incarnate. By the end of the night, when Wayne was fitfully, passively aggressively vilified by Jack, he nonchalantly made his way to the ceramic buddha in the corner of the bar. He bowed in front of it, and stood there long enough for all to notice. He had everyone fooled except the usual bar crew who all snickered behind his back, including the Buddha.

One late February night, I was serving a platter of cheese to a customer when Wayne walked in. I nearly dropped a wheel of brie on someone's head. Wayne was well-built and intimidating. He had a 1950's style haircut, short on the sides, high on the top. By the time he reached the bar Mara appeared from the basement. She spotted Wayne, marched directly to him, and stuck her finger in his face, "Why the hell are you here?"

"Can we please talk," Wayne said.

"How bloody dare you come into my place of business." Countless other insults spewed from her mouth while she darted her index finger in Wayne's face. She relentlessly pointed and pointed. A fit of frustration overcame him, his chest moved up and down rapidly, he raised his hand and slapped Mara in the face. The smack was loud and piercing. We all became still. Mara held her face. Wayne realized what he had done, and dashed out.

"That manky pig will not get his way with this screenplay!" Mara said. Determined to win a battle she had no business being in, she banged her fist on the bar. I handed her a glass of water to comfort her, "Thanks, I feel faint, darling." She swallowed the water and headed to the basement. Later, I learned she was interested in a three-story building on West 15thth Street. If Jack received the money he wanted for the screenplay, they could put a decent down payment on it.

While in the basement delivering glasses of brandy to Jack and Mara, Jack was on the phone with Wayne, "We're going to press assault and battery charges, and get a restraining order. How dare you harm my wife." The phone rested on Jack's ear, his blonde curly locks fell around his cheekbones. He started cutting up coke on the mirror as he talked into the phone. Mara stood next to Jack, writing things on paper while Jack read them into the phone, "You might have busted her jaw. She can't open her mouth. She's been crying ever since." Mara wrote more, and passed her notes to Jack who read into the phone. His acting was shockingly perfection, "She feels like she was publicly humiliated in her own bar. She's an emotional wreak. This is serious." Mara swallowed her brandy with one hungry gulp, her foot tapped the cement floor of the basement, her eyes on Jack. "She's my wife, she has every right to tell you what to do with our screenplay, every right, and don't tell me it's none of her business. If I wrote it, it belongs to her too." Mara grinned vindictively. And that was all that I heard Jack say. I was back upstairs within seconds.

Jack and Mara won. Jack got top billing and more money for the screenplay than Wayne. Wayne wanted an acting part in the film during contract negotiations, but he was denied because Mara made Jack threaten to pull the project if Wayne was granted an acting part. Jack told the director that Wayne had beaten Mara up. The director was appalled, and didn't want Wayne on the set. Jack had a starring role, a producing and writing credit and a fat check. It was a 6-week shooting schedule, and aimed for an early summer release.

When the movie, *Follow The Bone,* premiered at the Ziegfeld Theater, everyone in Jack Fresh's entourage was invited to go. I was asked to babysit Annie. Mara left us fifty bucks to order Chinese. We watched the *Little Mermaid.* I didn't mind. By that time, I knew all the words and we sang them together, our favorite song being, Under the Sea.... Ya, we in luck here, Down in the muck here, Under the Sea.

Scene Thirteen – Eric Clapton – *Cocaine*

Julia had officially told Rico to move on with his life. She told him there was no chance for them as a couple. She explained she was traveling and working. She concluded by saying she cared for him and that it wasn't him, it was all her.

"When someone says, it's all them and not you, you know they really want you out of their life. I guess she really didn't like me," Rico said.

"That's not true." I hoped not to be fired. Julia was in Tampa doing the play, *Burn This*. Soon I determined that instead of Rico firing me, he held on to me as his link to Julia. He became obsessed. He'd ask me every day if I had talked to her. He spoke of his pain, and of his hopes of getting back together with her. Meanwhile, his drug use escalated, and his self-esteem slipped away. He kept singing the same old song to me about his drug addiction; how he didn't want to do cocaine anymore. How each time he tried to stop, Mara asked him to call Suzie-Q for more dope. He became increasingly grubby. His hands shook. It was tragic and at times annoying to hear him say over and over, "I only wanted to use this shit occasionally. I think it has a hold on me." Each time I offered to take him to a rehab, he'd get indignant. He'd tell me those places were for junkies and ragefully scream at me. His temper scared me. Other times my twenty-four year old pride would become bruised, "Screw you! Up yours!" I'd croon. Then one day I watched him snort a line in the kitchen, "God, sometimes I love this shit!" and he did another line. Although he was deeply petrified, and caught in the grips of a serious addiction, he did love it. It had become his life. Cocaine had replaced his parents, his childhood, Jack and Mara and Julia and all who loved him. From that day on I treaded lightly when he spoke of his inability to quit. Our relationship changed, too. He was no longer the wise older brother type to my just arrived in New York greenness. I was now the older brother, the one in the know, the one who thought he was naïve and weak and in denial. I gave up on Rico for a while, and sometimes only listened to him to avoid igniting his frustrations.

Weeks passed and he became increasingly difficult to be around because his moods changed so drastically. One moment he would lovingly embrace me, proclaim I was the kindest person he knew, "You're a great friend. At least one good thing came out of my relationship with Julia." The next hour he hated me, called me a traitor, said I lied to him about Julia and that I was in cahoots with Mara to destroy him, "You're a little phony, did you tell Julia I picked on you, is that it? Did you go back to her crying, you little baby!" An hour later, he loved his life and said he was sorry for speaking to me the way he did. Then within a half hour, he told me how much he hated his life. Then he'd tell me how much he loved Julia, then he'd go on about how much he hated her. Followed by how much he wanted her back.

His paranoia escalated, too. With a burning in my chest, my hands clenched, I nodded intensely when he told me that ghosts lived in the basement. He said they spoke to him, that they weren't bad ghosts, but good ones. They protected him from the customers who he thought plotted against him. Once, he was so high he babbled on about how customers put a tape recorder in the stereo system near the bar and that the government was after him because he didn't pay his three hundred dollar tax bill the previous year.

By March, everything I did seemed to aggravate Rico. One night, according to him, I wasn't working fast enough. I broke a glass, and gave the wrong change to a customer. I was short one dime. He stormed out of the bar in a tantrum and went upstairs to Mara and Jack's apartment and complained that he couldn't work with me anymore. Moments later, Mara came into the bar, and smiled me.

"Jack is coming down to work with you. He's changing clothes, don't worry, darling, Rico is jealous of you, do see it for what it is." She then touched my arm gently, dotingly. "You're a fine chap. Forget about him."

Those rare moments of Mara's tenderness confused me, and at the same time gave me sheer joy. I hungered for her affections, and took the smallest crumbs of it she offered and devoured them hungrily.

Jack came into the bar, and Mara went back upstairs. That night, Jack and I got madly drunk together, and talked about our favorite movies and he asked me about my writing,

"Working on anything?"

"A play. It's giving me a hard time." I said.

"Let's plan on me reading something soon," Jack said. After he said it, I seriously considered washing his feet.

I stopped calling Esther because Jack and Mara had become my entire life. I was consumed by them and nothing else mattered to me. I received nasty messages from her for a few months and with each one she left, I became angry at her, like it was her fault, "Where are you, asshole?" she'd say. Sometimes I deleted the message before I listened to all of it, "You're such a moron. I thought we were friends. If you think that lousy actor is going to help you, you're nuts!" Finally, one day, there were no messages from Esther, or from any of my other friends. There was only some woman's voice telling me I had no new messages.

On my days off, I started hanging out in Mara and Jack's apartment because Mara wanted me to spend time with Annie, "She's a needy child and I can't be there for her all the time," Mara said. I agreed. On most afternoons we watched *Lion King*, made cookies and played endless games of checkers and other board games. One night, before Jack and Mara were to go out to an art opening in Soho, Annie and Mara had a horrible fight. Annie couldn't find her playing cards and was whiny, "Mommy where are my cards?" Jack sat in a chair doing what he always did. He blocked out all commotion. Then Mara yelled, "Why do you always have to be such an asshole, Annie? Why?" I became tense, stressed, bit the inside of my mouth, tasted blood. Not being able to bear the way Mara spoke to Annie, I put my frustrations into picking up Annie's toys, counting the seconds until Mara and Jack left, and when they finally did, Annie sulked, "I hate Mommy!" She said.

"Mommy is tired, she doesn't mean it. You don't really hate her. I have an idea. Draw a picture of Mommy and express how you really feel."

"Okay. But I really do hate her." I gave Annie some crayons and paper. She started to draw and color. I picked up a book, read on the sofa. After a while, I peeked in on Annie. She was sleeping. I didn't bother to look at what she drew. I went back to the sofa and slept.

I woke to screaming. It was Mara in Annie's room.

"This is what you think of me?" Jack sat across from me, rocked in his space, "But Leonardo told me to draw a picture of you," Annie's shrill tired voice traveled out to me. Immediately, I ran to get my coat. Mara followed me with Annie's drawing in her grip. She held it out for me to look at. It was a stick figure of a woman, above it she'd written in scribbles, *I hate Mommy. I wish she was dead.* She had drawn a knife that was stuck in the head of the woman, streaks of red splats, which I took for blood were all over the drawing. Next to that, was a stick figure of a little girl who had a big smile on her face. The sun was over her head and there was a rainbow, a big beautiful one. When Mara showed me Annie's drawing I clenched my teeth to prevent myself from laughing, from gloating, from loving the fact I was the impetus behind the drawing and the one who'd bought Annie the crayons in the first place.

"It's only a phase," my voice a peep.

"What the hell do you know!?" She screamed, and handed the drawing to Jack who examined it closely. He turned it this way and that way. At first he didn't say anything. Then he looked up at Mara and I. A stupefied expression was on his face. Then his eyes went back to the drawing and then he burst out laughing. It was deep and guttural. Mara smacked the back of his head. He fell out of his chair with a loud raucous thump. Mara started kicking him, "You're a nincompoop, an idiot! A waste of my time! I hate you, every lousy inch of you! You're a disgusting creature!" And still he roared with laughter. She tore the picture in little pieces and flung them at Jack and stormed off. Within minutes Annie appeared in pajamas. She held a toy unicorn, "Jack did you like what I drew?"

Scene Fourteen –
Amy Winehouse – *You Know I'm No Good*

By April I had completely lost myself. My world became small, and everything revolved around Mara and Jack. I become an integral part of the bar. Customers were calling me by my first name, and famous actors would actually acknowledge me. Jack was filming a movie uptown. He wasn't around much. He came home late, was remote and seemed disconnected, "It's a difficult shoot," he'd say. Other than that, he said very little when he was home. Mara complained, and nagged at him, picked fights and threw things at him to get a reaction. He'd grab his coat and leave without a word. Maybe once or twice he managed a whimper of disapproval, but when he left, he left for hours. Mara would storm around the apartment screaming at Annie for everything she did wrong from spilling her milk, to crying, to making a mess with her games and to being born. Mara would complain to me about Jack never being home. She'd lock herself in her bedroom, but before she did, she'd shout to Annie and I as if it was our fault, "He doesn't love me, he never did! He's an animal, a disgusting pig! A no good tosspot!" She'd slam her door shut and we'd have peace for a few hours.

Mid-April, Rico came to work early one day with his left eye horribly black. It was swollen and puffy. He said he had fallen down the basement stairs. He was limping and said his back was sore. "You've been done up like a kipper," Mara said to him. I concluded he was drunk when he fell, but learned later, it was far worse than a fall.

A month later, on the 15th of May, Mara called us together in the bar before opening for business. She said she had big news for all of us, "I'm expecting." She glowed. Everyone was stunned. I gave her a big hug, "Thanks, darling, I knew you would be chuffed. The doctor said despite my age, I am in tip-top shape! Plenty of woman have babies in their forties." she said. "I've decided that you will all be part of this sacred event." Honestly ecstatic about the news, I adored babies, and thought a baby was going to change Mara and Jack, and finally make them stop their partying. I was convinced they were on their way to becoming a wholesome family. Of course, I ignored the fact that Annie's arrival in the world didn't make Mara change, unless she was a lot worse before Annie was born. But still, I had hope.

I hugged Jack and congratulated him, "Thanks, Leonardo." Life was changing rapidly for him, and it showed on his quiet, still face. Frankie was ecstatic and clung to Mara, "We'll have a fabulous shower for you!" and Larry and Peter kissed and embraced Jack and Mara "We have to think of baby names!" Larry said, and Peter said, "I guess I'm going to be sort of a gay uncle!" All good cheer was around, except Rico who became exceedingly quiet as the night progressed. His eye was partly healed by then, only a small sliver of black and yellow existed above his eyelid.

I was mystified at Rico's lack of joy over the baby news, and decided he was internally comparing himself to Jack. After all, Jack had an acting career that seemed promising and his personal life was now going to be enhanced by the birth of a baby. And, there was Rico, working for his best friend and taking daily abuse from his wife. Not degreed, a coke addict, and dumped by his girlfriend. My heart started to ache for Rico. Wanting to console him, I asked if he wanted to walk through the East Village and get some Korean food. He agreed.

It was one of those electrifying spring nights when the wind was strong with a slight chill. People were out in herds. The smell of summer was faint, but the idea of its arrival ever present. We made our way down 1st Avenue, a cigarette hung out of Rico's mouth, he was anxious, and deep in thought.

"Rico, I want to say that you're a great guy, and you're going to meet a nice girl. You have so much going for you. You're a great bartender.

"Shut the hell up," he said this jokingly, but there was a sorrowfulness to his voice that hit me hard. He seemed empty and hopeless.

"No, really, I mean it," I tried my best to use my cheery voice.

"Thanks, man," he cleared his throat.

"Are you okay?" I asked. He shook his head yes. He then ran his hands across his face, "I dunno," his voice faint. He started to speak, but stopped himself as if saving himself from some sort of humiliation. He had gotten extremely thin, his clothes that had once fit him snugly, hung off him loosely.

"What's going on?" I asked. He shook his head again, "Nothing" We ordered a beef dish and a variety of Kimchee, ate, and made small talk. He started to speak about Julia. Mournfulness and vulnerability etched his voice, "Did she say she didn't like sex with me?" he asked. "No, hell no, Julia's not the type to talk about that stuff with me." He picked through the Kimchee, "So what was it about me she didn't like, go on tell me, I can take it." He was trying to act nonchalant, like he didn't care. When in fact if I told him the truth he would be crushed. It was his coke habit, his infatuation with Jack, his inability to finish college, and the way he played her by using Jack as leverage. He often said to her, "Jack will get you into films." It made Julia feel like a hooker.

"Julia is professional woman. She wants a career as an actor, that's her main focus. It's not about you personally." I was trying my hardest to sound sincere.

"Bullshit," he said, "Complete bullshit."

"No honest," I said. We left and started to walk down East 13th Street.

"I promised Jack I would never say anything about what—" he stopped himself.

"What are you talking about. What did you promise, Jack?"

"He's all I have. You have a family to go to. You wouldn't understand. I'm alone. When Jack was with Cora, there was none of this bullshit. She was family. We were all tight, a unit. Jack, his family, me, Cora. It was solid and real. Everyone got along. We all had plans. I had this picture in my mind that I was going to marry Julia. And Cora and Julia would become great friends. We'd all have kids together. Like a big family. I'm at my wit's end. I'm confused and disappointed in Jack. I really am. I can't talk about it, I can't. "

"I'm sorry. You're upset," I said.

"I hate talking this way. I hate feeling this way. It's bullshit. Nothing works out the way you plan it. Life is full of curve balls."

"Rico, what the hell? Come on. Jack's having a baby. It's great news, they love you, you'll be part of the baby's life. You haven't lost them. You'll meet a nice girl."

"Mara is trying to get me out of Jack's life. I feel it. I think Jack would allow it. Jack is under her spell. He's not thinking logically. I seriously think she's evil."

"To be honest, that thought has crossed my mind. She's pretty tough."

"Do you believe in that stuff, the devil, evil, all that hocus pocus stuff?"

"I think evil lives in all of us, and the challenge is to fight against it. I suppose some people don't care if they're behaving badly, or hurting others. I would presume some indulge in it. People like Mara only care about the end result, getting what they want. Life is a game for them. They know how to prey on the weak, they're master manipulators. They don't care how cruel or mean they are, they want what they want and nothing will stop them. They lack values and beliefs and morals. And sometimes, I wonder if life would be easier if I could be like that. I'm always feeling guilty. Sometimes I wish I were ruthless. I'm a sap," I said.

"I saw Jack for the first time tonight. I couldn't be happy for him because—whatever-" Rico's voice cracked. He wanted to say something, but couldn't find the words to articulate what he wanted to say. I wanted to somehow rescue him. But if I continued to speak cheerily of better days to come, it would've sounded phony because an eerie darkness started to fall on me; Rico knew something horrible, it was obvious. I remained silent and let him speak.

"We were boys together. And, ahhh," his face streamed with tears, he turned to hide his face from me. We walked down Avenue C toward East Houston. It was quiet, void of the crowds.

"Are you in love with Jack? It's okay if you are." He giggled and playfully pulled me close and kissed the top of my head.

"No I'm in love with you," he then sweetly laughed, "Leonardo you're a good kid. No I'm totally straight. I'm not in love with Jack. I guess I'm upset for a number of reasons and I feel confused because I know Jack is a broken man. When he was a kid, he was fun, and easy to be around. He was artistic, smart as hell and then one day he broke. He was never the same. Someone close to him snatched his soul away. I don't want to go into details about it, it wouldn't be fair to Jack, it's personal. But I'll say this. I believe in evil and once you're touched by it, it follows you around and it becomes your life. It feels normal. I wanna drink. Wanna get a drink?"

"Sure." We turned around, and went back up C Street.

"He's got himself in a total bind with Mara. We all thought that their marriage was one of Jack's indulgences; it wasn't going to last. Now he's having a baby. They are now forever entwined. It's pretty upsetting."

"But a baby is good news," I said. He stopped in front of an apartment building with cement steps right before East 14th Street and sat on the bottom step; they were old and chipped, painted a light coco brown. They led up to an old peeling red door. He lit another cigarette. Smoke billowed above him. The smell of the sewer was strong, dirty and unpleasant. The gutter was laden with food wrappers, and beer cans.

"Sit down for a second." It was grim sitting there. I turned my head toward 14th Street, and could hear voices of young people; they were happy and joyous. The sound of sirens came and went, lights of bars, bodegas and stores beckoned my attention. A teenager ran from corner to corner, laughing, as he was chased by his friends, and there we were, alone, away from the fun and lights of the city.

"I'll kill you if I find out you told a soul," Rico said. I nodded a promise. He started to speak, stubbed his cigarette out, and lit another, "A few months ago Jack went to a lawyer. He wanted to know the consequences of leaving Mara. I went with him. He wanted out. He told me he couldn't take her anymore. His exact words were 'help me, she's a psychopath, she's going to ruin me.

I need your help.' He begged me. During his relationship with Mara his parents have confronted him many times. They can't understand what he sees in her. His friends don't understand. We are all bewildered. We've told him that she is destroying his personal life. He has lost friends and family members. She is controlling all aspects of his life. He has never responded to any of us, he just listens. Then one day, he let it all out and confessed his unhappiness to me. He said he felt trapped, he told me he still loved Cora Tanner. He said he made a mistake. He wanted her back, missed her. He begged me to contact Cora and to break the ice, see if she would talk to him, absolutely begged me. Cora had made it clear to Jack that he had to stay away from her. She was adamant, angry, absolutely resolved in the fact that she didn't want anything to do with him. I agreed and went to Cora to see if she would consider talking to Jack. I made excuses for him, pleaded, spoke of his remorse, about the complexities of love, how Jack has never forgotten her. I laid it on thick. She wouldn't budge. She didn't want anything to do with Jack. She was done. Then, days later, she called me. She had softened and agreed to meet Jack. And so they met. Christ, I was so happy, better days were coming, I was certain of it. And so, the weeks that Jack was filming that movie up-town, Cora and Jack met. They rekindled their relationship, everything was forgotten and forgiven and then they made a plan."

"Holy shit. What was the plan?" My body became gangly and weak; it was absent of bones. "Jack was to go to the lawyer, which he did. He was going to serve Mara divorce papers. He was going to move-in with Cora. They were going to go to Italy for a while."

"This is blowing my mind." I rubbed my head, told Rico to give me a cigarette. And then I spoke. "Mara knew something was up. She knew, she's not stupid. All winter she complained because he was never home. Around Christmas time they were telling me all this great news, talked about how in love they were, and were planning a baby."

"I know, I think her baby plans were what pushed Jack over the edge. Sad thing is this; Mara swore she would never have another child. Jack said she was on the pill. She lied about that too. She trapped him. I bet she thinks this baby is saving their marriage."

"He can still divorce her."

"He can. But his lawyer advised him not to. He said Jack would have to pay her loads of money, and not only that, but how would it look for him to leave his wife while she's pregnant? It's career suicide. Plus he's up for a cable TV show. Anything scandalous would kill his career. The press would destroy him. His lawyer also said divorce was pointless if kids were involved because you're enmeshed forever no matter what. He also told Jack to think long and hard before he decided to file."

"Holy shit."

"She's evil."

"But he was having sex with her and was planning on leaving her. It's his fault too."

"Yes, true for the normal person that applies, but Jack is a sex addict. He can't control himself. Plus he's half in the bag all the time. She keeps him that way to control him."

"That's not an excuse."

"It's not an excuse, but it is what it is."

"What about Cora?"

"Jack wanted me to tell her."

"Wait you had to break up with her for Jack? Rico that's totally crazy. That's nuts. Even I wouldn't do that kind of shit."

"I know, but I did it anyway. That's how I got the black eye. Cora socked me. She said I was as bad as Jack, that I enabled him and all that crap. She told me we were real losers. She said a lot more but it doesn't bear repeating and she kept hitting me and hitting me, crying and kicking me, pulling my hair, telling me Jack would be nothing without her, it was seriously a bad scene. The cops came. She tore my shirt off and was grabbing and scratching me." He lifted up his shirt and showed me his back. All over were deep scratch marks that were scabbed over. I was momentarily silenced, and then I shrieked, "Holy shit!"

"The hell with Jack and Mara. I'm sick of them. Let's get stinking drunk!" he said. I nodded yes and we stopped at the first bar we came to. We drank, played pool, listened to music, and when we stumbled out onto 14th Street in the early morning hours, gusts of spring rain soaked us, at moments so forceful and blinding, we had to step in doorways.

Scene Fifteen – Bronski Beat – *Why?*

The weekend after the baby news Jack's family came to town to celebrate. His mother, Dina, a slender woman with a blonde shag haircut, with sad eyes and a kind smile, brought containers of homemade food from their home in New Haven; a magnificent beef stew, and a sweet cherry cake. It was a Sunday, and the bar was closed for the afternoon. Usually Jack and Mara used the bar for social gatherings because their apartment was small. I helped Dina set the tables in the bar, and heat the food in the kitchen. I exchanged small talk with her as everyone sat at the bar having cocktails. The food smelled warm and homey, like a summer herb garden; spring, hope, new beginnings.

Jack was with his father, they were picking Annie up from her father's house up-town, and she would be taken back to him after the celebration dinner.

Olena came to the dinner as well, and made her usual round of kissing everyone when she arrived. She told us how great Ian was. When nervous, or worried, Olena had a habit of fidgeting by putting her hair behind her ears and then pulling a strand of her curly red hair from behind her head and wrapping it around her index finger. On this day she it did compulsively. She went to the kitchen to help her Aunt Dina.

Larry and Peter sat at the bar with Mara, who was talking about the sacred event taking place inside her body, "The stars were aligned. We made love one night and I looked into Jack's eyes, we didn't have to speak, we said to one another through our eyes 'let's have a baby' It was so surreal, a spiritual connection on a level I don't think anyone would understand. And that night we had the same dream. We woke at the same time. He told me he dreamt he was riding a dolphin in a clear blue ocean. I was stunned because I had the same dream. It was fantastic, it really was."

"Wow! You had the same dream? For real?" Peter said.

"Yes, but it's not that big of a deal, it makes perfect sense, Jack and I are connected in a way I don't think many understand. This is all natural, because we are in tune to it."

"That makes sense. I really get it," Larry said. He ran his hands through his beard and looked at Mara intensely. He turned to me, his famous silly grin beamed on his face. I mouthed to him, "What the hell?" and he bit his upper lip, his face full of amusement.

"The water is life, love, and the dolphin is a symbol of safe travel, our journey in life together." She sipped wine. Larry rested his hand gently across his mouth. Peter had his arms around Larry. They both had stumped expressions on their faces.

"Let's go bow to the Buddha," Mara said. All three of them went to the Buddha in the corner and brought their hands together and bowed. If Mara was a Buddhist, than I was without a living doubt, Jesus Christ Superstar.

Rico was covering bottles of champagne with ice from behind the bar. Frankie came in, wearing a full length fake fur, it was ruby red. He held a small gift, a pacifier with a bow on it. He went directly to Mara. "Hello my darling!" He took off his coat, threw it on a chair, ruining one of my place settings; he glanced at me, "Hi, sorry." He handed Mara the pacifier and she cringed as if it were the most ridiculous thing she'd ever seen and tossed into the pile of gifts.

In the kitchen, Olena stood next to Dina. They were having a hushed conversation, and upon seeing me, they stopped speaking in mid-conversation. Dina's eyes were full, "Are you okay?" I asked. She nodded. One tear sprang from her eye, "I'm happy. That's all." Dina said. Olena bit her upper lip, shook her head, and motioned for me to leave her alone with her aunt. I left the kitchen.

Back in the bar area people joyously encircled Jack, and congratulated him. Shyly he gloated. Mara called me to her side. Both of us observed while Jack's family and friends fell over him.

"You would think he was carrying this child," Mara crossed her arms over her chest.

"This is exciting for all of you," I said.

She exhaled deeply, dramatically, and strengthened her stance.

"Darling I know you mean well, but I don't need your 3rd grade logic. At least not now. And listen carefully, when you serve me Dina's food, put as little on my plate as possible. I'm not a fan of *her* cooking and I have the collywobbles."

"Okay."

"They're so provincial. I hope they don't stay long. Jack cannot be around them too much. I have to protect him from them."

"Protect him? From what?" I said.

"If you have to ask me that question then you're as provincial as they are, you're a writer, please be more aware. Jack's father is numpty. He can hardly speak and chew gum at the same time. How they gave birth to a genius is a mystery. They don't know how brilliant Jack is, but I do, this is why the Gods have brought us together. Now go fill the water glasses and make sure you use plenty of ice, I'm heating up."

Jack's father Eddie was an auto mechanic. A jovial guy who was rough around the edges, had the same flaming red hair as

Olena, a chain smoker, a good and charming man that one could not help but love. He came from Ireland when he was three years old, and a hard-core believer in the American dream. Therefore, he was enormously proud of Jack, and intensely idolized him, yet was annoyingly obsessed with his son's fame. Dashes of harmless jealousy, and a one-sided competitiveness in their relationship made certain circumstances cringeworthy. Eddie would joke, take credit for his son's success, say he was the one who influenced him, "Jack got the entertaining gene from me. My own Ma said I danced the jig like no other kid she saw back in Ireland" After such lame statements, he'd laugh his hoarse and phlegmy laugh. We'd all force a chuckle, except Jack who usually looked like a whipped cream pie had been smashed in his face.

Dina was another story. She was all mother. Her love for Jack was pure, sincere, and simple. She only wanted him happy, and expressed quite frequently her confusion over her son's odd demeanor. I was drawn to Dina. She reminded me of my mother; strong willed, and not afraid to speak her mind. She oozed an abundance of love. Decency and truthfulness was evident in all she did. An overwhelming need for me to make her happy washed over me each time I was in contact with her.

"Sometimes I wish I could have a conversation with Jack. He never talks to me. I guess I gotta accept the way he is. I'll tell you this though, I'd like to spend some alone time with my son. Every time I try, Mara sticks her nose in our business, you'd think that she owns my son."

At the dinner, Dina sat next to Annie, who she adored and treated like her own granddaughter. Annie knew Dina loved her. This gave me immense comfort and relieved constant worry, "Dina loves me so much, Leonardo, and I love her too, and guess what? Dina told me I was a special girl." Her puny voice was always filled with excitement. When she knew Dina was coming into New York to spend time with her, Annie became animated, "I can't wait! Dina is coming, Dina is coming!" She'd clap and jump, and peek out the window while she waited for Dina's car to pull up. If Dina and Eddie were taking her to Connecticut for the weekend that was an even bigger thrill for Annie. She'd have her little bags packed hours before they'd come to pick her up.

"Are you excited for your new brother or sister?" Dina asked Annie.

"I guess," her voice was docile.

"It's going to be a lot of fun," I said. Mara eyed both of them disapprovingly,

"Annie, do you think you could stop thinking of yourself and act a little excited? If you like, I can put you in a taxi and send you back to your father's. I'm sure you can sulk with your father. He likes to sulk too."

"I'm not sulking," Annie's voice a mere squeak.

"I think your father is bad for you. Maybe you should go away to a boarding school. Maybe that will teach you how to act like a human being." Everyone eyed Mara. Tears started to stream down Annie's face. Olena immediately stood and took Annie to the bathroom, and when they were both out of sight, Mara spoke firmly to us. "I refuse to raise a whiny girl. We must all stop babying her, I don't want a cabbage for a daughter, do understand."

"Well, she's had a lot of changes these last months," Dina said. She put her spoon down and sipped her water.

"I know my daughter, Dina. She has had no changes. She thinks of herself."

"Most children do," Dina replied. The table became silent. Jack poured himself more wine. Larry piped up and complimented

Dina on her food, followed by everyone else's proclamations of deliciousness and thanks, except Frankie who puckered his lips and passed exasperating gestures to Mara.

"Thanks, boys," Dina said.

"Thank you, Ma. It was delicious, as always," Jack said.

"I wanted this dinner to be special," Dina sipped her water again.

"It was Ma. It's all good," Jack winked at his mother.

"See, now I am the barking mad one!" Mara said.

"Where is that coming from?" Jack asked.

"Annie has a remarkable way of making everyone think I'm a nutter!" Mara said.

"She's a child," Dina said tersely.

"Drop it," Eddie said.

"Drop what?" Dina glared at Eddie.

"Dina, by the way, no more Barbie dolls for Annie. Buy her books," Mara said.

"All girls play with dolls," Dina said.

"Okay, drop it," Eddie said sternly.

"I need some air. I feel properly sick." Mara stood, held her belly, and went out to the garden. Jack followed her. Everyone was silent until Annie came back to the table. Dina took Annie by the arm and pulled her close to her body.

"Is Mommy mad at me? Did she leave because of me?"

"No sweetheart. You did nothing wrong." Dina played with Annie's hair.

The smell of marijuana snuck its way into the bar. I told myself, no matter how evil Mara was, she wouldn't do drugs during her pregnancy. It was only my imagination.

After everyone left that night, I started cleaning up, going back and forth to the kitchen. Mara and Olena were sitting at the bar. Larry and Peter had left after dessert to go dancing at a local gay club where they were doing a 1980's retrospective of Jimmy Somerville dance music. The bar was empty except for Mara and Olena who spoke in muted voices that made me suspicious. I washed glasses and pricked up my ears.

"He is mine now, she has to accept this!" Mara balked.

"Aunt Dina really loved Cora Tanner. Give her time."

"Give her time! Must you remind me that his family properly hates me and still loves Tanner? I'm Jack's wife, his baby is inside of me. Do stop."

"Don't worry, I'll protect you. I promise," Olena said.

"They should thank me. I got their son away from that slapper! I have the hump with those people, I really do."

"They're jealous," Olena said.

They talked more about Jack's family. Apparently Jack's grandparents had numerous photos of Cora Tanner hanging on one wall of their house. Rico had told me about this, too.

"I told Jack he needs to tell his grandparents to take all the photos of her down straight away, and he did, but they didn't, and now I go there and all I see is that daft cow hanging on their walls. It's a damn shrine to Cora Tanner. I am Jack's wife!" Mara said. Olena's cell phone rang, "Hello Ian! Right now? Sure, I'll see you in a few!" Olena hung up, took her coat, her face aglow, and she dashed off. I was alone with Mara in the bar,

"This boyfriend is going to hurt her. He's a rotten sod," Mara said.

"I know, I have the same feeling."

"Silly Olena. She'll learn. Look, chum, I'm going upstairs. I need a back rub, can you do that for me? But only after you finish cleaning up this mess. I'm knackered." "Sure, of course," I said. "You're the dog's bollocks, really you are, see you soon."

After she left, I did what Rico usually does after he spoke to Mara. I picked up an empty wine glass and threw it at the door. It splattered everywhere. It felt damn good. I then swept it up fast. Later, I rubbed Mara's back until she fell sound asleep.

I went to meet Larry and Peter, who upon seeing me arrive at the disco, ran to me and pulled me onto the dance floor. Somerville's, *Don't Leave Me This Way* was playing. We went wild, danced, drank, grinded, joked, and flirted. After one long spin on the dance floor I stopped myself. There was Charlie at the bar, he looked at me and cheerily smiled, "Charlie!" I whooped, and ran to him, pulled him to the dance floor and brought him to Larry and Peter. The four of us twirled and danced for a good while. They put me in the center of their dancing bodies and boogied around me while Somerville's (Bronski Beat), *I Leel Love* blasted from the speakers. We dry humped, and roared over our silliness. They made me feel special because they probably knew I craved it, because they saw the neediness in me and probably sensed my confusion. Perhaps they were repairing something that was broken inside of themselves when they were young and gay. Maybe they wanted me to feel good about who I was and, quite possibly, they weren't thinking about me at all.

Before Charlie left me on the dance floor, he hugged me, and rubbed my shaved head, and kindly smiled at me. I drunkenly told him I loved him. He pulled me close to him, his body warm, he smelt like he always did of his spicy cologne. A smell I missed. My eyes were closed; within that ten second embrace I imagined that we could be together. He let me go and when I opened my eyes, I was alone on the dance floor. I watched him disappear amongst the crowd of gay men and the flashing colorful lights. I found my way to the bar, ordered a cosmopolitan, and continued to get properly pissed (as Mara would say.)

I spoke to a small group of big burly, sexy hairy guys, better known as "bears" who towered over me. When one started to put his arms around me, Larry escorted me away from them. "He belongs to us," he said.

We left the bar and I sluggishly walked between them, their arms around my shoulders. They started to tease the hell out of me, "Girl, listen to me," Larry said, and I stopped him briskly, "I love girls!" I said. "Honey, if one of those bears took you home, trust me, you'd be a girl before sun rise," Peter said. They both poked me. "I love the bears!" I said. "We all do, but trust me, not in the condition you're in." We stopped at a bodega and bought cans of beer and put them in brown paper bags. We walked and drank, "I want you guys to tell me the truth. Do you think I'm pathetic? Be honest." They cracked up. "Totally!" Larry said. "Screw you!" I said, and whacked his arm. More laughter. I obnoxiously slurred on about myself. Larry became serious, "You know Leonardo, there is going to come a time when you have to leave the bar and get on with your life. You know that right?" Larry said. We were walking up 1st Avenue. The air was fresh and nippy. I could hear birds tweeting in the trees. It was early morning, we were passing Bellevue Hospital.

"You're a writer. You need to write," Peter said. My head was spinning.

"I know. I know, God I know! I can't take much more of that English ninny, screw her! Hey, guess what? I kissed Charlie months ago and tonight I told him I loved him." I had the hiccups, and the spins, and nausea was coming fast.

"I'm sure Charlie loves you, too," Peter said.

"He wanted nothing to do with me. He left me there," I said just getting the words out of my mouth.

"Charlie is one of the nicest and most decent people you'll ever meet," Larry said.

"He's almost 50. How old are you, twenty?" Peter said.

"Screw you, I'm twenty-four. He's forty I dunno, forty something, he told me so," I said. They snickered.

"Well there goes my theory of Charlie being so decent. Forty! So did you guys do it? Do tell, give details!" Larry said.

"Is he a top or bottom?" Peter said.

"I'm serious, I told him I loved him. Oh, shit. I have to puke!" I went off to the side and vomited.

I woke late the next morning on Larry and Peter's sofa bed. Their apartment was neat, and stylish, fancy, more formal than I would have expected. Larry was coming at me with a tray of toasted bagels, water, coffee, and orange juice, "Morning sunshine!" He was in his t-shirt and PJ bottoms. He put the tray on a side table, and came into bed with me. I started to eat, "I'm sorry about last night. Was I bad?" I bit into a bagel. "Horrible, you're a horrible person. I have never been around a drunk gay man before, let alone one who pukes and who was trying to pick up bears and older men. Basically, you're scandalous. You're a despicable person." Larry took the bagel out of my hand, and I pulled it back, "Hands off my bagel, queen." I said jokingly. He giggled. Peter came into the room, and crawled into bed on the other side of me, "Well, look at little Miss Mary Sunshine! Sleep okay?" he said and poured himself a coffee. I put a pillow over my head, "I'm a loser! I think I told Charlie I loved him last night!" I cried out. Larry pulled the pillow off my head, "Telling someone you love them is the greatest thing you can say to a person," he looked at me earnestly, rubbed my head, poked my shoulder, and for the rest of the day we sat in bed, watched reruns of, *I Love Lucy*, laughed wildly, ordered out, and stuffed ourselves with pepperoni pizza.

Scene Sixteen – Red Hot Chili Peppers – *Under The Bridge*

Mara had the most severe case of pregnancy any of us had ever seen. I was at her beck and call all hours of the day. I was the only one dimwitted enough to *not* avoid her as everyone else did. I was Mara's main slave, peon, her skivvy, confident, and all-around bitch boy. In my own twisted, self-loathing way it made me feel special. Jack stayed clear of Mara, too, and so I was officially Jack's fill-in.

I also quickly became the peacemaker between Jack and Mara, whose fighting elevated. I'd fill Mara's head with all kinds of positive things, saying things to her like, "Between you and I, the other night Jack was telling Rico how amazing you were. God, Mara, Jack is crazy about you!" Sometimes those little fibs worked, and she'd calm down. I'd work on Jack too, who, was completely clueless about how to treat a pregnant woman, "Jack before you come home, pick up some flowers. After all, she's pregnant. It's a big deal. Mara needs to feel respected. I don't mean to be rude, but she feels dismissed by you." He'd do what was suggested, and this pleased her. Jack would thank me profusely for spending time with her, and for giving him advice. He'd sing my praises, "Thank God I can depend on you!" He was cutting coke on a small mirror, "Don't let Mara know I'm doing blow. I promised her I wouldn't as long as she was pregnant. She's dying to do it, and she can't." Two lines went up his nose. Shortly after, he started leaving town for three to four days, he said, to do commercials in LA, Florida, and London.

My days were busily spent going to the bodega, the diner, CVS, Starbucks, the bookstore, taking Mara to her doctor appointments, answering calls, and taking care of Annie. Basically I did everything for Mara except eat, poop, shower and grow her baby in my body. Whenever Mara went on her many hysterical rants, people would covertly ask me, "How do you do this? She's so unpleasant!" I would smile, "Oh, I don't mind it, she's awesome." Meanwhile, I wanted to bring a jack hammer to my head.

The bigger Mara's belly got, the more emotional and stressed she became, and Jack spent more time away. It got to the point where kind words and flowers could not placate Mara any longer. She was a raving monster. She got so upset one day with Olena and I for not coming back quick enough from the diner with her dinner, that she threw it at us. Meatloaf went everywhere. She then announced that she needed a rest from all of us nincompoops, "I want room service and a massage. I need to be pampered! Jack treats me like I'm a cow about to give birth to a calf! And you two are ungrateful and slothful!" Jack booked her two nights at the Regency Hotel on Park Ave. The only person she wanted to see was Jack who was allowed to go to the hotel late at night and sleep with her. I was assigned to take care of Annie with Olena, who was still pitifully obsessed with Ian.

"He kissed me goodbye last night. I almost melted. I can't stop thinking about him. I think I should tell him I love him. Maybe he's waiting for me to tell him."

"Wait. He kissed you?" I was stirring a pot of Kraft Macaroni and Cheese for Annie.

"It was like a slow peck on my face. He smells so good."

"So you haven't kissed him yet? Like kissed, kissed?"

"Not yet." Olena scoffed her macaroni and cheese down within seconds.

Jack came home from shooting another one of his fictional commercials. He was stopping to pick up a change of clothes and was leaving to meet Mara at the hotel, "This is outrageous. Mara called me screaming. She called me a dog with two dicks! She told me I'm cheating on her. She doesn't trust me at all," Jack said, pouring himself a brandy. A part of me wanted to explain to him that it was simple math; *When husband cheats on wife it's hard for wife to trust husband.* Like one plus one equals two. It was pretty basic stuff, but in the universe Jack lived in, such logic didn't exist. In his world four plus four equaled an 8-ball.

At seven months pregnant, Jack and Mara's fights were frequent and monumental. She'd throw things at him, and call him every low and vile name known to mankind. Things like, mingebag, maggot, arse-licker, lazy sod, a plonker and my favorite, a wanker. Jack would snap back and tell her that he was going to work in the bar with Rico, or go out for a walk. She'd chase him out the door and down the steps and throw shoes, and whatever else she could find, at him. When she did this, her belly bounced and wiggled, her breasts, that were large and full, flipped up and down, "I'm carrying your baby and you leave me alone! You liar! LIAR! Wanker!" She would then come back into the apartment and throw herself across the sofa and cry. I'd go to her and rub her back. She'd tell me Jack didn't care about anything but himself, how people blamed her for everything, how Jack was viewed as the perfect star, and how unfair life was. She'd tell me her boobs were sore, that she had trouble pooping, and that she feared her "muff" would never be the same. She told me that Annie was a big baby and giving birth to her tore her apart. I sat and listened, coddled her, and rubbed her swollen feet.

Jack was doing a bit part in a major Hollywood movie in South Dakota and was away for three weeks. I promised him I would not leave Mara's side. I napped with her in the same bed, acted as her protector, and did my usual everything. I was quite excited about the baby's birth and talked about it nonstop. Mara seemed to enjoy my enthusiasm. Most mornings we played out a silly routine where I'd press my ear to her stomach and say, "The baby said, 'Hello Leonardo!'" and she'd call me a nincompoop or a silly ninny. When the baby moved, she'd quickly put my hand on her belly and tell me to feel it. I was thrilled and we'd softly laugh and become watery eyed. We made fun of our unyielding gluttonous eating. We ate bags of potato chips and onion dip, and gorged on big deli sandwiches and cupcakes and Cheetos.

One night when she was sleepy, we lay facing each other. She rested her head on a pillow our eyes meeting. She told me she hoped her baby would do something important in the world, and wondered if it were a boy, would it look like her father, "Bloody animal," a tear dropped down her face. She then told me Annie was the embodiment of her mother, "Maybe that's why I'm so hard on her." And that's when her tears really flowed. I wiped them away, surprised that she let me. "I love Annie. Everyone thinks I'm mean , but she needs to be tough. She's weak and soft like my mother. She can't be weak. I won't allow it. The world eats soft women." She blew her nose. I told her to rest, that Annie would be fine.

One night while Jack was still away, I thought of baby names for the fun of it and I recited them to Mara. For boys; Thomas, Daniel, Robbie, Luke, Kevin, Vincent, Conor, Lewis, and if a girl; Charlotte, Ellie, Emily, Courtney, Nina, Jacqueline, Abagail, Molly, "Are you a complete pillock? Those names are ordinary, and infantile. My ninny former husband insisted on the name Annie. My daughter is named after a trite musical! This baby needs a special name, after all the stars and universe brought Jack and I together. It's all about Karma," she said.

"Well, what about Cosmo?" I said. She took in a deep breath. I thought she was going to slug me. Instead she sat up in bed, brought her hands together, and covered her mouth, "You're brilliant, darling, positively! Gobsmacked! I love it, Cosmo! Absobloodylootly!" She immediately called Jack, who on that day was traveling from South Dakota to San Antonio to shoot a few scenes, "Jack, darling, I thought of the most brilliant name for the baby, whether boy or girl, we shall call it, Cosmo! Yes, I know darling, it's perfect, isn't it? I love you too, do travel safe, see you fortnight, cheers. Ring me later." She hung up, "Jack loves it! Leonardo remember, once Cosmo is born, I'll need you more than ever, are you up for it?" I nodded yes, and smiled. She wrapped her arms around my shoulders, released me, and kissed my forehead, "Would you fancy some lunch, darling? I'm famished. I can ring for Chinese and some chocolate cake?"

One afternoon, mid-fall, Mara was adamant about cleaning the garden area and getting it ready for winter. She said she needed the exercise, was jumpy, restless, but wasn't as manic as she usually was. We unlocked the bar and went out back. She instructed me to stack the chairs and tables and bring them to the basement. She started to sweep, as I started to move the chairs, "We're going to go and see Jack's family for the weekend, it's Dina's birthday, and I am dreading it! They are so excruciatingly boring!"

"Mara they're really good people. I'm sure you'll have a fine time," I said.

"What don't you and Jack understand? They can't stand me. Oh, forget it! What's the point? I'll bear it somehow, darling. My belly hurts I need to sit. I'll be back out to help in a bit." She went into the basement. I began my work.

Soon after, while squirting down the garden, I looked up and noticed that Susie-Q was standing in the doorway, "Where's

Mara, sweetie?" I shut the water off, "She's in the basement. She's busy," I said. "Sweetie, she knows I'm coming." I went to her, "I said she's busy." She stepped toward me, "Sweetie, relax, she called me," her voice curt. She pushed past me, and started to climb down the stairs and into the basement, "She's pregnant, you know that, right?" I called after her. She stopped at the opening of the basement, her eyes batting, "I know she's pregnant, sweetie." She disappeared into the bleakness of the basement. I turned the water back on and continued to squirt the garden floor, became angry, then I shut the water off. I wanted proof that what I was suspecting was true. I quietly went into the basement.

I saw Mara's head go down on the desk through the junk of the basement, and next heard the sound of her snorting. My body went limp, how could she? I wanted to run in and tell her to stop. I wanted to shame her, have her placed in prison, and have her baby taken away from her the second it was born. But I remembered Esther's and Charlie's words and about the power Mara had because of Jack's fame. People would not believe me. The world would protect him, not me. Esther was right. I would be viewed as some low life wannabe writer with an agenda and would be attacked. In the end, I would be ousted, destroyed, and Mara would merrily continue with her coke habit anyway. Yet, was I choosing my own survival over the betterment of a little girl and an unborn child? Was it that simple? What kind of hellish dilemma was I in? Was life this cruel?

Walking home that afternoon my feet were heavy and my mind flip-flopped. An unborn baby was involved. Do something, you idiot! Do something! To hell with my life, my stupid, nonexistent writing career! But I became paralyzed with fear again, knowing that if I followed through with phone calls to social services or to Annie's father, I could potentially make things worse for Annie. If she was removed from Mara, then what? She could go with her father, but he was always traveling. She'd be in the hands of strangers. Did I really want to be responsible for removing Annie from her mother? I rationalized that foster care might be more damaging to Annie.

Once home, I laid across my bed, the sounds of sirens invaded my small room and added to my anxiety. Before I dozed off, at the end my self-doubt and debating, I firmly decided that the second Mara came back from Connecticut I was going to march myself to her apartment and tell her exactly how things were going to be. I was going to tell her that it was her duty to protect her unborn child. That using cocaine was lethal to her baby, and she needed to stop immediately. Determination to speak my mind possessed me. Nothing was going to stop me. I rehearsed over and over what I would say, editing myself, writing the entire spiel out in my mind. I was not going to contribute to the ills of this sick world. I was going to save those children. It was my civic duty.

Scene Seventeen –
John Lennon – *Beautiful Boy (Darling Boy)*

While Mara and Jack were in Connecticut visiting Jack's parents Mara started having labor pains. She was rushed to the hospital via ambulance and gave birth to a premature beautiful baby boy who they did indeed name, Cosmo. Rico told me the news when I arrived to work at the bar. Mara had to stay in the hospital for a few days due to dehydration, the baby would be there for a week or so, too. Rico told me not to call Jack or Mara, he was resolute about me not calling them; it almost felt that if I did, he would break my legs. I started to worry whether or not the baby was okay, and wondered why Jack or Mara never called me. But Rico was headstrong and told me the same thing each time I asked about them, "They told me to make sure not a single person called them under any circumstances."

When they finally came home three weeks later, Mara called me, "We're home. We need to talk. Come see me before work." Click. When I walked into her apartment she screeched at me with fists clinched, "I cannot believe you didn't come to see me in the hospital, it was so traumatic, everyone was all over Jack, like he gave birth. I needed you. You're a selfish arse!"

"Rico said you didn't want to see anyone. He said you wanted to be alone. He wouldn't tell me what hospital you were in; he basically forbid me to call you."

"Don't listen to that manky ninny! How many times do I have to tell you that he is jealous of you, he doesn't like that we're friends. Sometimes I think you are as stupid as Jack's father!"

"Why didn't you call me?" My voice meek.

"You wanted me to call you! My stomach was sliced opened. I couldn't move! I could hardly hold my baby and you expected me to call you!"

"I'm sorry, like I said, I was warned not to."

"I'll take care of that ninny. Now come with me. Come meet Cosmo."

Cosmo was an angel, small and sweet, he had clear little eyes and a head full of white hair. I was mesmerized.

"He's beyond incredible," I said. My smile so wide it hurt.

"Premature childbirth was such a bitch, man. Really, I'd like to see a man go through that." She picked Cosmo up, spoke sweetly to him, and we made our way to the sofa. Both of us cooed and touched little Cosmo's hands and feet in total amazement. Jack came in holding magnificently wrapped baby gifts that his friends had dropped off at the bar. He had a sincere gleeful peacefulness on his face, and proudly told me how he had never had such a feeling of love and completeness after seeing his son born. That night the three us marveled at Cosmo, all of us enthralled, sweetly happy with the miracle before us.

The next day, Mara lambasted Rico for not allowing me to call her in the hospital. She told him to take a week off without pay. I bartended and Olena waited tables, and one night Larry came in to wait tables and we had an absolute blast. Yet, this only made matters worse for Rico and I. When he returned to work the following week, he was nice enough to me, but the friction between us seemed unfixable.

Each evening before I reported to work at the bar I'd run upstairs to Mara and Jack's apartment to visit with Cosmo. I'd hold him, touch his little nose, and giggle when he smiled at me. At first Annie was quiet and withdrawn, but I attributed that to the fact she was astonished over the new addition to her family. Her eyes wide and curious, I figured she was probably processing what the new addition in her life meant to her. In time she was overjoyed, and pleased. She kept a close eye on her baby brother, spending time kneeling by his crib. Her tiny face sometimes sticking in between the bars.

Cosmo's birth and the joy it brought everyone filled me with such blissfulness that sometimes it felt as if I belonged to a family of my own. Each day my heart sang of new beginnings. I felt confident that Mara and Jack would be turning over a new leaf, one of sobriety, responsibility and love. Happy days were here.

Scene Eighteen – Ace of Base – *The Sign*

My first night babysitting Cosmo, Jack answered the door, "He cries all the time. You said this was going to be wonderful," he said this dryly, grudgingly, and walked away from me as if it were my fault I didn't warn him about the crying baby part. Mara quickly went over the babysitting instructions with me. The first thing she did was bring me to the crib and told me that when Cosmo needed to be fed to balance the bottle on a pillow while the plastic nipple of the bottle was in his mouth.

"If you balance the bottle next to his face on a pillow, and turn his head into it, he can drink on his own and you don't have to hold him. It takes forever for him to finish a bottle. You'll get right knackered feeding him."

"But he's too young for that. Babies need to be held," I said timidly.

"Whatever, mate. Hold him if you want. I'm just trying to make it easier for you," She walked away. I picked Cosmo up and held him to my shoulder. He was warm and soft and clean and smelled like baby powder. I rocked him most of the night while Annie sat at my feet.

Soon babysitting Cosmo became my main job. My bar duties went down to one night a week, and Rico resented the closeness I had with Mara and Jack. If we were all together, and if Rico gave me the slightest bit of trouble, Mara would ferociously protect me, "Leave him alone Nincompoop! Leonardo does more for us than you could ever imagine! You look like a junkie! You're a sorry excuse for a man!"

Naturally, Rico's hatred for me grew into gigantic proportions. He would give me one word answers and disparagingly snarl under his breath if I did something he didn't like. This included just about everything I did including being born and breathing. Yet I understood his anger, and remained quiet.

After babysitting one morning, I headed home to nap before returning that evening to work at the bar. The bar was closed, it was dimly lit, and when passing it I saw Rico. For a moment my eyes seemed to be stuck on him and an unnerving pity stung me. Poor Rico. He sat at a table alone, stared blankly, his hair out of place, he twitched. Reluctantly, I knocked on the bar's window, and he let me in.

"I haven't seen you in a long time," I said and he opened the door and let me in.

"I'm working tonight. I hope you're doing ok," I said.

"Why wouldn't I be? What? Did Mara send you down here to spy on me?" he barked.

"No, I only wanted to say hello. I'll see you later." My voice sour, I headed to the door.

"I'm the godfather. Jack and Mara both asked me." His words cracked as they came out of his mouth, he sounded childish. I think he feared I was going to snatch his godfather position away.

"I know. That's great Rico. That reminds me, I have to buy a gift for the baby. Maybe I'll go to *Baby Gap* now pick some stuff out. Wanna come along?" I said.

"No. I'm not up for it."

"It might be good to get out of here for a while. It might help."

"Help? What the hell does that mean? He was tapping his legs on the floor agitatedly.

"It's dark in here, let's turn on some lights," I said.

"No, no lights, I'm chilling out. Let me chill," he said.

"Rico, look I care about you, you mentioned to me more than once that your drug use was getting out of hand and I was thinking—"

"Don't -don't worry about me. I'm fine. I'm great. Anyway, listen I need to buy Cosmo a gift right?" he said trying to calm himself.

"Yes. That would be nice," I said.

"Do me a favor? Buy some stuff for him. Wrap it nice and stuff." He handed me money.

A half hour later I was in *Baby Gap* buying all kinds of clothes for Cosmo using Rico's cash. When I went to pay for the gifts I was giving the baby, my credit card was declined, and I decided to wait until I had some cash saved. I went back to the bar a few hours later with boxes wrapped. Rico beamed.

"Thanks, Leonardo. I'm sorry I snapped at you. I got some stuff on my mind," he said.

"Want some coffee?"

"No, I'm going to go to the basement to sleep, I'll see you later tonight," he said. I left, and went home. Olena was going to babysit Cosmo and Annie that night.

When Mara and Jack came into the bar before it opened Rico proudly gave them the gifts. Jack hugged him and they chatted about Cosmo while Mara opened the gifts. When she saw the *Gap* boxes she reacted as if someone had taken her cocaine stash and tossed it into the Hudson. She sighed deeply, mournfully, like someone kicked her in the gut, "*Baby Gap*? Rico, come on, mate, use your noodle for a change, why would I dress my child in such ludicrous clothes? They look like they're made for the children of farmers. But thanks, anyway." She tossed the boxes to the side stingily. She ordered a drink, and told Rico to make a call to Susie-Q. He did as ordered. For the rest of the night Rico acted like he was going shove the adorable *Gap* corduroy pants and thermal striped reversible hoodie down my throat.

The following evening, I had dinner with Mara and Olena in the apartment. We had Italian food sent in and ordered all of Jack's favorites; Veal Rollatini, Gnocchi, and a side of meatballs. We waited and waited for Jack, but he didn't come home so we ate without him. Mara cursed him to the heavens, wasn't feeling well, and relentlessly called the bar looking for Jack, but the line was busy and Jack's and Rico's cell phones were dead. Ever since Cosmo was born, Rico started taking the bar phone off the hook because Mara's phone calls were absurd and obsessive. She wanted this and that, and lamented to Rico for hours as he tried to tend bar; the baby wouldn't stop crying, she was having a breakdown, the apartment was too small, she couldn't wait to buy an apartment. Rico would get frustrated and irritated, "What the hell does she want me to do? Why isn't she calling Jack?" Rico made lame excuses to her to about the busy phone, "Customers were using the phone, I'm so sorry." But to me he said things like, "She's going to have to take care of her own baby, she wanted it, now deal with it! Crazy bastard!" After putting Cosmo to bed, Mara started calling the bar, and again, the line was busy. Their cell phones were still dead, "That nincompoop Rico has the bar phone off the hook again!" Mara slammed the phone down, "I will not be dismissed like some stupid nagging housewife!" She was flat-out on her bed, complained about a headache and her sinuses. She wanted Jack home immediately. She threw her phone across the room and it smashed against a porcelain carrousel music box that was a gift from Jack's aunt to Cosmo. The crashing sound was loud and threatening, and Annie jumped and Cosmo started crying. Olena instantly started sweeping up the mess. When she was done, from the depths of the barrel where she had tossed the broken pieces, Brahms lullaby started playing, it sounded defected like background music from some spooky horror movie.

"Leonardo! You go down to that bar and put the phone back on its cradle, and you tell Rico to answer the phone, furthermore, you tell that rotten junkie if he takes the phone off the hook again, he is fired. And you tell my husband to get his lousy bumsucker arse up here! "Olena started feeding Cosmo his bottle. I reached in the barrel and shut the music off.

"Leonardo, what are you waiting for? Get my husband!" She pointed to the door,

The bar was dead, Rico sat reading a newspaper, rock music played. As usual it was Queen. I went to hang up the phone, and Rico came to me.

"What the hell are you doing?"

"She told me to hang the phone up."

"Keep the phone off the hook. Screw her. Jack needs a break. I need a break!"

"She wants Jack. Where is he?"

"He's in the basement. He said not to bother him. He said he's working on something."

"Mara told me to get him."

"Dude, I said don't go down there. He needs to be alone."

"Mara wants me to."

"I don't care. Strict orders from Jack." I left the bar angry. What the hell was I going to say to Mara? If I told her Rico wouldn't allow me to see Jack, it would be an all-night war, and I was in no mood for their drama. The last time I obeyed Rico when Cosmo was born, I was scolded by Mara. Not this time. I decided that Rico was setting me up to be crucified by Mara.

He wanted me to look bad, he always did. Carefully sneaking to the garden area through a tight alley between buildings I went to the bulkhead doors that led to the basement and searched through my key chain for the key to the padlock. Strangely the door was unlocked and jammed with a piece of wood. Descending the old cement steps, I called out, "Jack? Jack Mara sent me to come get you. Jack?" A large crash of objects and commotion from deep within the basement echoed, Jack cried out, "I'll be right there!" I walked in semi-darkness to where the sound came from, "Jack, are you okay? I'm sorry, but Mara insisted that I come find you." Jack was right before me, he was shirtless, and pulling up his pants. He looked at me dolefully. Behind him, yards away in the middle of Mara's fallen antiques was Ian, stark naked, briskly putting on his clothes, he did not look up at me. Pretending not to notice, my throat tightened, "I'll tell Mara you'll be up soon." And, off I went.

Back in the apartment, Mara was sipping a brandy, "So, where the hell is Jack?" She said. "He said he'll be right up." I couldn't look at either one of them, "So what the hell was he doing!" Mara clamored. I didn't want Mara or Olena to read the unease on my face because it would lead to questions and more drama and more drama and yet more drama. So to distract them, I did my best to act nonchalant and started gathering Annie's clothes to put them in the laundry basket, and then I started picking through the leftover Italian food.

"Was Ian there yet? I'm supposed to see him in a bit," Olena called out.

"I didn't see Ian," I called back from the kitchen, my mouth full of Gnocchi.

"So where the hell is Jack!" Mara screamed.

"Jesus, Mara, he'll be right up," I put a meatball in my mouth. Poured myself a big glass of wine, drank it down like soda and immediately the stress left my body in a river of warmth that speedily traveled through my limbs.

Jack showed up twenty minutes later. He didn't look at me, went to Cosmo and picked him up out of the crib and brought him into the living room. Mara shook her head in disgust, she stood over him, her hands on her waist, her black robe almost open, "I'd rather be dead than married to an egomaniac like you." She turned her back on him, threw out endless insults, and slipped on her clothes. She snatched Olena by the elbow and practically dragged her out the door. Jack looked at me, "I'm all set if you want to go home," he said. I left too.

A month later, Ian was an extra on a cop show that Jack did some work on, and had acquired an agent, the same one Jack had. I never saw Ian in person again, only in small roles in Indie films and the sporadic TV commercial. After that night, whatever relationship Olena and Ian had, was over.

"He won't even talk to me. I call him and he doesn't call me back and he always did. What did I do wrong?" Olena said to me one day while we walked through Central Park. She was holding Annie's hand. Olena had tears rolling down her face, trying to hide them from Annie. I was pushing Cosmo in a small baby carriage.

"You're a great person, you'll find someone else," I said.

"Olena, why are you crying, are you mad at me?" Annie asked.

"No, Annie, how could I be mad at you, how could anyone be mad at you?"

"Mommy is always mad at me," Annie said.

"Your mother is mad at everyone," Olena said.

"That's true," Annie said. Olena giggled through her tears.

"Hey Annie, there's the zoo, go on, see how fast you can run!" Olena said. We stopped for a moment and watched as Annie excitedly ran through the park. There was such beauty in her little legs going as fast as they could and it was nice to witness her happy and free. It made me feel joyful and content, like I was doing something important and good. "When she's with you I don't worry about her," Olena said to me.

"I get scared for Annie sometimes. I only hope she'll be able to trust when she gets older," I said. Olena then burst out crying, "I thought Ian and I were going to get married and have children. He dumped me for no reason." I put my arms around her, softly kissed the top of her head. More tears spilled from her eyes, "Olena, I know, it's painful losing someone you love. I'm sorry. But you're going to meet a wonderful guy one day. It's going to be amazing. I know it." In the distance, across the green, Annie was at the entrance to the zoo, "Leonardo! Olena! Hurry! Let's go inside!" Annie cried out.

Olena would never know what I saw in the basement that night. If she knew of the gross deception from Jack and the first boy she loved, it could possibly damage her for years or perhaps her entire life. By not saying anything, I figured she would heal quicker, and eventually think her break up was because of something silly and lame. Telling Olena the truth wasn't worth the risk of messing with her ability to trust again.

Scene Nineteen – Tracy Chapman – *Give Me One Reason*

Cosmo was an adorable baby, and as he grew, I couldn't hold and love him enough. His eyes were big and blue, but sad, like Jack's. His lips full, like Mara's. He had locks of soft twirling white hair due to cowlicks all over his head. His legs were pudgy like his little nose. I loved running my finger under his chubby neck until he smiled. He smelled like sweet milk, and his skin was soft and pinkish. His cry was so loud that his wail reverberated in my ears hours later, and he took massive man-like dumps in his diapers that made us all choke and shudder.

Annie was thrilled with her new baby brother, and loved helping me when I babysat. She ran for diapers, found blankets and bottles, bent over the crib and said hello to him repeatedly. Her eyes gentle and curious, she took pride when Cosmo smiled or moved. She especially liked it when I held Cosmo. She would sit close to me and pat his head, "Hey Cosmo, hey there, here I am. Peek-a-Boo! Peek-a-Boo!"

Close to a year after Cosmo was born, Mara found a four story building to buy with the money Jack had made that year. It was located on West 15th Street between 9th & 10th Avenue. It needed a lot, and although it cost somewhere in the millions, Mara wanted to spend as little as she could during the demo process. She asked me to help her. Naturally, I obliged enthusiastically because I liked manual labor as much as I liked eating maggots off dead birds. "Once we have a bigger place, and Jack has his own office, he wants to start writing. I think you two would be a great writing team, he's practical and smart, and you're sensitive and something. Whatever it is, I know it's good and it would be a nice balance," she said. Excitement grew inside of me- -writing with Jack Fresh!

"That would be fantastic! I've been thinking that I really need to start paying more attention to my writing. I haven't worked on anything for such a long time." I said to Mara.

"Must you always talk about yourself?" Mara said. "Can you meet me tomorrow at the new building or not?"

Initially, Jack and I were going to tear down walls on each floor and make the building an empty shell. New walls would be built. We were to toss parts of the old walls down a long tubular chute that led to a dumpster on the street below. Plans changed.

The next day, I showed up in my old clothes ready to work and please. However, Jack couldn't help because he landed a job recording a book on tape for thirty-five thousand dollars. It was a self-help book, *How to be more Zen in your Everyday Life* "It's such a perfect book for Jack," Mara said to me in front of the building. I was not happy with myself for agreeing to do the task at hand, and now I was doing it alone. Zen, I was not. To get myself out of my funk, I told myself it was an honor to aid in the creation of their fancy new home. I was chosen and special. One day Jack and I would be writing in an office. Perhaps we'd be a famous writing team.

"I'll show you what needs to be done." Mara opened the door and we both went in together. We climbed the urine smelling stairs, and we humorously read graffiti on the walls that was interestingly expressing what I was feeling toward Mara; *eat shit and die, douche bag and cracker ass bitch.* Inside it was dark and dreary. Scattered about were old toilets, soda cans, beer bottles, wood piles, dead pigeons, broken glass, exposed wires, and clothes. A single light bulb hung from the ceiling. A wall of exposed brick was to the left. The entire place reminded me of a third world torture chamber. A rat the size of a puppy ran into an opening in the brick wall. My heart became an active ping-bong ball inside my chest cavity. Mara ignored the rat and started with specific instructions,

"Okay, so I need this wall down, and this wall down, and all this trash tossed down the chute." Mara started marking the walls with a black marker, "Be careful of pipes and electrical wiring, and if you come across any *live* wires leave the beams around them. Be careful, do not get yourself electrocuted. I have to run, do have fun, cheers, mate." She said "electrocuted" so causally you would think she was telling me to be careful of splinters.

"Is anyone else coming to help?" I asked obediently, cautiously, careful not to offend, my eyes fixated on the hole where the giant rat had disappeared.

"No. You're the only one we can depend on. We love you darling, we sincerely do. Your friendship with us is sacred." Mara gave me a kiss on both cheeks, like she was saying goodbye to me for good. Then she left. In full rage over the predicament, I rationalized that I was the chosen one, the one who was loved the most. Being careful not to get electrocuted, or bitten by that gargantuan rat, with the biggest sledge hammer in my hand, I went nuts. Walls came tumbling down. Each section of wall was tossed down the long chute that led to the dumpster on the street below. It was 8 am, and at that point I was determined to do a fantastic job to impress Jack and Mara. I worked until 1 am, and there was still more work to be done. The next day I was back by 10 am ready to work. Mara was already there, holding a cup of coffee for herself. She inspected my work, and smiled, pleased.

"Good job! I can have the contractors in here by Friday! They wanted to charge me fifty thousand dollars to demo this place." My arms were so sore that I worried they were going to pop out of their sockets. I started knocking down the one wall that was left. Mara eyed me.

"You're as strong as a bloody bull! It's brilliant!" she said.

"Thanks." When the last wall was down I tossed the rest of the garbage down the chute. A disco ball was the last to go down into the bowels of the dumpster, it landed with a distant quick crash. I even swept. It was 2:30am and I was done. I inhaled about six pounds of dust and for the next week, I coughed up plaster chunks from the 19th century.

"Leonardo, thank you so much," Jack hugged me. He then handed me 200 hundred dollars. At first I refused, but since I saved them fifty-thousand dollars, I took it. Now my rent would be paid.

The weeks that followed, I practically lived in expensive hardware stores, fancy household fixture stores and elegant tile stores. We picked out imported tiles from Italy, sinks, shower heads, paints, plaster board, and every kind of supply they needed to make their home an exquisite show piece. I went with Mara to pricey antique shops to buy light fixtures, furniture, drapes and art work. I spent days lifting and carrying items up flights of stairs, while she watched. "I'd help but my back is so bad, truly it is." I spoke to contractors, gave them Mara's instructions, bought contractors sandwiches, babysat Cosmo, and appeased Annie. They paid me enough to just get by, they fed me, and they told me over and over they loved me. They loved me.

When their new four million dollar home was ready, they planned on going to an all-inclusive trip to Barbados. Jack had made two films that spring and summer, and they both told me they needed rest, but were going to take the children. Frankie,

Larry and Peter were invited, their trip paid for by Jack and Mara. I was certain they were tricking me and would surprise me with a ticket. I went along with it, and told my parents I was going to Barbados. Days before they left, Mara told me she wanted to see me, it was another one of her "emergencies." Later that day I bought myself a bathing suit at a place in Chelsea. I chuckled and went to her place expecting an airline ticket by some sort of elaborate plan like opening a box within in a box within in a box. Or, maybe she would put a ticket in Cosmo's crib. When I arrived she was standing on a ladder in the front foyer. Light bulbs sat on the top step.

"The bloody bottom part of the light broke off and I can't get it out! I screwed it in too tightly and the bulb came off in my hand," she said. Perhaps my ticket was on the top step of the ladder, but there was no ticket there. I removed the bottom of the light bulb, replaced it with a new one. "Bravo, darling!" she said. I climbed down the ladder. "While we're away I'll need you here, darling, the plumbers are coming to install the jet whirlpool, and the dishwasher. And the painters are coming to paint the front room. Jack's desk is arriving, too."

I smiled widely, "I have you covered, no worries." On the way home I tried to return the bathing suit, but it was a final sale. My rage buried, muted, I blocked out my hurt. The first night they were gone I got drunk and danced. Another night I stayed awake in bed until 3am. I tried to go back to sleep; anger about being left out of the trip covered me in a slimy film of self-pity and disgust. I was allowing them to use me! I was an idiot! The sounds of cars zooming up Broadway kept me awake, the smell of freshly baked bagels floated through my window, and made me hungry. My breathing increased. I felt panicky. What the hell have I done? I started to think that maybe, just maybe the weakness in me was creating this entire situation to prove to myself I was worthless. I was scared. Nah. No. This was all good. I was being sensitive. I convinced myself that I needed intimacy, sex, and a bagel. It always helped. I called a guy I had fooled around with a week prior who lived a block away from me. We met at a small bar on 106th Street, drank gin and tonics, and had sex back at his place. That morning when I walked home, eating a bagel, Mara and Jack popped in my mind again, no, they weren't taking advantage of me, they loved me. I was doing it all willingly. They loved me.

When they came back from Barbados, Jack's parents and I helped Mara and Jack officially move into their new place. We schlepped up and down the stairs all day. That day, Mara decided she wanted to spend the night at the Regency Hotel, she was exhausted. Before she left she instructed us to put everything inside the building and she would sort it out after her rest, which meant I had more work to do. She kissed all of us goodbye.

"I need a rest, those renovations nearly killed me, and that vacation was no vacation! I will never bring the children again! It was a bloody week of work!" She said.

That night Olena took the kids to her place for the night. The next day Jack helped us move the best he could, but he was so hung over, all he could manage to carry was two boxes. He only stayed a few hours; said he was shooting a commercial uptown.

At the end of a long trying day of moving, Dina, Eddie and I went out for pizza.

"Why didn't they hire movers?" Dina asked me.

"Mara wanted to save money," I said.

"Why spend money when you have us," Dina let out a frustrated, disgusted sigh.

"Don't start, Dina," Eddie said.

"Is my son happy?" Dina asked.

"I think so," I said.

"Why wouldn't he be happy? Look at that place he's moving into. He's famous for crying out loud!" Eddie said. He bit into his pizza, mozzarella swung from his lip, and dripped off his chin. "It doesn't matter, Eddie, what the hell he has! Leonardo, I want to know what is going on with my son!" Dina said. Her hair a bit out of place from carrying boxes and climbing the stairs all day. I wanted to tell her that her son was a drug addict, a drunk, a puppet on a string, and that he needed rehab. But who was I to say such a thing? I was not a drug addict, but I certainly drank a lot. I didn't want to ruffle Dina's feathers, why make her worry, what could she do anyway? When Eddie left to return the rented truck, Dina looked at me, discontent washed over her face. "She overpowers our son. I do not like the way she treats Annie, or the way she goes out almost every night. Cosmo is a baby. Every time I call Jack's house, you answer. I blame my son, too. He wasn't raised this way!" she started to cry. I was silent.

"Is my son on drugs?" She asked.

"No. No. It's not Jack's fault, none of it. She's dreadful. She is." I couldn't believe the words came out of my mouth.

"I could tell you felt the same way."

"I love those kids. I worry about them," I pushed my pizza crust around my plate.

"I feel safe with you at their house. I worry about my son. Keep in touch with me, take care of them for me…"

"I promise I will," I said.

"I think she's the devil," Dina said. Her voice stern, convinced.

"You and everyone else," I said. Dina then stopped, blew her nose, she glared at me.

"So what does that make us?" She asked.

"Nincompoops," I said.

Scene Twenty – Simon & Garfunkel – *America*

That 4th of July my family and I sat in a boat in the middle of Boston Harbor waiting for fireworks to burst across the sky. My niece and nephew were huddled under the wings of my parents, and we all sipped cold beer. It was a warm night, but a slight chill was coming off the ocean. My brother-in-law sat next to me. In one month I was going to be 27 and my third year with Jack and Mara was coming up.

"What are you writing these days?" My brother-in-law asked me.

"I'm working on a play." Liar, liar big fat liar. I hadn't written anything in almost 6 months, and even then it was not good writing.

"I thought Jack was going to help you with your career. All you talk about is babysitting. You worked very hard to get into graduate school and spent all that money on tuition. For what? To babysit for a movie star?" my sister Emily said. I wanted to jump ship.

"I can't just come out and say help me with my career," I said. Shoving potato chips in my mouth. The harbor was filling up with boats.

"Why not?" my father said."

"Yeah, why not?" Emily said.

"Why not?" my little nephew Scott said, not understanding what he was saying. I handed him a juice box, popping a straw in the top of the box.

"Because he's my friend. It would be uncomfortable."

"Well, if he's your friend, it wouldn't be uncomfortable," my mother said.

"I agree with, Mom," Emily said.

"I do, too," my dad said.

"He and his wife have no issues asking you for help," Emily said.

"If you're such good friends, you need to ask him," my dad said. Everyone was looking at me, waiting for an answer. Instead I laid back, and watched the fireworks explode in the sky; reds, blues, whites, and greens.

"When you get back to New York, you tell Jack you need advice, you ask him to read some of your work, or at least ask him to recommend a literary agent," Emily said.

"Yup," I slowly nodded. The fireworks reflected off their faces, all of them waiting for me to say more.

"I agree. It's time. I'm going to ask him for some help," my voice cracked. They all nodded in unison, the sound of fireworks exploding took their eyes off me and they looked toward the multicolored sky, my head went downward toward the water where the fireworks reflected off the water's surface in faint, wavy, trickles that made me nauseous.

On the train back to New York, I talked to myself, *okay, I've had enough! This is it! I'm going to do it! I'm going to come right out and ask Jack for some sort of help. I'm going to do it, I swear I am! I'm going to do it first thing! I'm going to march right into their house and demand he help me!* The second the trained pulled into Penn Station, Jack called me, "Want to have dinner with us? Come down." This really meant, we'll buy you dinner if you babysit for us later.

Before I knew it, I was sitting in his fancy new living room. Their entire place was four floors of opulence; each floor, each room thoughtfully designed by a famous New York interior designer, some walls were covered in fabric, drapes were hung in doorways, striking and interesting art covered the walls, a black grand piano sat in one room, there were shiny new wooden floors throughout. The colors were deep light greens and soft plumy purples. One room was all white. When I arrived Mara was snorting coke at a small table in front of the large cherry-wood bookcase that dominated one wall of the massive room. It was full of old books that Mara had bought at various flea markets. I doubted the books had any intellectual value to her because I never saw her read. She had done a year of college in Europe, claimed to be a art history scholar, but she told me she was not degreed, "All professors are nincompoops! I quit. I tell people I went to Columbia. Who cares!"

"I want to do a reading of my new play," I spluttered each word as they come out of my mouth.

"What did you say?" Mara said, wiping her nose.

"Nothing," I said.

"I always liked theater. I started out in the theater." Jack came to attention and poured brandy into my half empty glass.

"A play reading sounds like fun," Jack said. Mara came over to us. She eyed me up and down. "I always wanted some kind of artist salon! That's what I wanted my bar to be. But Rico has turned it into a vulgar bar. It is important that art and the—" Jack interrupted her.

"Don't blame Rico. Come on, give the guy a break," Jack said.

"Don't defend that nincompoop! Are you brain dead, too? Really, Jack, what's wrong with you? You act like you're the stupidest man alive. Rico will bring you down. You need to listen to me, Rico will destroy you because he's jealous of you." She carried the mirror with the lines of coke to Jack. She became soft.

"Here baby, I'm sorry, but listen to me, Rico is not fully developed as a human being. Try and understand this. We've talked about letting go of bad things." She ran her hands through his hair. He didn't flinch; he indulged in the coke.

"Why don't we do a reading of Leonardo's play at the bar, we can do it on a Sunday afternoon before you open?" Jack said, rubbing his nose. She brought her hands together as if in prayer, and bowed. She then babbled on about art in textbook fashion. She started referring to the soul and expression of the human spirit, "I can see it all in front of me now, artists could come to my salon and read their work, show their paintings, and we could have deep and meaningful conversations about their art. It's a brilliant idea!" Her face went back to the mirror, she snorted a line, and kissed Jack's face, kneeling in front of him and putting her head on his lap. Her hands were extended around his hips. She spoke like some actress from a cheesy 1930's movie.

"Jack, our love and the creation of art is all that matters. Our life can't be about these small and insignificant people in your life. I'm the only one who will love you properly. We are soulmates, put on this earth for a reason. I know this to be our truth. We are here to create art and nurture artists, darling. Let go of the people who are out to hurt you. Rico is a bad man. Let's focus on art."

Jack then went for the mirror, snorted two more lines. Then he ate his dinner; three almonds and an *Ensure* vitamin drink. I sat biting my fingernails while Mara blathered on some more about the glory of art and something about her being the reincarnation of Gertrude Stein and Jack being Alice B. Toklas, which I suppose made me John Dos Passos.

"Tell us about your new play," Mara said. Shy, but thrilled they showed interest in my work, I perked up. It was the first time they didn't treat me like I was born to serve them. "It's about a domineering mother and her neurotic daughter," I said, naively not realizing I probably wrote a play about her and Annie ten years from now. Regardless, Mara liked the subject of the play. She told me my play would be the first project in her French style salon. I teased her and called her "Ms. Stein." She didn't think I was funny, "Stop! This is not a time for jokes, you nincompoop! This is about art! It's sacred!" My heart instantly stopped, blood rushed to my extremities, the taste of my lunch the day prior coated my mouth. "It was a bad joke," I said and cleared my throat. She continued to scold me, and I obediently listened, "Art is the highest order of God, and you laugh! You make jokes!" She squalled and pointed at me. "You are so right and I am so very wrong," I said. Before she put her nose to the mirror, she said, "Stop acting like a non-artist!" Her face moved across the mirror, she smiled. "Would you fancy some Chinese food?" she asked. I nodded yes, relieved, Chinese food, my friend, my savior.

I was to have my reading on a Sunday afternoon. My parents were excited and told me they would wait by the phone to hear the news about how the reading went.

"Finally he's doing something for you!" my dad said.

"Bravo!" my mom said from the extension.

Desperate for an audience, I had to apologize to my friends for avoiding them for the last three years, and made excuses that I was working on my career. Since they were as self-centered and driven as I was they understood, but only committed to coming when I mentioned that Jack was going to be there. Except Julia who was angry with me for disappearing from her life, and refused to come, but finally agreed after I profusely apologized and offered her the chance to read lead character.

"It's a great chance for Jack to see you act," I said. This made her furious, "I'll do it for you Leonardo. But I'll be honest, you dumped my ass for those people and I'm not happy about it. I don't care what Jack thinks of me as an actor. I get my own jobs. I don't need Jack and quite frankly neither do you."

Esther never returned my phone calls. There might have been one message from her that said, "You're an asshole!" but it could have been an old message. Mara insisted that Rico direct the reading. I was blown away by this, because for months he had been on her shit list. However, Rico was calling himself a director that month, and people were starting to believe him. The month before he was calling himself a writer. The only thing he wrote that month was a bad check for his rent. Despite my worry over Rico directing my reading, I was happy for him, it seemed to lighten his mood and I saw that it gave him a sense of importance. He spent days analyzing my script. Julia complained that Rico was directing. "This is going to be so uncomfortable. I feel you tricked me." I told her there was no trickery, it was just how things went down. She screamed into the phone, "Fine!" and hung up on me. When Mara heard that Julia was going to read, she was steaming angry, "She's a daft cow!" When Julia showed up, Mara stayed very close to Jack the entire time.

The day of my reading my head went numb, and my throat was closed with fright, inhaling and exhaling was a chore. I set chairs up in rows. Jack and Mara bought fancy pastries and I made coffee. Larry, Peter, Frankie and about 15 of my friends came, some I hadn't seen in years.

After the reading, Jack took my hand in his, his grip hard, and sincere, "Go talk to your friends. We'll talk in a bit." And off he went to fix himself a coffee. My face was flushed. It was the first time I had shown my work to him, and whatever he thought was going to be the golden word to me. What was he going to say? Was I worthy? Did I have talent? I waited for him to speak to me while the actors and my friends congratulated me on a fine job. Finally, Jack tapped me on the shoulder. Once again, he took my hand in his with the same earnest grip.

"Leonardo, nice work," he nodded with a serious, intense expression on his face.

"Oh, really? You mean it? The first act needs re-writes, and scene four is weak, but thanks," I said shyly.

"Mara and I want you to have dinner with us tonight to talk further about your work."

"Really, that sounds great," my heart was pounding.

"I think you're talented. It is a really good play," he patted my forearm.

"What did Mara think?" I asked him. By that time the actors were saying goodbye, and Mara was talking to Rico, waving her hands around in a scolding fashion. I later learned that she was telling him he should never direct again, that he did a horrible job, and that he was lucky the actors provided some talent for him to work with, except of course Julia who had no talent. If not for my writing, it would have been a major disaster, adding again, that my script was good but weak in areas. When Mara was done belittling Rico, she came toward me, I buckled up for my berating.

"You have passion, and it's from the heart. It will be done everywhere posthumously, and not a second sooner. I know these things, darling, I do, trust me. It is not your masterpiece, which I hope will soon come. I insist you do come to dinner. We have much to discuss."

"Sure," I said, thinking of the fifty venomous daggers I wanted to shoot in her head. I'd completely forgotten that I'd made dinner plans with the other actors and Julia. They were chatting and waiting for me.

"Can we have dinner with Rico and the other actors?" I asked. Mara cringed as if I farted and burped in her face at the same time.

"No. They are all so daft," she said.

"I forgot I made plans with Rico and Julia. I can't have dinner with you and Jack."

"What do you mean, you can't? This is a sacred moment! Jack and I want to talk about your play, you must. Those actors have mediocre talent. You must break bread with us." I glanced over at the half eaten Neapolitans, the fancy cream puffs, and empty cups of coffee. The chairs that were set in rows for the actors to sit, all of them showing up free of charge because they had passion for new plays.

"We can do it another time, come on Mara. He made plans," Jack said. He gave me a reassuring wink.

"I'll cancel," I heard myself say. Show biz came first. I was going to have dinner at Jack's house and talk about my play, and no one or nothing else mattered. Each minute I spent with them was an honor, a cherished moment. I proceeded to the group of actors waiting for me, and decided to say what I had to say,

"I wanted to say thank you everyone. You all did a great job. Something came up and I can't have dinner. I forgot I made plans and there's no way out of it," my voice cracked. Rico gruffly turned away from me. The other actors didn't seem to mind, but on the way out Julia came to me and calmly, softly, spoke, "Okay, I'm so pissed right now it isn't funny, but I am going to chalk this up as your almost three years of insanity. When you come back from this crazy turn and you get your butt away from them call me, but until then, don't bother," she kissed my face, and left with the other actors. I tried to speak further, and she held up her hand indicating that I should stop speaking, so I did.

Jack ordered in a simple dinner, penne with tomatoes, basil and olive oil, and chicken cutlets. They ate two spoonfuls, whereas, I gorged myself. Feelings of guilt for being a complete ass to my friends started to settle in. Was I that desperate to "make it" that I would treat the people I cared for so poorly? Was I that reckless with my relationships? How bad did I really need the world to love me? All these questions started to germinate in my mind the day of my reading, but it didn't stop my obsession to make it in show business.

Later, Mara was sprawled out on the floor with sofa pillows. I sat in a chair flipping through a book. "My headache is so bad tonight, darling, I don't understand these headaches." I brought her some aspirin and convinced her she was under the strain of being a wife and a mother and a business owner. "Being a woman in today's world is not easy." I often fed this type of bullshit to her and she liked it. She closed her eyes, ran her hand over her face and told me I understood her profoundly. "Only the gays can fully understand women and their lives and the difficulties being a women entails," she yawned. For a glam slam I added, "Think about it Mara, what other women could do all that you do for your husband and children? Not only that, you also run a business, you're amazing, you are, and you're such a great example for Annie." She reached over and stroked my arms. "Darling you're too kind to me," she wiped a tear from her eye. And I tasted venom on my tongue.

Jack joined us and sat in his chair. Candles were burning, Mozart played off a CD faintly, and soon the mirror came out. Jack started to cut the coke and make lines. Mara sat up and snorted her two lines and then she passed the mirror to Jack, then it went back to Mara.

"Would you fancy a line? Please do, it will make you feel lovely, darling," she held out the straw to me. I didn't want to do it, but thought, why not? It was a magical day, I'd had my first reading, why not? I stuck the straw too far up my nostril and my head went back in pain. "Ouch!" She leered at me. "Blimey! You've never done it before?" I nodded no. My nose was severely deviated and I couldn't suck anything up without hitting some cartilage. I was completely, wholeheartedly, mortified about not being able to snort professionally. My second attempt made a mess of the lines on the mirror. I tried again and they both had stunned expressions on their faces, clearly thinking I was an imbecile. "Forget it, darling, you're making a shambles," she said. I gave the mirror back to them and apologized.

"I can't do it," I giggled.

"I'll say!" she said. When they were finally riding high on coke, Jack started rubbing his hands together like he was washing them. Mara started biting down and licking her top teeth like a ravenous horse. Then they started talking about my play, they said it was about my pain and sorrow over not having children. They went on and on about how happy they were that I was part of their life, "You will be a major talent one day, darling," Mara said. She added, "I see it all. I see novels too, best sellers. Maybe one day you will write about us. I see you doing it years from now. Portray us nicely, darling, won't you?" she laughed.

"I feel foolish. All this time I've known you, and I didn't know. We should write a screenplay together," Jack said.

"That would be awesome," my voice meek, I coughed. Finally, finally, finally, hooray for me. Mara and Jack respected me. Even though they were so drugged a surgeon could have removed their spleen without them noticing, I hoped Jack was sincere.

A month passed while waiting for Jack to bring up the idea of us writing together. Too intimidated to ask him when we would start, I wallowed for days. I asked myself why Jack would want to write with a no-talent, loser like me? After sufficiently verbally abusing myself for a few weeks. I decided to muster up the courage to ask him about us writing together. I gave myself a deadline and waited another month. I'm not exactly sure why I waited a month, but looking back evidently, I needed a tad more emotional abuse.

Scene Twenty-One –
Katrina & The Waves – *Walking On Sunshine*

Weeks later, I was watching an Italian film, *The Star Maker* with Jack and Mara. It was the story of a pseudo talent scout who rides the poor back roads of 1950's Sicily with a sound truck, a camera, and a tent. Throughout the film he's allegedly seeking ordinary faces for the movies and tells the people of these small poor towns that he's conducting screen tests for a Roman studio, promising big dreams of stardom, but he is really scamming fees from the villagers for the price of their screentests. At the end of the film, when looking at the screentests, he is moved profoundly by the villagers who had expressed their deepest feelings. He realizes the wrong he has done, and redeems himself through the love of a young woman who is entwined with the village.

Jack and I loved the movie. We thought it touching and philosophical, and beautifully photographed. Mara went on about how the movie was badly made, the acting trite. "It was a silly movie for silly people." She couldn't understand the journey of a man whose initial evil turns into awareness and redemption. I loved the movie so much that I didn't bother refuting her. It never made any sense to argue with Mara because any attempt at an intellectual conversation would ultimately end with relentless berating and insults. That night Jack did as I did, he sat quietly and let her pontificate for two hours, our eyes nearly closed with sleepiness and boredom. "So, are you going to say anything? Or are you both going to sit there like two nincompoops!" I shrugged. Jack cracked his knuckles. "Mara, it was a great film, what do you want me to say? That I disliked it because you did?" As expected, she called us both "assholes" because we had no argument for her, and she went off to bed. Cosmo was in his crib, Annie was with her father. We drank brandy, I loosened up a bit, quickly grew a set of balls, and gathered up all the courage I had.

"Jack, you mentioned writing a screenplay with me. I think we should do it.

"Sure, that would be great. What are you thinking?" his eyes sleepy, nonchalant.

"I don't know, something spooky, psychological, like *Rosemary's Baby*," my voice assured, but at the same time every inch of my being trembled; even my toenails.

"That's one of my favorite movies."

"Mine too!" I said.

"Start writing one, show me thirty pages, we'll go from there."

"Alright, I'll get to work on it immediately," I said.

That night I walked up Broadway in a whirlwind of excitement. The fall air was fresh, crisp, and at that moment I loved my life in New York. I was full of anticipation, was weightless, my head as big as a Macy's Thanksgiving Day Parade balloon. *I was going to write a screenplay with Jack Fresh!* Finally it was happening. Finally, I would be someone. Finally, my due was here for putting up with his harebrained wife. My God, maybe I could even marry Anderson Cooper. My mind went into overdrive. I walked and walked, had a smile on my face from ear to ear, smiled at everyone; every high class business person, every street person, and every drugged up dirty drunk. I loved everyone. New York was my town that night. At Columbus Circle I decided to take a longer route along Central Park West. I picked up leaves that fell from trees and twirled them in my hand and pulled them apart and threw them in the air like confetti and roared with joy. I didn't care who thought I was crazy because chances were everyone else I passed was as crazy as me. This was New frigging York! When I reached 110th Street and took a left toward my building, panic set in; *what will I write about? Where will it take place? What if I can't give him a decent thirty pages? What If I write something he doesn't like, what did I get myself into? This was the real deal, the real thing, someone with great show biz connections, I will have to blow his socks off, push the envelope. Failure is NOT an option.* With one block to go, my feet picked up until I was gleefully running, and once home, I turned on my computer, worked until the sun rose, slept a few hours, went right back to work, took another quick nap, then worked into the night, and when done, I called my parents.

"Mom, I'm writing a screenplay with Jack!"

"You're kidding, that's wonderful!" my mom said. My dad got on the phone.

"Hey, that's great news. Do you have some kind of a contract?" he asked.

"Not yet," I said.

"Well, as long as you know what you're doing," my dad said.

"I know what I'm doing! Why did you say it like that, you treat me like I'm some kind of moron."

"I'm not saying that. You know him better than I do. I'll put your mother back on the phone," my father gave the phone to my mother.

"Leonardo, your father is being protective."

"There is nothing to be protective about. Jack and Mara are my friends," I said, but even I thought I sounded ridiculous.

Early evening I called Larry and Peter because I had not seen them in a while and wanted to check in. The last time I'd seen Larry he had lost weight. He said it was his new medications. "Plus I'm working out, and I'm feeling fabulous! We're on a going to bed early routine. We're getting old!" he'd joked. When I called them that night, Peter answered. He sounded distant, and somber. I asked him if he was okay and he told me he was exhausted. He reassured me they were doing well, and said they wanted to go dancing soon, but then he sighed deeply,

"Leonardo, you might as well know the truth. We're backing off from the bar and the other stuff, if you know what I mean. It was getting out of hand. Every time we were around Mara and Jack it turned into something that we didn't necessarily want it to be. The fact is Larry has to take care of himself," he said.

"I agree, and think that's great news. Good for you guys!"

I asked him about Charlie. He said Charlie was doing well. He had a new gig at a restaurant near his apartment and he was playing at a hotel uptown, and was happy. "I want to call him. But I feel funny," I said. Peter then explained that he thought Charlie needed a break from anything to do with Mara and Jack. "You might be a reminder. Don't take it personally. He likes you. But he and Jack are very old friends. I bet Charlie is thinking that any association with you at this point would mean drama and Charlie hates drama. He's a very sensitive guy. This entire Mara thing is unbearable for all of us," he said. We promised each other to talk soon. I was happy for them, and I hoped their decision would transform their lives.

Back at my computer I worked more, rewrote, focused, read pages outloud to the roaches that pranced across my feet. The first thirty pages would be perfect. I was determined to have Jack Fresh read the start of my screenplay and completely stun him. I was a star in the making.

Scene Twenty-Two –
Barry Manilow – *I Made It Through The Rain*

"Wow Leonardo, I am blown away," Jack said, my pages in his hands. I was loading up a tray with drinks for a table and almost spilled them.

"Really? You mean it? Are you sure? Come on?" my hands were wobbly, and the pinkish cosmopolitans on my tray were waving over.

"I said I liked it. What more do you want me to say," he sounded angry. I froze. *I tried to control myself, don't mess this up with your doubts, be professional, be confident, be sure of yourself, be like him, stop being so neurotic!*

"Well, that's great. Glad you like it," I tried to sound blasé, measuring my voice from that moment on; eliminating any tone of self-doubt. Jack told me to deliver the drinks and sit with him at a table after. *Here I am world, I have arrived! I was going to discuss my screenplay with an actor who was in the movies!*

"It's fantastic, *I wanted* to read more," Jack said. He pushed his long skinny fingers through his blonde tuft of hair. He had an intense look on his face.

"So this is something you would like to work on with me?"

"Definitely," he said.

"When do we start?" I coughed, clearing my throat, holding down my jumping leg.

"Tomorrow night. We'll have dinner and get right to it. I've been thinking a lot about it, and I have some ideas."

Rico glanced over at us. The resentment on his face grew so much that night, I was positive he was going to buy a chainsaw, a massive one, like the ones only found in Texas and big enough to cut down Red Woods, and then slowly, jubilantly dismember me finger by finger, toe by toe, joint by joint, limb by limb, the second he had a chance. When Jack was finished speaking to me, he stood. "I have to get going. See you tomorrow night. Great, great work." Meanwhile, my head was spinning with images of an Oscar and a Golden Globe and universal love and approval. I went into the bathroom and jumped up and down! Yes! I did it! I did it! I composed myself and went back to work. The rest of the night Rico was nasty to me; I wasn't working quick enough, I wasn't talking to the customers enough, I didn't smile enough, the list of how bad a waiter I was went on and on all night. It was easy to ignore him because I was writing my Oscar acceptance speech in my mind.

At the end of the night, I rolled up the gritty rug and started to mop the wide wooden floor panels. Rico sat at the bar doing a line of coke, drinking a beer. He had Elvis Costello on the stereo, something sad, and that meant a conversation about Julia. They both loved E. C. I was preparing for the long string of questions: What is Julia up to? How is she? Did she say I did a good job directing the reading? I don't understand why she doesn't like me. What did I do wrong? Do I have a chance? Who's the guy she's dating?

When I was done mopping the floor, I sat next to him and drank my beer.

"What were you and Jack talking about?"

"Not much, just talking."

"Want to go to the diner after we close up…look Leonardo, sorry I was being an asshole to you tonight. I'm just not feeling so great these days."

"Sure. Why not. No worries."

"So Jack liked what you wrote?"

"He told you about it?" I asked.

"Yup. That's great, Leonardo. Congratulations," he sounded about as sincere as the eight pebbles in his throat that he was trying to swallow. The questions about Julia commenced as expected. I sung a string of yups and nopes, and later in the diner while we ate our eggs, bacon, and pancakes, the same questions were met with the same yups and nopes. He then went on about his concern over his drug use in which I became annoyed and silent. It was a waste of time to give advice because he wouldn't listen. A long night was ensured, so I ordered a blueberry muffin and more bacon to keep me company and happy.

The next night at Jack's place, we ordered Thai food, and Mara couldn't have been nicer to me. She was actually thrilled about the screenplay. She even washed her hair before I came over.

"I'm proud of you, darling, I read what you wrote, bravo, really, Jack is so excited." She fixed me a plate of spicy, crispy duck, and a pile of rice. Annie sat next to me and was trying to show me how to use chop sticks, which was useless because they prevented me from shoveling food in my mouth at the accelerated rate I normally enjoyed. Cosmo was on Jack's lap, and he fed him some warm cereal. I reached my hand over to him and his small, plump hand gripped my pinkie finger. "Who's a good boy!' I said, and Cosmo giggled, warm cereal drooled out of his tiny mouth.

"Annie, after dinner, you must go straight away to bed. Leonardo and Jack have work to do. I'm working in the bar tonight. You must be a good little girl, make mother proud."

"But I want to play checkers with Leonardo," she moaned.

"Annie, you have school tomorrow, darling," she ran her hands lovingly through Annie's hair and kissed her face. "Another time, I promise, love."

"Okay, Mommy."

"I'll read you a story before bed." All was calm and pleasant, it was a 1950's family TV show right before my eyes. As promised, Mara read a story to Annie. Soon the kids were sleeping. Mara kissed Jack and I goodbye. "Work hard, darlings. I love you both so very much. Cheers," she left for the bar. I was amazed. My mind filled with quite a bit of "maybes". Maybe Mara was having a bad three years and now it was over. Maybe she saw the error of her ways, and had finally changed; turned over a new leaf. Maybe she was actually practicing Buddhism instead of proclaiming she was a Buddhist to help absolve herself of her wretched behavior. Maybe Larry and Peter had spoken to her. Maybe Mara laced my crispy duck with LSD and I was hallucinating. Whatever it was, that night it was clear, Mara's support with our screenplay was perfect and good.

Jack and I worked madly on the story outline. We wrote on small index cards, wrote out character descriptions, we drank beer and talked the story out. We took our main character on a wild journey. I had never seen Jack the way I saw him that night. He had come alive, talked with passion, acted out scenes, we argued about plot points, dialogue, complimented each other on our storyline and character development. He chuckled at jokes I put in the screenplay, thought of actors we might approach. He was like me in the fact that he yearned to live in the world of make-believe, a place that was safe and under our control. Sure he wasn't the best writer, and he needed ideas planted in his head to work from, and at times he had a hard time coming up with certain plot points, but when prompted, he was good. I was certain our screenplay was going to be outstanding. At the end of the night, Jack and I compiled our notes, and the next day I was to write scenes that we had discussed. I was to bring them to him the next night, and we were going to read them out loud to each other. At the end of the night, Jack handed me a hundred dollar bill. I was hesitant to take it, but I did.

I took the train home with the same feeling of bliss I had since I began working on the screenplay. Finally, my dreams were coming true. I no longer disliked Mara, no longer thought Jack was a weak imbecile. Rather, they were both the kindest, most giving, loving people I had ever known in my entire life. I rated them right up there with my parents. I started to think that Mara was only strict with Annie because she loved her. Besides who the hell was I to judge? So what if she called Annie an idiot. Mara had changed. Maybe all that Annie had endured would make her strong. I convinced myself I'd been overly dramatic and ungrateful.

The next night we met in the basement. He had his brandy, and I had my beer. He loved the new scenes, all except for one. He thought it wasn't dramatic enough. I made notes over the three pages of the scene, and told myself to make that scene the best scene ever written in motion picture history. We talked more about the story, drank, and joked, playfully insulted each other. We talked about our childhoods, our show business dreams, we concluded we had similar backgrounds and family dynamics. I had found a good friend, a brother in creativity. We talked about writing future screenplays together, how we could be a writing team and the more we talked, the more my creative juices flowed with ease. There was something outstandingly pleasing seeing Jack laugh and smile. Since I had known him, he was usually morose and passive, going through the motions of life, not caring if he went left or right, up or down. It seemed that he only wanted to be pulled along the daily routine of life and to get it over with as promptly as possible, numbing his waking hours with drink and drugs. The creative Jack contradicted all that.

Those first few weeks of working with Jack I had an urge to talk to him about his drug use and to mention that Larry and Peter had stopped using. I didn't dare though and concluded that maybe Peter and Larry wanted it kept private. Not confronting Jack, I made up my mind it was none of my business.

"Leonardo, you're a fantastic writer. Amazing," Jack said to me one night after he read a scene that was giving us trouble.

"Thanks."

"I have a great feeling about this, I really do."

"Me too, Jack, it's weird, this story is pouring out of me," I said.

For many weeks this was exactly how our collaboration unfolded; we'd meet almost every night except when Jack had an acting job, or when I wasn't working in the bar. I continued to babysit. Annie started calling me Uncle Leonardo which was extraordinarily pleasing to me. Things were going my way.

I received adulations from some of Jack's famous actor friends, too. They would drop in and have a drink and chat with Jack. He would introduce me as Leonardo, an "amazing writer." He introduced me to Candy Olsen. She had violet eyes and resembled Elizabeth Taylor. She was an Indie film star and was breaking into mainstream films. I shook her hand, "Leonardo is an incredible writer." Jack said. Candy smiled at me and said, in her famous childlike voice, "Then lets count on working together one day." My face heated up, not quite sure how to react to such a compliment and statement from an actress I greatly admired.

In a few months we had a good solid draft and I made the cover page for the script, the name of the screenplay was, *Frank*

Stein, by Jack Fresh and Leonardo Banani. The screenplay was an eerie film about a fanatical Doctor, named Frank Stein, who was deeply in love with his wife, Elsa. One day, Elsa is run down by a taxi. She becomes brain dead and paralyzed. Her body is a mangled mess. In the hospital where Doctor Stein practices medicine, he removes body parts from dead people and uses them to rebuild his wife in hopes of bringing her back to life. When he succeeds and she does come back to life, she starts randomly killing people. Doctor Stein is the only one who knows Elsa is committing the murders and eventually Doctor Stein is faced with the fact that he has to kill the woman he loves in order to stop her from killing people.

When I saw the title page come out of the printer, all I saw were Golden Globes and Oscars, and shaking hands with Meryl Streep who was asking me to write a part for her. When I brought the 120 page printed out screenplay to Jack, he looked over my shoulder, got a pencil, brought it to the title page, and crossed out our names. Then he wrote my name first, and his second.

"This is the first thing that has to be changed. Your name comes first, your idea, you wrote the first thirty pages."

"That's okay," I said.

"No. End of discussion." We read the screenplay out loud while the kids slept. Mara lay on the sofa. She was quiet. When we were done, she sat up.

"It's brill!"

"Thanks, Mara."

"But some of it is infantile. You need to change certain scenes. Like, when the Doctor says I love you to his wife," she said. Jack and I shrugged.

"Well, we have to do more drafts," I said.

"Yeah, of course," Jack said.

"I'm going to Boston to be with my family for Christmas. I think we should let this rest for a bit, and then get back to it in January," I said. Jack agreed, and the following day I left for Boston.

I was the hero in my family. My parents were excited about the screenplay; they told friends and family members, and I walked around town like I was Shakespeare. My sister Emily remained skeptical, always overprotective of me, she didn't show any excitement either way. She told me many times over Christmas week I was a great writer on my own with or without Jack Fresh.

After the New Year, we got back to work. We shortened scenes, added characters, took characters out, added scenes, and read it out load countless times. Finally, Beth, Jack's manager, read it. "It's like a work of literature," she said. I was never so happy in my entire life, in fact, if I were any happier champagne would have spurted out of my ears.

Then one rainy day in March, when we were close to another draft, I went to Jack's house to talk about what actors we wanted to star in our film. When I arrived, Jack was putting on his coat getting ready to leave, "Sorry, man, can't work today, I have an audition for that TV show I've been talking about. It's a good part, it's for some cable network. Let's work tomorrow." And he was gone.

Scene Twenty-Three – Fergie ft. Ludacris – *Glamorous*

Jack started filming his new TV series, *Love Me Do* that spring. It was a comedy and after the initial viewing by the critics, the buzz was that Jack was excellent and the show was going to be compared to a modern day, *Honeymooners*, but with an eerie twist. Jack's performance was highly praised. They said his comic timing, talent, and TV presence was similar to Art Carney. We were all thrilled for him.

Love Me Do, premiered at a movie theater in Times Square before it hit the TV waves. Everyone was invited to go; Rico, Larry, Peter, Frankie, Olena and Jack's parents. I was asked to babysit Cosmo and Annie. I was a little miffed that I was left out, but was told they needed me, "Who else can we trust, darling?" Mara had said, and Jack piped in, "You're like family, who cares about some silly premiere." My hurt feelings quickly vanished. After all, I was like family to a famous person, wasn't that enough?

A few weeks later, the show premiered on the cable network, and it was an instant success, a TV phenomenon. Within months, everyone in America tuned-in every Monday night to *Love me Do*. America was hooked. My parents told everyone they knew, including the bank tellers, and cashiers at the *Stop & Shop*, that I was friends with Jack Fresh. Inside a year, Jack Fresh was a household name. The show became critically acclaimed and it was held in as high esteem as some TV classics like, *I Love*

Cora, and *The Mary Tyler Moore* show. Although a comedy, it had a dark twisted side like no other show. Filmed in an artistic way; shaking camera, no laugh track, intense close ups, a multitude of A list actors doing cameos, and very hip music. It was breaking all kinds of viewing records. It was a must watch show, an artistic accomplishment and some said it was changing the way people watched and made TV shows. I saw bits of it, but I never watched a full episode because I couldn't afford cable.

After the show's premiere, Jack wanted to talk to me about our screenplay and Mara suggested we take a long walk by the river. "My two little darlings, my creative geniuses, go take a walk. I'll stay with the children." Mara was in one of her loving moods. I was a little guarded, but perhaps the cocaine she snorted prior to sending us out was extra pure. Jack and I took a walk up by the river. We took side streets and he wore a hat because fans had started to approach him and he said it was a bit overwhelming. We each held a beer in a brown bag from the bodega. The Hudson River was in front of us along with a view of New Jersey in the far off distance. Jack spoke of a verbal contractual agreement with me in regard to our screenplay. Every writing profit would be split fifty/fifty. I agreed.

"I want to expand a little too, I'm locked into this show, but I don't want to be trapped and I'm feeling trapped," he said.

"I understand," I said, wishing to one day be in such a trap.

"Now that my show is taking off it's the perfect chance for major studios to see what I can do."

"That's interesting," I said.

"I want to start directing and producing."

"Maybe I can co-direct and produce with you."

"I'll need you for rewrites. Anyway, I have this production company I established for taxes because with this new TV series,

I'm getting screwed on my taxes. I didn't pay taxes on some of the jobs I had in the past. If I produce this film under my company's name, it would help Mara and I. We're in a financial bind. The more you make the more they take. I can option the screenplay from you for twenty thousand dollars. It's for tax purposes. In the end I'll make it up to you," he said. "You're giving me twenty thousand dollars?" I ask. "No it will say that on paper. It will all come out in the wash, I promise," he said. "Okay," I agreed. Smiling happily, feeling like I was helping him out, and that this act of kindness would make us better friends. After all, we were family.

Back at his house he pulled out a contract and I gladly signed it.

When Jack was done filming his TV show at the end of the summer, we made a list of potential actors we thought would be great in the film.

"We'll win awards for this screenplay. I don't have a doubt in my mind."

"Really?" my heart instantly metamorphosed into a butterfly.

"George Jenkins read it. He loved it. He'd like to play the doctor's assistant," he said. George Jenkins was one of the stars in Jack's TV show. "Really, are you kidding?"

"No. I was thinking about showing other people on the show, too. I also like the idea of Andre Brent for Doctor Stein. My agent knows his agent."

"I was thinking the same thing!" I said.

"We also have a lot of guest actors on the show. I have all their contact numbers. Kelly Green was in an episode. She'd be great as the sister. I can call her."

"Kelly Green! You worked with Kelly Green? You can call her?"

"Yeah, she was pretty fantastic," Jack smiled.

"Show anyone you want," I had no idea Jack worked with these actors on the TV series, he was so secretive about the show, and I didn't ask many questions.

Jack's life changed dramatically as his show grew in popularity. There were endless elaborate gifts sent to him and Mara. Mara remodeled the townhouse with high-end furniture, and better appliances. They bought designer clothes and dined at expensive restaurants. Meanwhile, I had enough money to pay my rent, but was always broke. The more money they made the less they gave me for working for them. Mara stated acting like it was a privilege working for her. She started saying things like, *if you can't do it right then maybe we should hire someone, you should consider yourself lucky to be working with Jack*, and when she corrected me for forgetting something or not doing it exactly to her specifications she'd start off with… *I thought I told you to do it this way, how many times do I have to repeat myself*….blah blah blah

Jack was making late night show appearances. It was remarkable to witness, and also weirdly surreal and frightening, but it creepily drew me in. I abandoned my own life because in comparison to Jack and Mara's it was boring. The highlight of my life was going dancing Sunday nights with Larry (when he was feeling well enough) and Peter, and on occasion getting lucky with a hot guy. I didn't start a new writing project. I stopped going to theater. I forgot who I was. All my energy and hope was with what I wrote with Jack. Besides that, I was an extension of Jack and Mara and I didn't mind. At least I didn't have to deal with myself because that was entirely too much work and I believed I wasn't worth the time and effort fixing.

At the end of the show's first season, Jack and I took a taxi to *Duncan's,* a gourmet shop in the East 60's, known for their exceptional cuts of aged prime beef, imported cheeses, homemade pátes and imported truffles. Jack was hankering for a good steak and wanted to get some fresh air. He forgot his hat and glasses. While we roamed the aisles of the store, people swarmed up to him. They asked for autographs and photos to which he kindly obliged. Jack didn't look pleased or irritated; he looked more scared then anything. "Jesus. This is so- so eerie. I don't know if I'll ever get used to it." People continued to approach him, telling him what his show meant to them, as well as their personal stories. Jack smiled and nodded. One lady started poking him on his shoulder, "Oh my god! It's you! It's you!" Jack shifted away from her poking finger, his face covered in an expression of sheer fright, he laughed tensely. Meanwhile the store manager enthusiastically called his wife. Jack and I did our best to ignore him as we looked into the glass case filled with thick cut steaks. People gathered, stood around us, and thrillingly bellowed, "That's Jack Fresh," and Jack moved close to me and muttered, "Let's get this over with. Order us three porterhouse steaks." I did, and the butcher got to work. The store manager started to pace in circles while he talked to his wife on his cell phone, "Yes, he's right in front of me. Yes, Jack Fresh! Hey, Jack, can you say hi to my wife, come on, say hi," he brought the phone to Jack's face, and Jack politely declined. "My wife is expecting me home, but thank you," Jack smiled graciously. At check out, the manager gave him the meat as a gift. The bill was $117 for three humongous steaks. Once in the taxi, safe from his fans, Jack snapped his knuckles and let out a sigh, "I'll never do that again. Holy shit." His face became the usual pasty white it did when he was unnerved. "If you ignore your fans, you take a chance on making them angry and then you don't know what they'll do. If you acknowledge them too much, they'll want to talk to you all day. I find it's best to say hello and move on with a smile. They don't care about me anyway, they care about my fame. I guess it makes them feel special. I imagine most of them want to run home and tell people they saw someone famous. I feel like a nobody and they treat me like a somebody," he said. We exited the taxi and were on 8th Avenue.

"They were treating you like an object, like you weren't human. How about that lady poking you like you were a wax figure. Like you weren't real. That was nuts! The others treated you like you were a god."

"What? You don't think I'm godly?" He looked at me and smiled cynically.

"You're a human being. You're not someone to be used and prodded at. That was crazy," I said.

"I hate it and at the same time I crave it. How could anyone not love people drooling all over them. It's not easy to deal with," he said.

"Those people were out of control. They all seemed so, so… so desperate. It was sad," I said.

"Life is sad," he said.

"No, life is fascinating! Human beings are such a mystery. We want things and when we get them we don't want them. It's messy business being human. I mean those people hardly knew you and I swear it was like they worshipped you. Like they were lost and using you to help build themselves up. To fulfill something inside of themselves that's lacking… I dunno, Maybe? What do you think?" I asked.

"I think you're right. I think people are inherently lonely and insecure. We're always looking for something to fulfill a void that lives inside of us whether it's sex, drugs, relationships, celebrities, fame whatever…the human race is fucked up. I agree with you. I'm fucked up. You're fucked up. Let's face it everything is fucked," he said.

"Well if you put all that way, I guess life is sad and fucked up," we laughed.

"Human beings are like leeches, vampires sucking the blood out of things in order to survive. Maybe to feel something…. Vampires. I like that," he sounded pleased with himself. Besides for our writing partnership, this was one of the rare times he opened up to me. A huge part of me wanted to express my concern for his and Mara's drug and drinking habits, but I felt it would be too much to take on. Plus my drinking was up for discussion too, who was I to question them?

We walked home in an uncomfortable silence and I had reminded him that Mara told us to pick up toothpaste. In front of a Bodega, Jack coughed nervously, "Would you mind going in? I'll wait out here. I can't go through that again. I don't have the strength to fight off more vampires," he chuckled. I nodded to him that I would. Both of us stood in front of the bodega's glass door, it was covered in a circus-like mirrored door, our reflections beaming back at us. He looked different, like he had morphed into something timid and weak, unrecognizable. He left my side and went to the curb and lit a cigarette, a cloud of smoke billowed over his bowed head while he clandestinely looked from right to left for any approaching fans. Opening the door to the store I stopped and took a second look at my reflection. My body and face distorted by the mirror and the busy avenue behind me; I was no longer that innocent boy from Boston. At that moment something came over me that I couldn't decipher, some kind a crude reality and confusion. Was it Shame? Was I as bad as those gloating fans? Who was I to criticize them? When I entered the store the lights were so harsh I couldn't help but squint.

The weeks that followed, the world was inundated with everything Jack Fresh; dolls, cookbooks and special appearances across the country. He looked exhausted and looked disdainful when pressures were put on him. When I spoke to him, I practically bowed in his presence. When giving an interview Jack was told by his team that the primary goal was to make himself lovable so people would watch his TV show and buy products associated with it. His face was plastered on giant billboards in Times Square, at subway stops, on the sides of buses, and on every major magazine cover. So, even if you didn't like Jack or his show, it didn't matter because everywhere you looked there was Jack's face. People were thinking and talking about him without much choice, and the more talk there was, the more love people had for him. He had reached the status of a mega star, and for as long as that status was maintained it was clear he could live a charmed life and have his ass kissed endlessly. Jack could do no wrong. If he did he would be exonerated because his show was worth millions and millions of dollars and not only for him, but for everyone associated with the show. He was protected like Fort Knox. Jack Fresh was an industry. His power unprecedented and my power gone; I was falling for it, too. I thought myself lucky and honored to be his friend.

Each day became even more peculiar than the last. I'd never witnessed such opulence; gifts, privilege, fame, and overt sucking up. It was like I was pushed flat against a wall while observing Jack's life unfold in front of me. My eyes wide, shifting left to right, I was dismayed to see how people behaved around him. They were worse than me, their voices soft, almost apologetic, obnoxiously agreeable, a part of me felt bad for Jack. The only person who was genuine with him was Mara and she was flat out berserk.

Bearing witness to the overt deceit and gross hypocrisy of the media was another tricky predicament for me. The public was being incredibly duped by a false image of Jack that was created by his PR team. Most everything said about Jack in articles or on TV was carefully contrived. When Jack was on a late night talk show my eyes nearly popped out of their sockets. I twisted my fingers in my ears to make sure I was correctly hearing the same person whose dirty underwear I threw in the wash daily. Was this the same person whose blood alcohol level was usually at 2.7 or if poked with an icepick white powder would pour out of his body as if he were 198 pound sack of cocaine He told the host that Mara was British, but the way he said, "British," one would think Mara was part of the royal family, "She's related to a Duke. She has an interesting and fascinating lineage. She's very proper. She likes her afternoon tea, and she's an incredible mother." The truth: Using the word mother and Mara in the same sentence should be against the law. And she was from Liverpool. Her lineage was from a family of poor coal miners and she despised tea. Jack added that Mara was an art scholar. The truth: She was not degreed. I learned years later that while a student at Pace, she was kicked out for making racist comments. Two years later, she was escorted out of Hunter College because during a Q&A with Elie Wiesel, she proclaimed the Holocaust never took place. She told Mr. Wiesel it was a ploy used by Jews to take over Palestine. Years later, she tried to teach at a University. She used Jack's fame to get an interview with a stage-struck human resource employee. She said she was degreed in in England, but was promptly found out. On that same late night talk show, Jack said he liked spending time with his family. The truth: He was never home. He made-up stories about playing hide & seek with Annie in Central Park. The truth. He was confusing himself with me. He mentioned that he loved family dinners, "My wife is a terrific cook!" The truth: If Mara was handed an egg she would probably sit on it and wait for it to hatch. He said he was anti-drug. "I was never much of a partier." I nearly fell off my chair and busted an artery. He proclaimed he and Mara were devout Buddhist. He gave to the needy. Only when cameras were on him. All of his interviews contained endless fabrications that would further sanctify him and deceptively mislead the public. After a while, I made a conscious choice to stop watching such interviews. In fact I gave up watching TV because it was clear to me that a large part of show business was about glamour, image and money and little to with artistry or respect for it. I wanted to be real, truthful, genuine and not the frigging phony I was. After all, I was free to leave. On the other hand I was being sucked into something that was overwhelmingly enticing because the truth was being seen with Jack made me feel like I was famous and worthy. The worst part of it all was that I felt superior to other people and at the same time I loathed myself for feeling that way. In my gut I knew it was wrong. The truth of my situation was no longer a soft whisper of warning, it had become a constant whacking with a baseball to my skull each morning I woke.

Jack and Mara received endless invitations to celebrity parties and all-expense paid trips from various companies in exchange for Jack's presence. They were jetting off at least once or twice monthly leaving Annie and Cosmo with Jack's mother or with Olena and me. We started doing round the clock eight hour babysitting shifts. Dina would do the early morning to afternoon, and I'd come in after and work until twelve and Olena would take the overnight shift. Things became problematic one Friday because Dina was caught in traffic on the GW bridge. Olena had to work an extra three hours and missed a class, and was furious. I was sound asleep and I had shut off the ringer on my phone. Jack and Mara were in Barbados for four days. Olena and Dina argued. Then they yelled at me and told me I should have turned the volume on my phone higher. I got mad at them, tempers flared, nasty comments were made, and we hung up on one another. Dina and I quickly apologized and laughed at the absurdity of it all. Olena wouldn't let it go, and in a fit of childish rage called Mara in Barbados and grouched about the situation. The gates of hell opened. When Mara got home she told the three of us to come to her house for a meeting to discuss childcare.

The three us stood in her bedroom lined up like soldiers about to be court-martialed. Mara eyed us with grave disappointment. We didn't dare move. She told us how we let her down as she wildly looked in her closet. Boxes were being opened and silky blouses were flying every which way,

"Good damn it! I can't find those damn shoes!" Dresses were being chucked, more shoe boxes were flung. In between the tossing, she stopped and glared at all three of us.

"Can't you three figure childcare out, really? You can't do this one simple thing for Jack and I? Must we spend the money on a nanny? Is that what you all want? Some stranger to watch the children you all say you love so much? Really? Must I do everything? Damn it!"

She started digging through her closet again,

"Everyone thinks it's all glamour and travel and parties, let me tell you it's bloody work being married to a celebrity. Work! It's demanding and quite awful! I expect my family and dear friend to be able to handle childcare!" She then let out a screech of joy. "Here they are! Brilliant!" She pulled out two shoe boxes and opened them, took out two sets of shoes.

"'Ok, darlings. I need help deciding. Which pair do I wear tonight with the Vera Wang? The Choo's or the Manolo's?" I pointed to the Choo's. Dina pointed to the Manalo's and Olena finger went back and forth, "Bloody hell!" Mara screamed. She kicked us out and I did all I could not to vomit on her living-room floor as I exited the townhouse.

Another weekend, Olena and I were helping Mara pack for a ski weekend in Utah. An all-expense paid trip from MTV. Mara spent the day buying winter clothes and Olena and I followed her around town carrying her bags and helping her pick out outfits. By mid-afternoon we returned home and learned that Jack's mother had called and spoken to Jack. He said his mother didn't want to babysit because she didn't approve of Mara going away again. This was the third long weekend in a row. "How dare she!" Mara screeched. Jack added that his mother said it was mostly because Cosmo had a horrible cold and she didn't feel wholly comfortable taking care of Cosmo with him being so sick.

"They will never see our children again! They don't understand that you need me by your side!" Mara barked. She then asked Olena and I to stay the full weekend and babysit Annie and Cosmo. We agreed. While Mara watched us pack her suitcase, she curled herself up on the bed and pulled the silky white sheets around her body.

"I am so exhausted. I don't want to take this trip." Jack was holding Cosmo whose whooping cough sounded worse. He was whimpering and lethargic and white as powder.

"You don't have to go. I only have to sign some autographs and then I'll come home."

Mara sat up, pushed the sheets off her body and pointed callously at Jack.

"You'd like that, wouldn't you? For me to stay home, so you can screw some dumb actor!" she yelled so loudly I thought the windows were going to shatter. Jack didn't react.

"Cosmo is really sick. Maybe my mother is right, it might be best if you stayed home."

"Why doesn't your mother mind her own bloody business?"

"No, I think it makes sense, Cosmo is sick," Jack said.

"Olena and Leonardo will be fine with him," Mara crossed her arms over her chest.

Jack left the room with Cosmo. Olena then started removing the insides of pens and putting pot inside the cavity of them. She then made a small funnel with paper and filled writing pens with cocaine. She put the drug filled pens in Mara's suitcase.

"You're the bees knees, really darling!" Mara said with a smile.

Olena and I planned a fun weekend; movies, games, cookie-making, and late night chats after the kids went to bed. The morning after they left, Cosmo was hacking. I held him and paced the apartment, he would cry and cough, his nose ran, and at different times he gasped to catch his breath. It scared me, and I became angry and panicky, "Should we take him to the hospital?" That Saturday, I sat in a crowded emergency room at Columbia Presbyterian Hospital with a hacking Cosmo in my arms. Olena stayed home with Annie. Dina and Eddie, of course, came to the hospital from Connecticut and waited with me. Dina sat with her arms crossed over her chest, worry on her face, tears welling in her eyes. When Eddie left us for coffee or a bag of chips, Dina said more than once to me, "What kind of mother leaves her child when he's sick?" I never answered, but kept my eyes on Dina while she shook her head in disgust. Cosmo's lungs were clear, he had a very bad cold and was given an antibiotic.

Two weeks later Jack was due to bring his father to a Lakers game in LA. Eddie told everyone who would listen that his famous son was taking him across the country to a game. It was charming to witness how completely ecstatic Eddie was about his first trip out west. All of us indulged him for the pure fun of it. He was like a little kid excited about a trip to Disneyland. They planned to leave on Tuesday, Eddie and Dina came into Manhattan at our insistence. Rico and I planned a little going away party for Eddie. We asked Larry and Peter to come; they stopped by and of course brought a bottle of expensive champagne as well as a Lakers shirt and hat. It was great to see them, although a little shocking to see that Larry had become incredibly thin. Frankie had a cake made into the shape of basketball, and wore purple pants, a gold shirt, black shoes and a white cap. Rico was actually tolerable that day and we had a lot of laughs tossing around the basketball we bought for Eddie. We all seemed newly energized. We closed the bar early and had a party, ordered pizzas and cracked open Italian beers. We played music, danced around, and played cards. Jack thought this was great. Eddie was glowing. It was going to be his first time in California, time with his son. Eddie was insisting they drive to the Hollywood sign and walk on the strip to see all the stars on the sidewalk. Dina was thrilled. She bought Eddie all new outfits, a new suitcase and camera. Mara was silent as she observed and drank Kir Royales. After everyone left that night, Rico and I stayed behind and cleaned up. In the kitchen Jack and Mara fought while they snorted, their voices carried out to us.

"This all feels wrong! I will not allow anyone to use us! You asked your father to go with you after they refused to babysit for us? Are you bloody daft? They bloody walked in here tonight like they're entitled to a trip. And they get a party? For what? Who throws us a party? Who gives to us? It's always take, take, take! And you didn't ask me if I approved or maybe even wanted to go, you assumed it was okay to ask that knob father of yours. Jack, are you a complete ninny? Are you? Your father and mother have to learn that they cannot treat us this way! You must call this trip off straight away! They must be punished not rewarded! Bloody hell!"

"It's too late, Mara."

"Bloody hell it is. Call them and tell them the trip is cancelled! Our love is sacred!" She started throwing dishes at Jack, breaking one after another. "You don't love me! You never did!" Smash, crash, boom. "Call him now! I insist! Call him now!" Mara shrieked. Rico and I faced each other, our eyes squinting in anguish, Rico whispered to me, "Jack is such a pussy sometimes." Our bodies stiff as corpses as we pressed our ears to the kitchen door. Jack called his father and spoke to him.

"Dad, listen, I've decided to cancel the trip. Why? Because Mara wants to go." There was a long silent pause. Rico looked at me, he started shaking his head in disgust. We continued to listen. "Look you and Mom take a lot from us. We ask you to babysit and you refuse us. It's not right. It hurts Mara. When she's hurt. I'm hurt." There was another long pause. "End of discussion, Dad. Another time," Jack said. Moments passed and Mara and Jack walked out of the kitchen arm in arm. "Next time they will think twice. You have to train people. They will learn their lesson, all they do is take, take, take," Mara said. She kissed Jack's hand and they both walked past us as if we didn't exist.

"Jack's ashamed of himself," Rico said.

"He should be," I said.

"Eddie won't handle this well," Rico took a shot of bourbon and whipped it against the wall and shattered so badly bits of glass flew our way. It was the first time since I worked at the bar that I didn't grab a dust pan and broom and clean Rico's smashing glass mess. Instead I grabbed my coat and left. I called

Dina immediately while walking north up 2nd Avenue. "Hello," I muttered. Dina's sobs came intermittently though the phone, at first she could hardly speak, but managed to say, "Why is she so mean to us? What did we ever do to deserve this in our lives. It's not about the trip. This was about Eddie and Jack spending real time together. I can't talk now, call me. I gotta be with Eddie, he's so upset," she hung up.

That weekend I reluctantly babysat. Dina called me very late that Sunday night. "Eddie's devastated. Right now he's sitting in his chair and hasn't moved all day. He's been drinking his 7&7's one after another, and my Eddie is not a drinker. It's like he can't move from that frigging chair. He's been watching Midnight Cowboy over and over. It's their favorite movie. Jack and Eddie used to watch it all the time. I could cry. Just cry for days. Can I ask you something?"

"Sure," I said.

"You love your parents, right, you always say you do."

"Yes. I love them very much."

"So tell me, could you do this type of thing to your father?" she asked. My throat went dry. The truth would make her feel worse.

"Go on Leonardo, tell me. I can take it. Tell me."

"No I never would. Never. I couldn't hurt my parents. Never," I said.

"Because you love them, right?"

"Yes," my voice scarcely audible.

"She's a bastard and my son is no better! I've been saving for a new washer, but to hell with it. I'll do my laundry at my mother's house. I'm thinking about buying tickets and taking Eddie to California."

"You should, Dina," my voice soft, hers cracking with grief.

"I never dreamed this is the kind of person my son would marry. I feel cursed. Terribly cursed," she then started to sob. "I say it all the time, and I'll say it again, I lost my son to the devil and to the world." She took long pauses, talked through tears and frustration. "I come from a humble background. This stuff is over the top for me. I want my boy back. Fame is for the god damn birds!" She told me how she grew up with seven brothers in Providence. How she longed for another woman in their small family, and that she'd always dreamed she would have a daughter in-law to shop with, and to get their fingernails done together. "I tell you, we've been cursed. Mara has ruined my family." She ended the conversation asking me to pardon her because she was going through menopause. I told her she was speaking the truth, and that menopause couldn't be blamed.

Scene Twenty-Four –
Bob Dylan – *Knockin' on Heaven's Door*

Months passed. Wounds were healed. I was sitting with Mara when we got the phone call from Peter. I heard his voice come from Mara's phone as she held it to her ear. "Larry died," he said. Mara let out a horrible screech that hit my gut like a solid punch. The phone slid from her hand to the floor. I picked it up and asked Peter to repeat what he'd said. My mind slowed as I struggled to comprehended his words; *Larry died this morning*. Everything shut off inside of me as if a black curtain had been dropped over my body; there was absolute darkness and nothing to anchor me.

"Hello. Leonardo, are you there? I'll talk to you guys later. I have a bunch of phone calls to make. It will be okay, pal. It's okay." Peter's voice a mere sigh.

"Okay." I said, not being able to say more.

My world changed in mere seconds; darkness encompassed me as if I were going to drop to the ground, but a jolting fear came and I quickly found my grounding. I started to perspire. My mind raced. AIDS was no longer just a worry that lived in my mind, it was now a brutal reality that came into my world like predator in an action film kicking down doors and unmercifully shooting fire daggers and speeding bullets. Here it was, front and center, AIDS; that insidious monster who had now killed my friend. Who would be next? Peter? Frankie? Me?

The entire gay population? And would the world care? Instantaneously I hated being gay. I wanted to run and escape. Why couldn't I be straight? Why couldn't I be living in the suburbs with a wife and kids. Why was I created gay? This is not what I wanted for my life; to have the constant feeling people would reject me once they found out who I was? Knowing that they feared to touch me; use the same drinking glass as me, share the same eating utensils, eat the food I prepared and kiss me because I was gay; a potential carrier of a deadly disease. To feel every second of my life that this deadly monster was lurking around corners waiting to snatch me and unmercifully kill me in the most brutal way. To have the majority of the world watch such death and probably be delighted there was once less queer in the world. Gay pride? Nonsense! This was absolute misery, mostly caused by the world's lack of acceptance; the abuse and bullying; always something to remind us that being gay meant being treated less than human. How could anyone not psychologically suffer from the ugly consequences of such hatred and rejection by a society? How could anyone escape the self-loathing, the alcoholism, drug addition, sex addiction, narcissism, and maybe even the wish to be dead.

My breathing labored, I couldn't say a word. My attention was on Mara as she tenderly, staggeringly made her way along the perimeters of the living room, her hands covering her mouth, her eyes contemplatively shifting. I stood very still, tears fell uncontrollably. My heart raced, Larry's face was before me; there was his smile, his kind words.

Mara turned toward me, and gently said as if trying to convince herself that the news she heard moments prior was indeed real. "Larry gone? Dead? I can't believe it. This is so unfair. So wrong." She sat on the sofa and started to weep between long and strenuous respirations.

"Mara, I'm so sorry." I sat next to her, desperately wanting to make her feel better. After all, wasn't I responsible for all the agony in the world? Wasn't it my job on this earth to make people happy? To please. Weren't the ills of the world my fault? It all belonged to me because I was gay, and fundamentally a bad person.

"Larry, was the most decent person I knew. He was pure," she said, her head bowed.

"I know," I said.

"I need to be alone, Leonardo, I'm sorry. I need to rest. I can't talk about this now."

She kindly, lightly hugged me and held on to me for a moment. She emanated warmth and tenderness as if all the bitterness and acid that lived inside of her had dissipated and profound love and sadness had taken over her being. Yet my guard was up. She walked to her bedroom, and stopped when she heard my voice,

"Mara, what are you going to do in your bedroom? You're not going to lock yourself in there all day, are you? Maybe you shouldn't." I said.

I was surprised those words came out of my mouth, but they did and freely. She stopped walking and faced me. Fearful for a beratement, I felt myself step back. Her right hand inside her left, she twirled them slowly together. She appeared childlike, scared, her shoulders inward, her expression vacant and lost.

"Leonardo, I know you care, but save your voice. Save your time. I'm aware of my drug habit and my inability to stop. You're a good friend. Thank you, darling, truly." Her voice so soft I could hardly hear her. Tears crawled down her face, she wiped her nose with her hand and sniffled.

"I always be here for you." I said. She nodded, and continued to her bedroom, and quietly shut the door. I stood outside her bedroom. My voice stuttered when I spoke to the closed door, sadly assuming she was going to knock herself out with booze or drugs or both.

"I'm going to stay here. I love you, Mara. So did Larry. I'll be right here if you need anything. I'm not leaving." I said.

The sound of her weeping so deep and sorrowful it sounded like she was crying for all the other tragic things in her life; the other people who had abandoned her; her mother, her father, her past lovers and Jack who was now lost to his fame. It wasn't just about Larry dying, it was about *him* leaving her, as if he'd had a choice, as if he did it to hurt her.

I sat motionless on the sofa unable to move; my hands folded on my lap. I remained there for the better part of the afternoon not knowing quite what to do. I would never see Larry again. Never again witness his glowing smile, listen to his cutting wit, his offers of advice, and his gentle wisdom. Witness one of his practical jokes. Gone was the security I had in my mind that if I had needed anything I knew Larry would always come to the rescue. Gone was his overt kindness. Gone was the hope that I would grow to know him better, that we would become even better friends and that I would have him in my life forever.

When late afternoon arrived and lights illuminated the city, I called my parents; both were on the phone extension. I never told them of Larry's death. I didn't want to worry them. Instead, I told them I was thinking of them and every other mundane thing that came to mind. My voice forcibly cheery, I held back grief and my longing to be home with them. I spoke of a new restaurant I liked, an idea for a play, a movie I had seen, a book I read. Their voice calm and casual, happy to hear from me. I wanted to tell them I didn't want to grow up and be part of the unfair, ugly world. I wanted to be safe in their home; a child forever under their protective wing. At the end of the conversation they said the words I needed to hear and the sole reason I had called them in the first place, *We love you.*

The next day I woke early and went to a clinic in the West Village and had my third HIV test. I was convinced I had contracted it and that I would soon be gone from the world. I got tested for my parents. Safe sex was priority for me. But how safe was safe? There was always a chance of getting HIV. How much did those researchers and scientists really know? For weeks after Larry's death the very notion of sex numbed me from the waist down. I vowed never to have sex again, a vow, knowingly, I would ultimately break and then after submerge myself in the pool of internal shame for daring to put myself in jeopardy and for choosing to potentially cause pain for those who loved me. Human contact? Affection? Love? Sex? Was it worth the horrible death that most of the world had no pity for?

We learned of the troubles Larry had the last months of his life with the new medications. They did not work for him. His disease had advanced. He had developed full blown AIDS. We'd all believed his excuses, that he was busy with work as the reason for his absence from our lives. We never asked him about his health because before we ever could, Larry brought the subject up first, "I'm doing really well, the new medications are working fabulously," he would say reassuringly. I suppose it was his way of maintaining control, and avoiding our questions and in-depth conversations.

Larry and Peter met twenty years prior on Rehoboth Beach and it was Larry's wish to have his ashes spread at the spot on the beach where they'd met. Jack rented a luxury van, and Mara, Frankie, Rico, Peter, Olena, and Jack's parents, who followed us in their own car, drove to Delaware. It was a wet Sunday afternoon. I drove. At first Mara refused to allow Charlie to come, but in the end she agreed and there we all were.

The sky was gray, and snowflakes and spurts of icy rain stuck to the windshield. The ride was long and sorrowful, each of us lost in our grief trying to comprehend the enormity of Larry's passing. He was forty-five, young and vibrant, had fought the disease for almost ten years. When we finally spoke of our individual memories of him, we wept. No matter how much we loved him, and thought of the good times, the unfairness of his death played havoc in our minds.

We made our way to the spot on the beach where Peter wanted to scatter Larry's ashes. It was unbearably cold, our hands icy, our eyes full of tears both from the wind and our pain. The tide was high, the ocean was a piercing navy blue, it roared and hissed as is flowed and crashed to shore. Charlie's arms securely around Peter's back, they walked ahead of us. Charlie's words of hope to Peter, barely audible; sounded priestly; *you were both blessed, you will get through this, you were lucky, he loved you, I am here for you.* Each word that came my way jabbed me deeply. I wondered if my tears would ever stop; would the hollow numb feeling inside of me ever go away, would this sorrow cease? Mara and Jack held hands and walked yards behind them. Jack's face didn't show much, just a distant perplexed stare; he seemed lost in his thought. His skin color a sickly white. He seemed to be struggling to feel something and didn't say a word the entire ride to Delaware. He only managed little nervous coughs. His arm around Mara's shoulders, she was quiet and couldn't speak, and it was if Jack was holding her up. She had drunk almost half a bottle of brandy in the van. I was still worried about her; since the news of Larry's death she was on an alcohol and cocaine bender and had spent hours in bed. While on the beach she held a Kleenex to her nose and sniffled into it, her cries becoming louder with each step she took. Her eyes fixed on the shimmering distance,

I figured she was trying to comprehend Larry's death and the unfairness of it.

I lagged behind everyone, lost in my own world. For mere seconds my mind shifted. My imagination took over. It was another day, a dream, some hope. There was Larry, he was running toward us, waving, telling us to stop and to wait for him. He went to Mara and poked her shoulder and kissed the side of her face. He playfully tugged on Jack's hair. He pulled on my sleeve, "Joke's on you, kid!" he said. He told me he was not dead, but very much alive, his death was all a big prank and he boisterously laughed. I told Larry that I knew he was not dead because good and kind people don't die in such a horrible way. I told him I was glad he was alive, that he made me feel safe and that he gave me a sense of importance. He pulled me away from the others, we ran along the beach, chased seagulls and threw rocks into the ocean. I told him he was like my gay older brother. I looked up to him and loved him. He rubbed my head and told me I was dramatic, naïve and sweet and that I was special and unique to the world. He told me my life awaited me, he would protect me, he was on my side, all was good, happiness would prevail. There was no more sadness, no AIDS, life was fair and full of light. A new and good day for gay people would soon be here. Then as quickly as Larry appeared in my mind, reality came marching in. Larry was gone and there we were, preparing to say goodbye and to scatter his remains. I caught up with the others and we walked toward Peter, Charlie, Jack and Mara who were at the spot on the beach where Peter had chosen to release Larry's ashes.

Olena was silent and tearless as she pulled on her red hair and twisted strands of it around her finger. She was sad, I surmised she was unable to fully process Larry's death. Beside her was Frankie, who in honor of Larry, wore his big furry, red full length coat that Larry had begged Frankie to buy years ago when they were shopping,

"It was the funniest coat I had ever seen. Frankie had to have it!" Larry had told me.

Next to Frankie were Eddie and Dina, who held hands, their eyes reddened, Dina's words muffled through the gusts of cold wind.

"Poor boy, what a shame. He sent me birthday cards and Christmas cards. He was always so thoughtful. He said I was the mother he always wanted. It meant so much to me. He gave me chocolates for Valentine's day, can you imagine?"

"He called to remind me to buy you chocolates. He saved my butt last year. If it weren't for him, you would not have gotten a Valentine's day gift," Eddie said.

"You're not kidding," Dina said. We all laughed. Eddie coughed deeply.

"You know what it was about Larry that made him so wonderful? He made you feel like you were special, no matter who you were, he made you feel like you were important and he looked you right in the eyes when he talked to you. That's a sign of a very sincere person," Dina said.

Eddie blew his nose with his hanky, tried his hardest to contain himself; his eyes blinked quickly. He kept blowing air out of his mouth as he struggled to fight the emotion that built inside of him.

"I'm going to miss that guy," Eddie said.

"So where are his parents? I don't understand how a parent doesn't care their child has died. What kind of people do such things?" Dina said.

"Evil ones," Frankie said.

"What's wrong with this world? I don't understand people. You have a child and you love them no matter what. Gay, straight or frigging purple, you love them. You love your kids." Dina shook her head bewildered."

"Yes, but Larry didn't need his parents. He loved his life in New York. His dreams all came true. Peter was the love of his life. When he was young and when I first met him, he was practically iconic inside the gay population. He was all heart," Frankie said.

Frankie then looked over at me. I was still quietly sobbing, unable to speak.

"I know this is hard for you. It's good you're crying. It's when you stop crying you should worry. I've been burying friends for the last ten years. I don't know if there are any more tears inside of me to shed," he handed me a Kleenex.

"Leonardo, he thought you were quite special," Dina said.

"Look, kid, I haven't been very nice to you. And I'm sorry. When you lose as many friends as I have…you… you.. -I don't know, become a bitter old queen, I guess," Frankie said.

He put his arm around me. The fur of his coat tickled my nose and I couldn't help but silently laugh at the idea of Larry making Frankie buy that ridiculous red coat.

"Goddamn him for dying. I hate this day," Frankie said.

Rico wanted to be alone in the van for a bit, but had jogged to our side; his face forlorn, his jaw taunt. I knew he was repressing his grief. For all the resentment Rico and I had toward each other, I truly cared for him. I knew he was hurting, knew all his personal losses were plaguing him. While he walked by my side, we both fell behind everyone.

"You okay?" I asked.

"I'm okay. You okay?" Rico said.

"I can't stop thinking about him. I can see him right in front of me. I feel him here right now. It's like I want to reach out and grab him and tell him not to leave because he belongs with all of us," I said.

"I hear you, man. I want this to be over. It just sucks," Rico said. He took deep breaths, cleared his throat. He rammed his hands in his front pockets of his jeans, his teeth started to chatter, his stare distant and gray. One lone seagull glided over us, its squawking settled heavy on my ears, our feet crunching on the frozen sand,

"You wanna play pool this week at that place on 4th Avenue?" I asked.

"Sure, why the fuck not?" he said. I pushed my entire body into Rico and he pushed his body into me and we walked in silence to join the others.

Peter held onto the urn, his hands red from the cold, his eyes full. He pointed to a boarded up seasonal concession several yards away,

"That's where we first met. It was the summer of 1975. I knew I was gay, but I was scared. I came to this beach that day to be alone, to think, to figure stuff out. I was standing by that hut waiting to buy an ice cream cone and this tall gangly, handsome guy who had these amazing big green eyes says hello to me. I knew he was gay and I was petrified because it was the first time I'd ever spoken to a gay man. He buys me a pistachio ice cream and we walked along the beach. He started telling me that everything will get better. I didn't know what he was talking about and I didn't ask him. After a while, we went our sperate ways, but decided to meet that night on the beach. The minute I saw him again, I asked him what he meant by telling me things would get better? He smirked, that all knowing smirk of his, and he said that he knew what I was going through and no matter who tells me differently, being gay is a gift, it's beautiful. He held me by my shoulders and he kissed me. At that moment, I knew I loved him, and I always would. Larry was my everything. He made me feel like I was the center of his world. He gave my life purpose when I felt purposeless. He always made me laugh when I wanted to cry. A week before he died, he woke me up very early just as the sun started to come through the window blinds. He looked right into my eyes and he told me that wherever he was going, he was going to miss me. He wanted me to promise to keep him alive in my mind because that way he wouldn't be entirely dead. He said he wanted me and his friends to be brave when he died. He told me he wanted to be remembered as a kind person because he had encountered so much cruelty in his young life because he was gay. He insisted those people made him better, made his love stronger, so he loved them for it. He loved me. He loved all of you. He loved people. He loved being gay. He loved New York. He loved French toast. He loved big sweaters. He loved Jane Fonda. He loved to dance. He loved to play Frisbee in Central Park. He loved Provincetown. He loved pizza. He loved his life. Dear sweet Larry, you'll be in our minds forever. We love you."

Peter then uncovered the urn, turned toward the surf, and released the ashes. A puff of black and gray floated in the air until it dissipated. Our eyes steady on the sky. Tiny glimmers of sun peaked through the clouds casting shadows that briskly moved across the beach giving the impression we were being chased by them. The world abruptly looked different and I guess it was because Larry was no longer in it.

We said our goodbyes to Dina and Eddie who were heading back to Connecticut in their car. In the van back to New York, Rico sat in front with me, and Frankie and Jack in the middle seat, Peter sat next to them. Mara was at the other window. Charlie sat in the back seat with Olena. Mara lit a joint. Everyone refused when she passed it.

"I wish we had known. Only to say a proper goodbye. It would have been the decent thing to do," she said. The tone of her voice worried me; it was sharp and cutting.

"He didn't want to tell anyone, Mara. I'm sorry, his wish was for you to remember him healthy," Peter said. He looked out the van's window.

"It's deeply disturbing, darling, at least a visit, a farewell, we were his friends," she said. "Then all the more you should understand," Peter said.

"Thirty six friends. Dead. It never ends," Frankie said as if speaking to himself.

"Must be at least forty two for me," Charlie said.

"You lost all those friends to AIDS? My God," Olena said.

"There's a war out there against gays, little girl, this is all the government's fault, they want us all dead, don't you know?" Frankie said.

"Larry's case was unusual, the new meds are really good now. There will be a cure one day. I just know it. People are living. There's hope," Peter said.

"And unity. When AIDS first hit the gay population it was awful. Everyone was scared. People abandoned friends and lovers. People didn't know what the hell to do. We've come a long way thanks to many gay men and women who fought for our rights," Charlie said.

"Shit Jack, do you remember Domani? That was at the very start of all this AIDS stuff. That guy was built like a brick shit-house. Christ, that was a long time ago. I haven't thought of him in years-" Rico said.

"Rico, why bring that up now?" Jack said.

"Sorry, man, I was just, you know, thinking," Rico said.

"Who is Domani? You never mentioned a Domani? Another man from your past?" Mara said.

"I don't want to talk about it," Jack said.

"How much cock have you sucked anyway?" Mara said.

"Mara stop this, now! The past, is the past," Jack yelled.

"Every day I turn around there is someone from your past lurking in our life."

"Just shut up, for once in your life shut up." Jack said. His voice calm.

"Who the hell is Domani?" she screamed.

"A friend okay, a friend who died. I don't want to talk about it!" Jack said.

"You're a coward. You always will be," Mara said. Her voice sardonic and mocking.

"Just shut up!" Jack said.

"Fucking coward! Cock sucker!" Mara screeched. All went silent.

"Damn Regan. If that asshole took the proper action this wouldn't have become the epidemic it is, " Frankie said.

"It's been a hard day. We're all upset. Maybe we shouldn't talk about anything right now." Charlie said.

"Charlie don't be controlling. I'll speak if I need to," Frankie said. He turned his back to Charlie who let out an irritated sigh. All went quiet as we headed to the upper west side.

"Did he not love us? Did he think we didn't care? I'm positively distraught," Mara said.

"Give up Mara, you're drunk," Jack said.

"Can't you see how troubling this is for me? It's always about you and your boyfriends or should I say fuck-mates!" she said.

"Really Mara? Must you be so vulgar," Jack said.

"Really, Mara stop it," Peter said. His voice high pitched.

"Don't yell at me, you should have told us Larry was dying! Fuck you!" Mara said.

"This will not end well. Let's please stop this," Charlie said, his voice firm.

"I agree, we all need to calm down. This has been a hard day," Jack said.

"Of course you would agree with Charlie! Maybe you and Charlie should walk off into the sunset together. You both make me sick! Sick! " Mara said. She pulled away from Jack.

"Mara, all I am saying is now is not the time for any discord," Charlie said.

Mara moved her body and faced the back seat. Her voice came from her gut, it was venomous.

"Don't speak another word to me!" Mara said. Charlie exhaled. Peter angrily positioned himself on the edge of his seat. He turned to everyone, my eyes on him through the rearview mirror.

"Holy shit, Mara, what did you want me to do? Go against Larry's wishes? I understand your anger and that you're upset, but this behavior of yours needs to stop, this isn't only about you and your sorrow!" he cuffed the back of his seat.

"What the bloody hell are you saying to me!" Mara screamed.

"I'm saying this isn't about you today. I respect your grief, I really do. I'm sorry you're hurt. Larry didn't mean to hurt you. Larry didn't want to worry anyone and you just have to understand. It's that simple. He was scared and ashamed and all the poor guy did his last days on earth was apologize to me. He didn't want to die. That's all he kept saying, he didn't want to die. He didn't want to leave me. Now please, Mara, I am asking you, no, I'm begging you to shut up. Just. Shut. Up."

"Pull over, let me out!" Mara screamed.

"Mara stop it!" Jack said.

"Leonardo pull over now, bloody hell, I mean it!'

"We're all upset, let's all calm down," Jack said.

"I want out too!" Frankie said.

"Unreal," Charlie said.

"Leonardo pull over now!" she cried out. I brought the van over to 65th and Broadway. Mara jumped out of the van. Jack, Frankie, Rico and Olena jumped out after her. We watched Mara storm off. Jack yelled after her. They hailed a taxi and loaded in, and off they went. I resumed driving and headed to the east side to take Peter home.

"Truth be told, Larry couldn't stand her this last year. He woke up one day and said he was done with her, and her cruelty, her berating, and quite frankly, so was I. I'm done with her and that entire bar scene. The drugs and the bullshit. I hope she doesn't call me," he said.

"I don't think you have to worry about that," Charlie hissed.

Later that night in a Starbucks below Peter and Larry's apartment, Charlie and I sat with Peter.

"He really liked you Leonardo. He got a kick out of you. Charlie, he adored you. He thought you both had a way with Mara. Not many people can tolerate her."

"Are you going to be okay?" I asked.

"I think so. I don't know. But I'm certain Larry wanted me to live a good life."

"And you will. I promise," Charlie said.

"He wanted me to keep his memory alive, and that's what I plan on doing. Sometimes I ask myself, why Larry and not me? I should have AIDS. I'm negative and truth be told, when we opened our relationship for a few years, I had a lot of sex. More than Larry!"

"Is that possible?" Charlie said. We laughed.

"I don't regret any of it. It was an experience that's for sure. But we couldn't keep our relationship open for long. He'd get jealous, I'd get jealous. It didn't work for us. In the end, we decided all we really needed was each other," Peter said.

"Regrets? No. Who knew there was a monster out there lurking to get us. We were doing what was natural to us. We're gay men, it's what we do. We have an abundance of love to give," Charlie said. I

"And we're also pretty horny," Peter chuckled.

"Well, we only want to feel good," Charlie said.

"You were lucky to have a great love," I said.

"You're going to meet someone really nice one day. It will happen when you least expect it. Don't worry," Peter said. He stopped himself, heaved forward, tears came, his heaving so bad, Charlie took him by the hand and guided him outside. We stood on the corner of East 36th and1st. Charlie hugged him while Peter wept in his shoulder, small spots of rain drenched us.

"You guys were wonderful together. It was beautiful," Charlie said. My hand was on Peter's arm and I rubbed gently, not knowing quite what to do.

"I think I need to go home and get into bed. I don't like this. This is too much. I need to be strong," Peter started to clear his eyes, compose himself. Charlie gently put both his hands on Peter's face, their noses almost touching.

"Now listen to me, dear friend, you do not have to be strong right now. I'm giving you permission to be weak and to be messy, to cry, and to remember. It's not going to go away, don't look for that to happen. This pain belongs to you. It's Larry's gift. It's his love. One day you'll wake up and it won't feel as bad, and when that happens, we're all going dancing because Larry would love that. God knows he loved to twirl," Charlie said. He sadly giggled.

"That he did. But answer me this, does Leonardo have to come with us? I heard he pukes after dancing. You know how those young gay people are nowadays, no stamina," Peter said. He laughed through his tears.

"No. He's not invited," Charlie poked my arm.

"Good, he's a pain in the ass," Peter said.

"You're both rotten and I hate you both," Peter pulled me toward him, and kissed the top of my head.

"Good night my friends. I love you guys. I'll be okay. I have no choice but to be okay." We watched him go into his building. The rain had stopped.

"Do you want a ride back to Brooklyn? We might as well use the van before I return it tomorrow," I said. Charlie agreed.

"So who was Domani?" I asked as we went over the Brooklyn bridge.

"Sadly, Domani is Jack's albatross. Where do I begin? There are so many half-truths to this story. There's the version from when I first met Jack and the true confession I heard a few days ago. Anyway, Jack told me many years ago that Domani was only his roommate and good friend. Nothing more. Domani was a very handsome Jamaican guy. I saw a picture of him years ago. Jack carries a photo of him in his wallet. Big white teeth. Beautiful black skin and a gorgeous body. It was 1982. Jack had just moved to the city. They both lived in this crappy place in the Bowery. I have no idea how they met. Domani was a very talented boxer and had a great future ahead of him. Jack said Domani was this big, kind, highly intelligent, intuitive, and gentle guy. He would occasionally tell me through the years that Domani had this great laugh, infectious, loud and from his gut. Jack met his family a few times. They lived in Queens and were Seventh-day Adventists. Good people. Righteous. Super religious. Anyway, Damani started getting sick and he was not getting better so he went to the hospital. A week later, Jack came home to find Domani sitting on the apartment floor in the dark. He was in agony, really sick, sweating profusely, and sobbing and he told Jack he had some kind of blood cancer and that he didn't want to die. He was holding a bible to his heart. Really clutching it. He told Jack he was being punished by God and kept repeating he didn't want to die; he didn't want to die. He was sobbing uncontrollably. Anyway, Domani ended up back at the hospital because he could hardly breath. Jack went to him and found out Domani was in a unit with people with bad blood infections. Jack had to wear a gown, a mask, gloves. Domani took off his oxygen mask and told Jack they needed to pray for their souls. He said his illness was the wrath of God and that he deserved this thing called GRID (gay related immune disease.) That's what they called it before it was called AIDS. Anyway, Damani's family wanted nothing to do with Domani. He was basically all alone."

"But he had Jack," I said.

"A week ago, the day after Larry passed. Jack came to me high and drunk. He was in a bad way. The past was right in front of him. He confessed the truth of Domani, he couldn't stop bawling. Jack confessed that he and Domani had been lovers. It was Jack's first true love. He kept telling me how he could never forgive himself for what he did to Domani all those years ago; he was full of shame.

"What the hell did he do?" I asked.

"When Domani was dying, Jack panicked. He freaked out. He thought he was going to get AIDS too and that it was going to kill him. After he found out that Domani was infected, Jack ran back to their apartment. He packed up his stuff and moved out and went back home to Connecticut. He abandoned Domani. Domani called him for a few weeks, and Jack wouldn't take his calls. Then one day, the hospital called and told Jack that Domani died alone. Jack was told Domani was asking for him right up to the end. He requested that Jack get his belongings and bring them to his family in Queens. At the hospital they handed Jack a bag. Inside the bag was Domani's wallet, his jeans, a gold ring he won for boxing, and a note asking Jack to give his wallet and the gold ring to his family in Queens. Domani ended the letter telling Jack that he never loved anyone like he loved Jack, and that he understood why Jack had to leave him. He told Jack what really mattered was the fact that he had good memories. He told Jack to forgive himself. The next day Jack went to Queens to give Domani's stuff to his family. His father and mother answered the door, his mother was bawling, and by that time five of Domani's siblings were at the door bawling too, but the father was just angry and mean. He told Jack to get lost, and that Domani was an abomination and that Jack was too. He called Jack a disgusting queer, and told him to stay away. Jack left. It was a ugly, fearful time. No one knew what was going on. We just have to forgive ourselves. I'm sure we all did things that were not proud of during those early days of AIDS. Jack thought that when he first told me about Domani years ago, that I would assume he was infected and would abandon him. That's why he told me they were only friends. Jack is negative, but he lived in fear for many years," Charlie said.

I pulled up in front of his brownstone, absorbing all that he told me, feeling even more sorrow for Jack. At that moment, I decided that I had landed on probably the saddest group people in the entire world. The sensation that something was starting to warn or enlighten me overcame me; I couldn't decipher which, but clearly knew something was behind all this profound sadness for I seemed to be a magnet for it.

"Are you coming in? Christ, this was a hard day," he said. I shut the van off and nodded yes.

Charlie gave me a tour of his apartment. It was spacious, and filled with books. A cello sat in one corner of his living room. We chatted about the paintings that hung on his walls. They were from artist friends, some who had left New York and others who had died from AIDS. They were an interesting, eclectic collection of abstracts, stills, and portraits. His furniture was a mix of old and new, an antique claw legged sofa was adorned with an intricate red and burgundy throw. A brick walled kitchen with pans that hung over a large gas stove led to his bedroom. The tour ended there. We stood at the entrance. His room was plain and white. A mahogany bureau matched his bed-set that was huge and high; it was covered with a white cotton duvet. A black and white photo of two naked men in an embrace hung on the wall across from his bed. It was a Mapplethorpe print bought for him in the eighties by one of his former partners. The window blinds were closed, and the smallest specks of light peeked in the otherwise darkened room; the sound of wind roared outside,

"I'm unsure about this. I fear one day you'll say to yourself, that Charlie was an old pervert. That's why I held back for so long," he said.

"But you're only forty," I said, and smiled mockingly.

"I lied," he said.

"I know. Larry told me, and I don't care," I said softly.

"Son of a bitch. Good old Larry," he said and gave me a thumbs up, made a clicking noise with his tongue. He was shaky, but his lovely eyes twinkled. I reassuringly smiled at him, nodded, and went to his bed, sat and held myself up by my elbows. He was still in the doorway eyeing me. I waited for him to proclaim his dire need for me. I knew in my heart that wasn't going to happen and knew, unmistakably, what the night was going to mean for us; our need to be close, to comfort one another in our time of grief.

"Leonardo, I want you to meet someone your own age. I want you to be happy. I want you to understand that this can't be more than what this is going to be tonight."

"Come to me," I said. He walked into the room, lit a candle on his dresser, and his darkened room became flame orange, the scent of sandalwood pushed its way around. He approached me, stood over me, and held my face in his hand, knelt in front of me. He stroked my legs, my crotch, and he kissed me. He motioned for me to stand, and I obeyed, "Take your clothes off," he breathed. I removed my shirt, my shoes, my pants and my nerdy boxers. I stood before him naked, erect, my eyes steady on his exquisite face, he then took off his clothes. He was not in bad shape nor good, but was perfectly Charlie. He embraced me, was warm, and tender, he moved slow, took his time, and I followed his lead. His hands on my body, he touched me all over and I touched him. I backed myself onto his bed. He lay on top of me, and we kissed longingly, deeply, our bodies moving in a slow rhythm, the candle flickered, and we made love. We held each other until morning when I knew to leave.

Scene Twenty-Five – Lou Reed – *Walk On The Wild Side*

The cable network ordered more shows, and Jack was off filming his series at the Brooklyn Studio. We hardly saw him. Most of my time was spent with Mara. Her drug use became worse, she was snorting coke around the clock, and her headaches had become so severe there were days she couldn't take her head off her pillow without screaming. Rico knew a doctor and made an appointment for her, and she agreed to go. Diagnosis: ulceration of the mucous membrane of the nose. She was told that her nasal septum was on the verge of collapse.

Mara said the doctor was a nincompoop.

Picking Annie up from school became routine, especially when Mara was having one of her headache attacks or when she was grossly hung over. She'd call me in the afternoon, whimper, moan, plead, "I'm not feeling well darling, please get Annie for me. Make sure you're both quiet when you get home. I need my rest. Annie is so inconsiderate."

In front of her school Annie greeted me with a glum smile, her large school bag hung off her tiny shoulders weighing her down. She'd hold onto the straps around her armpits soldiering toward me. Once by my side, she'd extend her hand for mine. I'd take her pack, and off we'd go to the movies, candy hunting, or the zoo.

Annie was a perpetually sad child, and it bothered me deeply. I praised her nonstop, and did my best to build her self-confidence. When that seemed to fail, I went overboard with buying her candy and gave her whatever she wanted in hopes of seeing her in the throes of happiness. "Leonardo, can we get some candy?" she would ask. We'd walk through crowds of people while she explained in detail a candy ring she wanted, or a necklace made of sugar crystals. One day she asked me about Boston, and I told her all about it, and promised we'd take a trip there, and expressed she could become friends with my niece and nephew,

"They probably wouldn't like me, no one likes me. Mommy says I'm a nincompoop."

"How could anyone not like you? You're my best friend in New York City."

"I am not."

"Hello? Are too."

"I'm not!" she giggled.

"You are too."

"Really. Double-pinky-swear."

"I double-pinky-swear!" We locked pinky fingers. Her small hand slipped into my hand and onward we walked.

Annie was an extremely good looking girl and people would often stop and say, "What an adorable little girl you have." I'd nod proudly, and Annie would shyly smile. Being with Annie filled me with purpose and responsibility. When I was with her, I was out of all my gross self-indulgency, and my show business goals. Annie made me feel human, snapped me back to reality, taught me what mattered most. One day, Annie looked up at me and said, "I wish you were my daddy." She gripped my hand, and although her words were comforting and special, it triggered a loneliness inside of me, a longing for my personal goals. I still wanted my own children. What had happened to that goal? What had happened to me?

Homework time was a horror show. Mara forbid me to help Annie. I tried to explain to Mara how Annie needed help and that it was best that she was helped. Mara would attack me unmercifully, tell me I was weak like Annie, and call me a nincompoop. "How dare you tell me what's best for my child! She needs to suffer and figure out her own homework!" One time when Annie was begging for help, Mara had an instant change of heart and angrily went to Annie. She grabbed the homework assignment out of her hand, read it, and called her a nincompoop, "You can't figure this out?" Annie curled up in a ball on the floor. "I don't understand, Mommy." And Mara went off on her. "Because you're lazy, because you want everyone to do it for you, because you don't like to work!" That time, she allowed me to help her, screaming at both of us.

"If you want to be a nincompoop all your life and have everyone doing your work for you, go ahead, be a daft cow, it's your life. Be an idiot. So be it!" For the rest of the week, she referred to Annie as the "idiot".

After filming the second season of episodes, Jack asked the producers if he could write a few shows for the third season. They agreed. One night, Mara told me to go down to his office and get him for dinner. She had ordered out. "Poor darling has been working so hard." I knocked on his office door, and peeked my head in and softly opened the door. Jack sat at his desk and stared at the blank computer screen, his face illuminated, he appeared stark, and somewhat ghostly, like an overexposed photo. "What did I get myself into," he said grimly. He sipped his brandy, ran his hands through his hair. "Take a break. Mara ordered Chinese, all your favorites," I said. "Good idea. To hell with this!" he went upstairs into the living room, and sat on the sofa. Tensely, he picked through the Chinese containers that were on the coffee table. "I can't eat," he groaned, tilted back. Mara gazed at him while she nibbled on small bites of a crab Rangoon. "Darling, don't get discouraged. It will all come. Do eat." Jack remained quiet. "Poor baby," she moved closer to him, and kissed him on the lips. "You can do this, darling. You're an amazing talent," she said. Jack pursed his lips together and blew out a puff of exasperated air. "I have a week, and I've written nothing. Nothing. I can't foul this up! I have to go back downstairs. I'll be okay. It will come to me." Off he went back to his office. Mara forked through the General Tso Chicken, picking out small pieces of broccoli to crunch on.

"Poor darling, he's positively fit to be tied. The longer he spends on that script the longer it will take to focus on your project, and his first love is that screenplay, we all know it. What to do?" she said.

"Maybe I could help. Make some suggestions?"

"No you mustn't, he'd feel humiliated, overpowered, maybe even insulted. He is a man after all."

"I could try to work around all that ego stuff. I could kind of give him a kickstart. I know how Jack works."

"Well, it's not a terribly bad idea, you never know where things like this could lead with your writing career, and you'd be helping Jack out. Would you mind, darling?"

"I don't mind," I said. She put down her fork, and clasped her hands together.

"Perfect. I say go down to his office, have a nice chat, do this and that, and whatever. Don't make a big deal about it, get him started, and then Bob's your uncle."

"Okay! I can handle that."

"You're brill!"

I fixed a plate of food for Jack, loading it up with all that he liked, put it on a tray, and poured a glass of wine, which impressed Mara. "Nice touch, darling! Wait!" She ran to a bowl of flowers on the dining table, picked out a rose, put it in a small bud vase and placed it on the tray. She clapped and jumped in her space. "It's perfect! Tell him the rose is from me." I walked down the stairs balancing the tray, carefully knocked on Jack's office door. I entered, he was snorting.

"Mara said you have to eat. The rose is from her," I placed the tray on his desk.

"This is harder than I thought," he said.

"It will come to you. Can I sit?" I said.

"Sure. Please. I have the breakdowns on what each scene has to accomplish, but I can't seem to do it," he flung the small packet of breakdowns across his large desk.

"Try and think like you did when we wrote our script," I said

"The screenplay was easier. I have strict parameters, time restraints. This is TV."

I knew why Jack was having such a hard time. His drinking and cocaine use were more intense than when we wrote the screenplay; he now had mega stardom, he was under a huge amount of pressure both professionally and personally, and the demands on him were astronomical. I also knew from working with Jack that as a writer he was good, but couldn't hold his own. He needed to have words on paper to work with. He was unable to scoop the clay out of the barrel and spin the wheel, the pot needed to be formed first before he sat at the potter's wheel. That night I suggested that he write as much as possible and keep editing down, "I wish I could write as much as possible! I can't get a damn word out! Not one single word," he said.

"May I have a look?" I said. He nodded, "Knock yourself out." He handed me the show's breakdowns. I asked him questions about the show. "Do you mind if I make some suggestions?"

I asked. "Go for it," he said, and started to pick through the Chinese food with his fingers. I moved the computer screen toward me, moved the key board and mouse and started writing. Jack began to eat. He looked at the screen and gleefully howled at the jokes I wrote. He loved my scene directions, he added a few of his own. I stopped myself following Mara's instructions about not overpowering or insulting him. "You're going to be fine," I said and stood, "Excellent! Great, you're a life saver," he said. I left him to his work. His script would be part of the third season.

Right before the third season was to be filmed, Jack's manager/agent, Beth, a striking red head who I had met a few times to discuss our screenplay, had gotten us a meeting at *Across the Line Cinema,* a studio doing hot new films by hot new directors and writers. Our meeting was 10:00 am. Jack was shaky when we got out of the taxi.

"I need a drink."

"It's going to be okay," I said.

"I still think we should make this an Independent film. I really want to direct."

"Let's see what they say, this is a major studio."

Jack insisted on getting a drink. We found some dive bar, he ordered a whiskey straight up. He gulped it down, the bar was too dark for anyone to know who Jack was, so we were safe. Once back out in the sunlight, people stared at us, some smiled, some came up to Jack,

"It makes me feel different. I can't take a lot of this fame nonsense anymore," He started to scratch his arm, then the back of his head. He took deep breaths.

The meeting was on the 54th floor, a split level office with a spanning view of New York; Central Park in all its green lushness stared me in the face. It all seemed perfectly normal to be in the offices of a major movie studio, like it was all part of what I envisioned my life to be. Jack and I were led by a skinny woman to a conference room with a long impressive glass table, and another spectacular view of New York, this one facing west giving us a view of the Hudson. We were told to wait a few minutes. We were offered coffee. I declined and so did Jack, but as soon as the skinny woman left, I gorged myself with the fancy chocolates on a side table.

"You eat a lot," he said.

"These chocolates are expensive," I tossed a few in my pocket, drank some water, and within minutes two women walked into the meeting room. Both women were skinnier than the one who showed us in, they had pleasant smiles, were dressed meticulously, smelled lovely, one wore dangly bracelets, one had long flowing blonde hair and the other had brown. They both shook my hand, and gloated when they saw Jack and chatted about his TV show; how much they loved it, and congratulated his success. He was polite, quiet, and overly well-mannered. I told myself that Jack was a great lesson for me in social graces and to take heed because usually I wanted to vomit when I was around such overtly disingenuous bullshit. An odd creepy feeling socked me in my gut. I instantly became nauseous. Who the hell was I to criticize Jack? Look what I was putting up with so I could get a lucky break in show business. I was cleaning his toilets, changing his kid's shitty diapers, cooking for them, and taking copious amounts of abuse from his wife. Was I like Jack in a different form? As Jack spoke to the two women, he repulsed me, my hands shook. He had become this person I had never seen; his weird introverted-self was gone. He was assertive, and confident. Why couldn't he be this way with his wife, children, parents and friends? Did the people who loved him really matter to him? Was his passivity in his personal life fair to the ones who needed and loved him? Sure he spoke up once in a while, but more often than not, he didn't. Like Rico, I was doing all his dirty work and he came off smelling like lavender. I remained still in my seat. I knew what Mara complained about, felt bad for her, and that's when I stopped myself, that was going too far. Feeling bad for her was not an option. I stopped my wandering mind, and switched my focus to the two women in front of me. This was my big chance, screw Jack. Buckle up, grow up. I worked for this. The two women spoke about the script, they said it was dark, but funny, they asked us about specific scenes, said the dialogue was exceptional, and asked us to clarify a few character motivations, and we did.

"Well, if it was up to us, we'd make this film tomorrow. The LA office loved it too, but they recently lost a ton of money on *Heading to Hell.* We both back this screenplay, and what we suggest you guys do is attach a popular movie actress to the lead and come back to us. Then, I think we can convince the LA office."

We thanked them and left. Jack called his manager Beth, and she suggested we start talking about actors we wanted to approach.

In the taxi home, Jack suggested Cora Tanner for Doctor Stein's wife. I was shocked. There was no doubt it was a perfect part for Cora, but Mara would never allow it, and I wondered if Jack was thinking clearly. "I owe Cora," he said. I never let on that I knew that before Cosmo was born they had rekindled their relationship. Cora would never agree to be in our film considering the fact that she almost killed Rico with her bare hands. I couldn't figure out why Jack was suggesting something that would infuriate Mara especially because the possibilities of Cora agreeing to do the film were zero. That afternoon when

Jack told Mara his intentions, her sharp claws came out, and they were deathly threatening. She went for the kill. She ran around the house in a frenzy. Meanwhile, Jack sat quietly and watched her, a slight smile across his face.

"No way, no way, not that horrible ugly actress in your masterpiece! Why her? So you can make amends, is that the deal? How dare you suggest such a thing to me in my home? You stupid bumsucker." With those words came books, ashtrays and pillows flying towards Jack and me. Her vulgar tirade lasted hours, and it was mostly about how Jack wanted to have sex with Cora, and how he was a weakling, a sex addict, a fraud, a pig and a nincompoop.

"You want to shag that slag one last time! That bitch with the mouth like a race horse!" It was torturous listening to her, and I wanted to leave, and when I said I had to go, she yelled at me, "No, you can't leave me in my hour of need, you ninny! You must stay, in fact I demand you stay and witness the crucifixion of this insolent piece of shit called my husband! What kind of bloody bollocks is this! Cora Tanner!" She went on and on. I obediently stayed, my head in my hands, I gazed at the door, my toes curled. Jack tried to reason with her, but when she was high on coke, it was impossible. The night ended with Mara calling us stupid poofs, knobheads and finally slamming her bedroom door, and telling Jack to drop dead.

"I guess we can't ask Cora," I said. Jack burst out laughing, and couldn't stop, his face turned a deep red.

"There are plenty of other actresses, but Cora would have been perfect," Jack poured himself more brandy.

"I need to go," I said.

"Please stay. Have a drink with me."

"Why did you tell Mara about Cora, it seemed kind of a waste of time and a little mean."

"Maybe," he said and handed me a brandy. He downed his, poured another and downed that too.

"Did I tell you I saw a ghost the other night?"

"What's with you and Rico seeing ghosts?" I asked, trying to act as if I believed him, knowing these type of hallucinations came from heavy cocaine use.

"I was sitting here alone and there was a woman standing there," he pointed towards the kitchen where the light shined. In my estimation Jack was officially losing his mind. He poured another drink.

"Did you talk to her?"

"No, she was only standing there, crying"

"She was crying?"

"She was crying for my life," he said. I sighed when he said this to me. "Why the deep sigh?" he asked. "No reason," I coughed, cleared my throat, wanted to say something to him about his drinking, his drug addiction, but I held back. The rotten truth was there was no one in his life helping him. Like me, everyone was too scared to confront him, it was as if no one really cared for him, but they loved his celebrity status because being around Jack meant you had celebrity status, too. It was all so ugly because I stood by all these years and watched him destroy himself. I watched Mara do the same. Who was I?

He poured me another brandy, like a fool I took it, kicked off my shoes, moaned deeply spread out on the floor, none of this made sense to me. If anyone saw what I was tolerating no one would understand, there would be no pity nor should there be. My parents would be so ashamed of me. That killed me the most. What was this sick need for approval that I had? Was I such a damaged person? Jack hoovered over me.

"Leonardo, I want you to suck my cock," he started to unbuckle his pants. I sat up.

“Are you crazy, seriously,” I started putting my shoes on. I was leaving.

“Don’t you want to?” his voice meek, sad, he looked lost. Desperate.

“Jack, I have to go. This is too much.”

“I’m sorry. I shouldn’t have said that,” he said.

“It’s okay, forget it.”

“Please don’t go. Please.”

“Jack, I really want to go.”

“Please, don’t leave. I’m sorry I shouldn’t have said it, please stay. I’m begging you, stay, I won’t speak, stay. I can’t- I don’t want to be alone please. I can’t do this anymore, I don’t know who the hell I am anymore,” he went to his knees in front of me, and embraced me. Placing my arms awkwardly around him, he sobbed into my shoulder like a hurt child.

That night Jack fell asleep on the sofa, and I on the floor. The next morning he was off filming his series. Mara asked me to spend the day with her and the kids, and I did. About noon, while coloring in a book with Annie, Cosmo on a blanket next to us, the phone rang. Mara answered it in her bedroom, after a short while she came out, put her coat on and came to us.

“That was Jack, poor darling, I have to take a taxi to the studio. He’s stressed. He wants me to bring him a bottle of Vodka. He’s been working so hard.” Twelve hours later, they both came back stumbling drunk, without a phone call from either one of them the entire day.

During the filming of the show’s third season, a fourth season was ordered. That would mean Jack would have eight weeks off. During that eight week hiatus, he was going to film a movie and our project was put on semi-hold once again. I was getting impatient.

"As soon as I'm done filming this movie and shooting this fourth season, I promise we'll get our project under way. Beth said it will be a long process."

"It's okay, don't worry, Jack. I know you're busy." I found myself saying this to him over and over. I had invested so much time in this screenplay, and nothing seemed to be happening. I was determined to wait it out.

The first season of his show won all kinds of awards. Jack was nominated for a Golden Globe and an Emmy. He lost, but was nominated again the following year. The cast of his show won the first of many SAG awards. The third season progressed into even greater success. There was merchandise, clubs, web sites, fan parties, T-shirts, dolls and recipe books. Everywhere I went, Jack and his co-stars' faces were plastered all over New York City. Back home in Boston, on the highway into the city, there was a billboard with the cast of the show on it. Whenever I went home for visits and passed it, a part of me felt proud, the other conflicted. I saw what took place behind the billboards, it was like seeing the trap door before the rabbit came out of the magician's hat.

The second time they were to go to LA for the Golden Globe Awards was the time Frankie would be officially banished from their lives and from all of us. Mara wanted him to come over to dye her hair the usual jet black. Once in LA, she would have it styled. Annie was at her father's house. I was taking care of Cosmo.

When Frankie came to the townhouse to dye Mara's hair, I was feeding Cosmo small portions of chicken. His small lips oily and pink, he managed to speak in his little voice after each bite, "more, more, more," his eyelashes long and dark, his eyes popped out like gleaming blue lights. Mara was in an arm chair in the middle of their large kitchen. Bottles of hair dye sat on the gray granite countertop. Frankie took the bottle of dye and worked it into her hair. Jack was with his manager going over his contract for the next season because there was some kind of money conflict with the star of the show who wanted more money.

"If that fat pig gets more money for starring in that show, Jack better get a raise too. That dumb show would be nothing without Jack." Frankie was working the hair dye into Mara's hair with his hands like a child making a mud pie, up and around, twisting and working the slimy dark dye throughout her hair. It smelled like one of Cosmo's dirty diapers.

"This is a new dye. It's my own special concoction," Frankie said.

"It stings a bit. Are you sure it's good, darling?" Mara said.

"It will be okay," Frankie reassured her. When he was done, he took off the plastic gloves over the sink. Mara's hair was now a muddy, slimy mess wrapped around her boxy head in a giant twist that came to a point at the top. It looked like she had an ice cream cone smashed on the top of her head. Cosmo started banging the table while I tickled him under his chin and ran my hands through his hair, "Who's a good boy? Who's a good boy?" I said this while altering my voice to typical baby talk tone.

"I hate when you talk to him like that, he'll grow up to be a ninny. The last thing I need in my life is another nincompoop, stop it, mate."

"I'm sorry," I said, clearing my voice.

"Put him in his bed, if he doesn't take his nap, he'll be a bloody monster."

Frankie rinsed out plastic dye bottles under running water. "How much longer? It's burning," Mara said. Frankie glanced at the clock over the oak table. "Ten more minutes." It was two o'clock. I took Cosmo to his room and put him down. I closed the door and went back to the kitchen, took a bottle of water from the fridge, and sipped it, my eyes on Mara's slimy head. Frankie cut coke on a small mirror. It was nine past the hour. She had a minute left before her hair would be rinsed. She started to snort.

"You know, mate, Jack is the only actor on that show who can actually act, and that pig makes all the money. But it's out of our control. I am trying to convince Jack to fire Beth. She's a horrible manager, positively full of herself," Mara said, wretchedly. She snorted another line. Then Frankie shoved the straw up his nose.

"Then we have to share the jet with that skinny dumb actress with that dumb fluffy hair and her big Broadway star husband. She's a ninny." She was referring to Carla Jean Picot and her husband Michael Otter. Carla Jean was on another popular TV show produced by the same cable network.

"Michael Boomer is fabulous in *Hey Diddle*!" Frankie said.

"What's she like?" Frankie handed the straw to Mara.

"She's a skinny, ugly, bitch is what she's like. And that husband of hers is this all American, uninteresting, boring actor. Big Broadway star! They're both bloody disgraceful! No talent!" Mara said. It was twenty-minutes after the hour, and Frankie grabbed Mara by the arm and pulled her to the sink.

"Bloody bollocks!" she screamed.

"It's time, it's time!" his voice was full of panic, he trembled and ran his hands over Mara's head doing his best to wash the dye out of her hair. "Oh! God! Oh God!" he started showing me clumps of wet, slimy, gelatinous hair that came out of Mara's scalp.

"What's going on? My head is burning! Darling, is everything okay, you're scaring me!" Her face pushed down into the sink, her voice was muffled and sounded like she was calling out from the bottom of a well.

"Get me a towel!" Frankie said. I ran to the bathroom and got a towel thinking this was going to be worse than any bomb of mass destruction ever dropped, and the casualties monumental. I heard Frankie cry out again, "Leonardo, hurry! I need a towel!" I ran to the kitchen and gave him the towel. Mara was silent. He put the towel over her head and wrapped it tightly. Her eyes closed. Frankie handed her a paper towel to wipe her face. She sat back in the chair, and breathed heavily.

"My scalp is on fire! Never use that new stuff again!" Frankie rubbed the towel to dry her head, and then he lifted the towel off. Frankie's mouth dropped, mine dropped lower. When I saw Mara's head, I ran out of the kitchen. Mara called after me, "What's going on, mate! What? What's wrong! Leonardo, what's wrong?" Mara's head ironically looked like a black bald globe, and the hair that was left, and there wasn't much, represented shapes of various countries. I hid in Annie's room. My back pressed against the door, emotions came all at once; fright, amusement, and then the guilt over the revengeful thoughts that come when something bad happens to a person you deeply resent. Then the bomb hit. Mara's voice was so loud, so crazed, I could have sworn the walls were vibrating and crumbling. "Ahhh! You're a nincompoop! Look what you did to me! Look what you did to me! You idiot! You nincompoop! You moron!" I heard her pace in the living room. I peeked out the door. Frankie was in complete distress, and pathetically followed her around, "I'm so sorry, I am so sorry. Oh, my God, look what I did, I am so sorry, please I'll make it up to you, I am so sorry!" Mara then turned and went to him, and started smacking him all over his body. Frankie fell to the ground and curled in a ball. She hit and kicked him repeatedly, threw big books at him as he whimpered like a dog. "I'm bad, I'm bad, I'm a bad person, I'm not good, hit me, go on, hit me, I'm no good," he cried out. When she was done, he stood facing her, stunned, tears rolling down his face, snot streaming out of his nose, he was whimpering like a wounded animal. Mara covered her face with her hands, she was crying and hyperventilating, she sat down on the sofa. Her sobs were heartbreaking, childlike.

"Get out. Bugger off!" she said softly.

"Please Mara … I—I—I—" he started to back away toward the door.

"GET OUT! GET OUT!" she threw a book at him, and out he went.

I never saw Frankie again. Mara picked up a pillow and put her face into it. I went to her slowly, my heart sank for her. "Jack cheats on me." Tears streamed down her face. "All the time. All the time he does, bloody hell." I handed her a Kleenex and sat next to her on the sofa. I put my arms around her while she wept.

"I love you, darling. What would I do without you?" she said.

"I love you, too," I said.

"I'm ugly. Bald and ugly and fat and disgusting. No wonder Jack cheats on me."

"You're not fat," I said. She wept in my arms for a very long time, holding on to me, pulling me closer, tighter and tighter. "Please darling, don't let me go."

The night of the incident, before Jack came home, Mara told me to meet him in the foyer and tell him the news so he wouldn't be terribly shocked when he saw her. When he arrived home I told him what had happened, he shook his head and looked puzzled, "Jesus," he said. I then sighed sadly, he sort of smiled. I smiled back, and then I giggled, and then he giggled, and I told him how it all played out.

"Jack, look, you may be tempted to laugh when you see her, if you do, she'll kill you."

"Don't worry, I won't," he started to chuckle again.

"Don't even look at me, for God's sake!" I said.

"It will grow back, right?"

"Yes, of course," I said.

"She'll be fine. She took some valium and she's sleeping," I said.

Within in a day Mara had wrapped her head in a silky kerchief and she actually looked quite attractive, like Jackie O going yachting.

Olena and Mara had gone shopping for a wig, and found an expensive one uptown. She wore it to the Golden Globes. Olena and I babysat, and watched the show from the townhouse. Jack's show won in almost every category and was making television history like no other show before. Mara had teased her wig unmercifully. She refused help from hairdressers, and refused to wear the gowns the cable network provided. She ended up looking like a combination of a drag queen, a vampire, and a back-up singer from a 1960's Elvis Presley movie. Jack didn't win and Mara was furious when she came home two days later.

"That other stupid actor won, that non-talent idiot who runs around with his snappy gay jokes! Jack should have won!"

"Who cares? There'll be another year, and another after that," Jack said. He was showing me all the gifts in his Golden Globe gift bag.

"Is that a Rolex watch?" I said.

"It still bewilders me, when you're poor, you get nothing, and when you're rich, you get expensive gifts." He left me gawking at the Rolex and went to bed. Mara stayed up and told us how she was photographed, and that she was expecting to be in a few magazines. The next morning she told me to buy every magazine that covered the Golden Globes. She said she didn't want to wait for Jack's people to send them over. I spent the day scanning a pile of magazines. There was only one photo of her, but she was cut out of it. The photo was of Jack, however, you could see her baby finger by Jack's left hand. "All that bloody time wasted on the red carpet!" she snarled. "Get rid of these lousy snitch pads!" She angrily kicked the pile of magazines out of her path, all of them fanned out before me. She went storming to her bedroom and slammed the door.

A week later, when Jack had a break before shooting a movie, we made plans to meet at the townhouse in the early evening to work on some changes in our script. He called me midafternoon, his voice was muffled, "Come now. I have someone here that I need to get rid of."

"Should I call the police? Are you okay""

"I'm fine. Make any kind of excuse you can to get this person out of my house." Click. I immediately jumped in a taxi and was there in 20 minutes. Mara was out with Annie and Cosmo. When I arrived Jack was sitting with a vacant expression on his face across from an actor friend of his from LA. His name was Mickey. He was extraordinarily handsome. He wore tight jeans, and had shoulder length jet black hair. Jack introduced us. I greeted him hurriedly and turned to Jack.

"Jack, Beth is meeting us in 15 minutes, not to be rude but we really need to go," I said.

"Mickey, it was great seeing you, but I have to split," Jack said.

"Wait can you give me a second? We were best friends at one time, we did a lot together. We survived a lot of shit when we were starting out, remember when we were new to the City, and years later in LA? Remember that producer in the Hills? That was crazy shit. Remember? I saved your ass that night."

"I don't want to talk about show biz or LA or the past, that part of my life is gone, we're in my home. It was nice to see you. I have to run," Jack said.

"Jack we really need to go," I said.

"I need to ask you something," Mickey said.

"Do you need money? I can give you some money," Jack took out his wallet and handed

Mickey five one hundred dollar bills, and he took it.

"Thanks, man. Look Jackie, I need an audition for your show, things are tough."

"Sorry, man, I told you. I don't control that part of the show."

"Please, Jackie, I need some help. I'm sick, things are bad. Medications. My insurance. I need help. I want to work,"

"This is not good," Jack stood, steadied himself.

"You're kicking me out, aren't you? Don't be a prick, Jack I knew you when."

"It's time to go, Mickey," Jack started to usher him out.

"Hey, man, get your hands off me. Jack, I mean it."

"I'm asking you nicely to please leave my house," Jack started directing him to the staircase that led four flights down to the foyer,

"You're a dirty, fucking bitch! You always have been, the only difference between you and I is that you sucked and fucked the right people. This should have been me. I have more talent than you! This should have been me! You're a nothing! A nothing!" he yelled insanely and wouldn't stop, and he looked at me. "Don't trust this motherfucker. He'll suck every ounce of life out of you!" My body was instantaneously jarred. Jack socked him in his face, blood squirted out of Mickey's nose and he went down. Jack started kicking him and dragged him down the first flight of stairs, pushed him down the next flight and the next. Mickey brashly howled at him.

"Get your hands off me! I knew you when you were selling your ass! How can you do this to me, I need your help, man, we were friends!" Jack picked him up, and tossed him like a dirty rag into the foyer, and pushed him out onto the doorstep. He gave Mickey a final kick and shut the door. I peeked out at him, he was on the tip of his toes practically jumping forward, pointing at the house, his face deep pink as he bellowed at the building, "Phony! I knew you when you gave blow jobs in the back of limousines! Piece of shit! Phony! Asshole! I know who you are! I know you! I know you! I know you!" His voice seeped through every crack in the house and rebounded all around us as we walked back up the stairs to the living room.

I wiped his blood off the floor and Jack poured himself a drink. He acted like what took place moments before hadn't happened. He sat down and kicked his feet up. Mickey could no longer be heard, but his voice rang in my ears.

"I need to hire a cop to sit out front. I can't live like this."

"Jesus Jack, I never saw that side of you. Why the hell did you let him in?"

"He took me by surprise. I came home; he was waiting out front. He's gone, forget him. Anyway, I told Beth we wanted Andre Brent to play Doctor Stein. You agree, right?" Jack said.

"Sure. I love Andre Brent." Andre Brent was a popular 1960's actor, nominated for a few Oscars and had a TV show in the early eighties. In his heyday he did some great Indie films way before they were called Indie films.

"I think before we send it off to Andre we should tighten up the ending, the part when he shoots his wife in the head," he said.

"That sounds great," I said, thrilled to be working on our project again. We were back to work within seconds, swapping ideas, typing, and rearranging scenes.

Hours later, Jack was a little buzzed. He laid out on the sofa and became morose, consumed, stared at the ceiling, hands folded across his chest, eyes droopy, like he was going to fall asleep any second.

"Mickey did some bit parts in films. Poor bastard. I shouldn't have hit him. But he deserved it," Jack said, yawning.

"It was nice of you to give him money."

"He's sick. Hepatitis or HIV positive, it sucks. But he's trouble. I can't get him an audition. He's got a big mouth. He has plenty of talent, but his ass has been around so much that he's only known as a hustler. He ruined any chance he could've had as a legit actor. Plus, he made some gay porn, and people in the industry know it. He's poison goods. He was used over and over, tossed around. He was stupid enough to believe a lot of what those men promised him. Stardom. Everyone wants to be a star. His good looks were a curse for him, everyone wanted a piece of Mickey, and he let everyone have it. I bet you're thinking I should have helped him. But I gave him money. Right? I did help him."

I kept my eyes on Jack, not quite sure what to say, or how to react. Each time I learned something new about him, I was stupefied. It was like meeting a new person every day but that person lived in the same body. I never knew what to expect.

"Leonardo, why are you so quiet, say something?" There was anger in his voice, "Say something," he demanded. He picked up the upper half of his body from the sofa, and turned to me. "You think I'm a shithead don't you, say it. Jack Fresh is a shithead, say it!"

"You gave him money, that was good," I said.

"Say it, Jack Fresh is a selfish shithead. Say it."

"Stop, Jack."

"I know you're thinking it. I know you are. Let me tell you something. I struggled for years before I got my break. No one helped me, I did this all on my own. Why the hell should I help anyone, and don't mention this to Mara. I'm in no mood for her today."

"I won't. I promise," I said.

"Promises? Promises mean shit. I know you think I'm a shithead. I know you do." He let out a giant yawn, fell fast asleep, and started to snore.

Scene Twenty-Six – R.E.M. – *Night Swimming*

Jack had gone to Madrid to film a TV commercial. Mara had another nasal infection and couldn't fly, so she sent Olena with him. "Guess what? Mara doesn't trust Jack so she's sending me to babysit Jack in Spain! I guess I don't blame her. Either way, they're paying for the entire trip, can you imagine!" Olena was ecstatic. Before they left, Jack told me that he was taking our script with him. He wanted to carefully read it before it was sent out to more actors, and would contact me in a few days. After Madrid, Olena said they were going to spend some time in Barcelona much to Mara's chagrin, but since Olena was going with him, she reluctantly gave in. One of my friends from college was going to Paris for work, and she had asked me to watch her cat, Fiona, in exchange for the use of her cottage in Wellfleet. It was located far from the town center and was walking distance to a pond. I wanted to start a novel. Mara begged me to stay, but I told her it was for my mother's birthday, (I lied) and was granted clemency.

While on the Cape, I went to Orleans in the early morning and wrote in a small coffee shop where they made fancy chocolates and homemade marshmallows. I swam in the pond, walked barefoot in the grass, ate steamed clams, made a fish stew, bought fresh eggs, walked Nauset Beach, marveled at the cliffs, and danced my ass off at the *Crown & Anchor* in Provincetown. An outrageously handsome guy from Claxton,

Georgia asked me to dance. His name was Stewart, he had a southern drawl and proudly told me Claxton was the fruitcake capital of the world. I cracked up laughing after he told me. He didn't laugh, and said he didn't appreciate me making fun of him. We had a bit of a quarrel, and I tried to explain the irony, but he was having none of my jokes. I bought him a drink, and we ended up back at my cottage. To make amends, I told him I wanted to look online at various fruitcake companies in Claxton, "Christmas is right around the corner," I said. This pleased him. After that, I was in his good graces. We jumped on the bed while Fiona the cat decided to make an appearance. She perched herself on the dresser and watched as we nakedly, drunkenly, tossed around.

That entire week I felt like a human being again. I could hear my own voice, and feel my heart beat. I could breathe. There was silence. There was no Mara.

At the end of my week Jack emailed from Spain with ideas for rewrites to get to the action of the film quicker. I told him they were good ideas, but they would not work for various reasons, but I suggested another idea. He agreed, and I spent two days rewriting. I emailed him the changes. I received an email back from him 24 hours later:

Leonardo: I am proud of this script. Working with you has been one of the most profound experiences of my life, you're an amazing talent. I cannot believe how quickly you wrote those scenes. They are perfect. This script is like our child. We have nurtured it and it has grown into something really spectacular. Good job! Bravo! Love, Jack

When my week on the Cape was over the reality of going back to New York made my heart ache. Something was shifting.

A longing for a quiet life was planted in my mind. On the train ride back to the City my week on the Cape flashed before me; the icy pond, the fruitcake guy, the feel of grass under my feet, moonlight and stars, and the sounds of buoys. The moment I arrived in Penn Station I became anxious. From my core, the feeling of not belonging where I was in life plowed me over. I bought a dozen doughnuts at *Krispy Kremes*. They were sweetly, creamily delicious, and they made me feel cozy and loved. I bought a foot long ham and cheese sub sandwich with extra mayonnaise, and chowed that down while I walked through Times Square. That made me feel better, too. I got back to my place and I laid on my bed like a child, my hands on my sick, full belly. Tears came. I did not want to be in New York, but I was afraid to admit it to anyone. So my life continued in a place and situation I didn't want to be in, all so people wouldn't think I was a complete failure.

The next morning, Mara said she wanted to buy me a leather coat because the new coat I wore made me look like a, "country hick." She went on and on. "You have to start dressing better. You look like you're about to milk cows, it's embarrassing being seen with you." She said all this while caking mascara on and painting the tops of her eyes a deep almost black-brown. My mother had bought me my coat. It was a barn coat from the *LL Bean* catalogue.

"I'm sorry. You're right. I have no taste in clothes. I'm such a loser," I said.

"Yes, you are, but I will change all that, darling," she hauntingly smiled.

Once on the street, Mara pulled my arm into hers, locked like lovers. Suspicion grew with each step we took.

After trying on many coats, she decided on a brown leather jacket. "There, darling, now you look normal."

I looked like a gangster.

She told me to take off my old coat and toss it in a trash can on the corner of West Broadway and Chambers Street. "Go on now, off it goes." It was like tossing my beloved mother away. I started to hyperventilate, turned and looked, my eyes steady on the tips of the coat as it peeked out at me.

We had lunch in a diner. She hardly ate. I, of course, chowed down on a grease-drenched cheeseburger, and ate the rest of her butter soaked grilled cheese sandwich as orange blobs of cheddar oozed onto my empty plate,

"I don't know how you eat like you do."

"I have a great appetite."

"But you never gain, it's remarkable," she said.

"I dunno," I said.

"I hate to eat. I have no appetite anymore." She excused herself to go to the bathroom. I scanned the table like a scavenger to see if there was any more food to be eaten; a pickle on her plate and her fries. I woofed down a handful of fries, they tasted like oil sticks encased in a thin layer of potato. She returned, rubbing her nose. She sat down, started grinding her teeth, a small speck of coke under her moist nostril. I pointed to my own nostril to indicate that she had coke there, and she wiped it away with a napkin and then stuck her finger up her nose and gave it a twirl. My stomach rumbled.

"I worry about Jack, he's under so much pressure, darling," she said.

"I know, he's a great guy. He'll be okay."

"And how do you know this?" she asked and glared at me.

"Well, I know Jack. He'll be okay."

"I don't think he'll be okay. Okay? He's my husband, not yours."

"Okay." I said. I curled my toes in my worn sneakers. Mood shift had arrived.

"You think you know my husband better than me?" she showed her fangs, I knew to stay calm.

"No. No, no, of course not," I let out a string of silly giggles.

"You want to marry my husband?" she mocked my giggling.

"What?"

"I read the screenplay again last night. It needs work. It lacks sacredness," she said.

"Really?" I took the pickle off her plate and ate it. I smiled timidly.

"I wanted that pickle," she tapped her fingers on the formica table.

"I can order more."

"Please do," she snapped.

I waved my half eaten pickle to the waitress, "more pickles" I mouthed to the waitress and within seconds a plate of pickles was in front of her, and she shoved the plate towards me.

"I don't want the fucking pickles!" I picked up a pickle and crunched into it, my fingers trembled.

"Are you fucking my husband?"

"What the hell! No!" I said. She twisted her mouth, crossed her hands over her chest. She changed the conversation quickly.

"That screenplay needs so much work," she picked her nose again.

I acted like I didn't hear her. I did not want to ask her what she meant because it would have opened an unwanted dialogue.

"The film's setting should take place in the 1930's."

"But it's a modern day take on the Frankenstein story."

"I know what it is! But I still think it should take place in the 1930's. I'm going to talk to Jack about it as soon as he gets back from Spain."

"Jack and I agreed it was going to take place in modern day," I said, trying to sound jovial.

"I don't care what you and Jack decide. You and Jack don't have a bloody clue! This script has to take place in the 1930's. And, I also think you have to think of a design concept, it has to be written in the script, you must write a psychological analysis of it and attach it to the script."

"You don't do that." Pretending indigestion had arrived. I held on to my stomach, "I should go home, I'm not feeling well," I said.

"Who says what you can and can't *do* in a script? Who? The ninny's in Hollywood?"

"When you write a screenplay, the set designer takes care of that. They look at the writing and do their thing. That why they have designers."

"I see how shows are lit on Jack's TV show. I go on set. What the hell do you know? I know you went to some fancy school, we must not forget that! But you know shit. You don't have a sense of timing. Your character development is not good either. You have so much to learn, darling, trust me."

"Mara, now listen, I know my weaknesses as a writer, but character development is not one of my weaknesses.

"You do realize you're lucky Jack has taken the time to write this script with you." She put cash on the table. I took cash out of my pocket and put it on top of her cash.

"Yeah, I know," I said. My face heating up.

"I told Jack I want to do the set design. Jack is going to direct."

"Oh?"

"There are things I require."

"Require?" I smiled.

"Changes to the script. I will make them with Jack."

"You can't make changes. Jack and I make the changes."

"Jack and you? He's my husband. I read the email he sent you. And how he compared that trite script to your, and his, child. He's absurd and so are you!"

"Mara, I don't want to talk about this. Let's forget about this for now."

"Fine." She put on her coat, and I followed her outside. Once on the street she told me she had errands to do, and hailed a taxi and left me standing alone. I went back to the trash bin, and fetched my old coat out of the trash and put it back on. I carried the leather coat home.

Scene Twenty-Seven –
Grateful Dead – *Friend of The Devil*

I was never with Jack and Mara on Monday night when Jack's show aired because they chose to stay in and watch the show alone. I saw the show once, and didn't understand the massive attention it was getting. Jack was stunned by it too. He told me the critical acclaim his show was receiving was usually paid for by wealthy producers. "It's all a game, a big fucking game, tell people they must see a TV show, and they believe they must see it, tell people it's a classic and they believe it is, tell people it's groundbreaking and people believe it is. All of it is rotten, liars, cheaters, sad, desperate people. Art my ass," Jack said to me one night when he was so drunk I had to help him climb the stairs to the living room,

The few times I saw the show there were moments of great hilarity, and Jack was brilliant. On a Tuesday, three weeks after I got back to New York, my Dad called me.

"Did Jack ever read any of your plays?" his voice sounded off.

"Yeah, sure, all of them," I said. Maybe a year ago I had given him a bunch of my plays to read, they sat in his office on a shelf, same spot, unread.

"Did he read, *Come and Get It?* Did he?" My play, *Come and Get It*, was produced in graduate school. It was the type of play that people loved. It was humorous, heartwarming, easy to follow, and I had gotten a small amount of attention for it when it was produced in graduate school. It was a comedy/drama about a family coming to terms with a gay son, but they were dealing with it through his gay dog.

"Did you see Jack's show tonight? He wrote tonight's show."

"I didn't see it. I don't watch the show."

"There's a scene in the show that is identical to a scene in *Come and Get It.* The jokes were the same, almost verbatim, you have a very distinct sense of humor."

"What are you saying? Jack stole from me? I don't think Jack needs to steal from me."

"Yes. He stole from you."

"That's nuts. So many stories are alike. It happens. I helped him here and there with a few of those TV show scripts. So what?"

"So what? Now you're telling me you help him write some of those scripts without being paid? Why are you refusing to hear this?"

"Dad, get a grip. I have to go."

"Watch the show," he said. We hung up. From that day forward I refused to watch Jack's show, ever. I avoided it every chance I had, and resented my father for being negative, and thought him old and crazy.

Scene Twenty-Eight –
Nina Simone – *I Put a Spell On You*

Jack brought Jennifer Langston, the actor who played his wife on the TV show, home. He wanted her to be a part of our project and thought it would be fun for all of us to meet one another. She had a knockout body, was stunningly attractive, and a fine and skilled actor. When they both came into the room I was playing checkers with Annie on the floor. Mara had been in and out of the bathroom all night, sniffing and coughing, complaining about her usual headache, pacing around the apartment yelling, "Where the hell is Jack!" Every so often Annie and I would look up from our checker game and look at each other, our eyes full of fear. "He called two hours ago and said he was on his way home!"

At the moment Jack and Jennifer came into the livingroom, blood rushed to my limbs. Mara stopped her spooky and restless pacing. At first she didn't say anything. Jennifer went to Mara. "Hi, Mara. How have you been?" she extended her hand. Mara eyeballed Jennifer's hand like she was going to chop it off and eat it, bones and all.

"Mara, I wanted Leonardo to meet Jennifer. I think she'd be great in our film. Let's order Chinese," Jack said. Jennifer came to me. "You must be Leonardo?" I nodded yes, my eyes went directly to Mara, who still eyed Jennifer. "I read the screenplay, it's wild, I love it, great job!" She smiled at me. My eyes moved from Jack, to Mara, to Jennifer, to Annie. "Thank you," I managed to say. Then crash.

"Why did you bring her here?" Mara's voice splattered all over us like shattering glass, "You slag! You whore! Get out of my house!"

"Mara, stop it, what the fuck!" Jack said. Jennifer cleared her throat.

"Okay, well, it was nice meeting you," Jennifer said. Her voice tense, sweet, earnest, she went towards the front door.

"Mara, for crying out loud! This is Jennifer, from the show," Jack said, as if Mara had to be reminded. "I want her to maybe be Doctor Stein's wife in the screenplay Leonardo and I wrote. Didn't you hear me?"

By that time, Jennifer had quietly left the house.

"Why did you bring that bitch here? Why, Jack, why? To rub it in my face? I see it every week, how you both kiss and fondle each other on that stupid show, and you bring this bimbo into my home? Are you crazy? Did she suck you off in the limo here?" Jack shook his head in disgust, and went into the kitchen. I heard him pour himself a drink. Annie eyed Mara who stared at the hall door blankly. I cracked my knuckles. "Mara, are you okay?" I inched my way to her. "Bugger off, Leonardo!" She then screeched into the kitchen. "You're a nincompoop! How else do you want me to react? 'Oh, it's nice to meet you, it's so nice to see you on TV kissing my husband!' Are you a complete nutter? Are you?" Mara slumped on the sofa,

"Annie, get ready for bed. Now!" Annie ran to her bedroom.

Jack came out of the kitchen and sat down on the sofa next to Mara. He flipped through a magazine, and said hello to me. I mustered a wave and a smile. Jack then asked Mara how her day was.

"Fine darling," she kissed him.

"I'll order dinner, would you fancy that chicken dish you like, and dumplings, yes?" she said to me.

"Sure, sounds great," I said.

"Some shrimp and broccoli, too," Jack said.

"Sure, baby, anything you want," she said to Jack. Mara then called the restaurant. After we ate, they asked me to sleep over because they wanted to go out for a few drinks. I obliged.

An hour later they left in a lover's bliss.

Scene Twenty-Nine – Coldplay – *Yellow*

The demands on Jack because of the public responses to his show, were rapidly escalating every day. Every person in his life wanted something from him; auditions, interviews, money, and the press followed him all over New York. His life was not his own. His mother called periodically, and if Jack was out with Mara, we'd talk about the same old stuff. She would tell me how she was losing her son, tell me a story of how Mara insulted her, and how they struggled to maintain their tempers, and how Mara was always threatening Jack's parents when they had small family arguments about how they would not see their grandchildren again. The notion of that absolutely terrified Dina. Usually, I was lost for words when she went on about her frustrations with Mara but I'd listen attentively. At the same time it angered me, and again I felt something shifting inside of me. Why the hell was everyone allowing this crazy person to dominate our lives? Why? Because her husband was famous? One night I changed the subject and talked about things that I hoped would ease her worry,

"When Jack and I worked on this screenplay it was like he came alive," I said.

"He told me how much he liked working with you. I love the screenplay. It's so spooky. But very funny, too. You have a great sense of humor," her mood changed to light and easy. She spoke about Jack as a boy and how he had an active imagination and would play for hours alone, making up stories and pretending.

"He was always happiest when he was creating when he was a boy. He really was a sweet boy. Never gave us an ounce of trouble. But he was always in his head. I'm glad you're his friend, Leonardo. I often fear something bad will happen to him."

"I'm glad I'm his friend too. Jack is a smart guy. I think he's going to wake up one day and look around and make serious life changes." I said.

"We can hope." Dina said.

When I hung up after talking to Dina, a part of me wished I'd told her that her son was a drug addict, a drunk, and that he needed help. I felt guilty and dishonest placating her as I did, but I wanted her to be happy, and free of worry because the fact remained that nothing was going to change as long as Mara was in his life. All the same, the yearning to confront Jack about his drug use grew and grew. He was tired all the time, cranky, didn't eat much, and he seemed even more lifeless than he was when I first met him.

Later that night, when Jack and Mara came to the top floor to go to bed I heard them in their bedroom. They were in deep discussion about our screenplay,

"I want to rewrite the scene in the morgue, and the opening scene of the screenplay is so weak," Mara said. My body tingled with frustration. It was almost like she wanted me to hear their conversation.

"I agree, baby," Jack said.

"Leonardo is a good writer, but we need to get darker with it. I think the entire film should have no music, and it has to take place in the 1930's. We should get started on that straight away," Mara said.

"Beth said that we should be hearing from Andre Brent soon," Jack said.

"I'm excited for us. You've done a great job on this screenplay, but it can be better." I sat up in bed; *us! US!* Excited for "Us!" Beads of perspiration were forming on my forehead. I wanted to march out into the living room, tell her off, and banish her to hell. Finally, there was silence for a few moments, then there was ruffling, next the sound of a bed creaking, and then Mara screaming hungrily.

"Do it! Harder! ! Give it to me!" It went on for a while, and I pulled my pillow over my head. Vomit hit the back of my throat. Suddenly there was something beside me. I jumped, Annie was standing by my bed, her face illuminated by the streetlights.

"Why is Mama yelling like that? Is she sick?"

"Yes, you mother is a very, very, sick woman, but she'll be okay, go back to bed, and cover your head with a pillow. She'll stop yelling soon. She doesn't want to see anyone tonight.

"Is she mad at me?"

"No, Annie, how can anyone be mad at you," I stood and guided her back to her bed and tucked her in. By that time, Mara's howling had stopped.

The next morning played out like a nightmare. I heard Annie wake up and get out of bed. Her usual routine was to wash up, make her own lunch, and when she had her coat on and was ready to go to school, she was then permitted to wake her mother so she could walk her to school. Some mornings I walked her, but on that morning Annie wanted her mother, "I'm worried about Mommy. Does she feel better?" I was brought out of sleep by the sounds of Annie rustling through her dresser drawers, she lamented and sighed, something was not going right for her. Her voice cried out, "Mommy." There was no way Annie was ready to be walked to school.

"Mommy, Mommy, wake up, I have no clean clothes to wear. Mommy!"

"What? Annie, you're going to be late for school again!" Mara's voice was startlingly loud and viscous. Cosmo started to cry. I jumped out of bed, and went immediately to his room. He was in my arms in seconds. Mara stomped past me and screamed, her voice escalated with each step she took. Her hair flying every which way. She was in her underwear, topless, her breasts flying left to right. Mara went into Annie's room, Annie followed, I did too, Cosmo still in my arms,

"Nothing to wear! Nothing to wear! Why didn't you find something last night! Why are you doing this now?!" Mara started to fling things out of Annie's dresser, items that Annie outgrown, or not school appropriate. Jack remained in bed, and Cosmo continued to screech.

"There is nothing clean for me to wear. I told you last night!" Annie said. Mara then pulled Annie into the laundry room and we followed. Mara pointed to a pile of Annie's dirty laundry. "Annie! This is your fault!" Mara picked clothes up out of the pile and threw them at Annie after inspecting each piece of clothing. Annie stood there helpless, as articles of clothing were being thrown at her, pushing them off her small body, crying. Mara found something that was semi-clean,

"Here, wear this!"

"But I wore that yesterday, everyone will laugh at me!"

"Oh, poor crybaby, acting all sad in front of Leonardo, so Leonardo will think I'm a bad mother, poor Annie, poor, poor crybaby Annie! Wear this and shut up." Cosmo had stopped crying, and I put him back in his crib.

"What about my lunch!" Annie wept while putting on her outfit.

"Annie!" Mara punched the wall. I immediately went to both of them.

"Mara, go back to bed. I'll get her lunch. It will be okay. I'll take care of it. I'll walk her to school." "Thanks, mate," Mara let out a big exhausted sigh, and sauntered back to bed. Jack's voice floated my way. "Mara what's going on?" his voice sleepy, distant.

I made Annie a turkey sandwich, washed her face, and we were off. It was spring, the sun was high, the sound of car horns surrounded us as they zoomed up 8th Avenue. The few trees that lined the street were starting to bloom,

"I can't do anything right," Annie said.

"That's not true. Mommy's not feeling well, that's all. It's okay, forget about it."

"She never feels good, and she's always yelling at me."

"Tell me about your Daddy?" I asked. I had only met him twice, his name was Henry, a chef at a popular upper east side restaurant. He was quiet, unassuming, serious, and gentle. Someone I could never imagine with Mara, yet he was probably a wild man who liked to be tied up, whipped, and told he was a bad boy.

"Mommy hates him. She says he is a nincompoop."

"What do you think of him?"

"I love my Daddy, but Mommy always picks on him. She always tells him that he might not see me ever again."

"Why?"

"Because he sometimes forgets to pay to see me."

"You mean he forgets to pay child support?"

"Yes, that's it. Daddy says Mommy and Jack have a lot of money."

"Would you ever want to live with him?"

"I think Mommy would be mad at me and never want to see me ever again."

"Why do you think that?"

"Because she told me she would never see me again because she hates Daddy."

Once in front of the school I went to my knees and hugged Annie tightly, "Have a fantastic day. You're a great little girl and I love you." She hugged me, her puny arms around my neck, she squeezed me hard. "I love you too, Leonardo." After I watched her walk into the school, I decided it was too tormenting to bear witness to any more abuse or chaos. I couldn't do it any longer. I was leaving Jack and Mara's life for good. It was going to be difficult, and the thoughts of parting from those children made the bottom of my stomach feel like hot coals, but it was time. Walking back to the townhouse, my phone rang,

"Darling, can you pick up some bagels, lox, and coffee for Jack and I and some smoked white fish. And some orange juice? I'm right knackered. And....can I ask you a huge favor? Would you mind washing the kitchen floor? It's filthy, you do such a good job, darling. Oh, buy some Mr. Clean, it works best."

"Okay," I said. My voice tense. I swiftly hung up. Something terrifying overcame me, it was like a massive storm cloud; a tunnel of absolute fury. There was no escape. All I could see was gray and black, then red. My mind spun. All logic vanished. I smashed the cell Mara had bought me on the sidewalk. I stomped on it madly; plastic pieces went flying, wires were exposed and buttons popped out. People were looking and I didn't care. What the hell was I doing? The same old song started playing in my mind. Was I that pathetic of a person? Was I this needy? Did I want to make it in show business this badly? Was I nuts? I was sick of my complaining and whining. The prison door was open. And the truth was, Mara and Jack could well afford domestic help, but Mara was too cheap and greedy to pay for it. She'd often say to me, "Why should I pay someone to clean my house? I can do it! I can take care of my own children! Who do these lazy show-business bitches think they are? People should do their own dirty work!" Hilariously,

Mara actually believed she did her own housework, and took care of her children. (Olena and I did the majority of her housecleaning for a third of the cost of a housekeeper) The very notion of her thinking she took care of her home and children was so beyond outlandish to Olena and I that at times we howled in uncontrollable fits of laughter. Mara was unbale to see the truth of who she was as a woman, a wife, a mother, a daughter, and a citizen.

When I was done demolishing the cell phone, I composed myself, picked up the pieces and threw them in the trash and walked to a cell phone store I'd seen and grungily took out my credit card and bought a new phone. I knew it would take me years to pay it off, but it was worth it. I had my own phone, my own number and even though it took a long two hours to set up my new phone, I had a sense of independence and pride. When done shopping for what Mara wanted, I started to think of a good excuse to tell her why I no longer had the phone she had bought me a few years ago and why I suddenly had a new one. When I arrived at the townhouse, as I expected, Mara was a wreak.

"Where have you been? I was worried sick! Sick! I called and called and called and no answer! I wonder about you lately! I really do! I used to be able to depend on you. Now look at you! I also wanted you to pick up some laundry detergent. Olena was supposed to do it, but she's so undependable these days too! I got you that phone for a reason, to answer it! Damn it, Leonardo! I was calling and calling and calling!" she marched from one corner of the room to the other. I stood holding the bag of groceries. I remained silent.

"Can you speak? Have you gone mad on me too!" she asked. One of her hands was on her forehead, the other on her hip. Her left foot extended, she tapped it on the floor waiting for my answer.

"After I dropped Annie off, I was walking back here, and someone pushed me to the ground. They grabbed the phone from my hand and ran off. I chased them for blocks. They got away. It was horrible. I was scared," My voice not very convincing.

"Oh darling, darling are you okay?" she came to me and rubbed my arm. Her eyes on the bag.

"I'm fine, just startled," I said.

"You could have at least called," she took the bag from my hand and looked inside and sniffed. "These smell lovely, divine. I'm famished."

"I couldn't find the words to tell you I was mugged. I didn't want to upset you," I said.

"I'm glad you're okay. You seem fine. Shall we call the cops?"

"No what could they do?"

"Well, as long as you're okay," she said with concern the size of the poppy seeds on the bagel she was shoving in her mouth.

"I'll get the laundry soap when I'm done with the floors."

"In the meantime, we'll have to get you a new phone. More money," she sighed irritatingly.

"I bought one."

"You bought one?"

"It's smaller. Updated. It's time I had my own phone. Everyone is getting them nowadays."

"Is that so?"

"I mean why should you pay for my new phone? That first one was very expensive."

"Indeed it was."

"I know. I'm sorry. I'll owe you babysitting hours."

"Well, fair enough," she said. I went for the bottle of Mr. Clean, the bucket, the mop and started swishing the mop around the floor. I felt horrible lying to her even though I did it to save my ass, but still it was wrong. The lemony smell of the cleaner almost knocked me over and my guilt vanished. She chomped on her bagel and kept eyeing me. Cream cheese gathered on the corners of her mouth.

"What's your new number?" she asked. I acted as if I didn't hear her.

"Leonardo? What's your new number?" she asked again. I glided the mop along the floor and made large wet circles that I imagine were secret exit ways I could jump into and escape.

"Leonardo!" she put her bagel down.

"What?" I stopped and looked dead pan at her.

"What is the bloody number?"

"What?" I said.

"Are you daft? The bloody number for your new phone! What is it?" she said. It took every muscular fiber in my entire body to not tell her to fuck off, but instead I glared at her. My hands tautly around the mop's handle, I gave her each digit slowly, methodically trying to control the anger inside of me . When I was done. She frowned at me. "You've gone completely bonkers! I don't know who you are anymore. You're odd!" she grabbed her half eaten bagel, the bag of bagels, her coffee and went to her bedroom and slammed the door. I continued to mop and started to make swirls on the floor that read SOS.

Scene Thirty – Eminem – *Lose Yourself*

I was babysitting when my mother called me at Jack's house.

"I read the screenplay you wrote with Jack, so did your father, and so did Emily."

"Mom not this again. You read it months ago. What's up?"

"We all read it again. Honey, last night, Jack's show was written by Jack again."

"I don't have cable. I told you. I don't watch it."

"It's on again Thursday night. You should watch it."

"Okay, what now?"

"Do you remember the scene when the Doctor removes the leg off a dead person and he has this surreal dream of legs chasing him around?"

"I wrote it, of course I do."

"Honey, it was on the show last night. He's stealing from you."

"Mom, it's a coincidence."

"No Leonardo, people don't have dreams about being chased by legs, he's stealing from you, and you're refusing to see it. I'm worried about you."

"He's my friend, Ma. So what? One scene."

"I know this is scary. I know it's hard to face, but he's stealing from you."

"It doesn't matter; we're going to get our screenplay produced It doesn't matter. Artists steal from one another all the time. Look, Ma, the baby is crying, I have to go," I hung up, and picked up Cosmo. He clung to me. He had this habit of nestling his head on my shoulder, it was real, pure and innocent, so different from what I was going through. I felt like his father, confident and proud of the care I gave him. After dinner, Annie started to choose what movie she wanted to watch. The phone rang. It was Jack's manager, Beth.

"Hey Leonardo, I've been trying to call Jack, no answer. Look, good news, Andre Brent read the screenplay; he loves it, and he wants you guys to fly out to LA and have lunch with him."

"Are you kidding?"

"No, I'm not kidding! He thinks it's the best thing he's read in years."

"Come on!"

"I'm serious. If he signs on to do this, it's a made movie."

"Oh, my God! I'll tell Jack as soon as he gets home!" All this bullshit was worth it. In addition, I had Annie and Cosmo in my life, I loved them, how bad was all this. Really?

"Thank you, Beth, thank you so much! I am so excited, I mean, wow! Wow! Andre Brent! I loved him in *Twelve Miles to Yonkers* and *Forget Chicago*! Holy cow, Andre Brent! Are you sure, absolutely sure he said he loved it?" I said.

"I'm sure. Yes. It's great news. I got off the phone with his manager moments ago."

"Wow, this is just great! Great! Wow!"

"Congratulations," Beth said.

"Thanks," I put Annie's movie in and placed Cosmo on a blanket in front of the TV. Annie lay next to him. I walked to the kitchen with the phone still pressed to my ear.

"You should have your agent call me, that's your friend, Gwen, right?"

"Yes. Sure thing. I'll call her when I hang up," I said.

"Leonardo, I'd like to talk you about something else," she sounded hesitant.

"Sure."

"I don't want Jack to know about this conversation."

"Okay," I said.

"I'm concerned about his drinking and whatever else he might be doing."

I answered her quietly, cautiously, "I don't know," I said.

"What's up with Jack and his sexuality?"

"What? What do you mean? Why is that important?" I asked.

"If the media gets a hold of some of the stuff I'm hearing, it won't be good."

"What stuff?" I asked.

"George Jenkins told me he sees day players, men in and out of his dressing room. He saw Mara come on the set with bottles of vodka and brandy. People are talking about him. There is a lot of money involved, and Jack could lose it all. One male day player said Jack fondled him and was making passes at him, the actor told his agent who told me. Please don't say anything. The actor doesn't want to say anything. He's scared, doesn't want to jeopardize his career."

"I don't know about any of that stuff."

"I know you're protecting him. I love Jack too."

"Then why don't you say something to him."

"It's his personal life. I only manage his career, not his life."

"Why doesn't George Jenkins say something to him if he's so concerned?"

"You're right. I only want him to be careful, fame can mess a person up."

"Look, okay, I do see things and it does bother me. I'm scared too."

"But he's your friend."

"You're his manager."

"Are you fearing that he'll get angry and bag the screenplay?"

"Are you fearing that he'll bag you as his manager?" There was a long silence. When Beth finally spoke, her voice had changed, it was real, troubled,

"I wish I was young again and did something else with my life. I have a client who got out of rehab two months ago. He went to LA to promote his movie, and there was a bag of coke waiting for him when he got to his hotel room. It's gross. I hate it. Then, there's the public, no one cares for them really, everyone envies them, everyone uses them, and it's so disgusting. Everyone is so desperate."

"I hear you," I said. My voice low, knowing all she said was true. We hung up and I told her Jack would call her back soon. I then called Gwen in LA.

"If you come to LA, we have to see each other. It's been awhile," Gwen's voice was melodious, positive as always, and it made me smile.

"Jack's manager wants to talk to you, too, at some point."

"Okay, sounds good. Talk soon," Gwen hung up.

I then called my parents.

"Mom, Dad, I'm almost positive I am going to Hollywood to meet with Andre Brent! Can you believe this?" I stood at the doorway to the room where the kids were now sleeping in front of the TV.

"Oh my God! Andre Brent is my favorite! Are you kidding?" my mom said.

"That's terrific, good job, Leonardo," my dad said.

"See, Dad, I told you I knew what I was doing."

After I hung up, I put the kids to bed and soon after I heard Jack and Mara. She was talking about our screenplay again; talking about other scenes that needed to be changed. I went to the guest bedroom before they could see me and pretended to be sleeping while absolute frustration and anger invaded me.

Scene Thirty-One – Peggy Lee – *Is That All There Is?*

A few days before we were to go to LA to meet Andre Brent, Jack called me and announced that Mara was coming to LA with us. I was walking up Broadway and had just bought jeans and a shirt for the trip. His tone was low and solemn, my hands started to shake. I stepped into a doorway, my eyes fixated on construction workers pouring wet cement onto a sidewalk being repaired. I became unsteady on my feet. Would this freak show of a ride ever end? "Hello, Leonardo, hello are you there?" he said. "Yes, I'm here, Jack." The construction workers spread the cement with wooden plows, made it smooth. Jack's voice was distant, a million miles away. "Mara has officially decided that she's designing the set for the movie. It might not be that bad, she has some good ideas," he said meekly.

I had no doubts that Mara was on a mission to ruin and destroy our brilliant screenplay. She was going to sabotage it, do all that it took to keep Jack under her dark callous wing and to isolate him from friends and family, and Jack would allow it because he was weak, because he wasn't man enough to stand up to her. So it was my time to be cut, for the kill, the slaughter, the abomination. "I'm sure it will be fine," I said to Jack, and hung up the phone. I walked across the street without looking. Cars beeped knocking me out of my haze of disappointment, aware that if I didn't cross the street my feet would be stuck in cement forever.

Scene Thirty-Two – Kinks – *Celluloid Heroes*

When we first arrived in LA my fear was replaced with joy. It was a sunny place and I was distracted by my glamorous surroundings. My mood shifted into optimism. Jack had gotten a suite at the Four Seasons Hotel in Beverly Hills. There were free snacks in fancy jars, a view of hills, big soft towels, and a giant pool that was blue and clear. When we checked in, I realized I was famished, "I'm hungry," I said. "Of course you are," Jack said. Mara puckered her lips in annoyance. "Sign lunch to the suite," Jack said. Mara stepped forward, "And stay down as long as you want. I want to be alone with Jack," she pulled Jack close. "We're going to shag."

I went to the Cabana Restaurant, ordered a big tropical drink, a double salmon sandwich, and let my body absorb the sun; it was warm and good, and I fell asleep. My phone rang, it was Gwen, "Welcome to Hollywood!" She told me she was coming in a few hours to pick me up to spend time with me. I went to the suite, took a bath and let water pulsate all around my naked self while I drank wine, and ate snacks; here was the fabulousness I wanted. My mind wandered. Was I *really* being taken advantage of by Jack and Mara? After all, Jack was paying for all this, who was I, some ungrateful swine?

Late afternoon, Gwen picked me up. It was fantastic to see her, she was still brilliant as I remembered. We hugged tightly, giggled over the excitement of seeing one another and talked about our budding careers. Gwen was bony and soft, delicate to the touch, but strong and practical. I trusted her. We had planned on a quick ride through the Hollywood Hills and off we went in her BMW convertible; sun and balminess was all around us as Gwen sped through the dusty hills. The smell of dirt and the dryness of the air made my nose itch. She drove for a bit and parked at the Hollywood sign. Before me the city of Los Angeles; it spanned for what seemed like forever, the view was lovely and perhaps one day my life would be here with my own family. My phone rang, and I saw that it was Mara calling. I answered. She sounded upset, desperate.

"How long are you going to be? Jack and I had a horrible fight, he's a manky, disgusting animal, he walked out on me. I need you here, darling. I can't be alone, everything is closing in on me, it's simply terrible!"

"I'm with my friend, Gwen. I have to talk to her about things, she's my agent and I—"

"Agent! Huh! They are all disgusting and vile! I need you!"

"I really can't," I kept my eyes on Gwen who was perplexed.

"You can't or you won't! We paid for this trip out here, we're practically handing you a career! Most people never get a chance like this, and you want to refuse me comfort for some agent that can be replaced at the snap of a finger, Jack will get you an agent! Are you serious?"

"Mara, it's not like that and-" Click she hung up on me. Without thinking, I dialed Mara's number.

"I'm on my way," I said.

"Thanks, darling I'm sorry I yelled, I love you. I'm so sorry! I am. You're brilliant you really are!" she said.

I explained to Gwen that Mara needed me back at the hotel, and she glared at me oddly, "What do you mean you need to go back? What's wrong?" I started to hyperventilate, my hands shook, I rambled. "I've messed up, I've really messed up. I need to get back to the hotel," I said. Gwen turned around, headed back and I told her everything, the entire story of Jack and Mara, and how I had babysat Annie. How I babysat Cosmo since birth, knew their habits, what they liked to eat, when they slept, when Cosmo first walked, and then Annie, how she was sweet and timid, a great checker player, and that I wanted to protect them and that I didn't know how, and that I was a lousy person and I couldn't leave them, but knew I had to. And how I had to get away from Jack and Mara because they were killing me, it was unhealthy and bizarre.

"I sacrificed my morals, my self-worth and for what? For what? Here it is, my dream coming true, and to hell with it! I didn't think I was going to fall in love with two little kids along the way. I didn't know." It was all coming out; the ugly truth.

"Leonardo, you don't need Jack Fresh, and loving those kids is worth so much more than some screenplay. Honestly, I know it sounds phony, but it's the truth. Those two children will remember you for the rest of their lives, no one forgets feeling loved and needed. That's a huge gift, a total blessing. I see all kinds of crap out here, people lie, they use each other, what you did for those kids was real, and it was important. Go to your meeting, stay calm, let it play out and see what happens. Relax. I will protect you on the business end of this, but you need to protect yourself and stop allowing them to use you."

Gwen drove down from the hills, she dropped me off in front of the hotel, and I kissed her goodbye. "You'll be okay," she said.

"Have a good meeting and call me when you get back to New York," she blew me a kiss and drove off. I stood watching her until she was completely gone. At that moment I don't think I ever felt so alone in all my life.

Walking into the suite I called out Mara's name, there was no answer. I checked all the rooms, heard music, it was coming from the bathroom. I knocked on the door.

"I'm back, are you okay?"

"You may enter," Mara said. Clouds of steam came toward to me, giggling came my way, stepping further into the bathroom, right before me in the whirlpool was a naked Mara and Jack with soap bubbles around their chests.

"Hi, man, sorry, Jack came back. I should have called you," she kicked her leg up and pranced her foot across Jack's chest. "He's come to his senses."

"Hi Leonardo. A producer friend of mine sent a case of Pino Noir from his winery in Napa. It's great stuff! Help yourself. It's very good," he lifted his foot and waved it in front of Mara 's face. "Look darling his and her towels!" she snagged Jack's foot and stuck his big toe in her mouth and playfully bit it. I shut the door, saw the case of wine, and contemplated grabbing two bottles and cracking one over her head and the other over his.

We met Andre at The Polo Lounge at the Beverly Hills Hotel the next day. The space was stunning; white table cloths, and white iron chairs, the scent of the air was sweet, flowery, yet hot and heavy. Beads of perspiration formed on my head. We sat near fiscus trees, the floor was smooth red brick, pink rhododendrons were everywhere. I wore a new pair of shoes, gray slacks, and a baby blue polo shirt. I gave myself a close shave, made myself neat and clean and ready. We sat and ordered cocktails. Jack sat very still, and remained quiet. Mara was back and forth to the bathroom and each time she returned she rubbed her nose. While waiting for Andre, a handsome man came up to us, he practically bowed as if he were before royalty, directing his attention to Jack,

"Hi, big, uh, fan, wanted to say hello." Jack shook his hand. Mara rolled her eyes while Jack signed an autograph. When the man left and was out of sight, Mara snapped at Jack.

"Too bad I came with you, isn't it? You could have given him a wank!" Mara said.

"Mara, not now," Jack said. A fly came toward me, and I swatted it away.

"I hate this town. I have such a headache," Mara said. She acted as if she *had* to be there, as if her presence was required, as if it was a chore, and she would rather be home with her children.

"You didn't have to come," Jack snarled. I kept a blank expression on my face and savored his every word, smacked the fly with the menu and killed it, then swiped it off the table.

"You would have loved to come out here without me, wouldn't you? Wouldn't you? So then you could shag every dumb actor or model that came your way, you want that, don't you!" she said. People stared.

"Will you please be quiet?" Jack said.

"You're such a ninny! Big TV star, big show off."

"All I said was you didn't have to come here, and you're acting like you had to. You didn't have to come here," Jack said.

"Fine, I'll go pack my bags and leave!" She got ready to leave and I tried to hide my glee and gigantic smile when across the dining room, Andre Brent came our way. Jack growled at Mara. "He's here, will you please calm down," Jack said.

"Asshole," She groaned and pulled her drink close to her in a self-satisfying way.

When Andre arrived at our table, we all stood. He was much shorter than he appeared on TV. His skin tanned, clear, he was in his late sixties. He almost didn't look real to me, like he was made from wax. He shook our hands and we sat.

"I was tense all morning thinking about meeting you guys. A big star like you, and a young writer. Why would anyone want an old actor like me in their film?" he said.

"Andre, I can assure you this is an amazing honor for us," Jack said. I nodded and agreed, and we all laughed anxiously. He ordered mineral water and Mara ordered another drink.

The three of us ordered the Salad Nicosie. Andre ordered a bowl of fresh blueberries, and popped them in his mouth as he talked, they made a slight cracking sound that I found amusing. I was instantly in awe of him, and listened attentively as he spoke. Mara, not growing up in America, didn't know or respect the fact that we were sitting with one of the country's most beloved actors; she seemed unaffected, but mostly threatened by the attention we were giving Andre. She picked at her nose, periodically, swung in her seat, monitored every word Andre said, and payed very close attention to Jack's responses, making faces that mostly consisted of disapproving grimaces.

"When I got the script I read it immediately, and I couldn't believe it. It's one of the best scripts I've read in years," Jack smiled at me, Mara snarled.

Andre was a kind, generous, and open man, with an elegant lovely demeanor, not only was he a revered actor, but a strong voice for women's rights, and he famously protested the Vietnam war. I told him of my admiration for his political work and work in film and TV. He shyly thanked me. Mara rolled her eyes as if thoroughly revolted with each word from my mouth. I sank in my chair. She was doing her best to shame me. Andre might have noticed the dynamic, knew we were anxious, so he started to make the conversation light, and easy. He talked about making a film with Marlon Brando, and from there he told stories about Rod Steiger, Mickey Rooney, and Bette Davis, and with each passing second I couldn't believe Andre Brent was sitting with us in a restaurant in Hollywood; it all seemed weird, but completely thrilling. My dreams, no matter how hard they were to achieve, seemed to be coming true. Andre talked about Jack's show, how he admired Jack's work, and thought he had a great range. He then focused on me, asked about my theater work, told me he loved theater, and that when he started out as a young actor, his only desire was to work on stage. We spoke of our favorite playwrights; Pinter, Ionesco, and O'Neill. He then told us he had no idea his career would take off as it did when he was young and in New York where he lived in a small apartment in the West Village. I was mesmerized by his decency, and modesty.

"I only wanted to act. I knew I wasn't that great looking, I knew I wasn't movie star material. I thought I would do regional theater work, but someone saw me in a play, liked my work, and the rest, as they say, is history. I was never desperate; it came to me. It's an odd business," he put a blueberry in his mouth. His voice rang in my ears; *I was never desperate; it came to me.*

"So, fellas, what are the plans with the screenplay?" he said, his smile full of childlike innocence, not an ounce of arrogance, I wanted his wholesomeness, his humble manner,

Jack began to speak, "Well, Andre, you're our first and only choice for Doctor Stein, we want you, and we hope that-" Mara cut Jack off. I arranged my seat to fully face Andre, my back completely to her, which was a waste of time because she practically leaned over the table into Andre's face.

"Well, I will be designing the movie, so let's start there," she said.

Andre giggled, "Okay." He eyed Jack and I. My face went blank. Jack became a beaten dog. Andre's eyes went to Mara, and he started to blink as if someone threw sand in his eyes. Jack's face went towards his salad, and Mara prattled on.

"I see it all done in tones of reds, something dreamy, surreal. The lighting dark, but misty. I envision the costumes to be circa 1930's, oh, Jack and I will be changing it to the 1930's. The entire movie is going to be brilliant," Mara said.

I'd had enough.

"We're not changing it to the 1930's, that has not been determined," I said.

"The reason I like the script is because it's a classic story in modern day New York. Wow," Andre roared with laughter. "Some of that stuff is very dark, some very funny stuff. Wonderful scenes."

"Thanks," Jack and I said in unison.

"I also think I'd put you in a wig," Mara piped up.

"A wig?" Andre said, he scratched the top of his head. Jack continued to stare at his salad, my eyes bore through Mara, she had white powder marks under her left nostril.

"Yes, a wig, a white one, big and curly, to make you look insane. Also, since you are a doctor in the film, you would wear your scrubs throughout, even when you take that long walk in Central Park with the first victim's mother, it's a positively perfect idea, don't you think? I see this as a very Ingmar Bergman film, like the *Seventh Seal.* I also think it would be brilliant in black and white."

"Black and white? Interesting," Andre started to look skeptical, undoubtedly he thought Mara was a lunatic which was messing with our credibility. His eyes started to move from me to Jack to the exit, we were losing him,

"You don't like that idea?" her voice defensive. I feared she was going to call Andre a nincompoop at any given moment. I was squeezing my hands under the table wondering if anyone could possibly despise a person as much as I despised her, was it humanly possible?

"I think black and white is fine, but it's hard to make movies in black and white. It's costly," Andre said. He placed more berries in his mouth. As she continued her cocaine generated twaddle my eyes were glued on Jack; *say something, stop your crazy wife, she's going to ruin everything! Say something, you whipped weasel!* Finally, Jack did speak up, and politely told Andre that Mara's ideas were only ideas. But Mara shut Jack up quickly, she gave him an eye that told him to be quiet. Andre's eyes widened, and she went on and on. I wanted to speak-up, rebuke her, defend our screenplay, but greatly feared Mara's ridicule, and being publicly shamed, also knowing if I did, I took a chance of being viewed by Andre as the cad, the chauvinist pig shutting down a woman.

And so, Mara continued. She took over the meeting, and silenced Jack and I each time we spoke. Slowly I started to detach and dissociate, slumping in the chair, I wanted to sleep the nightmare away. After an hour of that debacle, I could not deny the obvious. Mara had made a mockery of us, had taken our screenplay and misrepresented it in a way that confused Andre, and befuddled Jack and I. "These ideas are quite different than what's on paper," Andre said, and soon he was saying goodbye, and shaking our hands. We all stood, and when he left he rubbed his elbow apprehensively, and turned to us one last time. Bewildered, he gave us a wave from across the dining room. It was more than clear he was turned off by Mara's poor ideas, her nonsensical rambling, and overpowering personality. I was sure that if Andre was given the choice of meeting us again or having rat poison injected into his eye balls that he'd go for the injection.

Scene Thirty-Three – Dave Matthews Band – *Crash Into Me*

The Saturday night after getting back from LA, Mara and Olena came to the bar an hour before it closed to pick up the money from the register. They were smashed. While they waited for the bar to close, they sat at a table drinking, laughing, giggling, and gossiping. I stood at the bar and listened. The sight of Mara was tough considering LA had turned into such a fiasco. If my glares at her were sharp darts, she would have been depleted of blood in thirty seconds flat. When she spoke to Olena, she slurred feebly, "Darling I told you the second I laid eyes on Ian I knew he was a poof, it was all a disaster in the making. You were chasing him down like an absolute nutter so I never dared say a word," she gulped down her Cosmopolitan, Olena shook her head in disbelief.

"When I saw him today making out with that guy in Washington Square, it all made sense to me," she said.

"Bang to the rights, darling, bang to the rights."

"I should have known!" Olena finished her drink.

"Now really, darling, were you *that* gobsmacked?" she said. Olena spoke softly, "I guess not." Mara curtly called over to Rico and demanded two more Cosmopolitans.

"You'd have to be deaf, dumb, and blind not to know he was a bleeding fairy, you must wake up, darling! The real tragedy is that you didn't keep that sausage jockey around. Darling, listen to me, everyone knows poofs make the best of friends, they're like pets really, they'll do anything to please, it's absolutely fact that poofs are desperate for love and acceptance because the world deplores them; therefore, they're quite simple to train. It's a shame really, poor dears, they really are a girl's best friend. Who needs a mutt or a puss when you can have a poof." They both laughed hysterically.

I stood over them and put their drinks in front of them. Mara looked up at me, "Isn't that right, darling?" Mara eyed Olena mockingly, they both cracked up. "Anything you say, Mara," I said. "See what I mean, darling, they're agreeable too!" More laughter. I walked away, my stomach ached, it was on overload from producing extra bile with each word Mara spewed.

As the night came to a close, Olena left. Mara sat at the bar, slumped in her chair. On the stereo, was Queen's, *Don't Stop Me Now*. Mara spoke drunkenly about Ayn Rand, "Rand said it herself in her masterpiece, *Fountainhead*, a man's first duty is to himself! Screw everyone! People are selfish, and that's brilliant, it's the one absolute truth of life! To hell with you all!" She banged on the bar. Rico ignored her, then in the next breath she said, "I miss Larry. He was the only decent one out of all you wankers! I want Larry back!" She wept, and babbled, and made no sense. "Larry! Darling, Larry!" We ignored her. I picked up drinks to serve to my last remaining customer. "Deliver those drinks and get over here! We need to talk, mate! I mean it!" her voice venomous. I placed the drinks in front of the customers, went back to the bar where Mara sat. "What's up, Mara?" My voice full of annoyance. She put her hand on my shoulder, draped herself onto me. She could hardly speak.

"You don't love me. No one loves me. Larry loved me. But you don't!"

"Maybe it's time for you to go home," I said. She sat right up, and tried to point at me, but it was more like a sloppy twirl of her finger.

"Don't you tell me what to do, you nincompoop!" she forcefully jabbed her finger in my chest. "You're hurting me," I said.

"So bloody what! Hurting you? Big college boy, Mr. Perfect, Mr. Good Deed! You're a real drag! Really you are! Damn poofs are all alike!"

"I'll get you a taxi," I said. And that's when she slapped my face. After immediately realizing what she had done she held her hands over her mouth, forced tears, "Oh, shit, I didn't mean it, oh my God, I didn't mean it, darling, I swear!" she pulled me toward her, started hugging me. I stood with my hands by my side.

"Say you forgive me, darling, please, say it!" she said.

"I forgive you. You need to go home." Some of my steady customers called out to her and told her to stop, she looked at them, and pleaded, her voice full of false sadness, patting me kindly like a mutt or a puss.

"No, no, no, he's my good, mate, my good mate, Leonardo is my mate. My darling!" Her eyes rolled to the back of her head, she then slumped the upper half of herself on the bar. "I'm not good! Truly, bloody awful!" She covered her head with her arms, and wept and whined. Then, there was beautiful silence. We assumed she'd passed out. We didn't bother checking nor did we care. It was routine Mara. We continued to work until Rico locked the door. When we were ready to leave, Rico tapped Mara on the head,

"We're leaving. Hello. Wake up," his voice sullen. She raised her head, rubbed her face, cleared her throat,

"Bloody hell! Get your stinking hands off me! I need sales slips and all the cash. Now!" Rico put it all in front of her. She started to sloppily count. I was putting my coat on ready to leave.

"Wait! No one leave! All that was made was two thousand and thirty two? That's it?" "We made three thousand thirty-eight, you counted wrong," Rico said.

"Bollocks! Count it in front of me. Right this instant!" she said, and Rico did, he was right, three thousand thirty-eight.

"Plus I took ten bucks. I bought myself some dinner, sorry. He threw ten into the pile of money. Three thousand forty-eight," Rico said.

"You took ten dollars from the register?" Mara asked.

"I meant to put it back. There it is." Mara picked up the ten dollars, crumpled it and threw it at Rico, it bounced off his nose.

"I don't want your lousy money. I do everything for everyone, and people take advantage of me! Piss off! You're bent as a nine bob note!" She then pushed the cash across the bar and it went flying everywhere. She then stumbled out of the bar, her face smeared with mascara, her hair on ends, we giggled at her infantile dramatics, compiled the cash, and left for home. Walking out we saw Mara steps away, swaying in the gutter, illuminated by headlights, a black silhouette. She was a vison of outright idiocy, she tried desperately to hail a taxi, waving both her hands, screaming out, "Taxi! Taxi! Taxi! Blooming idiots! Stop! Damn it! Stop!" Her drunken voice jetting toward us. One taxi finally stopped, she crawled in and she was off. Rico shrugged, "See you next week," he said, "Yup, see you later," I mumbled, and we parted ways. It was the last time I would ever see Rico.

The next day, Rico was fired for stealing and was banned from the bar forever. He would not take my phone calls. I left him numerous messages, went to his apartment, but remembered that at that junction in his life he had been evicted from his apartment in Manhattan and was renting a room in a basement in the Bronx, I had no way of finding him. I went to Jack, pleaded with him to help Rico. He said his hands were tied, adding, "Rico turned into a junkie, and he needs help, there's nothing I can do. In time I'll reach out to him. But he stole from us, why are you protecting him?" his voice nonchalant. "He didn't steal from you. He needs you now, Jack," I said and he shrugged, "He'll turned up in six months sniffing around, don't worry about it." Finally, I called Julia, told her everything. I knew if she called, Rico, there was a chance he would answer his phone. A day or two later, Julia called me back, she was exhausted and distraught. She and a friend found Rico in his rented room. "It was filthy, he hadn't eaten in days, had no money, was withdrawing from coke, how could Jack allow this? Rico is supposed to be Jack's best friend? Are you kidding me?" She then told me they had gotten Rico into an inpatient drug rehab in the City, it was a horrible place, state run, but a start. She wanted me to ask Jack to pay for a private rehab. "Tell him his best friend is in a disgusting place, and he has no insurance. Beg him if you have to. Rico deserves more than this."

"Of course. I'll call him now," I said.

I called Jack and told him about Rico, "Okay, good for him," he said, and changed the subject quickly. He said he had a spectacular news that would make me very, very happy. "Get down here!" He hung up, and I jumped in a taxi, figured it would be better to speak to him in person about paying for Rico's rehab. When I saw Jack he was smiling, I was out of breath, determined, and concerned for Rico, nothing else mattered,

"Look Jack this is embarrassing. I'd never ask this if I didn't think it was important."

"What?" he said. I explained in depth about Rico.

"I'm not paying for that. Maybe Rico needs to learn a lesson. We warned him."

"Jack, he's your best friend."

"I'm not going to do it. He'll be fine."

"Julia says the place is horrid. Rico deserves more."

"I work hard for my money."

"Jack, listen, I'm telling you that Rico needs your help."

"Leonardo, I said no. End it. Now listen I have exciting news." He ran his hands through his hair and smiled widely at me,

"Andre said yes, but before he signs anything things need to be clear."

"I don't blame him for wanting clarity after the spectacle Mara made of us," my voice hostile, not so much about the situation with the crappy events in LA, but for his refusal to help Rico. I glared at him and he didn't seem to notice.

"Mara is very excited, I told Andre's agent we'd make things clear, and not to worry. And get this, Jaffe Cash might be interested in playing Doctor Stein's wife! Beth called an hour ago, and we might be having a meeting with her tonight. She read the script and thinks it's genius, but she has some reservations about the violence, I think we can convince her."

"That's good news. Can we talk about Rico?"

"Rico, Rico, Rico… Leonardo, this is great news about the screenplay. You should be very excited." Jack was beaming. Jaffe was on the "A" list of Hollywood actors, she was tiny, hot, cute, had short blonde hair. I was a huge fan, but at that moment I no longer cared about the screenplay,

Jack poured us a celebratory brandy. We toasted. I didn't drink.

"We won't take *no* for an answer, we'll convince her. Drink up!" Jack said.

"I don't feel like drinking," I said.

"Mara is so proud of you."

"That's good."

"Mara loves you so much, Leonardo."

"She slapped me. In the face."

"She told me. She said she'd never forgive herself."

"She shouldn't," I said.

"God you're in a mood! Let it go, this is all fantastic news. Let's have a drink."

"What about Rico?" I said.

"Rico, again? Forget about him, he's a loser."

"Jack stop it, the guy idolizes you."

"How is that my issue?" he said.

"Do you not care about him?"

"Are you not understanding me. Jaffe Cash is considering acting in our movie. Rico will be fine. Now listen, Mara and I changed the script to the 1930's, and we changed the Passover scene to a Christmas scene. We've been up for days," Jack said. He wiped his lips, poured more brandy. I wanted to slaughter him, and then Mara.

"But Doctor Stein is Jewish? Plus Andre was not keen on the 1930's idea," I said and covered my face in agony.

"I can handle all that," Jack barked,

"But I don't want it changed," I said.

"We made Doctor Stein convert into Christianity in a very short scene in the beginning."

"Jack, you can't change the screenplay without asking me first. This is our project, you and me, we both wrote this, not Mara. Those changes are wrong. It knocks everything off. I'm not happy. In fact, I am pissed off." I stood, started pacing, Jack's eyes had that usual glassy-high stare that meant a split in his awareness and presence and I didn't know who I was going to get next, it could be any number of his thirty-six personalities.

"Jack, something has to change, here. Look, we have to keep this professional. I do not want Mara involved in this."

"She's the designer, and I am the director," he said.

"And I am the writer, and I have been more than patient. There's a lot of bullshit I've had to deal with. I'm sick of being pushed around."

"You're exaggerating. Mara has been very nice to you. You sit in our house, eat our food, and drink our liquor."

"And I babysit your kids. I wash your clothes, I clean your house, I get your dinner. I'm at Mara's beck and call, helped you with the writing of your TV scripts, and did your job as father and husband."

"Fuck you," he said.

"No, fuck you! Your wife is destroying our work, and you're allowing it."

"She's not ruining anything," Jack's voice was full of disgust for me.

The phone rang. It was Beth. He hung up, spoke to me directly, his voice stern, but distant.

"We're meeting Jaffe in an hour at her place in the Village, and I am not happy with your attitude. I'll meet you out front in an hour. I need to chill out. And you never helped me write those scripts for the show, you better get that out of your head and never repeat that bullshit."

"Whatever, Jack. But in the meantime, you need to reconsider helping Rico."

"Why do you care so much about him anyway, he doesn't even like you."

"I don't care if he doesn't like me, he's a human being and he needs help."

"I'll see you out front in an hour," he went to his bedroom and slammed the door.

Emotionally wrought, I ran out of their apartment and walked up to 8th Avenue, my breathing heavy, hoping calmness would come. I called Julia.

"He said no, the prick said no. That narcissistic piece of dog crap said no!"

"He's disgusting."

"I have to figure a way out of this. It's madness."

"Leonardo, you know what you need to do. Do it. This was never you."

When the time came, I waited out front for Jack. He was twenty minutes late. When he came down, stress had taken him.

"Hi." I said.

"I'm sorry about all that," he said.

"It's fine."

"Mara is home, she wants you to stay home with her."

"I'll go meet Jaffe, you stay home with your wife," I said.

"But Mara feels left, out and Olena is not around to babysit."

"That's not my problem."

"Can you please run up and tell her you'll say hello to Jaffe and then make some excuse and leave and come home and be with her. It's the least you can do for Mara."

"I'll call her," I took out my cellphone.

"Can you please go up and tell her, please make this easier," he said.

I glared at him, "Go on, do it. Please. At least tell her in person," he said and he turned from me. And I mindlessly went upstairs. Mara was sitting on the sofa, holding Cosmo, and Annie was sleeping in her room.

"I'm going to meet Jaffe and come right back. We need to talk."

"I need to go with Jack, you stay with the kids. You don't know anything about show business. You'll ruin everything," she went to hand me Cosmo, and I backed away.

"I know, you're right, I'm a nincompoop, but all the same, I'm going, period." and I left not paying attention to the insults she growled after me.

On the taxi ride, images of Rico in a dreadful hospital room played out in my mind; was he okay? How bad was it?

Jaffe greeted us with a kiss, "Hi guys. Come in. Welcome." Jaffe was smaller than expected. She was mellow, genuine, her smile mesmerizing. She wore torn jeans and an orange halter,

"Hey how 'bout some wine?" she handed us glasses of red. She sauntered over to her sofas, and we followed her.

"Jack, I so dig your show, it's amazing."

"Thanks, Jaffe, nice place," Jack said.

Jaffe's place was wide and spanned the length of the top floor of a newly converted building that had once been a hospital. Large floor to ceiling windows provided a grand view of the West Village. There were two white sofas in the center of the space, purple throw pillows were scattered about. A glass coffee table was in front of us, a bowl of apples sat on top.

"The screenplay is really twisted, real dark, spooky," she crossed her legs Indian style, and sat in the center of one of the sofas.

"We really want you to be part of this project. We're almost positive Andre Brent wants to play the doctor," I said.

"He's almost thirty years older than me," she sat on her hands, a look of concern came.

"I know, but you'd be great together," Jack said.

"Putting casting to the side I feel a bit apprehensive about the violence," she said.

"I understand. We can make changes, so far we've changed it so that it takes place in the 1930's," He said.

"But more than likely we're not keeping it that way," I said.

"But good chance it's going to take place in the 1930's," Jack said.

"I like that it takes place in present day," Jaffe said. By the end of the meeting we had at least gotten Jaffe to think about being in the film, and Jaffe promised she would keep an open mind. Meanwhile, I wanted Jack to get the hell away from me. Once back in front of Jack's apartment, he asked me to come up.

"No, I want to go home."

"Why?"

"I'm tired."

"Forget about earlier." Jack ran his hands down my back, patted my shoulder reassuringly. I shifted away from him to get his hands off me.

"You're in love with me aren't you. It's okay," he said.

"Are you out of your tree?"

"We can get a hotel right now and be together, that's what you really want isn't it, that's what they all want," he then came to me and tried to kiss me on my lips, and I briskly pushed him away.

"Get the hell away from me, Jack. That's gross. What the hell!" I backed away from him.

"We're all stressed, it's going to be okay. I didn't mean any of that," he said.

"Jack, I'm done."

"Done with what."

"All of this," I said.

He let out a sigh, "Leonardo, let's have a drink, relax. Let's talk this out. You gotta understand that Mara cares for you, she wants to be part of the project too."

"You can't make changes in a script without permission from me."

"Will you come up? Let's talk,"

"Hell no!"

"I'm begging you. Come see the kids, they love you."

"I'm begging you to help Rico."

"Oh, my god, Rico again! You're unreal, okay, okay I'll help him. Give Julia my number and I'll have someone make arrangements. Now please just come up stairs," he said.

The minute we went upstairs we were bombarded with questions from Mara, "Where the hell have you both been!"

"She didn't say yes, and she didn't say no. But I think we can get her to do it," Jack said.

"Of course she didn't give you a definite answer, of course she didn't. You're both weak!" she said. My eyes bore through her, it was like seeing her for the first time, she was foolish, and pathetically tragic. She was off on a spin of nonstop reprimanding, and there Jack and I sat, our heads bowed, "Both of you are idiots for leaving me here alone! If I had been there, I could have gotten her to say yes! I know you want to shag her, I know you do, Jack!"

"Calm down!" Jack said to her.

"What did she say? Go on, tell me!" She pointed her finger in Jack's face.

"She wants to think about it," Jack said. He pushed her hand out of his face and walked away, and she tailed him around the apartment.

"She's an idiot! Think about what? You have to convince her. She's a dumb actress, a puppet like you, but her name is big money, Andre is big money! Bigger the stars, more money we make! You cannot take no for an answer. Think of the money, Jack! The money! We can buy that home in California, another one upstate. Think!"

"I want to give her time," Jack poured himself a drink, offered me one. I refused. "You want to shag her, don't you? I know you do! You want to wait and see if she'll let you, and then you'll beg her to be in this trite film! Tell me, damn you!" She pointed her finger in his face.

"Will you stop it!" Jack said in a low, defeated voice.

"I need to take Jack out for a drink. He can't think here. He's not making sense!" Not waiting for my answer, Mara practically pushed him down the stairs while telling him he was a failure and a spineless man.

After they left, I went into Annie's bedroom and stood in the doorway, she was sleeping soundly, my heart sank, poor kid, she was so sensitive, a good little girl with a big heart who yearned for tenderness and love. I had a constant worry about her, and should have done more. I went into Cosmo's room, he was rocking himself into one of his deep slumbers. Mara wasn't as brutal to him as she was to Annie. That gave me some relief, but whose to say what the coming years would bring for him. At that moment my mind played tricks on me. I saw Annie and Cosmo twenty years from now; would they be addicted to drugs, would they be messed up, mixed up, confused and feel they were never loved properly, would they remember me? Would they tell me one day that I should have saved them from their lunatic parents, would they be criminals, land in jail, rob banks, be vandals, or do whatever they could for the world's attention? I sat myself in the middle of the living room floor and brought my hands to my face. My dreams had come true; I had my kids, but they weren't mine. I had my screenplay, but it was being taken away by a crazed drug addict.

Scene Thirty-Four – Gladys Knight & The Pips – *Midnight Train to Georgia*

My first week back in Boston I stayed with my parents in my childhood bedroom. I read, slept, and detoxed from a life that I was glad to be free of. I told my parents not to worry, that it was the flu. They left me alone. I made it clear to them that I needed time to think and make some kind of life plan. Most mornings there was a pit in my belly. The absence of Annie and Cosmo hit me hard. They had been in my life for three years, and now I was cut off from them. It was like death. After weeks of being home, the loss and absence of them let up, after all, I knew they were alive, I knew that there were other people in their life that loved and cared for them; they had their grandparents, Annie had her dad, they had Olena. They would be okay.

I found a waiter's job in Boston. I went through the motions of humbly serving steaks and creamed spinach to successful people my own age, collected tips greedily, and saved my money and wrote a new play in my free time. My mind started to come back, and my thinking actually was logical. I was on a writing frenzy. Each morning my feet were on the floor by nine o'clock, instead of three-thirty in the afternoon. The morning sun greeted me merrily; it seemed brighter, more orange, and the sky was a deeper blue, everything was clear and focused. Yet I had moments when serving food to my customers, or driving to work or laying in my bed when thoughts of the day I left

Jack and Mara played out in my mind over and over. There was the occasional dream of them and I would wake and become panicky. In those seconds of fright, I missed them, longed for them, but knew my days with them were over because they fed the unhealthy hungry part of me and no matter how often my emotions flip-flopped, I knew there was no choice but to stay away from them.

The day after we met Jaffe, I fed Cosmo and Annie breakfast, and soon after Annie mournfully told me she had a ton of homework to do, and placed a pile of worksheets in front of me, her head in her small hands, her eyes watered, tears dropped. I reassured her that I was going to help her, but she kept crying, "Why are you crying, I'm going to help you." I said. "The kids in school call me dumb, and they call me names." My heart sank to my toes, "Well those kids are idiots, you're lovely and smart and good. You're the best kid I know." She cried louder, "Mommy told me last night you were a nincompoop! I hate Mommy and I want to live with my Dad or you. Can I live with you?" She started whaling, and it became loud and sorrowful, it seemed like all the disappointments in her little life had reached a crescendo, and it happened on the worst possible morning. I wondered if in her little mind she instinctually knew I wouldn't be seeing her for quite a while. Why would Mara tell Annie I was a nincompoop the night before? Did Annie hear us arguing that night? My plan that morning was to help Annie with her homework, tell her that I would not see her for a while, write some sort of letter to Jack and Mara, leave, and be done with this pitiful situation. But it wasn't that easy.

When Mara heard Annie's droning, things happened so rapidly there was no time to process what was taking place. Everything spun into madness. I could have left, but I was compelled to stay and to somehow protect Annie. Within seconds she viciously shook Annie and started hysterically screaming at her; she was lazy, she was no good, she was stupid, and she said that it was not surprising she had no friends. I was holding Cosmo. Tears streamed down Annie's face, she was crying out for me, "Leonardo! Leonardo! Leonardo!" My stomach did quick harsh flips while Mara brutally pulled Annie into the living room and made her sit on the sofa in front of the giant book case. Mara then pointed her finger in Annie's face, her hair askew, mascara from the night before running down her cheeks like a black murky river, her blood shot eyes bulged out, she looked like an escapee from the depths of hell. "You want to be lazy! You want to act dumb! You want to be selfish, bloody hell!" Mara found the biggest book on the bookshelf and threw it on Annie's lap, then told her to read the entire book and when done reading it, Annie she was to give a verbal report on what she had read. Mara meant it. I looked at the book on Annie's lap. I remember skimming through it years ago, I couldn't read the first page of that colossal book even if I tried; the print was fine, and the book very old and intricate, a collection of the philosophical theories of Nietzsche, Rousseau, Socrates, and Spinoza,

"Bollocks! Stop your whining, grow up, this is life! You damn nincompoop!" Her British accent thick and cutting, it sent chills down my spine, and it fed my anger. "Leonardo!" Annie screamed.

"Leave her alone!" I shouted loudly, and so furiously, it was like my voice came from some other place than me. Annie stopped. Mara stopped. All went dead. "Leave her alone. I'm serious, she's just a little girl. She needs your love, not your constant criticizing," I said. Mara walked toward me slowly as if she had a knife in her hand and was going to cut my throat.

"She's my daughter, have you gone bloody mad? You can't tell me what to do in my house." I walked directly toward her, our faces met, and that's when I saw what existed inside of her; hatred. It glowed from her and it was blinding, raw and bold and in dark colors, but it wasn't hatred for Annie or me or anyone else in her life, it was hatred that she had purely for herself. At that moment I knew she existed to make others feel as bad as she did, it was her life's mission to ridicule and shame, it gave her power, and it sickly eased her own inner pain,

"Annie is perfect, she's sweet and kind and you're jealous of her because you don't understand such lovely attributes, you think they're weak, and small, but they are grand and far beyond anything you would ever be able to comprehend. You disgust me."

"How dare you talk to me like this! You nincompoop!"

"Quiet! You're a bully, and you're cruel and unfair, and mean. I'm done with your lies and deceit, your nastiness, and every other stinking thing about you. This is a warning. You best never treat these kids poorly again because from this day forward I'll be watching you until these kids are old enough to walk out of this house and get away from the likes of you and Jack. You need to know that my mission from this day forward is going to be their safety. Do you understand?" I pointed my finger at her, and she backed up, and for a split second fright washed over her face. Jack came into the room.

"What the hell is going on? Why are you yelling, Leonardo?"

"I'm yelling because I am sick of your wife and the way she treats Annie and me, and everyone else in your life. Open your eyes, Jack."

"Get out of my house!" Mara came towards me, Jack stood between us.

"You're sick," I yelled.

"I want you out of my house!"

"I want to say goodbye to Annie first."

"Everyone, calm down," Jack said.

"You're going to allow him to talk to me that way?"

"Mommy, stop!" Annie cried out.

"This is your fault!" Mara screamed at Annie.

"It's never Annie's fault. Annie you're a special girl, you must never forget that."

"Annie go to your room, and you stay there. And take your brother with you."

"I don't want Leonardo to leave."

"Annie! Move now!" She ran to me, hugged me, took Cosmo and left for her room.

"Now listen, I'm going to leave, but I'm going to say a decent goodbye to Annie and Cosmo first and if you don't like it, then call the police because I would love nothing more than to have a chat with the police. I love your kids, they mean everything to me. It's the only good that will ever come from either of you. You don't know how lucky you are to have them, it makes me sick that you don't know that," I left the room.

I sat next to Annie in her room, I picked up her notebook and wrote my number down.

"I'm going to go to Boston for a bit, but I'll be back."

"Do you have to go?" she was sobbing.

"Yes, but I'll come back and visit."

"Okay."

"I still want you to come to Boston one day and hang out with my niece and nephew."

"Okay," her voice was very low; she sniffled and wiped her nose with her sleeve.

"Olena will be here, and Grandma Dina and Grandad Eddie, you have everyone."

"I know," her voice became even lower.

"And I'll call you, too."

"Okay."

"We're still friends, forever. I want you to remember that."

"Everyone leaves because they hate Mommy. That's why you're leaving."

"It will all work out, everything always does." I put my arms around her and gave her a squeeze, she didn't respond, her body was limp, lifeless.

"Annie, I have an idea, ask your Daddy if you can live with him."

"I told you. Mommy would never let me."

"You could ask again. Ask him today, call your daddy today."

"Mommy would hate me. I'm scared to do that."

"You don't have to be scared anymore. Sometimes you have to stick up for yourself, like in school when those kids say bad things to you, tell them to be quiet, and guess what? Anyone who doesn't like you is a nincompoop!" I said. She smiled sadly, and I kissed the top of her head. "Annie, I love you. You're the best girl I know, and you make sure you never forget that. Promise?"

"I promise."

"Double pinky swear promise," I said. We locked our pinky fingers, shook and I left her. I then went to Cosmo's room, picked him up, kissed him, and said goodbye. He pulled on my ears, playfully fingered my face, and all I thought of was that he was so young that he would never remember me or how much I loved and cared for him. I would never forget either one of them.

Those last moments with Jack and Mara are foggy and distant, but I recall that when I walked out of their house, Jack balanced himself against the kitchen counter, his face expressionless, his blonde curly hair a mess, his mouth open, trying to comprehend all that had taken place the night before and moments prior. My eyes on him, all I could think of was here, he was, Jack Fresh, a man with great fame, money, good kids, a nice home, and he was the saddest looking person I have ever seen. It became clear to me that he married a woman who would be his lifelong embodiment of punishment, his self-induced reminder to himself that he was worthless, and undeserving of all his good fortune and to see that in him shook me to the bone because it was exactly who I was, too. What other reason could it be? Why would I stick around such abuse and chaos. I deserved better.

"Jack, you need to stop. You need to take care of yourself. It's sick. All of it," I said.

"Help me, man, help me. Bring me to a rehab. Throw me in with Rico." He was acting, and badly, there was no truth in his voice, it was empty, shallow, meaningless, mere words.

"I'll take you now, we can find a rehab, a good one, we can call your parents and they can come and take care of Annie and Cosmo and we can help Mara. She needs help."

"My love for Mara is inconceivable. Leave her out of this. You don't understand our love." He stepped closer to me as to intimidate me, but I stepped closer. God! I was sick of his phoniness. His bullshit. His lies and rotten deceit. At that moment he mutated into lump of slime right before my eyes. He disgusted me and I wanted to punch him, really hard, in the face.

"Love? Look Jack, this pretentious and deceiving bullshit is not working anymore with me. Jack you cheat on Mara all the time. Everyone knows, she knows, she's not stupid. This isn't some romantic French novel. This is reality. You're both addicts and you need help. If you love her, help her, for fuck sake! Help her!"

"I resent this, all of it," his voice calm, collected.

"Would you like to know what I resent? That you think you've fooled people. Okay, the public maybe, but not the people who know you. Especially not me," I said. He shifted his chin, put his hands on the back of his head and nodded from left to right while letting out, what seemed to be, small gasps of fear. As he was about to speak, Mara entered the kitchen. "Leonardo, we should talk. I don't like this. I've been unreasonable, bloody hell, I've been unreasonable! But you've changed ever since you wrote this screenplay, your ego has inflated. You need to stop and come back to who you really are," Jack kept his eyes on me.

I shook my head in revulsion. "Enough," I said, and left.

While standing outside the building that I had demolished a few years ago, I had a sinking feeling. It would be a place I'd never forget, a place that housed a world renowned TV star and his wife, and besides the little children that resided there, regrets instantly came. I convinced myself that day it was all over, but little did I know I would return to that townhouse in a year.

I wandered the streets of New York for hours. My mind raced with a mixture of emotions and I couldn't seem to focus. I was happy, then sad and back to being happy. For the last four years of my life, I'd endured a great deal of heartache, was used, and abused, all of which I willingly accepted. I refused to think of myself as a victim because I chose to keep myself captive for every co-dependent, self-loathing reason imaginable. All those unanswered questions I had for the past few years pricked my mind like tiny daggers; the unfairness of bad people being rewarded with the better things of life and why good people were sometimes left behind. Was I a good person? Did I deserve more? Yes, and yes I told myself. I would get through all this bullshit. I needed to get out of New York and focus on my life. I was 28 years old-old enough to know that all the rotten things in life are temporary, and that nothing remains the same. It was a matter of getting through those bad moments that felt paralyzing. Life was unfair, pure and simple and I had to accept it. I walked down to the West Village, and crossed over to the East Village. Late afternoon and semi-darkness fell over the city. A slight October chill was in the air, the sky a brownish orange, my hands were in the pockets of my jeans to keep them warm. My mind became calm; relief and clarity came and I felt ready for a long sleep. I headed home. I could feel myself breathe and finally, my nerves were settled and sparks of joy went off all around me. When I thought about how I told Mara off. I giggled a bit; all those years of anger and frustration finally out of my mind and placed back on her. I wish I had said more to her! But wow, did I really say all that to her? Did I really stick up for myself and Annie and Cosmo? Before long, I was going back to the West Side from Gramercy Park and I ended up in the West 40's, I was going to take the Number One train uptown. My head looking downward, my eyes on my feet, a slight smile on my face as I walked and contemplated my next move. Abruptly a loud and thundering chanting came from behind me. It stopped me in my tracks, shook me to my core, it was a collection of many angry voices that were deep and guttural. Policemen on horses were coming toward me, and I heard the sound of police whistles. Within seconds, from behind me, like water gushing into an empty space, thousands of men and women filled the street. They were marching, and holding signs that read, *Homophobia Kills, Stop Hate Crimes, Where is your rage?* All of them repeating, *Justice Justice Justice! No more! No More! No More!* I had never seen unity and anger in such a large number of people. I was awestruck, and immobile, and managed to step into a doorway while more people passed me, all of them shouting and marching. A young man my age stepped in the doorway to tie his shoelaces, he put his sign next to where I stood, *Justice For Matthew* it read. "What's going on," I asked him. He looked up at me, and told me a young gay man was killed in Wyoming. "Haven't you heard?" I shook my head no. "He was tied to a fence, beaten, and left to die. He was killed because he was gay. Are you gay? Why aren't you marching? Every queer in this city should be marching! Are you queer? Are you?" he asked. I slowly nodded yes. "Then where the fuck is your rage!" I stood motionless, and he shouted at me again, "Where is your rage!" He came so close I could smell his breath, dry and sweet, like grape soda, his eyes filled with a combination of pride and sorrow, "Wake up! Wake up! Where is your rage!" He looked right through me. "I didn't know. I didn't know…someone was killed," I said, my voice meek. "Don't just stand there, brother! Rage!" he turned from me, picked up his sign, and held it up high, and shouted louder, "Justice For Matthew!" and off he marched. Without much thought, I stepped out from the doorway and joined the crowd. My first steps were awkward, my legs felt numb, and I felt shyness and embarrassment, but it only lasted seconds. Soon my self-consciousness vanished and I was part of it all, it wasn't about me anymore, it was about all of us, we were all Matthews. I started to shout loudly, words rolled off my tongue. I couldn't distinguish my voice from the others as it merged and became one, "No more! Where's your rage! Justice for Matthew! No more! Where's your rage!" My arms firmly reaching toward the sky, fists clutched, demanding, marching, and proud. There I was. Me. A gratified queer. I wasn't alone anymore. The more I screamed, the more my temper elevated. Finally anger had arrived in explosive volcanic proportions. My mind was inundated with fury over the mistreatment of gay people. At that moment I realized

I never truly comprehended the enormity of disappointment and discontent that lived inside of me. Where the hell had I been? I had ignored myself the years spent with Jack and Mara; allowed myself to crawl into a cocoon of abuse that felt safe and normal and deserving. They had taken advantage of my vulnerability, my kindness and good heart. But it wasn't only them to blame, it was mostly me and the false beliefs I had of myself that fed my life choices. I could have been loved properly. There were good gay men who tried to date me, but I never valued myself enough to accept their affections. Most off all, there was my nagging regret for not feeling worthy enough to stick up for myself during my school years. From a very young age I had allowed the world to push me down and keep me down, but I could have stood. I could have taken the hands of my gay brothers and stood proud, but I valued my shame more than my pride and self-perseverance. The rest of that evening I marched with honor, "Justice for Matthew, Justice for Matthew!" I yelled and screamed and shouted and it came from my feet up to my gut and into my lungs and poured out of my mouth with freedom and ease. My voice, powerful, forceful and mighty, it carried through the streets of New York like a roaring lion. I hoped my growl was the loudest of them all; one the entire world could single out and hear. Later that night my throat was sore. I could hardly speak, but when morning came my voice was back but it sounded different; conquering, full of glory, adult, manly, grounded, confident and ready for what would come next.

Scene Thirty-Five – Abba – *Knowing Me, Knowing You*

I was back home for about a year, it was summer, and Boston was in the middle of a massive heat wave. The exaltation of being home started to fade. I stated to worry about my nonexistent career and personal life, but told myself to be patient. I was in the process of great change. After all, learning to love yourself is not the easiest thing to do after years of believing you're a shithead. I wore T-shirts around town that said stuff on them like, *Gay and Proud*, *Gay Power*, and *Queer* and my favorite *I'm Not Gay but My Boyfriend Is.* No one seemed to care, much to my chagrin, because I was totally prepared and honestly dying to tell off any idiot homophobe that dared to give me any trouble. Plus *Will & Grace* was on TV and everyone was starting to really love the gays and I was cashing in, finally.

At my sister's annual Fourth of July party, I cracked a molar on a walnut that was inside a brownie. When it happened, I was so completely enraged that the idea of clubbing myself to death with a flag pole was probably the least violent way I wanted to do away with myself. The next day while sitting in the waiting room at my dentist, I flipped through a cheesy celebrity magazine and my eyes caught a photo of Jack and Mara at some glitzy award show. Immediately, my back stiffened. I stared at the photo of them for some time until it became a blur, and a sad longing emerged. They were on a red carpet with gleaming smiles, both squeaky clean, a model of all American perfection.

When I finally brought myself to read the small article under the photo my longing was replaced by a surge of a familiar darkness that made its way out of hiding.

... Jack's wife Mara was born in London and is a "An Art scholar." Jack says she is the glue that keeps the family together. "Nothing matters but my family, I am a family man at heart, we stay in almost every night and cook elaborate dinners, and we play games or watch old movies together with our children. We love children, perhaps one day we'll adopt more, after all, children give the world hope. Fresh and his wife are devoted Buddhists.

More lies jumped off the page in a mismatch of gross contradictions, my breathing increased and I became tense. I tried not to completely break down, it was such a rotten hoax played on the world, nothing made sense. That familiar feeling about how life was unfair and there was no justice in the world started to consume me like a flesh eating bacteria. My mood became despondent, and bitter. I asked myself over and over; why do bad people get good things? Why are Jack and Mara blessed with the better things in life when they are rotten to the core? Why am I hanging on to this? Didn't I resolve this long ago? But damn there I was again thinking how Jack Fresh achieved his goals in the most sinister of ways, it was unfair and wrong, over and over those same words, unfair and wrong, unfair and wrong... This wasn't how it was supposed to be. Most of my life I was taught that goodness was met with goodness. Was this another lie? After my internal tantrum, I left the dentist office wanting to kick telephone poles and shout to strangers about the unfairness of the lousy world I lived in. While driving home that day in my shit-box of a car; the muffler practically dragging along the streets, the air conditioner stopped. I madly pressed buttons, hissed and cursed, but to no avail. Perspiring profusely, my anger grew. This was it? This is what awareness was? This is life? Bad people get good things? Air conditioners break in record breaking heat? Teeth crack? Fuck this.

I pulled into the driveway of my parent's home. My mom was planting her flowers and my dad was watering the lawn. They seemed happy and content. When they saw me, they stopped what they were doing and waved. I felt bad that they had such a colossal failure for a son, and actually thought they were kind of dimwitted because they thought I was perfect. I wanted to bawl, not just cry, but pull my eyes out of my head and ring them dry. I exited the car, "Dad squirt me down!" I said, and stood before him, "Go on seriously, wet me down." My arms extended like some kind of sacrificed martyr, my parents roared with laughter. My dad brought the hose up and water gushed all over me, my mom shook her head in glee, my dad chuckled as I danced under the water. I forced a smile, but felt myself cry, I groaned and bellowed like a man on fire, until every inch of me was wet and dripping with icy water.

"Feel better?" my dad asked.

"Yes, that was brilliant, thanks, darling," I said trying my hardest to hide my sadness, while using my best British accent, I walked toward the house. "Hey Queen Elizabeth, go through the basement! Don't you dare get my floors wet," my mother called after me." I faked a laugh, "Cheers mum," and off I went to the basement, stripped down, and when I was completely naked, the house phone rang. "Hello?" I said, my eyes scanning my father's work table, my mother's petunias waiting to be planted. "I'm looking for Leonardo," said the voice. "This is he," I said. "My name is Helen Delany artistic director of Liberty Stages in New York, I finished reading the play that you submitted a while ago, *Come and Get it*, do you have an agent?"

When September approached, my family was overjoyed. I acted excited in front of them, but as my day of departure for New York drew near, hesitation stung me. I was afraid of running into Jack and Mara. Although New York is overwhelmingly large, there was a synchronicity there that sometimes terrified me, you never knew who you would run into.

Helen Delany and I immediately became fast friends. She was sincere and thoroughly dedicated to good theater. She had started the theater company on her own thirty years ago after a divorce. She raised two children on her own, and had a knack for raising money for her small theater company. The best part of it all was that she respected me, my education and talent. When I first got back to New York I lived in a small European style hotel on York Avenue, but when rehearsals started that winter, Helen invited me to stay with her; I happily obliged.

We came from entirely different backgrounds. Helen used the word "summer" as a verb, which I thought was hilarious. Her roots were steeped in wealth. Her family from upstate New York. It was amusing that she thought everyone had her kind of money. "My friend is selling a lovely pied-à-terre on 36th and 2nd, if you would like to take a look. I can arrange a viewing, it's a real steal at 1.2." *Sure Helen I'll write a check for it now.* Perhaps she thought I had money because of the fancy graduate school I went to, but little did she know I would be paying that loan back for the rest of my life. I was never exposed to the kind of money Helen had, or the lifestyle. It fascinated me, but I didn't indulge my fascination nor was I impressed by it. Money and position meant nothing to me now. I had learned from my experience with Mara and Jack to stay close to who I was, where I came from, to pay attention to my motives, and to keep all parts of my life truthful and wholesome.

Helen had shoulder length gray hair, and kept it straight and simple, her eyes a cornflower blue, she was thin and graceful. She was quirky and different, unequivocally positive. She didn't spend much money on clothes, but wore expensive French perfume. She smelled like Lily of the Valley and irises. She advocated that, "perfectly fine things" could be found at the thrift stores. She was forgetful, clumsy, giggled easily, and was amusingly hyper. She'd forget her cell phone almost daily, would lose her house keys, and forever have a locksmith at the house with whom she was on a first name basis. She would mistakenly put her red lip liner on her eye brows, thinking it was her eye brow pencil, and I would jokingly say "You did it again" and I'd hand her a Kleenex, and she would chuckle, "Thank you, dear." She was always hurried for meetings, cocktail parties, or dinner with friends, and consistently, put her blouse on inside out.

After my first reading at the theater, she had to run to a cocktail party immediately after, she unzipped a small duffle bag, pulled out a sequined dress, went into the bathroom, slipped it on, came out, I zipped her up, she brushed her hair, put on some lipstick, "I'll see you back at my house in forty-five minutes. I have to make an appearance at this darn cocktail party." She jumped in a taxi and was off.

Helen's home was a four level brownstone, with original works of art and French antiques, and with a restaurant type of kitchen. Throughout our friendship I often found myself cooking for Helen in the evenings. She'd watch as I made different kinds of dishes, and she'd talk to me and tell me stories. "Mother always instilled the importance of creativity, I was very lucky, when I was a child I would spend hours playing with other children and putting on plays. Father had a small stage built for me in our backyard at our summer home in South Hampton."

"I used to do that too, I put on plays in my father's dirty garage, no one came because I had no friends," I said. Helen thought I was joking.

"Where did you summer?" she asked me one day.

"We went to Cape Cod and stayed at the *Holiday Inn*. Right off Route 6."

"I love the Holiday Inn; there is no sense in spending money on those big hotels," she said.

That fall we worked constantly on rewrites. More workshops followed through that winter. I spent much of my time at Helen's house, isolated. That first month back in New York was vastly different from my last experience, and my view of the City changed. New York was a hopeful, thrilling place with endless possibilities. Darkness lifted. I was swaddled by light, and possibilities.

Peter called and we made arrangements to meet at the Monster in the West Village. We embraced, proclaimed how much we missed each other, ordered mojitos, and chatted for hours. He looked older, and the usual twinkle in his eye was gone; replaced with age and wisdom, but he was happy, or at least said he was. He had grown a beard. He said it made him feel closer to Larry. "I know it's odd, but I loved Larry's beard!" He also let his hair grow. He looked lumberjackish. "Death changes you in profound ways. I don't worry about things as much as I did. I've been volunteering at a gay teen homeless shelter. My priorities are so different now, it's like Larry is putting all these wonderful ideas in my head. Everything I do is for Larry, for both of us. I want his life to have mattered," he said. He also said he was forcing himself to date, but confessed he didn't want another relationship, and sex was starting to bore him. "It feels empty now. Sometimes I think Larry was the only one for me. There will never be another, Larry. I'm kind of a loner, and guess what? I like it!" he said. We talked briefly about Charlie. I told Peter that I would call him in time but that I didn't want to give him the wrong idea, or make him uncomfortable. He had made himself clear the night we had slept together. "Charlie's an old scaredy-cat. He's been hurt a lot," Peter said, and then told me that Charlie was overjoyed about my play, and was excited about seeing it. He mentioned they were both thinking about renting a house in Provincetown that coming summer, and if they did, they wanted me to visit. The night ended with a walk up Christopher Street, and a slice of Pizza at Two Boots, another embrace and a promise to see me opening night of my play.

My play was to open in April, and I would be staying with Helen for the duration of the show. I sat in on the auditions, then the rehearsals, rewrote madly, and sometimes I'd sit and watch as the set was built or while actors were being fitted for costumes. I observed as Helen directed, was overwhelmingly satisfied that she understood my play. I accepted her respect and professionalism, appreciated our friendship that was based on mutual admiration for each other's work. I savored the excitement of every second and told myself over and over, it was happening, it was real, my play was being produced in New York and I didn't have to mop anyone's dirty floor.

My parents and my sister and her husband came to New York for opening night. Julia came early and brought me roses. We hugged long and hard. She was up for a movie part, a minor role, but a small scene with Harrison Ford. I was thrilled for her. After greeting my family and their smiling proud faces, I brought them to their seats. I became nervous, bobbed around the theater and lobby, unable to focus. To my surprise, Olena was there with Dina and Eddie. Dina came up to me and gave me a warm embrace and told me she missed me, "I saw the advertisement in the Times, I had to come. I wanted to see you," she said, "How are the children?" I asked.

"They're good. I told Annie I was seeing you, she was so happy, she talks about you all the time. She went on and on about you; Leonardo told me do my homework this way, and Leonardo makes the best pancakes. They're good Leonardo, really good, we see them a lot. Don't worry we're on it." I nodded to her, my emotions elevated, happy they came, yet it was tricky. I started to think of Annie and Cosmo, I missed them so much. I felt bad, but I told myself I couldn't let it consume me. I had to focus on my play.

Minutes before the play started, Peter and Charlie came in. They jabbed me, taunted me, rubbed my head, and rushed to their seats, "break a leg, girl!" Peter said. I gave them the middle finger and they did the same back. They both broadly smiled, both mouthed congratulations to me and gave me thumbs up. Minutes before my play started I escaped into a dark corner of the theater and witlessly bit my fingernails, scared and qualmy, thinking this was going to be complete exposure. I finally found my seat next to my parents who beamed proudly. Helen was behind me. She leaned over, and spoke in my ear, "Keep smiling no matter what, dear." There wasn't a damn thing I could do about it now anyway, so I smiled the biggest and fakest smile I could possibly muster, and as the lights went down, it hit me. Happiness and joy collided with great fear. Would I make a fool of myself? Fail miserably? It was like this little play at this small off-Broadway theater was all or nothing for me. It was going to be the ultimate test of me mattering in the world of entrainment. Every pulse point in my body throbbed, my ears buzzed.

When the play was over, people stood and applauded. They liked the play. However, since most of the people in the audience were friends, and family of the cast and crew, it made sense they would like it, or at least pretend to. The following weeks would be the real test of truth and I contemplated taping the tips of my fingers with gauze so I wouldn't bite them off.

The first week the play ran, I remained insecure and fearful and was not happy with my reactions; that hapless part of me came sniffing around, and I did some inner battling. The day after opening night, Charlie called, "You know it's a fine play, don't be afraid to admit it. It's yours and it's damn good!"

Two weeks into production Helen told me a New York Times theater critic was in the audience days prior and a review would be out soon. I would have to suffer and wait, "If the review is excellent you'll have other productions, and if they're published, you'll be on your way to a playwriting career." Each day I scanned the theater arts section and each day my heart sunk when my precious review didn't appear. The old me had appeared in full force by that time, and I found myself waiting for acceptance, to be approved of on terms that were not my own, but on the terms of people and critics. I kept telling myself I liked my play, was proud of it, no matter what the outcome, it would be okay. I would survive. All that sounded great, but it was no use, I was obsessed while waiting for that review to come out.

One night after the play, my cell phone rang, it was Olena, she wanted to meet. I was apprehensive, but curious, so we met at an Irish Pub in the West 40's, "Let's get a drink. I'm near the theater," Olena said. Within a half hour, I was sitting across from her. She looked pretty, and even glowed, but as we started to talk something else on her face started to reveal itself to me, some sort of deep worry.

"So, how are Annie and Cosmo?" I smiled mournfully.

"Annie lives with her father, I guess Dina contacted him, it's all very hush hush."

"That is the best news ever!"

"Mara pretends she cares, and uses it for attention, but she's glad Annie is gone. When I'm a parent I swear I'll never be like her. Never."

"You sound angry."

"She's a lousy human being."

"Tell me about Cosmo."

"So cute and mischievous," she said.

"Does he still spit out his food?" I laughed.

"Oh yeah, and he's getting big!" she said. I had not seen him in over a year.

On Olena's fourth beer her eyes became wet and doleful, she had a dopey smile on her face. "Remember when Jack was in Spain filming that beer commercial and Mara wanted me to go with him to keep an eye on him?"

"Yeah, I remember," I rolled my eyes.

"You have to swear to never tell anyone what I am about to tell you."

"Okay," I twisted my jaw, could only imagine what took place in Spain.

"I'm in love with Jack," she said. I rearranged myself in my seat, wondering if she said what I thought she said.

"I am, it's sick, I know, he's my first cousin, but I'm in love with him. I can't get him out of my head," she said. I wasn't sure if she was serious or not, I was trying to wholly comprehend what she told me. "One night we went out, Madrid is such a romantic city, and we got drunk. Really drunk. Things got out of hand."

"What do you mean?" I sipped my beer, became alarmed, but acted unruffled.

"We made out."

"Oh," her words prodded me like a hot poker, I was lost for words.

"We got naked. I was scared, but I also liked it. In the end though, I freaked out and left his room. He was so drunk, and was kind of forceful, but it wasn't like he raped me. It wasn't like he was being mean or anything, after all, I took my clothes off willingly, I was drunk. It was my fault. If Mara ever knew, that would be the end of me. You think I'm a bad person, don't you? I can tell, you think it's sick. Stop looking at me like that," she said.

"Olena that was not your fault. You need to stay very far away from both of them."

"Do you think Jack is sexy?" Olena asked.

"I never thought of Jack in that way."

"Mara always said you were in love with Jack. I have to be honest. I hate her," she fumbled with the cardboard coaster.

"Mara thought everyone was in love with Jack, but that was not the case."

"Please don't tell anyone about Spain."

"Stay away from them," I said

"I think I'm in trouble to be honest. I don't know how to… forget it."

"Trouble? What's going on?"

"Forget it, I'm just confused and stuff. Forget it. You look all funny, forget it! Stop looking at me like that, Leonardo!"

"You opened the conversation saying you were in love with Jack, then you talk about Spain which was a long time ago. He's your family, he should know better and then you say you're in trouble. How do you want me to react? I'm concerned."

"He didn't rape me. I swear we didn't do anything. We didn't. We don't even talk about Spain, we don't do anything now, never did, everything is back to normal. Forget I said anything. Forget I said I loved him. It's been a bad few weeks. I had to do something and I feel badly about it. I'm having a hard time. I'll be fine. Honest," her eyes filled with tears.

“Why do you keep using the word rape? And what bad thing did you do? I’m worried.”

“I said forget it,” her voice soft, frightened, her eyes were everywhere but on me.

“Are you sure? Olena, what’s up, did he hurt you?” I asked.

“Please forget it. Forget what I said. Look I need to go.” She started slipping out of the booth, and I took her by the arm. “Olena, what’s wrong? Tell me.”

“Nothing I need to go. I just need to go. Just forget this conversation!” And she ran off, and that was the last time I saw her. Walking back to Helen’s brownstone, I was drowning in guilt, I handled her confession horribly. I shamed her and didn’t mean to, but my concerns were for her safety only. Obviously, she was seeking my help, and I majorly messed up. When I arrived at Helen’s, we ordered Ramen for dinner, and for the first time probably in my life, I couldn’t eat.

One night after a very good performance I walked out of the theater, ready to grab a taxi home when I received a tap on my shoulder, “Congratulations.” At first I didn’t recognize her. It was Esther, my first New York friend. She appeared surprisingly different, her hair was cut in a pixie, naturally auburn, and it showed off her angular face. She was calm, and had a wide clear smile on her face. She kissed me and shook my shoulders, “You did it! I knew you would!” She smelled good, like flowery perfume, and it warmed me,

“Esther! You look great,” I said.

“It’s been a long time. I’m so proud of you. It’s a great show. Wow! Good for you.”

“Thank you,” I said.

“There is a good part in there for Meryl Streep.”

"You're too much. If only."

"Wanna get some tea and pie?" I understand if you don't."

"Of course I do! It's really you! Esther!" I said, and put my arms around her and we walked to a diner around the corner, our heads hunched almost as if we were embarrassed about our past behavior. We sat across from each other, both a bit shy, knowing we had to resolve something between us.

"Guess what?" she said.

"What? You're not really Esther?"

"No, ummm… Leonardo, my dad died," she shrugged and stared off.

"I'm so sorry. That's tough. Shit, Esther," I reached over and our hands locked.

"He had cancer. I took care of him until his death. It was very strange, but profound. He held my hand while he was dying. When he died he let go of my hand, but I felt like he was still holding it. It was surreal. I still feel like he's holding it."

"Are you okay?"

"I'm okay now. Hey, I'm sorry for being such an asshole to you."

"No, no, no, you helped me a lot, plus you had some really good pot. Besides, it's all in the past. I suppose it wasn't easy being around me either. I'm neurotic and self-centered, it's gross."

"Remember the first time we smoked in Riverside Park."

"Crazy! We ate acorns. What's up with that?" We laughed so hard our eyes watered.

"Your play is passionate and sensitive. It is you. I was sorry to lose you as a friend."

"I'm sorry I dumped your ass."

"I'm sorry I let you dump my ass."

"Let's try again." I said.

"Life is full of trying and failing isn't it? I was so mean to my father for so many years. I was angry about losing my mom.

I weirdly blamed him and he had nothing to do with it. I am so thankful I had a chance to say I was sorry to him. All he said to me was that he loved me, and he said it over and over those last days of his life. He'd talk about the day I was born and how happy he and my mom were. He said I was their prize. Can you imagine? They were poor when I was born, just students, they lived way up in Washington Heights. He said I was this shiny star in his life, his gift from God. Can you imagine? He wanted me to have a good life. I learned a lot about him those last months. He was this poor kid from upstate. When he was real small, he used an outhouse. Can you imagine? I never knew that about him. He said I was the reason he worked so hard. I had a good dad, and I wasted a lot of time being angry. After he died I kept thinking, why would he love me so much when I was so mean to him? Let's face it, I was rotten to him, my guilt was astronomical. But I remembered what you had said to me once. You said that he loved me before I even knew myself and these past weeks I suddenly understood what you meant. That helps me, not all the time, but it's something I hold onto."

"At least I was good for something," I said.

"You were good for a lot more. You're not as bad as you think. Hey, guess what? I'm teaching the fourth grade," she said.

That's fantastic!"

"It's pretty great!"

"I bet. I like your hair."

"Thanks, I feel very adult. I wanted it to look very Cynthia Nixon," she tugged on the ends of her hair.

"Well, you succeeded," I smiled.

"I should get going, I have an early day, I still get shaky facing all those kids each morning, but I love them, this is the best thing I've ever done in my life."

"This is on me," I took the check in my hand, paid and we walked out to the street. I got her a taxi. We hugged for what seemed like forever. She giggled, smacked my ass like old times, "I still love your ass!" Once in the taxi, she rolled down the window and shouted, "Congratulations Leonardo! You did it! Yes!" The taxi sped off with her hand madly waving to me, I waved back and stood until her taxi merged into traffic and I could no longer tell which taxi she was in.

Weeks later, Helen threw a dinner party to raise money for the theater company, it was a long night of meeting people, and by the end of the night we were exhausted. I crashed in bed and slept through the morning. I dreamt of a phone ringing non-stop. When coming out of the deepest sleep I think I ever had, I realized the phone ringing was not a dream,

"Hello?" my voice was groggy,

"I've been trying to call you all morning!" It was Peter, his voice was high pitched, joyful.

"I was in a dead sleep."

"You got a quarter page in the New York Times! Plus a picture! A quarter page! You got a rave review! A RAVE review!"

"I did?" I perked up, it was almost as if I couldn't feel or trust or believe it.

"Yes, you did! I'm so very proud of you! It's wonderful news," he then read the review to me. My call waiting beeped, "I have call waiting! It's Charlie," I said. "Go!" he said.

"Well, well, congratulations to you!" Charlie said.

"I can't believe it!"

"I'm not surprised one single bit!" he said. My call waiting beeped again,

"I have call waiting!" I said and it played out like that for an hour, Julia, Esther, Gwen, and then Helen called from the theater. She was beyond proud.

I hung up from Helen and ran to the corner bodega to get a paper, and there it was, my rave review. My name in the New York Times. For an instant I was thrilled as I walked back to the house; I had gotten a good review in the New York Times. Me!

I called my parents, who were ecstatic, my father got off the phone and told me he was going to the *7-11* to pick up The New York Times. Later that day, my mother told me my father had picked up twenty copies of my review.

"That's a bit extreme, isn't it?" I said.

"It's the New York Times, son! Your father wanted as many copies as he could find in case he lost one, he wanted backups. He's so proud. We all are!"

"But why twenty?"

"He has an idea to use eight of them as placemats. He's going to laminate them."

"Mom are you shitting me?"

"He thinks he's being artsy like you, just go with it. He loves that laminating machine at Office Max," she said.

Later that day something overcame my twenty-eight year old mind. I decided that something was wrong inside of me. I had spent the last few hours talking about myself, my play, my career. It was grossly egocentric. I was finally validated in the world, and what better way but through the New York Times, but still… Wasn't I supposed to feel like a somebody now? So what was that doomed feeling inside? How would I react if I had gotten a bad review, what would that have meant to me? Would I have spent the rest of my life hoping to be validated by people and critics. Would I have jumped off the

Brooklyn Bridge? I wasn't strong enough for this type of thing. It wasn't me. I became overwrought with apprehension because right in front of me was a glowing review of my play, and I was happy but as the hours passed I was no different, there was no magic, no earth shattering light beaming down from the havens blessing me and telling me I was special. And, was this what I expected, and wanted? Was I an artist, or was I seeking recognition? Approval? Love? At that moment I resolved that a good review could possibly change my career path for the better, but it wouldn't change who I was as a person or a writer. I would always be stuck with me, and I was the one who was able to change what needed to be changed and not a critic or person who liked or disliked my work could validate me as a person. With that I knew I belonged exactly where I was regarding my career because to my core, I felt like I deserved it because I'd worked hard on that play. It meant, no more, no less; it was a small half crumb of success, a start to something if I wanted it. Besides, it wasn't like I wrote Death of a Salesman. I wrote a small play and it was done in a small off-Broadway theater and in the broad scheme of things, it wouldn't mean much to the world, but to me it was a big deal. With all that in mind, I sprang from my bed, clutched my review read it and over and over and over, and jumped for joy, embraced it for what it was, a professional victory, no more or no less. But I wasn't a complete phony, I did have moments when I thought that critic was by far the smartest person known to mankind.

Scene Thirty-Six – Lesley Gore – *You Don't Own Me*

The night my play closed, I was naturally sad, but grateful, and I looked forward to whatever would come my way. Helen was reading my newest play, and another production at her theater seemed hopeful the following year. My play was getting booked in other theaters across the country, things were rolling along. My plan was to return to Boston, to live on Cape Cod for a bit and to start another project. I was also thinking about teaching, and I was applying to many colleges for an adjunct teaching position. I hoped to meet someone soon, and start a family of my own. I knew nature would take its course.

Late one night a few days before I was to leave for Boston I received a call very late from Mara, "Leonardo, darling is that you?" For a brief moment I was sent back in time and felt the weakness in me rise, "Yes. Mara, it's me," I said. "Darling, it's been a donkey's ear, we've missed you. I know things in the past went sour, but Jack and I were speaking and we miss you terribly. We read your review weeks ago and we're so proud of you. Jack and I were thinking it would be brilliant to see you. He wants to cook you a celebratory dinner, he's learning to cook. And Annie is with me this week. She would absolutely be thrilled to see you. Cosmo has grown so much, darling, would you consider dinner, tomorrow night?" she asked. I found myself agreeing only because I would be able to see Annie and Cosmo.

"And guess what, darling, Jack bought a limousine, it's fabulous, it's from the 1970's, a real retro number, it's in perfect condition, we've done it all over inside, it's quite lovely. We can send it for you, would you fancy that?"

The next day I was inside a retro 1970's limo that was outrageously impressive, and completely refurbished with a TV, booze, and snacks. When the driver pulled in front of Jack and Mara's townhouse, memories flashed before me and they came fast and were relentless. My body became tense; there I was running up and down the front stairs, running errands, leaving at all hours, the constant cowing, the sacrificing of who I was and what I stood for. I was scared to remember it all, but even more frightened that I would forget it. When my finger pressed the buzzer, I felt a multitude of regret, but the idea of seeing Annie and Cosmo helped ground me. There were now security cameras attached to the townhouse and a policeman on duty sat in a car across the street. Mara had warned me, "Bloody fans started knocking on our door!" Mara greeted me with a wide smile. She had not changed, her hair and make-up all the same, even the cruelty behind her smile remained intact. The house smelled of garlic and meat, it was a warm smell, homey and safe, a major inconsistency, and red flags went off. I saw all this before. The first night Jack and I worked on the screenplay. Something was wanted from me. Their overt kindness always meant a favor was going to be asked; were they going to ask me to cut their toenails, demolish another townhouse, wash their floors...stand on my head for their amusement?

"Darling! How are you, it's been a long time, look at you, you're all dressed up, aren't you the lush one, come in." She embraced me and it took every ounce of energy I had to reciprocate her embrace.

"Everything is going well," I said.

"Jack is making you Veal Osso Buco. He knows you like to eat. He's been braising those bloody shanks all day!" she giggled as if we were picking up right where we left off, like no time had passed, no hard feelings existed, her jovial demeanor was making me leery by the second.

"We closed the bar, have you heard? Fans were coming in, it was positively nightmarish, darling! Let me tell you this, it's not the wild animal to fear, it's the unevolved human being to fear, what a dreadful bunch! Complete cannibals!"

Annie came in from the bedroom. She had grown in the year and a half I was away. She was shy at first, and gave me a silly grin, and gave me a quick, shy wave. I went directly to her, my arms wrapped around her, I kissed the top of her head.

"How are you?"

"I missed you," she hugged me tightly, smiled, then beamed, "I lost my front tooth!" she said. "Wow, how about that!" I said. Her small hand slipped into mine.

"She lives with her father now, its' really for the best, isn't that right Annie? We're getting along brilliantly, it's much better this way." Annie kept her eyes on me, "Leonardo, look at Cosmo!" she said. Cosmo came running my way, waddling across the floor, he was not shy or timid, and he had grown so much that I hardly recognized him. He showed me a small plastic figure, "It's a Tawnsformer," he said, as he came to me and reached for me. I picked him up.

"He means, Transformer," Annie said.

"Hey buddy," he put his arms around my neck. He had not forgotten me.

"Hi Leonardo," he spoke with a lisp and showed me his plastic figurine, bending it in different ways. "It goes like this and then like this and like this," he said.

Jack came from the kitchen, his hair cut short, close to his head, he appeared taller.

"Leonardo! How are you?" He put his arms around my shoulder. Cosmo was pushed closer into me by the weight of Jack's squeeze. Cosmo giggled and squeezed Jack's large nose. Jack smelled like garlic and herbs, beads of perspiration on his forehead,

"So you started cooking?" I said.

"Yes! I love it. Mara bought me cookbooks!"

"He's very good at it. He made a wonderful lobster Fra Diavolo over linguini the other night, scrumptious, really!" Mara said.

"Come in the kitchen with me, I have to check on the veal." I tagged behind him slowly, feeling skittish, my hands were clammy. Mara took Cosmo and went into the den. Once in the kitchen, Annie came back to me, she sat at the kitchen table beside me, and kept her eyes on me.

"So what's it feel like to get a love letter from the New York Times?"

"It feels good," my voice sure and poised.

"Good! We're proud of you, and we weren't surprised." He reached up and pulled down plates. Annie stood and took the plates from Jack and I watched as she methodically set the table, "Annie you have grown up so much!" She gave me a grin and took pride in each plate she placed on the table. Mara came into the kitchen, put her arms around Jack and they kissed. "It smells lovely, baby," she said. I wondered when those veal shanks would be flying across the kitchen in a fit of anger, hoping not any time soon because it smelled and looked amazing, if anything I was going to get a good meal out of this. My mouth watered.

We had dinner and everything seemed perfect, delicious. I sat next to the children, joked with them. Annie told me all about school, a new friend, and how she liked math and art class,

"She's gotten to be quite the math whiz, really she has," Mara said. Annie seemed more confident. Living with her father was proving to be good for her.

After the kids went to bed, I announced that it was time for me to leave. "So fast? Please have a drink, sit with us. I have exciting things to discuss," Jack said. "What's the rush, darling?" Mara piped in. I reluctantly agreed, my curiosity being the deciding factor in staying a bit longer. I had gotten to see the children and at this point nothing mattered. We sat in our same positions, me on the sofa, Mara on the floor surrounded by pillows, Jack in his chair, legs crossed, brandy in his hand. Out came the mirror. She started to snort. I was offered a drink, but refused. They insisted, but I refused again, making an excuse that I had a meeting first thing in the morning, and I had to leave soon.

"Darling it was a rough turn for us back then. Jack's fame and all. The new baby. So much pressure, darling," Mara said

"We all said things to one another that we didn't mean, we've missed you." Jack said.

I remained quiet and listened because when I told them off a year and a half ago, I meant every single word including the conjunctions. As they went on, I gave them a string of ahh huhs, and nods.

"So this is what I've been thinking, Leonardo."

"Listen darling, it's a marvelous idea!" Mara said.

"I want to go to the cable network and propose our screenplay and have them make a TV series with it. What do you think of that?"

"That sounds interesting," It was almost like I could see Jack putting a carrot on the stick and swinging it in front of my mouth, but my mouth was closed tautly.

"I can call Beth and she can set up a meeting. You wouldn't even have to go," he said.

"It's a brilliant idea, really, TV is very hot now," Mara said.

"It would pay well," Jack said.

"Lots of money, darling that's the point isn't it. Let's face it."

"I guess it would," I indulged them for the fun of it.

"We're thinking about buying a place in LA. Darling you could buy your own house, have those children you want," Mara said.

"I was also thinking we could write another screenplay together. What do you think of that?" Jack said.

"That sounds interesting," I said for the second time.

"I can tell you have grown. You look at peace. You've matured," Mara said. Her skin had a whitish-bluish tone to it.

"My mother said Olena, Peter and Charlie went to your play," Jack said.

"It was nice to see them. How is Olena?" I said, looking at Jack.

"We haven't seen her," Mara said. Her tone stark, bitter. I beamed alarm.

"She was reminiscing about the trip you two took to Spain," I said.

"Is that so?" Jack said as he sipped his brandy.

"Well, apparently darling, if truth be told, she got herself in a pickle. Some boy she fell in love with, we never met the bloke, but long dramatic story short, she got herself preggers and Jack and I had to give her money to take care of it. Everyone comes to us with their money troubles. We have expenses, too. We haven't seen or heard from her since. She's an emotionally wrought girl, you know. The highly strung type," Mara said. Jack examined his fingernails, acting indifferent.

"You sure I can't fix you a drink, Leonardo?" Jack said.

"I'm fine, Jack," I pronounced his name purposely snarky as it snapped off my tongue harshly.

"Is Peter doing well? I always think of Larry," Jack said. He was glaring at me.

"He was a good, man, that Larry. Bless his heart," Mara said.

"Since we're going down memory lane, Julia told me Rico was still clean, and working in a restaurant uptown. I'm happy for him. Thanks for helping him," I said. Jack briskly got up, an air of irritation followed him. "You sure I can't fix you a drink?" he asked pouring himself another. I nodded no. Mara became stern, adjusted her body,

"We can't have Rico in our lives anymore. That rehab cost us a small fortune. Never again. He was bringing Jack down, there is so much a person can do for another person. Bottom line, Rico is dodgy and he can't be around our children. Once a junkie always a junkie. Rehab or not. We need to protect ourselves and our children. We wish him the best." Mara went for the mirror again, and when done sat up, and stretched her arms. "I started yoga, and we're even thinking about adopting babies, lots of them! Namaste, darling." My eyeballs were glued to the door. I had had enough of them. I made up a silly excuse that I had to leave, and dashed toward the door, not wanting to see the kids, sadly knowing I had to let them go, but feeling confident that Annie was with her father, and they had Jack's parents. There was little or nothing else I could do. The situation with the children would never resolve itself with me. It was like dropping children in the deep end of a pool and hoping they would learn how to swim, knowing if you dove in to save them, you'd be shot in the head along with the children. It was an awful line to walk.

First thing the next morning Gwen called me, she was flabbergasted,

"Jack's manager, Beth said you agreed to turn the screenplay you wrote with Jack into a TV series. Is this true? Leonardo, this is an awfully bad idea."

"I never agreed to that, never!" I said.

"Clearly Jack is setting you up. Who knows what he is up to? Let me fish around for curiosity sake. I'll talk to his manager again and try get more information."

In two hours, Gwen called me back. I was packing my bags, I was on my way to catch a train to Boston,

"I spoke with Beth. Wow. This is the deal. Dear old Jack Fresh wants to go to the network with your deal in place which would mean a considerably less amount of money for you. Jack wants top writing credit, creative rights, and credits for being the soul creator, which means a huge amount of money for him. He also wanted his wife to have producing credits. In other words, you would be a staff writer and you're the one who initially created the script. It's Wayne Jackson all over again. The real clincher is this; part of Jack's contract with the cable network is to develop a new series; he's two years behind on that contractual agreement. My take on this is that he's desperate to meet his obligation and at the same time trying to make more money. Beth said he hasn't written a thing. I also learned from a source that there have been several complaints about his sexual harassment of men and women on the set of his TV show. He's skating on thin ice. Bottom line, is he's trying to use you again because he thinks he can. Listen Leonardo, people like him always fall. He's a fraud, many already know who he is. Sit tight, trust me he will be found out."

"I used to think that, but he's doing great. He lives in the lap of luxury."

"But look how he's gotten what he has? He's a thief, a liar and a cheater. Everyone knows he was a hustler, he earned all that he has dishonestly. Is everything he has worth that? Seriously, it may sound cliché but look at him. Really, think of him as a person, look at the legacy he's leaving behind. I'd rather see you dig ditches than achieve anything the way Jack Fresh did. Leonardo, the sad truth of life is this; good things happen to very bad people which proves none of that stuff matters. It's all an illusion. It's not important. Successful people aren't specially blessed by some higher deity. I don't know about you Leonardo, but my God could care less about the riches of humans, or screenplays, or show business, or Oscars or Golden Globes and every other award, but my God cares plenty for love and truth. You're a writer, you're the real deal and Jack knows it. He wants to eat you up. As I said to you before, the single reason you were put in their lives was for those children you love so much. Period. Let this other nonsense go. You're going to be fine."

My phone beeped, Jack's name flashed on my small screen. "Gwen it's him, Jack is calling me now."

"Tell him you're not interested and hang up. Be done with this. Look, I'm going over a contract for you, a theater in St Louis loves your play, they want to do it next fall. Focus on that! Let's talk soon." I clicked through, didn't say anything for what seemed forever, my packed duffel bag at my feet.

"Jack," I said, my voice somber and dull.

"We need to meet. I have more ideas," he sounded like nothing was wrong.

"I can't, I'm catching a three o'clock at Penn Station for Boston."

"Take a later train."

"Sorry, Jack, I'm not interested."

"I'll come there, let's talk. Tell me where in Penn to meet you."

"No, I'm not interested."

"What do you mean you're not interested? This screenplay is our child. It's beautiful, it's our work, it's great. This is what you've been waiting for, it's here. What's wrong with you? There's no money in theater. It's nothing. Theater is used by established actors who aren't working; loser actors who want to show the world they're not sell-outs, to prove to the world, 'they are a real artist' it's bullshit. Theater is dead. Leonardo, come back to us."

"That's how you think of other actors? I have to go. Jack, this is all over." I said.

"Over?" he started to laugh. "Hold on, Mara wants to speak to you."

"Leonardo darling, we'll order Chinese like the old days, we'll talk this out. Leonardo are you there, darling? Leonardo? Leonardo?

"Leonardo, Leonardo? Hello, you there?" Jack was back on the phone.

"Jack. Goodbye," I hung up.

I took my duffel bag, said my farewells to Helen and promised to see her soon. She kissed my face, squeezed both my hands with her skeleton like hands, and shook them meaningfully as I left.

Once on the street, I flipped open my phone, saw Jack's name, was tempted call him and tell them I was on my way to the townhouse. Doubts ran rapidly through my mind, but I knew it was important to listen to people who loved me, and to hold on to those people for dear life. Perhaps I would have to continue to listen to them for a very long time. I closed my phone and hailed a taxi.

On the ride to Penn Station every bus, and bus stop and taxi and space that was free, displayed new posters of Jack's smiling face. When my taxi entered Times Square, looming over me was another display of Jack's face, this one massive, splashy, many stories high, maybe eight thousand feet. It dominated the southern triangle of the square, and it loomed bizarrely for all to see. Jack's smile was as big as his retro-limousine, his eyes as large as six windows, they twinkled and gazed at the millions of people who looked up to him each day.

Penn station was packed with people coming and going, and I hurried to buy a ticket. I passed even more posters of Jack. I bought a book and a snack, and waited for my gate to be called. My father was to pick me up in Boston, and that night my sister Emily planned a celebratory party for me. I was excited to be going home, to be free, and to explore the next chapter of my life. My book in my hands, I started to read, and in time my gate was called. I made my way toward the staircase while feeling happy and self-satisfied over my restraint in not calling Jack, but as quickly as that thought came, my phone rang. It was him. I stopped in the middle of the station, my eyes glanced at a row of posters of Jack. I answered without thinking,

"Jack," I started to breathe heavily.

"I'm here. I'm at Penn. Turn around." At that moment everything was in slow motion; the people who bustled past me to catch trains, the sound of the announcements, the piped in music over the PA system, and the click of shoes on the concrete floor of the station. Then Jack and I face to face, the row of posters behind him. "We love you. You're all we have. There's no one else. Everyone is gone. We have no one. It's you, Leonardo, we choose you. Please come back to us," he said. Then there was a voice, it was a joyous cry, distant, but it was clear, and it came closer and closer, until it pierced my ears, "Jack Fresh! It's Jack Fresh!" and a young woman ran up to him, then a woman and her son, then two women, three men, five women, seven, eight and more, and more and more, all of them proclaiming their love for Jack, and his TV show. I stepped away, more voices were heard, "Look, it's Jack Fresh!" and more people looked, and even more came, a crowd formed around him, and within seconds it grew into gigantic proportions until Jack was in the center, being consumed hungrily like a raw slab of meat covered by flies until police came and controlled the mob and pulled him from the people and he stood alone, separated. Jack's face was visible over the crowd. Our eyes met, and his smile disappeared because we both knew the adulations were false and fleeting. His eyes begged to be rescued, to be protected, but he also knew the crowds were necessary for him to survive because it helped him feel something that he longed for. It would never be enough because he was soulless. He had no sense of purpose. Had no love in his heart, and he knew it. He used people, and stole from them and he devoured them just like his fans and everyone else responsible for his career. He was innately evil and he knew that too, and he hated himself for it, but he loved it more. He was a force not to reckon with, but to run from. I took steps back, my heart pounded, my book fell from my hand. I kept walking until I found myself downstairs running toward my train and past more posters of his face that were plastered on the walls of the platform and as I passed them, they merged into one another until they were nothing but figments of flashing colors that had no rhyme or reason.

The End – Natasha Bedingfield – *Unwritten*

Many months later I was living in my rented cottage on Cape Cod. When I first moved into the cottage I pinned a poster from the New York productions of my play on my bedroom wall to inspire me when I wrote. It was a small space in a remote area of Wellfleet where each morning the sounds of birds could be heard singing inside the pitch pines, and in the evening the sound of the ocean's surf echoed. It was perfect.

Charlie and Peter had come to Provincetown in late August, we had dinner and danced as planned. Larry was with us every step we took on the dance floor, every twirl, and every grind, and we wore his memory in our smiles and in each burst of silly laughter. Later that night, Charlie bought us pistachio ice cream cones at Spiritus, we toasted Larry with them, and we walked up Commercial Street until it was time for me to say goodbye and we agreed to see each other again soon.

By mid-September most of the summer tourists had gone, all was peaceful and quiet. Solitude had become my friend along with the morning sun, and the night sky that held stars for miles up the coast. That coming spring I would be traveling to several theaters to see other productions of my play, there would be more money, and more time to write. The following fall, I was hired to teach at a small college in Ohio, and the approaching summer I was to teach children with learning disabilities a few days a week at a local camp.

I spent my days writing, and in the early evening swam in a local pond. The water was icy, and it made my entire body quake with chills, but I loved how it made me feel. It curiously comforted me, and each day I looked forward to it. I'd float on my back, letting the water take me where it would. As each day passed, my previous life with Jack and Mara become a distinct memory. One night I returned to the cottage from a long swim, wet and chilled. I flicked on the TV and started changing channels. I came upon Jack's TV show. They were showing early episodes, an all-night marathon of reruns. I sat and shivered, water dripped off me, my eyes fixated on the TV show until I was dry and warmth had come. The first two shows I watched motionless. They were shows that Jack had received writing credits for and was nominated for a Golden Globe. Scene after scene, my words, my work, played out before me, scenes from my play and from our screenplay, the times I helped him write. He had taken my words, my thoughts, who I was and what I believed, and he made them his own. I shut the TV off, and the lights. I crawled into bed. There was nothing for me to do at that moment but to follow the shadows made by the clouds and moon that webbed and streamed and shifted across my bedroom wall. For a mere second, a flash of light stopped on the posters of my play, my name glowed, and I smiled, and then within seconds, without warning, my name was gone, lost in darkness. I had no fear because there would always be morning, the sun, a new day and I would always have my words and they would flow out of me with confidence and self-assurance and they would speak of truths, of love and loss and of injustices. They would come from me, but they would belong to the world.

Fade Out

Acknowledgments

A very special thanks to Suzanne Pavlos; first editor of this book, her hard work, friendship and dedication to this project was immeasurable. Thank you Steve Turtell, Courtney Jago, Amy Murray and Becky Mitchell Mcleod; second readers and supporters of this novel. Thanks to Mike Mintz, Linda Sanders, Sara Buff and Jesse for friendship and encouragement. Thanks to Robbie, Kevin, Nina, Vincent, Emily, Kathy, Maryanne and Denise.

Always, Vin and Nina.

About the Author

John C. Picardi is a graduate of Johnson and Wales University, The University of Massachusetts at Boston and Carnegie Mellon University. He is the author of the awarding winning play, The Sweepers, and Seven Rabbits on a Pole They are published by Samuel French and have been produced off-Broadway and across the United States. He is the author of the novel, Oliver Pepper's Pickle. He is also a painter and trained chef. He lives in Massachusetts.

Made in the USA
Middletown, DE
25 July 2021